Genevieve is a writer from Melbourne. She writes romantic comedies, content, and really long text messages.

Since studying creative writing at the University of Adelaide, she has worked as a copywriter, social media manager, and producer in Adelaide, Sydney, and Melbourne.

Genevieve loves croissants, Phoebe Waller-Bridge, Joni Mitchell, stories about complicated women and female friendships, and her dog, Viktor. She hates being called Gen.

T0357999

No

Hungover, underpaid

Hard

and overwhelmed

Feelings

Genevieve Novak

HarperCollins*Publishers*

HarperCollins*Publishers*
Australia • Brazil • Canada • France • Germany • Holland • India
Italy • Japan • Mexico • New Zealand • Poland • Spain • Sweden
Switzerland • United Kingdom • United States of America

HarperCollins acknowledges the Traditional Custodians
of the land upon which we live and work, and pays respect
to Elders past and present.

First published in Australia in 2022
This edition published in 2023
by HarperCollins*Publishers* Australia Pty Limited
Gadigal Country
Level 13, 201 Elizabeth Street, Sydney NSW 2000
ABN 36 009 913 517
harpercollins.com.au

A catalogue record for this book is available from the National Library of Australia

ISBN 978 1 4607 6189 2 (paperback)
ISBN 978 1 4607 1475 1 (ebook)
ISBN 978 1 4607 4238 9 (audio book)

Cover design by Mietta Yans, HarperCollins Design Studio
Cover image by Ulas&Merve/stocksy.com/1965628
Author photograph by Miranda Stokkel
Typeset in Bembo Std by Kirby Jones
Printed and bound in Australia by McPherson's Printing Group

For Sam and Erin. I'll love you forever.

CHAPTER ONE

I've just left the 42,613th bad date of my life, and I know this is a bad idea.

'You around?' I ask into the phone before he's even said hello. I'm just glad he picked up. 'Do you fancy a visit from the best, funniest, coolest girl in the world?'

'Why?' I can hear him smiling. 'Do you know her?'

'That's enough out of you,' I say, passing the train turnstiles at North Richmond and turning in the direction of his street. 'I'm just around the corner.'

'Meet you downstairs in a bit,' he says and hangs up.

There. This will make everything better.

I'm ignoring about a dozen messages in the group chat. If I open them, I'll have to tell my friends how the guy was four inches shorter than he claimed to be, made two hours feel like twelve by talking nonstop about cryptocurrency, and texted me before I'd even made it to Flinders Street Station, saying, 'Hi Penny. Wanted to let you know that I won't be pursuing this any further. Take care.' Then one of them will offer to come over to commiserate, and I'll have to explain where I am, and then I'll be in trouble.

'Urgh, babe,' Annie would say, exasperated, like she has all the answers even though she's as hopeless as I am. 'We need to stop this cycle of self-abuse. Have you tried Hinge?'

'*Where is your self-respect?*' Bec would ask, stern as a high-school maths teacher. '*When are you going to find someone nice and sensible, like Evan?*' And I'd roll my eyes so hard I'd give myself a hernia.

'*I exist on validation from emotionally unavailable men, biscuits, and cheap wine,*' I would tell them. '*And it's easier to get off with Max than a Tiny Teddy.*'

Some self-sabotaging part of me wants to be disappointed by every new match, polite coffee date, wine-soaked disaster. I'm holding out for Max. Not that he's interested in being my boyfriend, mind you. He's very clear about that. '*This is fun, Penny,*' he says all the time, '*we're so good at being friends.*' But what else do you call it when you see each other for pizza, sex, and Netflix every week? He texts me almost every day, and, anyway, we agreed to keep things casual, so it's fine. It's really fine.

He wouldn't come as my date to my brother's wedding in October ('*People would assume we're together,*' he said when I asked him. '*I don't want you to have to explain that all night, babe.*') so I had to take Annie, and I accidentally got champagne drunk and cried in the toilets. She found me and gave me the telling off I needed. After an emergency coffee and a makeup wipe, I pinkie-promised her I'd get my shit together. I would stop crying, stop waiting for Max to remember how much he cares about me, and find someone to hold my hand in public. I would start doing Pilates, drink more water, and keep my houseplants alive. I would also find a way to make my boss like me, or at least stop begging for her approval like a nervous little whippet.

That was three months ago, and I've been trying really hard. Honest. I've only killed one measly succulent, but I swear it was suicidal when I got it.

Maybe it's the Aperol Spritz buzz giving me permission to be a drama queen, but I just can't bear the thought of going home and opening Tinder again. I don't want to dissect the entire date in the group chat to a chorus of '*The next one will be better!*' I don't want to lay out my clothes for work and obsess about what stupid mistake I'll make at the office tomorrow to warrant one of Margot's scathing looks. I've just spent $44 on cocktails to get me through an excruciating one-sided conversation with the world's least interesting man. I want to end my night on a high, and seeing Max usually does the trick. I don't care how I'll feel about myself later.

It's like swapping cigarettes for a vape pen: I still get the nicotine hit and there's a chance the whole thing will blow up in my face.

Besides, this new Zara dress has become a personal polyester sweat lodge in the unrelenting January heat. I'm shamelessly fanning my armpits on my way down Victoria Street and I might die of heat exhaustion by the time I get home. I need Max to take it off. To save my life.

I see him as I dash between stalled traffic on Nicholson Street, armed with a six-pack of cider and a packet of condoms from the Aldi on the corner, and call out. He looks up from his phone, exits out of the app he was in, and pockets it. He smiles and I melt.

It should be illegal for one person to be this good looking. He belongs in prison.

Even back at uni, I always felt like a piglet smeared in lipstick when I stood next to him. He'd turn up to our 8 am lectures, after a thousand cheap vodkas the night before, looking like he'd made a wrong turn at the end of a Saint Laurent runway. And as we scrape towards our late twenties, and a steady diet of sauv blanc and 7-Eleven sandwiches threatens to turn my cheekbones into jowls, he's only getting dreamier. All tall and lithe and long-limbed, like an indie frontman who lives on free-trade espresso and Radiohead deep cuts. His dark hair hangs over his eyes for the pleasure of pushing it back. Add in a day or two's stubble and an arrogant little smirk, well, I'm helpless. Back when I was allowed to spend the night, I would creep out of bed at daybreak to pat on concealer, comb my brows and smudge mascara into the roots of my eyelashes, then pretend to wake up fresh and radiant, and I still wouldn't look as pretty as him. Nothing is fair.

'All dressed up for me,' he says as I arrive, bumping his jaw against my cheek. I accidentally kiss him on the ear.

Fuck's sake.

'Yeah, well, thought I'd try.'

'For once,' he jibes, and before I can even scoff, he's got his hand in my hair and we're kissing, and my bratty response dies in my throat. So familiar with this routine by now, we're on autopilot stumbling blindly towards the staircase, against the wall, in his hallway, at his front door, against the arm of his couch.

'Are your housemates home?' I ask, pulling at the hem of his T-shirt anyway.

'Don't worry,' he says, which isn't an answer, but I don't want to argue and ruin the night. I know his rules. I've been following them long enough.

Just because things are familiar doesn't mean they're boring. Even if I know every beat of this old song, it's still exciting. And you don't sleep with someone this many times without figuring out what they like. As I reach this thought — we have done this a million times, haven't we? — my mind starts to reel. He's kissing my neck and I'm counting. I came round to 'watch a movie' at least three times over the past month; I know this because I gave him a lavender plant for Christmas and I have to try not to take it personally every time I visit and find it parched and barely clinging to life. And there were all the times the month before when we played Risk with his housemates, and when we got wasted at Oktoberfest and watched a dachshund race, and before that when …

'How long have we been doing this for?' I ask, careful to keep my voice low and light. It doesn't seem to slow him down.

'Like, five minutes?' He's working on the zip of my dress, and I'm acutely aware of how I don't want to let it wrinkle on the floor. The crepe will be hell to iron. 'Am I boring you?'

'Not *this*,' I say. 'This. *This* this. *Us* this.'

Max straightens up, and my throat constricts. He's annoyed, and I've ruined it, and my brain isn't fast enough to fix it, and why am I like this? Couldn't I have just not said anything?

'If you don't want to hang out anymore, Penny, we don't have to.'

'I didn't say that!' I cry. 'It's been a while, that's all. I wanted to check in.'

'We've talked about this,' he snaps. 'I thought we didn't want to be that couple, all the heteronormative monogamy "checking in" bullshit.'

You heard that, right? *Couple*? It wasn't just me? Okay. Don't push it. Don't react, don't spook him. Breathe in, breathe out. We've been here before. I know how to handle this.

'You're right,' I say. I soften, smile and reach for his waistband. 'I was being a dickhead. You're completely right. Come back here.'

In his bedroom a while later, I am naked and content. I was especially impressed by the flattering light cast by his T-shirt hanging over his lamp, and that moment we had in the middle there when he kissed me and bumped his nose against mine affectionately, and that he's gone to the kitchen to get us the ciders I brought over. This is what Bec and Annie don't give him enough credit for: when Max is in a good mood, he's lovely. When he's lovely, it's smooth sailing. And that word is still echoing in my head and filling me up with happy butterflies: *couple*. It took a moment of tension, but I knew this was where we've been stumbling towards all these long months. I don't know what I was worried about, really. We clearly adore each other, and I'm sure if I invite him to brunch next weekend and the weather's good and mimosas are on the table, everything will start falling into place, and I won't ever have to go on another Tinder date again.

I'm mentally sorting through my wardrobe for the dress I'll wear to brunch, picturing us holding hands under the table, considering what colour my nails should be, wondering if I should find a cafe with transparent supply chain practices so we don't have to interrogate the waiter about the workers' conditions on the farm that supplies their avocados. Daydreaming, basically, like a lovesick teenager who's one half of a *couple*. I'll invite him on Thursday. Really casual, like I've hardly thought about it.

When he returns, he's only holding one bottle. The warm, affectionate expression I was looking for is instead one of polite expectation.

Oh no.

'Do you want to get an Uber home, or are you just going to walk?'

CHAPTER TWO

Usually I'd be hypervigilant about walking through this neighbourhood alone at night, but I'm propelled by fury.

At Max for his infuriating Maxness, at whatshisname earlier for wasting my time and money, at my friends for making me go on that stupid date in the first place, and at whoever circulated the concept of casual relationships that always, always screw over whoever cares the most. Mostly I'm angry at myself for falling into this again. There's surely nothing worse than watching yourself make predictable mistakes. Why didn't I just go home and eat pasta over the sink like a normal single loser? Don't I know better? Why do I do this to myself? The Bec of my mind's eye is right: where is my self-respect?

I'm so lost in the dissection of my weak and needy character, and every wrong decision I've ever made, and how this wouldn't be happening if I had a flatter stomach or a better haircut, that I hardly notice my commute. I barge through throngs of people on Victoria Street, avoid a group staggering out of the pub, storm past someone taking their bins out, stomp up my front steps, and, finding my keys missing from my clutch, let out a loud and cathartic *'FUCK!'*

All the lights are off inside, but my housemate's bike is locked up on the veranda so he can't be far. Hating myself and these stupid fake leather heels more with every pinching step,

I make for the pub on the corner. If Leo isn't there, the night will end with me scaling the fence and hoping for an open window to wriggle through.

The pub is half empty, which is understandable. It's a shithole of a place. Between the decor — jaundiced lights and threadbare carpet — and the clientele — puce-faced, big-tummied sports spectators — my crumpled dress and pash-rash-pink face stand out like a neon sign that radiates '*Slut!! Idiot!!*'. I wrinkle my nose at the glassy-eyed sixty-something who smirks at my arrival. I've no patience left for anyone.

Oh, thank goodness. There's Leo. We exchange a little wave as I line up for the bartender's attention. Wine is much, much needed. Hook me up to a sauv blanc drip.

I met Leo through Bec. They were old acquaintances from uni, and he went along to her and Evan's housewarming party last year. While Annie was busy sucking face with her girlfriend of the week, I found myself hovering by the communal bowls of Kettle Chips and untouched crudités. Leo was there too, seemingly too sober to socialise freely. He leaned in conspiratorially and asked if I'd support him in hurling Evan's speakers out the window if one more James Blunt song came on the party playlist. Just like that, we formed an alliance. We got to talking, and eventually it came out that I needed to get out of my dank, crunchy sharehouse, where aerosol deodorant had recently been banned, and it so happened that he had a spare room available. A few weeks later, I moved into his tidy little two-bedroom worker's cottage in Richmond, a suburb that is part cool, part convenient, part dodgy. There are innumerable dumpling restaurants on the high street, two train stations nearby, and more than enough bars in which to drown all my sorrows on any night of the week. It's walking distance to my office, and I can afford the rent without selling my underwear on the internet. Not that that's so lucrative anymore. Not that I've looked into it.

My bedroom is oddly narrow and gets about six minutes of sun a day, but the rest of the house is full of light, and it has boy luxuries like an enormous television and good Wi-Fi. The expansive kitchen is great for all the cooking I never get around to doing, and there's a courtyard out the back where, when I'm lucky, a neighbourhood cat sometimes stops by for a cuddle.

Leo has hung thoughtfully curated art prints in the living room, rather than the posters of *Pulp Fiction* and *The Dark Knight* that so many millennial men have blu-tacked to their walls. His bookcases are filled to bursting, with shelves and shelves of well-loved novels spanning Salinger and Ishiguro to Austen and Klosterman, as well as niche magazines and glossy coffee table books I like to pull out when I have people over, to pretend I'm cultured enough to read *Architectural Digest*. The furniture is eclectic enough to know he didn't pick it all out of an IKEA catalogue: a refurbished steamer trunk here, a linen lampshade there, a whiff of rattan to keep things interesting. He has matching cutlery and an even number of coffee cups. Leo is a real adult.

I've been living there over a year, but until recently, we only ever texted each other about the gas bill. He spent almost every night at his girlfriend's house. I only ever caught sight of her once, her topknot bobbing as she called over her shoulder that she'd see him at her place later, 'Love you, bye!' I'd been too lost in whatever all-consuming life crisis I'd been going through at the time – perhaps Max had forgotten to end a text with kisses, or my recurring eyebrow pimple was back – and didn't feel like introducing myself. I assume they broke up recently because now there's Bonsoy in the fridge and a conveyor belt of women in the hallway on a weekend morning, and he's been around a lot. Sometimes he invites me to the pub or asks if there's anything I need from the shop. He seems like a pleasant enough guy, if a bit promiscuous. But aren't we all?

'You wouldn't believe the night I've had,' I announce, dropping into the seat opposite him. He acknowledges me briefly with his eyebrows over the rim of his pint glass, before his gaze flickers back to the tennis match on the big screen above the bar. 'I forgot my keys. And I had a bad date. And I'm on a walk of shame.'

'What?' he asks, turning his attention back to me long enough to look amused. How validating. 'Was it so bad you had to screw him to shut him up?'

'*No!* I'm on a walk of shame from *another guy's house!*'

'Sounds like a busy night.'

'Yes, I'm extremely popular.' I pause. 'It's complicated.'

'Apparently. Go on,' he says. 'Indulge me.'

'I promised my friends I'd go on dates to get over my ex. But then I went and saw the ex. Actually, I see him quite a lot.'

'Ah, that old story.'

'We dated at uni and then we broke up and now we're *just friends*,' I explain, making a face for emphasis. 'And now, the big giant stupid idiot that I am, I read too much into it again, and he's sent me home.'

Leo looks sympathetic, but I can't tell if it's for me, or for Federer's sloppy forehand on the television. I'll take it. I need it more than Federer does.

I met Max in a post-modernism seminar at uni and we spent eleven lovely months kissing between library stacks and staying up all night on cheap weed and circular chats about whether Palahniuk is any good once you're no longer an angsty teenager. But when I suggested we get a flat together, he said he felt suffocated. Maybe I thought it was more serious than it really was. Maybe I just wasn't that interesting once I set my sights on an office job instead of following him into a master's in comparative poetry. In the end, he met someone else. Amber. Urgh. I can't even think her name without wanting to cram a doughnut in my mouth. She's so hot that she could host *Love Island*, and she almost never wears a bra, so when you're lurking her Instagram for the twelfth time this week, her nipples follow you around like the watchful eyes of the *Mona Lisa*. She also regularly posts videos of herself doing yoga headstands and deep lunges, while her crusty-eyed shih tzu licks itself in the background. She and Max got together around the time I was finishing my degree, and they took a gap year together in South America while I sat at the bottom of a bottle of Tanqueray.

After nearly a year of wallowing, I pulled myself together, downloaded three dating apps and began to navigate my life without our private jokes or his face on my home screen. Over the next few years I got used to being alone, went on good and fine and bad and awful dates, enrolled in French lessons, took up spin classes for two weeks every couple of months, and learned to enjoy having a queen-sized bed to myself. Just when I was starting to forget he existed at all, he messaged me. It's like they have a radar for that kind of thing.

'And — I've just remembered — I took cider over with me, and he fucking kept it.'

'Shit,' says Leo, looking affronted. 'Should we call the police?'

'Oh, shut up. Let me brood.'

There: he smiles. Mission accomplished. Friendly conversation achieved. He returns to the tennis, and I'm back to my supercut of humiliation, replaying it all to find the exact moment I let everything fall apart.

Maybe you can't reignite an old flame, and all this trying has been for nothing. Maybe Max never got over Amber. What kind of masochist would put themselves through all of this and still persevere?

'It's just that all the signs are there that he wants to get back together,' I press on. 'Help me. Give me a male perspective here.'

'Forget that guy,' Leo says. 'Find someone else.'

'It's not that easy,' I argue. 'You don't even know the full story.'

'It's never that complicated,' he says, looking unconvinced.

'Sometimes it is,' I huff. 'Or have you forgotten how relationships work since you started campaigning for Bachelor of the Year?'

'I'm not Bachelor of the Year yet,' he says. 'It's only January. Many, many months of casual sex left before I get the gold medal in bacheloring.'

'Gross,' I say, downing half my wine in response, and he laughs. Regardless, my mood is a little lighter than it was ten minutes ago, and the yucky shame has eased a bit.

He gets out his phone during the ad break, and I can tell what he's busy with by the left–right swipe of his thumb. The sight of a newly single man indifferently whipping through profiles when less than a month ago he was his girlfriend's unofficial tenant does nothing to endear the institution of singledom to me. He swipes left, left, left, right, left, right, left, left: a series of split-second decisions based on one image. It's easy for him, isn't it? Men with that kind of annoying impossibly thick hair, who are very tall and have a half-decent wardrobe, never have trouble finding dates. He could get a girlfriend as easily as ordering a kebab.

'I'm going to die alone,' I say with an exaggerated sob. 'No one will ever love me.'

'Probably.'

'*Hey!*'

Leo laughs.

'But what are you on the apps for if not to — urgh — *find love?*'

He gives me a look that plainly says, '*What do you think?*' and I scoff.

'Look at this,' he says and leans over to show me his phone, swiping through a series of profiles. 'People are only on here for one thing. Some people end up hanging out after the refractory period ends. Most don't.'

'That's so depressing.'

The silence we fall into is comfortable, punctuated by the obscene grunts of tennis players, the gentle thud of glasses being set down onto the table, and the rapid-fire chime of message notifications on Leo's phone.

'I've been summoned to the deep north,' he says, fiddling with his keychain. 'Take my key and let yourself in.'

'Stay,' I whine, almost pathetic enough to be persuasive. 'Get inappropriately drunk for a weeknight with me. You have to. It's in my rental agreement.'

'I must've missed that in the fine print. Seriously, though, relax,' says Leo, so sincere and pitying it's embarrassing. 'Your ex is a dick. You'll find someone else.'

'But what if I don't want anyone else? I only want to be with him.'

'Then I guess you're fucked.'

CHAPTER THREE

Obnoxious sunshine streams through my partially opened blinds and curdles the prosecco still in my bloodstream. It's already so hot, and there's a thumping in my temples, and my mouth feels like I've swallowed sand. I hate everything. I want to hook myself up to a vitamin drip, order pizza, and watch *Parks and Rec*, not sit hunched over my laptop sucking back watery coffee all day, and fielding phone calls from clients and tickets from developers.

No messages from Max overnight; no surprises there. Annie has sent the group chat a screenshot of her 5 am five-kilometre run, the sociopath. On Instagram, influencers are hawking laxative teas and fast fashion brands they don't wear. My fitness app reminds me to step on the scales, but, like, *can it just not?* Three new matches …

When Max said the word *couple* just a few hours ago, I assumed I'd be permanently deactivating these apps, but here I am. I keep them to keep my mind off Max. If I think about him for too long, I'll convince myself to text him and, before I know it, I'll be right here again. With swiping part of my daily routine, at least I give myself the illusion of choice.

Stefan, 30. What's your deal? His profile says, '*ENTJ, rugby, beer, dogs*', but the only photo where he isn't flanked by four identical guys in too-tight blazers and boat shoes is a gym selfie with his head cut off. I can't date someone with abs; I'd feel too gross in comparison to ever have sex with the lights on. Unmatch.

Bazza, 28. Good grief, why did I ever swipe right on someone named Bazza? Unmatch. Sorry. I don't make the rules.

Adam, 31. Hello. Don't you love when someone way too hot for you matches with you? It was probably an accident, but let's be optimistic. On a good hair day, with the right light, and two days after my period when my tummy is really flat, I can pass for a 7. In Adelaide or Hobart, I could even be an 8.5. Should I move? Anyway, he doesn't have a bio so he could be an idiot, but I don't care. He's six foot two and doesn't have a single photo at the races in an ill-fitted Jack London suit. What more could a girl ask for?

We only matched forty minutes ago, so I'm not going to say hi yet. Too keen. But if we get to talking late this afternoon, we could get a drink on Sunday, and if I wear a padded bra and it all goes well, we could be engaged by my birthday.

My phone buzzes and snaps me out of my daydream about how I'd do my hair for the wedding. Ooh, five new messages in the group chat.

> **Bec Cooper (06:31):** How was it??
> **Annie Lin (06:34):** Are you in love?
> **Annie Lin (06:35):** Are you pregnant?
> **Annie Lin (06:35):** If you're pregnant, are you going to name it after me?
> **Bec Cooper (06:37):** If she was pregnant, she would name it after Carly Rae Jepsen

I completely forgot I had a date last night.

Penelope Moore (06:38): Not pregnant, idiots.

Penelope Moore (06:38): Really shit. He's already unmatched me lmao

Bec Cooper (06:40): Oh babe :(that's not ideal

Annie Lin (06:45): He is obviously a complete moron

Bec Cooper (06:47): We hate him!

Penelope Moore (6:47): HATE him

How good are best friends? Sated by their loyalty, I silence my next alarm and return to my daily doom-scroll. Eventually, though, I can't put off the call of secure employment any longer.

Under the restoratively strong and scalding spray of the shower, I use my best shampoo and an excessive measure of shower oil, hoping that L'Occitane is French for *hangover cure*. It's not. When that doesn't help, I try two paracetamol and a banana, and fantasise about a buttery cheese toastie from the cafe near the office.

Right. Let's set our intentions for the day. That's my self-care homework, along with writing in my gratitude journal, which I never do, and practising self-compassion, which sounds like woo-woo bullshit. I consult my reflection for answers, and it says, '*I can't be bothered with any of this shit.*'

I'm an account manager at a digital agency, which sounds more interesting than it is. It's my job to figure out what the client wants and then find a way to make that happen. Mostly I coordinate the build of websites and apps, then make ads to get you to visit them. Have you ever been talking about something then inundated with creepy ads on your phone about it? I make those. Sorry. Lately, I'm pretty sure I only go to the office for the free biscuits.

My office is in Cremorne, the next suburb over, and slogging up the big hill on Church Street is the only cardio I get. My sunglasses, bless them, try their very hardest to shield my eyes from the sun and my late night from passers-by.

A couple of people from the development team are in early. The fluorescent lighting is especially punishing and throws the angry zit on my chin into harsh relief. It's barely past 8 am and the air conditioning is already struggling.

My to-do list is a mile long. I have to do a traffic report for Deco Cinemas and have a meeting with the ever-uncooperative marketing manager at Clean Juice Co, and I'll need to practically blow one of the devs to get that scheduling API live on the Jackson & Smith Realty site by tonight. I'd rather get a bikini wax.

Dumping my bag on the floor and slouching into my seat, I steel myself to open my inbox. Let's see the damage. It's the usual slew of technical updates from the devs, activity reports and conversion stats for a few websites, and, hooray, a chilly email from a client. Someone left them a one-star review, and they're upset I didn't find a way to cover it up overnight. And they've cc'd Margot. Grrrreat.

The office is supposed to be airy and modern like an aeroplane hangar, but the rows of pine desks and flatpack furniture makes it feel more like a Scandinavian prison. Beanbag chairs and the occasional office dog are to make us seem young and cool, and the casual dress code and Friday drinks are supposed to make up for the long hours and sub*(-sub-sub)*-optimal pay.

I used to work in a big ad agency with huge teams for everything. Although the clients were household names and the work got a lot of attention, I was running out of quippy ways to sell dog treats and would get frustrated at having to run each decision up a chain of twelve people before I could publish anything. It all got a bit mundane, and I longed for change. I wanted to do something fun and challenging and creative, so I interviewed for an Account Manager job here at Scout Digital. I had one interview with Margot and we spent about twelve seconds going over my resume, and half an hour bonding over Fenty highlighters and a mutual obsession with *The Crown*. She called to offer me the job before I'd even made it to the train station. It meant a pay cut, but she assured me I would more than make up the difference when I was promoted to Account Director at the end of my probation period.

The breakneck pace of things has taken some getting used to. At my old job, when I wrote taglines for school stationery packs and built case studies for pharmaceuticals, the work was so dull it was practically a waking coma. Here, I get overwhelmed and need to excuse myself to do emergency meditation sessions in the toilets more often than I should admit.

And Margot and I aren't exactly the pals we were when I joined. Sometimes when I'm talking to her, she gets the kind of blank expression I associate with digging for keys in the bottom of your handbag. And if she thinks I've been chatting to someone in the kitchen a bit too long, she catches my eye and pointedly taps her Apple Watch. I'm still trying to work off the humiliation of her talking over me in my own pitch last week. Lately, just thinking of her name makes my stomach twist. I have to keep telling myself I'm imagining it.

While I watch the clock and sprint out the door at 5 pm, she makes a point of telling everyone that she was here until nearly midnight the night before. She can silence a room with a look, and she's never short on suggestions for how I could have handled myself in a meeting. But it's all constructive. You don't need to be best friends with your boss.

I have a little fantasy in the back of my mind, so secret I hardly ever visit it. I like to imagine the last few months have been a perverse hazing ritual where Margot has been pushing all my buttons to see if I can hack it in a senior role. In the fantasy, I'm wearing something fabulous and unwrinkled — a print dress that makes me look feminine, powerful, effortlessly chic, and very, very smart — and I'm making a presentation, and I'm throwing out stats and facts and ideas that leave the clients slack-jawed (and maybe a bit hot; the dress's fault, obviously), and Margot smiles and gives me an impressed little nod. I get a five-figure raise, and I become the kind of woman I've always wanted to be. I keep fresh flowers on my desk, the elbows of my blazers aren't permanently crushed, my fringe cooperates every single day, and I can pick up the tab on a night out with my friends without having to use the iPhone calculator to work out how to split $73 three ways.

But Margot can't smile; her Botox prevents it. And I'm not sure that dress even exists because I've been looking for it my entire life.

Except she as good as promised me the AD role in my interview. Four of my clients pay agency fees that make up more than a third of our monthly revenue. And just last month I launched a new e-store two weeks before the deadline and fourteen hours under budget. Maybe I should go on The Iconic and search for that elusive power dress one more time.

No!

Stop!

We aren't thinking about it. Stop that right now.

Fuck it, I need a coffee. Caffeine will soothe my woes.

Penelope Moore (08:09): @*Bec Cooper* Coffee?
Bec Cooper (08:11): Meet you in 5 x

It's handy that Bec works nearby or I might never see her. She and Evan work side by side at a coworking space behind Richmond

Station. She's a graphic designer and he's an entrepreneur, whatever that's supposed to mean. I don't know how she does it. Working next to your partner every day sounds like the ultimate romance killer. Imagine learning the love of your life microwaves fish, or uses dumb workplace jargon like 'We'll circle back to this later' or 'Let's have a thought shower about that.'

When they met at a (semi-ironic) speed dating event a year and a half ago, their relationship went from zero to full throttle almost immediately. It was almost enough to make you believe in love at first sight (retch). But now we don't see her very much, and when we do, she keeps one eye on her phone. She has shelved her life-of-the-party persona to wander around furniture showrooms all weekend and use the word *we* at a competitive rate. What can Annie and I do? Ask her to care about her boyfriend less? I went to that speed dating night too. All I got was a cold sore.

I hope I've quelled any further discussions of last night's date-tastrophe. I don't really want to talk about it, not with Bec, who is too blinded by her own happiness to remember what a shitshow most first dates are. It was such a waste of time that I've actually begun blacking it out. Post Bad Date Memory Loss Syndrome: it's a real thing, you know? Look it up on WebMD.

I don't have to be at my desk until 9 am, so we meet at our cafe. We mostly like it because of the sexy barista who always remembers our orders. We don't know his name, but it's too late to ask, so now he's just Sexy Barista. I never much fancied men in uniform, but those with access to wholesale espresso and croissant suppliers? *Ooh.*

'Is it possible to be sexually attracted to a toastie?'

'Absolutely,' says Bec through a mouth full of bread and cheese and tomato.

'I love Sexy Barista. When I say one sugar, he knows I really want two.'

'You should ask him out!'

'Hard pass,' I groan. 'Do other people's friends ever stop trying to get them laid?'

I know it's gross, but the only sexy barista I want is Max. He works at a cafe in Collingwood that I've never been to, and I can never find the right excuse to casually drop by.

'You can't live your whole life juggling Tinder dates and hangovers.'

'Why not? It's working great so far. Last week someone asked me to send him pictures of my feet to wank to.'

She cringes.

'He offered me fifty dollars! I considered it.'

'If Evan and I ever break up, I'm becoming a nun,' says Bec. 'Why do you put up with all that stuff?'

'What choice do I have? If someone tried to hit on me in a bar, I'd assume they'd slipped something in my drink.'

'You don't open yourself to possibilities.'

'But I am open to possibilities,' I say, frowning. 'I use the apps. I go out with people all the time. I just don't like any of them.'

'You don't like anyone because your standards are so high. What about that finance guy you went out with? Back in November? He was cute.'

'He was twenty-five minutes late and told a story about his pet rabbit drowning itself.'

'So?'

'Even his rabbit didn't want to be with him! Why should I?'

'If I held Evan to your impossible standards, we wouldn't be together,' she says, and I frown harder. 'This book I'm reading says you have to commit to loving the *whole* person. Do I love spending half my weekend with him on a golf course? No, but I love having someone to watch *MasterChef* with. Compromise. Acceptance. Togetherness. You're complicit in your own unhappiness.'

'I'm fine. *I'm* not drowning myself in my water dish.'

'One day,' Bec says, assuming a smug and high-eyebrowed expression, 'you'll find a real relationship and you'll learn about sacrifice and compromise. Love is a *verb*.'

I can tell she's memorised this line from one of her self-help books, and she's very proud of it. I avoid responding by taking a big sip of my latte.

Aren't your friends supposed to gas you up and tell you that you deserve the best of the best of the best? What kind of best friend tells you to lower your standards?

Maybe she has a point. Maybe golf barely scratches the surface of all the annoying, unattractive things about Evan, and there's no end to the things she has to overlook to make their relationship work. But do I have to start making compromises from the minute I meet someone? Shouldn't that come later, when I've already fallen in love with them, and I just have to accept that they clip their toenails on the toilet or call their mum before bed every night?

'We just want you to be happy,' she says with a mighty eye-roll.

'No one's *happy*,' I tell her. 'This isn't a Nancy Meyers film. Happiness isn't a flat plane that you climb up onto and coast on. People just have nice moments here and there to stop them throwing themselves onto train tracks.'

Apparently I talk about suicide more before 9 am than most people do all day. All year even.

'Do you actually think that?' she asks.

I make a non-committal face.

'When's your appointment with that therapist?'

I find this a touch condescending, like not agreeing with her automatically makes me mentally ill. But there's no point arguing. According to Bec, she alone understands the complexities of building a life worth living, and my lingering headache has sapped any energy I might have had to contradict her. She announces that she has a teleconference in ten minutes, and I need to make my way back to a staff meeting, anyway, so we peck cheeks and part ways, perhaps a little less enthusiastically than usual.

She means well. I should learn to take it as a sign of affection and let it go.

I would do better to channel my energy into impressing Margot with my impeccable social media management skills or thoughtful compliments about today's outfit. Maybe I'll corner her over office drinks to have an intense discussion about our shared love of NARS lip crayons, and any icky awkwardness will dissolve into an office marriage. Then she'll have to acknowledge how good I am at my job. I might as well go ahead and change my email signature to *Penny Moore, Account Director*.

A while later, when I'm on my third instant coffee and beginning the monumental task of choosing between a banh mi or a baked potato for lunch, Margot appears at my desk.

'Can I speak with you?' she asks. My breath hitches in surprise, and I burn my throat on a sip of scalding Blend 43. It's not really a question. Before I can do more than wheeze a '*yes*', she has turned on her heel and made for the conference room, and I'm expected to follow.

Margot compensates for being very short by wearing stilettos, even on Fridays, and takes five little steps for my one long stride. I want to ask if she has big plans for the weekend, but my voice comes out hoarse, so I try to pass the whole thing off as a cough.

'So …' she says from the head of the table. She could have sat anywhere but took fifteen extra tiny steps to make a point. Power dynamics are in play.

'So!' I plaster on a smile of manufactured confidence and positivity. I feel like my oesophagus has tied itself in a knot.

'This is uncomfortable,' she says, and I laugh politely.

'Yeah, isn't —'

'I know when you first joined the team, we talked about you hopping up to director level at the end of your probation.'

'Yes! I'm so —'

'I do appreciate your interest, Penelope,' she says.

I wish she would let me finish my sentences. And I wish she wouldn't call me Penelope.

'But …'

'Oh.'

My stomach sinks. The knot in my throat squeezes ever tighter.

'The senior team feels that you're still a little green for the step up to that role.'

'Oh.'

'We do appreciate your interest,' she repeats.

'Okay.'

'Perhaps in a few years,' she says, giving my hand a little pat. Her hands are alarmingly cold for an office with such bad air conditioning.

A few years? A few *years*?

'Okay.'

'Okay?'

'Yeah, no, yes, I understand.'

'Anything else?'

'No,' I say automatically. 'No, well — if there's anything I can do. To, um, convince you. That I could do the job.'

'I'll have a think,' she says, smiling thinly.

I try to match it and fail.

Margot excuses herself, and I'm surprised to find my teeth clenched.

This is why I didn't want to think about it. I knew it wasn't going to happen. If you have to wonder, the answer is always no. Maybe I should change my email signature to *Penny Moore, Idiot* instead.

CHAPTER FOUR

Between Bec's inability-slash-refusal to unravel herself from her couple cocoon, Annie's relentless pursuit of hitting every career milestone ahead of schedule, and my pathetic compulsion to keep all my plans vague in case Max calls last minute and wants to see me, it has been weeks since we've all been in the same place at the same time. So when Bec messages us and asks us to dinner on Wednesday night and says it's really, really important, I'm inclined to make the time.

Usually when we get dinner, we go for dumplings in the city because you can bring your own wine and my runty paycheque prefers a night out that costs less than $30. But Bec has already booked us a table at Entrecote in South Yarra. Her news needs to be delivered somewhere nice, she said.

I have to take a train and a tram to get there and find myself sandwiched between another commuter's sweaty back and the door. My life is so glamorous.

My phone buzzes and, trying not to elbow anyone in the face, I fish it out of my bag to find a message from Max. With a jolt, I realise that I've forgotten to think about him for four whole days. This might be the longest I've ever gone without thinking of him. It makes me feel strangely guilty. Looking down at his message (*Max Fitzgerald (17:40): Want to get baked and watch Four Corners? Miss you beautiful xx*), I'm struck both by surprise at this unusual display of affection and what it could mean. Is he apologising for kicking me out the other night?

I can't tell my friends about this. By now they are truly sick of analysing every little thing he ever does. I don't want to tell them because I'm so uninterested in being that girl: obsessed with finding a boyfriend, so set on being validated by men that I can't hold a conversation about anything else. No thank you, not today, not ever.

I know I'm not supposed to believe in any of that shit, by the way. I shouldn't think that the key to happiness is a husband, or that low self-esteem can be solved with the right lipstick and $500 at Agent Provocateur. This is real life. I'm not Carrie fucking Bradshaw.

If there's a spider in the house, I use a glass and a piece of paper and take it outside. To open a tight jar, I pour hot water over it or give it a good whack against the benchtop. I taught myself to fix a leaky tap with a YouTube tutorial. I don't own any dresses that I need help zipping up. Trust me, I'm good. I've got this whole single girl thing sorted.

But sometimes I get a bit sad. Once in a while — come in close so I can whisper it — I wish I had *someone*.

It's like I'm waiting for my life to start. So far, these situationships and setbacks are part of a cold open, and I'm ready for someone to roll the opening credits. I'm sick of the holding pattern, but I don't know how to land on my own.

When I'm hungover, dreading another week of work and feeling bloated and low, I start to wonder, *Why not me?* I've tried so hard with Max, watched my phone for so many hours, soldiered through so many romcoms and revised my Tinder bio so many times. It's so easy to pick myself apart. If I had Bec's collarbones or Annie's quick wit. If I had more interesting hobbies, if I didn't get nervous and lose my train of thought so often, if I could make cooler references. If I put myself out there more, if I learned how to do full body contouring, if I went running more often. Sometimes, the serotonin drops and the sun dims and I know, I'm sure, the real truth is that I'm just not lovable. And it becomes all too easy to crawl into bed and stay there for a week, diving into these ugly thoughts for other horrible truths to anchor me there.

But I can't get into all of that on a Wednesday night. Not because my friends wouldn't rush to tell me I'm wrong, because they would. I just know I can't talk about any of it without unloading about all of it. I decide to put an embargo on all Max talk, at least until tomorrow.

'Don't worry,' I call as I spot Annie in the corner of the Botanical, the chic bar next door to Entrecôte. She has an icy gin and tonic waiting for me, and I've never loved her more. 'The most beautiful girl you know has arrived.'

'What are you talking about?' she replies. 'I got here ten minutes ago.'

'I said most beautiful, not most obnoxious.'

She flicks water at me from her sweating glass.

When the weather is above thirty degrees, I swear, G&Ts are basically Gatorade. We need them. For electrolytes. I down half of mine in the first sip, and we launch into catching up while we wait for chronically late Bec.

'So,' Annie begins, tossing her perfect blow dry over her shoulder, 'how does it feel knowing that your best friend is up for senior associate?' She's a lawyer who works out before I'm even awake, and she has a weekly standing appointment at the nail salon near her house. She's who I want to be when I grow up.

'Stop it!' I cry. 'Already?'

'Ahead of the curve, babe.' She shrugs, delighted with herself. 'Just really smart and great at my job. Racing up the corporate ladder. Ooh! Should we get champagne? Let's celebrate.'

'We should wait for Bec,' I tell her, thinking how I'd prefer to pay for a third of a bottle rather than a half. This dinner alone will put me on a diet of tinned spaghetti on toast all week.

'True,' says Annie, making a point of checking the time on her phone. 'So, it's not official or anything, but it came up with my boss, Lydia, you know —'

'Ten feet tall, cheekbones, terrifying?'

'She's asked me onto this huge litigation case; it'll go to the Supreme Court —'

'Oh my god!'

'*Massive.* And she said — well, she implied: heavily — that if I do well with it, I can look at a title upgrade and my own office in a few months.'

'That's amazing!'

'It'll mean basically living in the office, though,' she says, grimacing. 'Seriously, I'm going to start keeping clothes in my desk drawer. I'll probably work until midnight most nights. I've even said I'll go in on the weekend.'

'Work on a Saturday? That's sacrilege.'

'Mountains of research to do. There'll be a whole team behind it.'

'I like to imagine you're Cher Horowitz highlighting the September third calls.'

'If only. I wish any of the clerks looked like Alicia Silverstone.'

'Well then, what's the point? You should quit and find a firm with prettier lawyers. Where does whatsherface work? Has she replied to you yet? It's been days.'

'Fuck Lillian.' Annie rolls her eyes. 'Five dates in and she disappears for four days. She replied today, finally —'

'Finally!'

'She said she'd been slammed at work, but I did a tiny bit of completely harmless stalking on the socials, and she spent the weekend on a yacht on Sydney Harbour with her ex-girlfriend. There were tagged photos. She's a dick.'

'Fuck Lillian,' I say, loyally outraged.

We spit at the very idea of her, and the conversation churns into a dissection of her worst traits. That's what friends are for. Lillian isn't the worst of them. You should have seen the shitshow three months she spent being love-bombed by Amanda, ending in a weeping meltdown in a Witchery change room when Amanda broke it off via text. Or the long-distance disaster that had Annie driving to Albury every other weekend, which ended when it turned out the girl was married to a man. It's one sordid drama after another.

Quietly, I'm a little relieved. How would it be if all of my friends were not just coupled up, but wildly successful and happy with their careers? I'd go from lovably frazzled to downright pitiable. Sometimes I catch a look on Bec's face when I talk about a particularly painful Margot barb or some sad Max anecdote, and her furrowed brow and pursed lips make me feel pathetic. At least with Annie's floundering love life, I feel like someone's equal.

Somewhere between our first and second drinks, I ask Annie, 'Are you happy?'

'You've been talking to Bec too long. What has she said now?'

'I mean it. Are you?'

'In what way?' she asks.

'Like, broadly. Career, wardrobe —' I pull a queasy face '— relationships.'

'Mm,' she stalls, pushing the ice in her drink around with the cucumber garnish. 'I'm happy enough. Not everything is where I want it to be. But it's relative, you know? If I'm feeling shit about Lillian —' we flip each other off '— or any girl, then it comforts me to know that my career is going well, even if my love life isn't.'

'What about when none of it is going very well?'

'You're just in a little rough patch, babe,' she says kindly, giving my hand a squeeze. 'You're in a rain cloud right now. It'll pass.'

'When?' I ask, my voice small.

'Soon. I promise.'

She passes me her cocktail napkin to dab at the corners of my eyes and pulls a stupid face to make me laugh. It stops real tears before they have a chance to form.

We're officially in danger of losing our reservation, so we head next door and order another cocktail while waiting for Bec. I always get a hangover if I have more than two drinks, so why stop there? Might as well make a night of it.

'About fucking time,' calls Annie, waving Bec over. 'You only live down the street. How can you be twenty fucking minutes late? I'm fucking starving.'

'Honestly, Annie,' Bec hisses. 'Can you watch your *effs*? We're in South Yarra.'

'People in South Yarra say fuck too.'

'Yeah, I bet they even use it as a verb sometimes,' I add, and Bec scowls.

'Well, can you not say the F-word for one minute? I have news. Big news.'

'Sounds like someone has news,' mutters Annie, and I snort into my glass.

Here in this noisy restaurant, full of gin and in-jokes, being stupid with my two favourite people in the world, I'm okay. The nonstop internal panic dims to a barely audible hum. I'm safe here with the people I love most. So often I feel like I'm running out of things to say, like I have so little going on in my life and head that I'm simply out of conversation to make. How much can I talk about what I'm watching on Netflix, or Emily Ratajkowski's abs, or how sad my boss and my not-boyfriend make me? That's why I keep a *New York Magazine* subscription, so I can binge on news and use it in conversation: a weird cult at Sarah Lawrence; why millennials are flocking to astrology like religion; which lip balms Cara Delevingne can't live without. What do other people fill up their time with? CrossFit? Volunteering at the RSPCA? Molly? But here, it doesn't matter. I'm with my girls.

'Sorry,' I say. 'We'll be nice. We want to know your news.'

Bec looks unimpressed. I think she gets tired of having to be the mum of the group. Finally, she can't hold on to her bad mood any longer and she cries out, 'I'm engaged!'

Annie and I freeze. Time has simply stopped. Bec's smile is so wide that it might crack her face in two. I can see her wisdom teeth. Her jewelled left hand is hanging in the air between us.

'Aren't you going to say anything?'

'But you're only twenty-six,' says Annie.

'What has that got to do with anything?'

'Your parents still pay your phone bill.'

'So *what*?' sighs Bec, impatient.

'So how can you have a *husband*?'

'My mum had two kids by the age of twenty-four.'

'Yeah, in the nineties, when there was nothing good on TV.'

'I should have known you'd be like this,' snaps Bec, pulling her diamond out of our face. It's pear shaped. And the band is yellow gold. How did she keep from vomiting long enough to say yes? 'But I expected more of you, Penny.'

'Of me?' I ask. 'What did I do?'

'You did nothing. Your best friend is engaged, and you have nothing to say.'

'Babe, I'm just — we're just surprised! I'm happy for you! We both are! Annie, tell her.'

'Of course we are!' says Annie, rushing to our defence. 'That's great, babe, really!'

Bec sniffs, chewing on the inside of her cheek and refusing to look at us.

'Evan is so lovely,' I say, with false conviction. I've only met him a handful of times, and we've never exactly had any meaningful conversation, but he seems nice enough. 'You're going to be so happy together.'

'I know we are,' says Bec.

'Engaged!' cries Annie, milking it. 'A wedding!'

'You look so good in white.'

'Yes, I do,' says Bec, pursed lips beginning to give way to something like a smirk.

'And a wedding registry is a great way to make someone buy you one of those Le Creuset things you always make eyes at.'

'Will you make sure it's the wasabi-coloured one?' she asks. 'If my mother gets me the teal, I'll never speak to her again.'

'There's our girl!' Annie beams. 'Let's get champagne! Congratulations!'

The world has changed, but no one else in the restaurant seems to notice. Doesn't the two-top next to us understand that the next chapter of Bec's life has suddenly started? Why aren't they as shocked and disturbed and frightened as I am? Is it just me or does she seem older? I bet she could explain what stamp duty is now.

How many more dinners like this do we have left, I wonder. How long will it be before we're having to specify that our catch-ups are not baby friendly? Will she even be able to come to dinners, or will her commute from the inevitable holiday house on the peninsula be a convenient excuse for the friendship to fade to nothing?

This is all wrong, wrong, wrong. Why is she doing this? Who even gets married anymore? Didn't our generation collectively agree to adopt some Scandi model for long-term cohabitation without needing to get confetti and taffeta involved? And, anyway, why does *she* get to go first? How long before Annie joins her, and I have no one? I keep trying to catch Annie's eye to share a look of panic, or disappointment, or disbelief, but she's focused on Bec's retelling of the proposal. Where's the solidarity? Why isn't she more panicked that we're both stuck in first-date hell while one of our friends has jumped the queue? And god, what's wedding planning going to be like? You should have seen how many times Bec dragged us out shopping for the perfect dress for her twenty-fifth birthday party. Her capacity for dramatics exceeds even mine, and I fear there aren't enough sequins in the world to satiate her bridal appetite.

Why am I thinking like this in the first place? Why can't I just be happy for her?

I do a passable job of masking my panic with a face full of bubbles and bread. The night passes quickly, and my glass never gets empty, and when we pay our bill I have to enter my PIN three times before I get it right, but it's okay, it's fine, I just have to hold it in until I get home.

Annie and Bec head east, and I north. I hardly notice as I clench my teeth, dig my nails into my palm, absently scratch my arms. Under the fluorescent light of the 246 bus, I try to practise gratitude for my friendships, but all that comes out are unhelpful comparisons.

Maybe I would get promoted at lightspeed like Annie if I had the discipline to work after 5 pm once or twice a week.

Maybe Bec deserves her happiness more, some karmic privilege I can't identify. And maybe some of us are just destined to be kind of lonely and average at everything. Maybe I should give up and get a stress-free menial job and make peace with my mediocrity. I don't know why they're friends with me anyway. My loud, silly, wonderful friends, who have earned every joyful moment, who probably feel dragged down whenever my name pops up in the group chat. In this hot pool of shame and self-loathing, I'm dipping beneath the surface and giving over to it with such lethargy that I barely feel the full sting of seeing Max's message from three hours ago.

Max Fitzgerald (18:16): Sorry, wrong person. X

CHAPTER FIVE

It isn't until I get a reminder notification on Wednesday morning that I remember the therapy session I booked weeks ago. The girls made me promise to go after the anxiety attack I had in the crowded H&M sale section last month. I had every intention of cancelling the session, but now it's too late and I'd have to pay the full fee, so I might as well just get it over with. I text Margot a hundred apologies and set off, disgruntled.

So here I am in this sleek waiting room, fourteen floors above Collins Street, pretending not to hate the music the receptionist has on — some woodwind shit on a Spotify playlist that's probably called *Mindful Meditations for Miserable Mondays* or whatever — with sweat patches steadily bleeding out of the armpits of my shirt.

It's 9:04 am. I'm about to get up and tell the receptionist I've had an emergency text and I have to go, when a door in the hallway opens and a voice dryly calls out, 'Penelope?'

Ugh, fine. Too late. I swing my bag over my shoulder and follow her into her office.

She's probably only ten years older than me, and it takes me by surprise. How did this thirty-something find time to get a master's in psychology and set up a practice with good enough SEO to land her on the front page of the search '*anxiety depression therapist inner east Melbourne*'? She even sort of looks like me, tallish and pale, with lazily balayaged hair in a sloppy bun and wearing a top I've seen at Gorman. There's a purple stain on her collar.

Her office has one tiny window that looks out onto a flat grey wall. The room itself is home to a cheap red IKEA couch, an uncomfortable-looking wire chair and a little desk cluttered with a tissue box, half a dozen cracked pens, a cactus and a smattering of pastry flakes next to a balled-up brown paper bag. That's probably where the stain came from. The clock on the wall ticks loudly, like it has an agenda. It doesn't exactly inspire comfort.

'Are you a Penelope or a Penny?' Dr Minnick asks, turning to me as she perches thick-rimmed glasses on her nose. I have a pair just like them.

'I'm a Penny.'

'I'm a Jennifer and I *loathe* when people call me Jenny. I always check.'

'Ha,' I laugh politely. 'Considerate.'

'Right, so.' She opens up a notebook and fixes me with an expectant look. 'Dive right in? Dig up all the good stuff?'

'Yeah, why not?'

'Okay. Tell me why you're here.'

'Um. Well. I'm anxious. And depressed, but only sometimes.'

'Anxious all the time?'

'Most of the time. It's not debilitating. I get on with my life. It's just a bit hard sometimes. All the noise in my head.'

'Okay. I know it's a cliche, but I have to ask,' she says, clicking blue ink into her retractable pen, 'what's your relationship with your parents like?'

Here we go. This conversation. Therapists always want to drill down into this and won't accept that it isn't important. It isn't like these sessions are cheap. At best, I'm out of pocket

$125 while they yammer on about how we're all shaped by childhood experiences, but *I'm* not — at least not by this one — and we never get anywhere.

'I'm close to my dad,' I say. 'Well, close enough. He moved out to the country a couple of years ago, so I don't see him much, but we talk a couple of times a week.'

'And your mum?'

'I don't have one,' I tell her, jaw set and ready to argue. I drag the pendant on my necklace against its chain. 'She left when I was a baby. I don't have any memories of her. We've never had any contact. I have my dad and my brother, and they're great, and they love me, and I don't have a massive gaping hole in my heart about it. Everyone always insists I do, but I don't. Talking about it just feels like a waste of time. She may as well have never even existed. If it was that significant, my brother would be in therapy too, and he's not. He has a husband and they just moved to London and they're deliriously happy, so my problems must come from somewhere else.'

I'm ready for her to challenge me, to tell me it *is* significant and we *will* be talking about it, and I'm ready to use it as an excuse to storm out and refuse to pay for a session that only lasted three minutes. That would be gratifying. I could get breakfast somewhere on my way back to the office. Maybe a bagel from 5 & Dime.

'Okay,' she says instead. 'And you've been in therapy before?'

'Um.' All that indignation has nowhere to go, and I have to choke it down. 'Yes. A couple of times.'

'Why did you stop?'

'It gets expensive.' I shrug. 'And it feels a bit pointless. Like, if I'm not having a tough time with anything in particular, it feels like I'm just going to therapy to complain a bit, but there's no actual progress. I can complain about my life to my friends, and the bar tab is less than the bill here.'

'Finding a psychologist you work well with can be challenging,' she says, scribbling on her notepad. I'd love to read all my therapists' notes about me someday. Or maybe I wouldn't. Some things you never want to know.

'Maybe I only want something to be wrong with me so I can explain away my bullshit. Maybe I'm just lazy and self-indulgent.'

'Those are strong words to use about yourself.'

'Does self-deprecation have to be a symptom of self-loathing?' I grimace. 'Can't I just be funny?'

'Well, I think it's interesting that criticism is the first thing you reach for,' she says, not rising to meet or counter my tone.

'But who sits around listing all the reasons they're great? Arseholes.'

'Give me three reasons you're great, then. Free pass for conceit, go on.'

'Uh.' I'm stumped. 'I'm smart, I guess.'

'Smart, that's one.'

'I'm … nice?'

'You don't sound sure.'

'I don't yell at waiters or anything. I put my spare change in those RSPCA receptacles at the shop. I remember my friends' birthdays. I recycle. Does that make me nice?'

'You tell me,' she says. 'Do you want me to write down "*nice*"?'

'No,' I grumble, slumping down against the couch cushions. 'I'm not that nice. I hate my boss. I resent my friends' happy relationships. That's not nice.'

'Why do you do that?'

'Because I'm petty and jealous and awful?' I offer sarcastically for her to raise her eyebrows at.

'But that's not *why* you do it,' she says, eyebrows resolutely steady. How annoying. 'People don't yell at waiters because they're arseholes. They do it because they feel powerless and yelling at someone makes them feel important. Why do you resent your friends' happiness?'

'I don't know. Because I don't have it. Or because they get a partner and I'm not the centre of attention anymore. Like, we text all day and see each other every weekend and support each other through everything, then Bec gets a boyfriend and he does all that for her, so she doesn't need me, but I still need those things from her.'

'Do you feel like your friend Bec has replaced you with her partner?'

'Well, she still has someone to see every weekend, and I'm lucky if I get whatever scraps of her time are left. It's like our friendship isn't important now that she has her relationship.'

'What about when you have a partner?'

'Ha!' I bark, and I feel my face get hot. 'Not applicable.'

'Sounds like there's a bigger story behind that. Do you struggle to find a partner?'

'That's one way of putting it. I'm sort of … it's nothing, honestly. Like, it's actually nothing. I still see my ex a lot. *A lot* a lot. But it's not a relationship.'

'What's his name?'

'Max.'

'Max,' she says, scribbling it down. 'You two are still friends?'

'Well, that's the word we use. But we aren't really. We don't go to bars, or visit NGV exhibitions, or braid each other's hair. I've asked, but he — y'know. He thinks that would confuse things. Mostly we just watch movies in his room and have sex, and then I go home.'

'You don't sound happy about that.'

'It's fine.'

'Would you like it to be different?'

'Yeah, but he gets funny about it if I bring it up.'

'How long has that been the agreement between you two?'

'A year or so. A little less.'

'Why do you keep doing it if it isn't what you want?'

'What choice do I have?' I ask, getting a bit annoyed again. 'I want to be with him, and this is the only way I can do that.'

'Why do you want to be with him?'

I'm chewing hard on the inside of my cheek, and I stare at the floor to avoid giving her a blatantly irritated look. What kind of question is that? 'Because I do. He's smart and interesting and we were happy together.'

'And why do you think he doesn't want a relationship with you? *You're* smart and interesting.'

'Because,' I snap, 'I'm too needy or too fat or too not enough in a million other ways.'

'But you're not too needy or too fat or too generally deficient for him to sleep with regularly.'

Dr Minnick keeps her voice light and pleasant, with no inflection for me to draw her real thoughts out of. She's a diplomat. My mouth is full of the metallic taste of blood. The filthy look I'm not bold enough to give her directly is boring a hole in her cheap grey rug. I shrug again. She doesn't know him at all. Who does she think she is, talking about him like that? Max was a perfectly wonderful boyfriend before, back when I knew how to be fun and carefree and could fit into the occasional size eight. How dare she?

'What I hear is that you've got a lot of self-criticism to explain away your unhappiness. It's not "*The timing isn't right*" or "*Max is afraid of commitment*". According to you, it's all your fault.'

She waits for me to respond, but I don't.

'And what does holding on to that blame do to you? You're carrying it around, bringing your self-diagnosed deficiencies to his door and apologising for them. How does that feel?'

I wearily shrug again. At this rate, I'm going to throw my shoulders out. 'Pretty shit.'

'But you're used to feeling pretty shit, aren't you?'

'Yeah,' I say, laughing despite myself. 'It's familiar territory.'

'I think you're probably more comfortable there. I think that's why you keep going back. Every time you see him and feel shit, it reinforces the negative things you believe about yourself.'

'Maybe. I don't know.'

'And then you get angry that other people around you aren't drowning in all the same self-loathing as you are. You resent their ability to form stable relationships.'

'I don't want my friends to hate themselves, or to be alone. They don't deserve that.'

'Do you deserve that?'

'I didn't say that. There are just areas I could improve on. My ... brain, my body, my personality, I don't know.'

'Listen, I don't want to cut you off. I want to tell you what I think I've learned about you so far, and you can tell me if you agree or not.'

'Yeah, okay.'

She takes a breath and adjusts her glasses, reading off her notes. I steel myself for the worst. I should have left before we got into any of this. My brain conjures an image of Winona Rider in *Girl, Interrupted* saying, '*What's your diag-nonsense?*'

I wish I had the bone structure to pull off her pixie cut and boatneck tops.

'So, neurologically speaking, our brains love shortcuts. When you revisit an old habit, a familiar pattern, your brain goes, "*Okay, yep, I've been here before, I know how to react to this,*" and you get a hit of dopamine. When you get an answer right at a pub quiz: dopamine. The sound of a new text message: dopamine. A bit of affection from Max: dopamine. You get the picture.'

'Right.'

'When I asked you to tell me three nice things about yourself, you came up with one positive and three negative things. You're great at criticising yourself.'

'Isn't everyone? That's normal.'

'Well, "normal" and "healthy" aren't necessarily the same thing.'

'Okay.'

'I'm interested in finding out where this negative self-belief comes from,' she continues. 'Somewhere along the way, you came to believe that you're fundamentally insufficient, no matter how much your dad and brother and your friends tell you they love you. You don't believe them, but you do believe Max when he says — not verbally, necessarily, but through his actions — that you're not enough. So you stay in that cycle because it feels good to have your beliefs validated.'

'So, what, I'm a glutton for punishment?' I ask, barely biting back my incredulous tone. 'I'm with Max because I hate myself?'

'Because it's familiar,' she says softly. 'Because it's what you feel you deserve.'

'But that doesn't explain the shit with Bec,' I argue. 'If I believed that I deserve to be miserable, wouldn't I love the excuse to feel sorry for myself?'

'It doesn't mean it doesn't hurt. Actually, I think that's why it hurts so much. Someone else might think, *Bec's priorities have shifted, I'll have to find someone else to text all day and see every weekend*. But you think, *She's replaced me and abandoned me*, and you list all the reasons why she might want to do something like that. You feel things so deeply because after years of criticising yourself, you've worn your emotional resilience down to nothing. Bec, Max — it's the same pattern. Why not walk away from these relationships if they're so unsatisfying? Why continue to expect something from them that they aren't willing or able to give? Because we love being right, even when it hurts.'

Dr Minnick holds her wastebin out for me, and that's the first time I realise my hands are full of shredded tissues. The lap of my trousers is covered in freckles of white lint, tacky with it, and my collar is wet from tears. It feels like we've been in this little room for hours, and I feel bullied and scared and ashamed, all of it, all at once. And annoyed with myself for not knowing all of this stuff already and at needing some stranger with a snaggletooth and a curling motivational poster on the wall to point it out to me.

She smiles kindly as I drop the damp, disgusting tissues in the bin. Sitting still feels lazy and wrong, so I pick up my bag. The strap is brittle and cold in my hand.

'There's a lot we can work on together,' she tells me. 'You did a really good job today.'

I make a noise between a laugh and a sob.

'It's not always going to be this hard. We're going to get you to a better place, and you're going to learn how to be proud of yourself too.'

I nod, rendered mute, and pull out the last tissue in the box to wipe my nose.

We spend the last five minutes of the session practising breathing exercises. I think they're a crock of shit, but I'll take any excuse to stop the relentless cross-examination of my worst habits and deepest wounds, so I do them without complaint.

'Have a glass of water, take it easy today, and give yourself a break,' says Dr Minnick when I'm allowed to open my eyes again.

'Thanks. Thank you,' I say, shielding myself in the performance of digging my wallet out of my bag to pay at reception, too mortified for eye contact and too tired for anything else.

The thick humidity of Collins Street has given way to hard rain, and I stand and let it hit me, as people around me dash between shopfront awnings. They're probably staring. I take in great gulping, desperate lungfuls of air, and I wonder why I paid Dr Minnick to make me feel like this. Am I so transparent: a walking sandwich board for a list of insecurities and pain points? How many sessions does it take, exactly, to clean out twenty-six years of hurt and hate? Will I ever actually get there, or will I be this frayed and exposed nerve forever?

CHAPTER SIX

I've decided to ignore everything Dr Minnick said.

I cried the whole train ride to work. Then I cried on the phone to my dad as I took shelter under the overpass on Swan Street, though I couldn't tell him what I was crying about. I just told him I was having a bad day and I missed him, which was most of the truth. And then I cried again in the disabled toilets as I scrubbed off the mascara rings under my eyes. And in the indignity of squatting under the hand-dryer to sort my hair out, I thought of Dr Minnick's frizzy, haphazard bun and realised she was no role model. Why believe the psychoanalysis of a woman with a jam stain on her top? Who said she knows best? No one. Not me. She's just invented a narrative around me; that doesn't make it true.

Fuck her. I'm fine. I'm great! What's more, I've come up with my own plan for how to cope with Max.

For a week, I wait at least two hours before responding to any of Max's texts.

I want to tell you that I'm consumed with work, or that I've taken up microdosing LSD and managed to push it all out of my mind as part of the search for a greater purpose, but it's not true. I go frantic-searching for my phone every time it makes a sound. I only wear outfits with pockets, so I can have it on me everywhere I go. I keep it face-up on my desk and glance at it every five seconds. If I'm in a long meeting, I'll sneak off to the bathroom to check it as often as I can get away with. I chew through my battery by mid-morning.

Most of the time the pings are just from the group chat or Candy Crush (why do I still have that?), but sometimes it's him, and I get this hot flash all over that has nothing to do with the weak office air conditioning.

I don't start writing back straightaway. I made a promise to myself. And I don't want to give him the satisfaction of seeing my three little dots appearing and disappearing. After he messages me, I go on a posting spree on Instagram, or leave Facebook Messenger open so he can sit and stare at the green dot next to my name and feel the full weight of my silence. I've been on the other side of that green dot. I've carried that feeling around with me everywhere for a year. Now he's the one double- or even triple-texting for once, and, well, I don't hate it.

It goes something like this:

Max Fitzgerald (11:12): Had the weirdest dream I was back at uni getting roasted by that philistine from our politics tute
Max Fitzgerald (12:27): I'm having thesis-itis, want to come round and distract me tonight?
Max Fitzgerald (12:56): Pennnnn. If you're nice I might even throw in a pizza to sweeten the deal xx
Penelope Moore (15:12): Can't tonight, sorry pal x
Max Fitzgerald (15:12): Even if it's four cheese pizza? xx

I invent wild fantasies that it's all been a big misunderstanding, and he's wanted me all along; all I needed to do was stop being so high maintenance about it. Dr Minnick was wrong, and this is proof that the only thing standing between me, Max, and Sunday trips down the Aldi middle aisle has been my inability to play it cool. I figure I'll only need to keep this up for another couple of days.

But no matter how busy I am, or how good it feels when his name pops up on my phone, I still find time to dig at that unhelpful corner of my mind that wonders who he had meant to text that day. When it's long past bedtime, I'm still awake, carefully scrolling through the Instagrams of every woman I know he has ever interacted with.

But game-playing is tiring, and I'm ready to switch off my brain and talk and think about anything else. After showering off the sweat and stress of the day, I wipe off the mirror and sternly tell my reflection, 'No boy talk tonight, got it? None at all. We're better than this.' And it's true. I'm a smart and (ahem) hilarious woman with interests and opinions, and there are far better things to lend my mind to than whether some guy thinks I'm cute, or how long I can play hard to get to teach him a lesson. It's enough.

In my bathrobe, towel turban and a clay mask, I'm working on the perfect Friday night kick-off. I've got Lizzo blasting, a coffee capsule, and some ancient Kahlua I've scavenged from the back of the pantry, and I'm ready to ring in the weekend with a pep in my step and a warm buzz in my extremities. I might go for a mani-pedi tomorrow and buy some flowers for my room. Maybe I'll finally learn how to meal prep and not eat three dinners by Sunday night. I am gearing up for this to be the best, easiest, most productive weekend of *my entire life*! I fucking love this song!

'What Kate Hudson movie montage are you living in?' comes Leo's voice from nowhere.

'Oh my *god*!' I cry, drenched in my homemade espresso martini. 'I just nearly *died*.'

'And what a way to go,' he laughs. 'Sexy outfit.'

'Surprised to *death*! I wasn't expecting an audience.'

'Date cancelled last minute,' he says with a shrug, and helps himself to my Kahlua. 'I see you have big plans too, Mrs Doubtfire.'

'I'm going out,' I say, trying to use the sleeve not soaked in coffee and booze to wipe off my mask. 'I was making myself beautiful before you gave me a heart attack.'

'Plans with the big bad ex?'

'No. We're ignoring him.'

'Good girl.'

There is a pause and a second of eye contact in which it occurs to me that I'm very nearly naked. I clear my throat and pull the lapels of my bathrobe tighter.

'I'd better get ready,' I say, breaking the silence. 'Places to go, people to see. I'm extremely popular, you know.'

In the reflection of the microwave door, I'm pink from rubbing my mask on my sleeve, and my towel turban has pulled my left eyebrow up by half an inch. I resolve to be a lot more dressed in the kitchen now that my housemate is home so often.

'Where are you off to?' he asks, pushing himself up to sit on the kitchen counter.

'My friend moved house. We're going to celebrate, but I think she just wants us to help her put all her IKEA stuff together.'

'Can I come?' he asks. 'I'm alright with an Allen key.'

'Oh!' That's a surprising request. But we've lived together for over a year and he hasn't displayed any sociopathic or otherwise annoying tendencies, so what's the harm? 'Let me ask Annie. So long as you're *really* good with an Allen key ...'

'Is that lame, inviting myself along? I only have about two friends anymore.'

Oof. I guess his ex got custody of all their friends in the breakup.

'Bring wine and split the Uber and you've got a deal,' I say, and he brightens up. And they say making friends as an adult is difficult. Pfft.

CHAPTER SEVEN

'Visitors!' cries Annie, throwing her front door open to us. 'Lovely Penelope! And Leo! Come in and be impressed!'

'Lovely apartment, lovely apartment owner,' he says, pecking her cheek.

'Bec brought Evan,' she tells us with a funny, hard smile.

'Oh, nice,' says Leo, and he makes his way over to them. I always forget I only know Leo through Bec. They've been friends longer than she and I have, in fact, but I hardly ever hear her talk about him.

Meeting my deliberately blank face with a resigned shrug, Annie drops the topic; there's no sense ruining a perfectly good Friday night. Leo pops the cork on his bottle (Piper Heidsieck: nice but not too nice — looks like he got the memo) and the mood resets.

As ever, Annie is ahead of the curve: the first of the three of us to get a mortgage.

For a solid two months last year, Annie and I spent every Saturday morning visiting open houses in search of the perfect first home for her. From expansive penthouse studios to dark ground-floor flats, from rickety old two-bedroom places above Indian restaurants to glossy, soulless apartments with chrome tap fittings and walls thinner than paper, we searched and searched until we found a place with the right energy for her.

She ended up buying herself a bright new one-bedroom apartment at the northern end of Collingwood, on the corner of Smith Street where all the intimidatingly cool people hang out. She has a little balcony just big enough for the three of us to sit on and get blitzed on spritzes all summer, a dreamy walk-in wardrobe, and a rain shower head. The building boasts amenities like a sauna, cinema room, and rooftop community garden. What more could anyone need?

'I love it here,' I tell Leo as he pours champagne into a mug for me. 'I'm moving in. Find another housemate.'

'You'd miss me too much,' he scoffs. 'Who would you pilfer biscuits from?'

'I'll buy my own biscuits when I live here.'

'Maybe you could buy your own biscuits where you already live.'

'Why would I do that when I have you? Isn't there a biscuit clause in my lease?'

'I should never have made you a legal tenant. Biggest mistake of my life.'

'Too late,' I beam. 'You're stuck with me now.'

It's true: I've stolen about three of his dark chocolate Tim Tams in the last two days. Fine, eight. There's a fun familiarity between us lately. He's been home most nights this week, and we have debated about the best burgers within our delivery zone and squabbled about what to watch on Netflix. He knocked on my bedroom door to approve his outfit for a date on Wednesday, and if there's a man alive who can pull off corduroy pants, it's him. Who knew? It's nice having a proper housemate instead of a rarely present house ghost.

I've never spent this much one-on-one time with a housemate before. Before this I lived in a grimy Carlton North sharehouse with four strangers. My clothes stank of their stale weed no matter how many times I washed them, and I swear sitting on the couch gave me a rash, but it was on a tram line and I hadn't needed to pay a bond to move in. When my housemates began to talk about cancelling the gas and electricity supply in an effort to fight climate change and save us each $15 a month, I knew I was done. I couldn't move back home because Dad had moved to the country, so it was kismet that I met Leo. I threw myself at the cheap room in the house he had recently bought.

How old is he, even? I can't imagine anyone in my age bracket can afford to buy an entire house in the inner suburbs. Even Annie could only buy a one-bedroom apartment with considerable help from her parents. I don't even know what he does for a living. I know he and Bec met in a design elective, but how many graphic designers can afford the Tom Ford sunglasses I keep meaning to accidentally borrow from him and never return? Maybe he comes from money. Maybe his battered paperbacks are hiding a private-school kid who grew up playing lacrosse and going on ski trips with the other blazer-wearing Young Liberals of Toorak. Looking at him, though, I can't see it. I see a silly, earnest twenty(thirty?)-something who rides a bike to work and buys outrageously expensive cartons of eggs from farms with the best living conditions for the hens. I shouldn't jump to conclusions about his secret inner posh boy. I should just appreciate my affordable little room, and spring for my own biscuits now and then.

'Right, Annie,' says Leo, when we've all had enough time to let our drinks fizzle into our extremities. 'Put me to work. Hit me with your Malms and your Kallaxes and Björns and Blomkvists and every other Swedish thing you've got. I can follow an instruction manual like you wouldn't believe.'

We split up and get to work. Bec and Evan coo at each other over the build of a single dining chair (*Aw babe, just like when we got our dining set! Remember?*' she says, and he says to all of us, '*We* must *have you round for a dinner party. I've got a recipe for a pork shoulder that'll make you believe in God,*' and I consider taking a vow of vegetarianism to get out of it). I kind of wish Bec had just ditched us for a sedate Friday night in with Evan like usual. Annie and I look in boxes for glassware and plates, but all we find are books and towels and a thirsty little monstera plant. Bec supervises the boys as they heave the washing machine into place. Leo and I put a bed frame together with minimal swearing and drag Annie's mattress onto it, high-fiving each other for getting through it without a tantrum.

The ease with which he fits into our little group is sweet, but it makes me self-conscious. I'm jealous of how comfortable he is with himself: sprawled across the floor, all limbs and gestures as he's telling us a story about the time his trousers got caught in his bike chain and he had to give a presentation at work with only one and a half pant legs. I can never take up space like that. Even now, my ankles are twisted around each other, my shoulders are hunched, and I'm measuring my sips to make sure I don't monopolise the conversation. I'm like a chihuahua on the verge of a nervous breakdown.

I don't know how long I've wanted to be as small as possible. My body has always felt like a problem to be solved, something I feel burdened with and disappointed by. I suck my stomach in when I notice the clean curve of Annie's waist, her dainty wrists uncorking another bottle. Maybe all my problems would be solved if I got the fat sucked out of my thighs. Things just fall into place more easily for skinny-legged women. Look at Alexa Chung. I get my phone out to surreptitiously google '*South Korea plastic surgery tourism*' to research later.

I don't think I'm hideous. Mostly I like my face, my thick hair, my straight nose. I can keep up with Max — there he is again, *tsht!* — in sparring matches about Greek mythology, Vonnegut, David Lynch. His mum likes me. I get him thoughtful gifts. I suck him off even when I don't feel like it. I proofread bits of his thesis and let him use my Netflix password. I don't complain when I pay his half of the UberEats order. And yet sometimes I just wonder if he would be more accessible if I could sit in a crop top without looking like a half-melted ice cream.

Leo lets out a bark-like laugh at a story Evan is telling about an angel investor for his latest venture — what's an angel investor, and why do all of Evan's stories make him sound like he's Mark Zuckerberg without the creepy haircut? — and I'm pulled out of my spiral just in time. Another drink and five more minutes of tallying up the ways I feel like I'm failing and we would enter the drunk-crying danger zone.

Annie's half-furnished flat has turned into a mess of cardboard, loose screws, instruction manuals, and oily napkins. We've demolished four pizzas and five and a half bottles of sparkling. Perhaps guzzling prosecco to quench our thirst was unwise. It's hard to keep track of how many glasses you've had when you're using a University of Melbourne mug for a flute.

'How's your love life, Penny?' asks Evan. I choke on a sip. 'Bec says you're into the barista at work. I won't ask you, Annie — not enough hours in the day!'

'My love life is on pause,' I tell him coolly. That's a bit personal. I don't think he even knows my last name. And that jab at Annie was unnecessary. Bec is rubbing his back under his T-shirt, and it takes effort to keep my scowl to myself.

'You really ought to do something about that,' continues Bec. She's glassy-eyed. 'If you don't hurry up, all the good ones will be taken.'

'Nothing wrong with a sabbatical,' says Leo in my defence.

'Is that what you're doing?' she sneers.

'*Darling,*' says Evan weakly.

Leo focuses on screwing a hinge into place.

'Let's get you some water,' says Annie, breaking the room's chill before it has a chance to set. She grasps Bec's forearm and pulls her towards the kitchen. 'Come on, Drunky Drunkerson. Hydration pitstop.'

'What's wrong with you?' I hiss at Bec under the sound of the running tap. 'Why are you being rude to Leo?'

'Don't you know?' whispers Bec. 'He just left his fiancée at the altar.'

I force a mug of water into her hand. 'Drink this. All of it.'

'She's the loveliest girl,' she continues. 'We've had brunch a few times.'

'You have brunch without us?' asks Annie.

'They had a five-year plan,' says Bec. 'They were all set to get married and then — *bye!* What a *prick.* None of us know what happened. He just woke up one day and ruined her life. Penny, does he have a new girlfriend, is that what it is?'

'I don't think so,' I say uneasily. It feels disloyal to whisper about his love life when he's nothing but nice to me. 'I don't think he's seeing anyone in particular.'

She looks disgusted, and tips the water down the sink. 'I'm going back over. I don't want Evan getting any ideas.'

'So, this is how it's going to be now, huh?' Annie murmurs.

I shrug. She tops up my drink. We watch Bec and Evan *Lady and the Tramp* a piece of capricciosa, and I feel a bit sick.

'You don't mind that I brought Leo, right?'

'Of course not. You asked, and Leo isn't the one making twattish comments about my love life. I think I have a right to not feel like the third wheel in my own flat.'

'Do you think that's true? About his girlfriend?'

'Don't listen to her. She's being a dick. She's on a pre-wedding starvation diet and she's had five mugs of wine. Who cares?'

'He does have a lot of fuckboy qualities, though.'

'Like what?'

'I don't know. A vinyl collection. The inability to maintain interest after a first date. A premium Bumble membership. A drawer full of weird sex toys?'

'One of those twenty-four-carat gold vibrators!' Annie squeaks, and I cackle into my cup.

'He probably sends women home with a gift bag —'

'With a little framed picture of himself —'

'A protein bar to restore her energy after a night of passionate grunting —'

'And an Uber discount code —'

'*Twenty percent off when you enter #OneNightWithLeo.*'

'What are you two laughing about?' calls Bec. 'Is it about me?'

'Not everything is about you,' snaps a pink-faced Annie, wiping her eyes.

'Pen,' says Leo. 'Can you make yourself useful and pass me the little screws?'

The night fizzles out. I help Annie wipe off her lipstick, and make sure she has a glass of water and a sleeve of Nurofen next to her unmade bed. Evan lumps a heavy-lidded Bec into an Uber. The balmy January air matches my warm, slow faculties.

One of us should book an Uber to head home, but Leo nods his head left, and without speaking, we decide to seek out a nightcap.

I've had too many and I'll pay for it later. I'm already dreaming of pancakes, a double shot latte and a long nap in the sunny spot on the couch tomorrow. Still, I chirp, 'Negroni, please!' to the bartender at Smithward. It's dimly lit and crucially quiet, even as the night rages on around it. Never too loud, not too cool.

'Gossip time,' I sing as we find an empty table in the back. 'I heard a rumour about you tonight.'

'Please, respect celebrity privacy,' says Leo. 'Talk to my PR rep about it. Have my people call your people.'

'Shush, I just mean — oh, water, yes, good idea — and I've been dying to know anyway, and now I can ask. Tell me: girlfriend. What happened? Why are you home all the time all of a sudden? Are you as much of a dog as Bec says?'

'Oh, are we drunk enough for the ex talk?'

'Yes!' I cry, both in response to him and the arrival of our drinks. What's more refreshing than the cool fruity sting of a freshly poured cocktail?

'Do we have to?'

'You *have* to tell me or Bec is going to keep telling people that you're out there ditching women at the altar and stomping on their hearts. You'll get a reputation.'

'That's not what happened.'

'Set the record straight then, fuckboy.'

'Shit, alright,' he says, humouring me with a performative sip of his drink. 'We were together for nearly five years. *Fuck*, that sounds like a long time. And it was fine, y'know — *fine*. We were pretty happy. We hadn't moved in together yet because her cat was about nineteen years old and totally blind, and we thought it was cruel to move him from his home. We just decided to wait it out, and it was easier for me to stay over there every night. Anyway, all our friends were starting to take the next step, and my feed was nonstop "life announcements" and people adopting greyhounds. She was sending me links to rings she liked, we were having conversations about good suburbs to raise kids in, and it all seemed pretty inevitable. Then one day we were having breakfast and it came up again — we were making fun of cash bars at weddings or something — and I wasn't excited. Nothing had even changed. Not really. We were still the same people. I still care about her. I think she's a nice person. But being together for a long time didn't seem like a good enough reason to stay together. In another five years, we were still going to be doing fine — not unhappy, not excited — and that sounded miserable. So I ended it. And now I have a reputation, apparently. In hindsight, it's pretty obvious I'd been making excuses for a year or two: excuses to live apart so I didn't have to commit, and excuses to stay together so I wouldn't have to deal with the fall-out. It wasn't fair to either of us.'

'Christ,' I say. The ice in our drinks has melted, and I'm tracing patterns on the table. I can't think of anything scarier than that: investing so much time and thought and energy and love in someone, building a life together and counting on a future, only to have it change completely over a cup of coffee one morning. To have a clear picture of the life ahead of you, and then to have it evaporate in an instant.

'It happens,' he shrugs. There's no regret in it. 'I just fell out of love with her.'

'Been there. Been on the other side of that,' I say, and my shrug is full of the sadness missing from his.

Leo considers me. To give myself the excuse to look away, I ruffle my fringe, flatten it down, flick it into place. Six mugs of prosecco and half a negroni brought us here. I could have just asked him about his job or something. Then I wouldn't feel like I'm sitting under a spotlight.

'Your ex. The one we're mad at. Have you asked him to get back together?'

'Kind of. Sure. He knows.'

'But have you asked? Told him what you want: no qualifiers, no bullshit?'

'I can't just sit him down and say, "*Hey! Be my boyfriend!*" That's psychotic. That's way too needy. He would hate that. I have to kind of … sneak it in.'

Leo raises his eyebrows.

'Are you telling me that a girl could just tell you she wants a relationship with you, and you wouldn't think she was the clingiest, neediest person on the planet?'

'Not if that's what I wanted too. Not if I liked her.'

'So now he doesn't even *like* me?'

'I didn't say that,' he says patiently, countering my rising pitch. 'I'm sure he likes you. You're very likeable. You should just tell him what you want.'

'What if he says no? I'd be *mortified*. Putting myself out there and being shot down? He'd ignore my texts for weeks.'

'Penny,' Leo says, putting his glass down heavily. 'If he said no, why the fuck would you still be texting him? Why would you want to be with someone who doesn't want to be with you?'

I don't have an answer for him. I don't even have an answer for myself. I feel my eyes get hot. Oh no. We are not crying here, not in this dim bar, outnumbered by bored bartenders ready to giggle about the drunk girl with mascara running down her cheeks. I drain my glass, counting on the crisp taste of gin to balance me out. It's all getting a bit real in here. This conversation needs to go somewhere lighter. I have to get out.

'Hey,' says Leo warmly. He's probably also panicked that I'll burst into tears and make a scene. 'Gelato pitstop on the way home? C'mon, on me.'

CHAPTER EIGHT

Penelope Moore (01:07): I needto talk to yo vvvcinpotant pls??vv 💜 💜 🐥 💜

Amped up on the sickly combination of a fruity drink and a double scoop of tiramisu gelato, I shout a '*bye!*' over my shoulder to Leo, and I'm off. It's way too late to be navigating Richmond backstreets alone, but I'm teetering on the edge of a second wind, and nothing — not the blaring music from the karaoke bar on the corner, the drunk patrons spilling out of the pub, a huddle of mini-skirted girls consoling their crying friend, poor thing — can stop me. I'm a woman on a mission. And I need to pee.

I check my phone as I round the corner to his front door. *Seen: 01:12.* That was nine minutes ago. Great! He's awake. Armed with all the precision my blurring focus can muster, I push the intercom button for flat #9. A brief buzz would probably do, but time is moving too fast around me and I don't trust it, no sir, and the bzzzzzzzzzzzz is pretty quiet, so I lean into it and let it ring out a while longer. Oh! Someone's coming out the front door and I can zip inside past them. How perfect, how convenient!

Up the stairs two at a time, and I'm so glad Max's building security is so crap or else I'd be out of luck. Did you see me make it up three flights without slipping even once? I'm a lot of things — lots! Wonderful things AND bad things and that's okay! I'm human and I'm great! — but my balance is something no one can take away from me. Girls with legs like giraffes can't trust their balance like I can. Take that, social expectations of beauty! Take that, Alexa Chung!

I hammer knocks like machine gunfire on his door — *taptaptaptaptaptaptaptaptap* — politeness fading fast and giving way to urgency as impatience presses on my bladder.

'Fuck, Pen, it's one in the fucking morning,' says Max, opening the door.

God, he's good looking.

'I need to pee!' serves as hello.

Usually when I use the bathroom here, I'm paranoid about its proximity to the front door. Can people in the hallway hear me? What about the people in the living room? I don't even trust the running tap; I use a scrunched-up ball of toilet paper to deafen the noise my bodily function makes. Heaven forbid anything spoil the whole sexy carefree perfect delightful mysterious aura I'm always trying to cultivate. No wonder I'm always so tired.

As I wash my hands, I wonder what kind of master's student is dropping $40 on Aesop soap. He probably nicked the bottle from some swanky bar and has been topping it up with dishwashing liquid ever since. I use my clean wet hands to tidy up the flick of my cat-eye and rumple my hair. Per*fection*. I'm ready.

'RIGHT. Where have you gone? Can I have some water?'

He's on the sofa looking crinkly and delicious. Hey! That's my Spice Girls T-shirt he's wearing. I've been looking for it for a year! He gets up to fill a glass in the sink. I'm braver with his back turned.

'You and I both know this is *fucking* ridiculous. No, shhhhh!' I throw my hand up as he opens his mouth to talk. 'I'm talking, it's my talk time. You don't get to sleep with me for a *year* and steal my T-shirt and send me ten memes a day and just IGNORE the rest of my life. I have FRIENDS and a JOB and a HOUSEMATE and a HOUSE and you don't spend any time with them! You've never been to my house! It's ten minutes THAT — no — I don't — THAT way, I think — and look, listen, I like a good weeknight sesh as much as anyone but that is *not* friend shit. You're a bad friend and you aren't my friend, Max. You're my *boy*friend and you know it and you better start acting like it, alright? That's what you are, and you have been this whole time, and not acknowledging it doesn't make it not true. Climate change deniers, you know? This is the SAME THING. The ice caps are melting and those sad photos of those skinny polar bears are *fucked up* and just because people don't say it's true doesn't mean those polar bears aren't skinny and starving! And it's the SAME — oh my god I'm talking so fast I'm dizzy, do you ever get that? My mouth is so dry, it's like I'm talking too fast to even get oxygen in my brain — wouldn't that be the most embarrassing way to die? Fucking yelling at your idiot half-boyfriend? Anyway, that's what you ARE, but full. Full time. And you know that I know you know that you know that, and I'm done acting like it's cool when it's NOT, okay? OKAY?'

From down the hallway, one of Max's housemates shouts, 'Shut the FUCK UP!' and it snaps me out of my tangent. I can't tell yet if I'm embarrassed, but I feel quite sober.

'Okay, Penny,' says Max quietly.

'Okay?'

'Alright. We can try that.'

Am I so drunk that I'm hallucinating, or did you hear that too? Did that tactic — being honest about my feelings, asking

for what I want without dressing it up in a façade of aloofness —
actually work? Is it possible that Leo is, like, really smart? He has
a dog-eared copy of *Crime and Punishment* on the coffee table,
and he's always watching these quiet, intense foreign miniseries
on SBS, but I always assumed these were red herrings. Why
didn't anyone tell me about this trick before? How many nights
have I stayed awake looking for clues that Max gave a shit? All
this time, I could have just … done something about it?

'Oh,' I say. 'Well. Good. Glad we got that sorted.' I don't
know what to do with all the space my shouting has left in the
room.

'D'you want to go to bed?'

'Spend the night here?'

'Yeah, go on,' he says, and I feel his warm hand on my back,
and he's soft and open, and I feel safe.

'I could do that.'

I feel silly after all that, but heat is spreading through my
limbs at the sight of his little smile. He kisses me, and it's
sweet and warm and brief and devoid of the usual urgency.
It's affectionate and familiar, just like when he belonged to
me before. I'd forgotten all about being kissed like that, but
now that I've been reminded, I don't know how I ever thought
about anything else. All the nerves and skittish insecurities I
usually feel here are quietened by this small, simple gesture,
and the whole world feels right again.

CHAPTER NINE

Sometimes the universe changes its mind. Sometimes a benevolent god chooses to shine on you, and after weeks and months of hurricanes, the sun breaks through storm clouds, and things are bright and life is good again.

My luck must finally, *finally* be changing, because I somehow wake without a hangover.

Max's alarm blasts into the sleepy silence of his bedroom, and he reaches over me to turn it off. I smile into a kiss as I register that he's let me sleep on his side of the bed. His breath is hot and sweet, and I forget to worry about how my makeup must have smudged and caked while I was sleeping. I didn't have to pretend to fall asleep halfway through an episode of *Curb Your Enthusiasm* to spend the night here. The second alarm rings, and he makes a happy little noise and heads off to start the water for a shower.

I don't think I've ever seen this bedroom in daylight. The walls are the blueish white of skim milk, and two neat rows of record sleeves decorate the wall opposite us: a mishmash of Arcade Fire and Bon Iver and Childish Gambino and Daft Punk and Sonic Youth. The open wardrobe holds a mess of T-shirts, unironed op-shop button downs and Docs. His desk is littered with coffee mugs, notebooks and incense ashes. It's sweet to think of him there, grinding away at his thesis, scrolling through Instagram and thinking of me when he finds a dumb post that adds to an ongoing list of private jokes. How strange, I've never imagined him thinking of me when I'm not around. I only imagine him completely forgetting that I exist.

'C'mon,' he says, reappearing and throwing a stiff, faded purple towel my way. 'I've got to open the cafe. Work calls, but shower sex calls louder.'

Who am I to argue with that?

Today's sky is the idyllic endless blue that refuses to be captured by an iPhone camera. A pleasant breeze follows my easy walk home from Max's cafe, soundtracked by the peachy-easy-cool company of Haim and The Aces. I've stolen back my T-shirt and keep catching the scent of him, and I can hardly keep myself from dancing at the pedestrian crossing. Everything is wonderful. I'm floating on electric air.

He has drawn my name on the side of my coffee cup, a heart for the *o* in Penelope, and it makes me so giddy I forget to hate the taste of oat milk.

In my haze of contentment and girl band joy, I buy a bunch of pink peonies from the florist to brighten my bedroom. All week I'll look at them and remember the morning I woke up to the thing I've wanted for such a long time.

Last night with Leo already feels like weeks ago, but I haven't forgotten. I make a pitstop at the cafe near our house for croissants and coffee for him, but he's already there. He must have invited someone over late last night, because he's surely too cool for breakfast dates, and he's sitting across from a woman with impossibly long wavy hair. (What salon do you go to, Mermaid Hair Girl? Would I need to take out a mortgage for a blow-out there?) It's early for him to be awake, but I guess it's pretty easy to get up and eat carbohydrates when you wake up next to someone beautiful — as we both now know (*ha!*).

'Of all the gin joints,' he says, spotting me.

'Well, it's a convenient gin joint. Short commute.'

I catch Mermaid Hair's politely puzzled expression and realise I must be a sight. Faded Spice Girls T-shirt, half-dry hair pulled into a careless topknot and the lingering shadow of last night's eyeliner bleeding into my undereye bags isn't my most show-stopping look. *Who is this girl?* she must be thinking. *And why is my Tinder match smiling at her after spending the night with me?*

'This is Penny,' he tells her flatly. Ooh, what's that tone for?

'I'm Leo's housemate. Hi! Your hair is *amazing*.'

'I'm —'

'You're in a good mood,' interrupts Leo.

'I had a good night.' I give a coy shrug. 'I was going to bring you a coffee. Thanks for saving me four dollars!'

'You'll just have to add it to the list of all the wonderful things I bring to your life.'

'Unstacking the dishwasher, remembering to bring the bins in after rubbish day, saving me in the middle of the night if a murderer were to break in ...' I say, and he laughs.

Mermaid Hair's latte glass clinks down hard on its saucer, and he stills.

'Anyway! I'm going home. So nice to meet you! Seriously, such pretty hair.'

I leave them to it and turn down my street. I fancy a cup of tea and a nap on the couch. Their morning-after breakfast couldn't contrast mine more. Max let me take my pick of the vegan muffin selection and held my face while he kissed me up against the espresso machine.

As I put my peonies in water and set them on my dresser, my phone pings with a message and my mood is lifted higher still:

Max Fitzgerald (07:49): ❤❤❤

Leo is a fucking genius.

CHAPTER TEN

'Let's go to the pub,' says Leo before I've even opened my eyes.

'How much damage do you think my liver can take in one weekend?' I grumble from the couch. I knew I couldn't avoid a hangover altogether. There's a rude pounding behind my eyes. I want a greasy burger and a full sugar Coke and a pet to cuddle.

'Come on,' he whines. 'Staying home is for Sundays. We'll get a massive bowl of chips.'

'Leave me here to die. But bring home chips.'

'Up up up up up! The night is young! And so are we!'

'I liked you so much better when we never spoke.'

'That's not true,' he says. 'I'm the best. Go on, if you don't come with me, I'll have to sit in a pub alone like a sex offender.'

'What does that mean?'

'I don't know. Are you coming?'

'Are you buying?'

'There's the Penny we know and love. Let's go! Half an hour!'

He's lucky the water pressure in his house is excellent. I take my time in the shower, hoping the steam opens my pores to ease the booze bloat in my face, and treat myself to the charcoal mask I reserve for special occasions.

I wonder if I should invite Max. I'll message him. I'm sure he and Leo will get on. They can both talk about anything, although where Leo has the effervescent enthusiasm of a puppy, Max is full of the quiet intensity of a Siamese cat. Still, I like them both, so they'll like each other. It'll be nice to sit at a bar with Max and pull this relationship out of the confines of his apartment.

> **Penelope Moore (18:01):** Going to the pub w my housemate. Join? xx
> **Max Fitzgerald (18:08):** Exhausted
> **Max Fitzgerald (18:09):** Come round after?
> **Penelope Moore (18:10):** I'll message you on my way home, you can come to mine x

Oh, well. Another time. I should message Annie and Bec to see if they want to come. Annie and Bec! In my sleepy stale state I forgot to give them the news.

> **Penelope Moore (17:55):** So, news!!
> **Penelope Moore (17:55):** Max and I have got back together, for real this time

Within a minute or two, they've both seen the message, but haven't replied. That's disappointing. But their hangovers are probably as unpleasant as mine; I'm sure they're just dozing. We'll catch up soon, and they'll be as excited for me as I am.

Down the hall Leo is blasting The Strokes, and it helps. I love a theme song. In minutes, I've pulled on a passable outfit and begun the task of strategically dusting on bronzer for the illusion of health.

'You almost look human again,' says Leo once I emerge from my room.

'Best looking human you've seen all day. Hey! No! Who was that goddess at the cafe this morning?'

'Serena,' he shrugs.

'Who is Serena? She's too good looking to be seen with you.'

He laughs but doesn't offer more. 'Let's get some chips into your face so you stop asking annoying little questions, hey?'

'That's never slowed me down before.'

We bicker all the way down Victoria Street and into The Aviary. We make it to a booth, feeding off each other's bullshit with lovely ease. While Leo heads to the bar to get a round, I check my phone.

Bec Cooper (18:35): Oh wow

Annie Lin (18:41): That's great, babe

Annie Lin (18:41): Happy for you

Bec Cooper (18:44): When did you start seeing him again?

I do my best not to read into their lack of enthusiasm. I don't want to go digging for the subtext of their missing exclamation marks. It won't take me anywhere positive. They have hugged me through Max-induced hysteria one or twelve times too many, and I can't fault them for being cautious. Annie is still on the Hinge circuit from hell and gets irked every time someone around her manages to get a third or fourth date — and aren't I guilty of taking my friend's happy news and making it about myself too? Didn't I do that just last week?

Leo reappears with two pints and a table number, and I put my phone back in my bag and channel all my meditation practice into putting it out of my mind.

'I've never asked what you do,' he says, setting my glass down. 'Did I hear you say you were an accountant?'

'Oh, god no. I'm an account *manager*. I work at a digital agency. I manage clients and projects and cry a lot.'

'Is that in the job description?'

'Yeah, every job ad is like, "*Applicant must: 1. Have experience with Shopify and WordPress; 2. Shop exclusively at Gorman; 3. Love getting paid fuck-all; 4. Be able to type and have a breakdown simultaneously.*"'

'Then you must be the queen of account managers.'

'I can cry with the best of them.'

'You're so impressive.'

'Aren't I?' I pretend to toss my hair over my shoulder. 'I don't know what you do, either. You could be a professional hitman for all I know. Are you?'

'If I told you, I'd have to kill you,' he says, and I laugh. 'I'm an architect.'

'That's sexy,' I hear myself say before I even catch myself thinking it. He barks out a laugh, and I feel myself go lobster red. 'Buildings,' I say, my mind rushing for a way to paper over it. 'Love buildings. I go into buildings all the time.'

'I'll pass on your feedback to the CEO of buildings. They're Penny-approved.'

'I'd really appreciate — *ooh*, chips! If you're one of those psychopaths who pours tomato sauce over the whole bowl, I'm moving out.'

'That behaviour deserves the death penalty.'

My slip of the tongue is forgotten in the presence of icy cider and steaming chips.

'So …' I say through a mouthful of molten potato. I won't stop until I'm at least four percent chip. 'This girlfriend of yours —'

'You're obsessed with this.'

'I'm just fascinated by the whole thing. I don't know anyone else who's even had a relationship that long. You went from being Mr Girlfriend to Mr One Night Stand. You switched genres!'

'I think you think I'm more promiscuous than I am.'

'Come on, what's wrong with you? Did you have a traumatic childhood or something?'

When Leo laughs, it takes over his whole face. It crinkles his eyes, and his smile stretches as wide and wild as the Cheshire cat's. It makes me smile too, just seeing it.

'Are you going to analyse me?' he asks.

I get the feeling I could ask him the most invasive questions and he would answer me without any hesitation. He's someone who knows exactly who he is, but what's more he *likes* himself. Maybe it's the inherent confidence of an adult male, or maybe there's just nothing in him worth disliking.

'Yes,' I say. 'Give me a minute to grow a beard and ask around for some *nosé* and I'll be your personal Freud.'

'Excellent.'

'Well?'

'My childhood was perfectly fine,' he says, rolling his eyes. 'It was just my mum and brother, but it was lovely. There was a house with a yard in Camberwell, fresh air, bikes, karate lessons, a golden retriever, all that shit.'

'Sounds terrible,' I say. 'You poor thing, struggling through that idyllic childhood.'

'I suffered so,' he sniffs.

'Is your brother older or younger?'

'Older. Lachlan. He lives in Sydney now, but we get along.'

'Leo and Lachlan?' I smirk. 'Really?'

'Okay, I take it back. That's my childhood trauma. People used to assume we were twins because he's only a year older and I was a fat baby.'

'Oh, I fucking love fat babies, though.'

'Their chubby legs!'

'Like little croissants!'

Leo absently scratches at his collarbone, and I notice a tattoo there, though I can't make it out. How many does he have, I wonder, and where, and what do they mean to him? I'm too afraid of needles to even get cosmetic injectables. Although that might change. I worry that I'm going to wake up and look like Gordon Ramsay any day now.

'What about you?' he asks.

'Same, really. Just my dad and my brother. He's older too and lives in London with his husband.'

'Good excuse to go visit,' says Leo. 'I probably go to London more than I go to Sydney.'

'You don't see your brother much?'

'Not lately. He visits us. I'm convinced that he moved away so I'd be the one who has to help Mum set up her smart TV, or move her furniture when she wants to rearrange her living room, or get her printer working for the ten millionth time. Who needs a fucking printer?'

'So it's Leo to the rescue, huh?'

'I'm a superhero, baby! Look at how thick my hair is.' He tips his head towards me, and I reach out to give it a tug. 'Bruce Wayne wishes.'

'I need to get whatever shampoo you're using,' I whine. 'That's not fair.'

'It's your shampoo, actually,' he says. He pushes his hand through his hair to push it back and it falls into place perfectly. How annoying. 'I'm a dirty little thief.'

'You use my shampoo?! Wear my underwear too, why don't you.'

'Is your underwear drawer not a communal space?'

It's crude and gross, and I laugh. He certainly doesn't have the slick moves of a repressed misogynist fuckboy, but perhaps that's something he turns on when the moment is right: when they're a bottle of wine into it and that sexy Arctic Monkeys album is playing and it's time for someone's hair to go into a ponytail and her bra to go flying.

Still, that has nothing to do with me. Good for him. Here at this table, it's just two people who share a house and an enthusiasm for hot chips and silliness. We slip seamlessly from work talk (his latest sustainability project, my credit union client) to shit-talking *Game of Thrones* (I got four seasons into it before realising that one old white guy was actually three different old white guys; a story that delights him), from a mutual brain crush on Jacinda Ardern to a wonderful story about his childhood dog, who could open the fridge and followed him to school every day. Before I know it, we're at the bottom of our third round, and the pub has filled considerably.

En route to the bar for one more drink — I make him swear it's my last one — I take a detour to the bathroom. Hangovers make my skin ravenous for makeup. Isn't the headache and perma-hunger enough punishment without my pores drinking in my foundation and melting my eyeliner into my eye wrinkles? Luckily, no matter how small my bag is, I always have room for a little pot of concealer, a mascara, an eyebrow pencil and my backup *Dragon Girl* lip crayon from NARS. This little kit, courtesy of the women doing god's work at Mecca, can save almost any makeup crisis.

'That red is perfect on you,' says a petite woman in a *fucking* cool white jumpsuit as I stand back from the mirror to assess my eyebrow touch-up.

There is nowhere like the ladies' room for making fleeting female friendships.

'Forget lipstick,' I tell her. 'When did Bianca Jagger start hanging out in Richmond? I'm obsessed with your outfit.'

'That's exactly what I was going for!' she says excitedly. 'Look, this is weird, but I wanted to ask. Are you here with that *gorgeous* guy in the black shirt?'

'Leo? He's my housemate.'

'Is he spoken for?' she asks. 'My friends and I have been gawking.'

'He's single,' I say, settling right into my role as housemate-cum-wing woman. 'Sorts his laundry, leaves the toilet seat down. Do you want me to introduce you?'

'Would you?' she squeaks. 'Would that be so awkward?'

'Totally fine! Come with me to the bar and we'll go back to our table together.'

In the ten minutes it takes to get our drinks, I learn that Katie, alias Jumpsuit Girl, works for a bank, got her jumpsuit at an alice McCALL sample sale, and has *never, ever, I swear*, asked someone to wing woman for her before. She's chatty and sweet and, more importantly, she gives me the opportunity to excuse myself from the crowded bar and head home.

'I've brought you a new friend,' I announce, and Leo looks up from his phone. 'Leo, meet Katie. Katie has great taste in jumpsuits. And, oh no, what's this? I only have two drinks. Katie, you'll just have to have mine. No, it's fine! I'm going to go home.'

'You're shameless,' he laughs and has the good grace to look mildly embarrassed.

'Have fun, kids!'

By the time I reach the door, they're already chatting freely, and I'm pleased with myself. Hell, yeah. What are friends for if not to help get you laid?

*

A while later, as I float somewhere between daydream and real dream, consciousness comes calling by the cold air of a sheet being pulled back.

'Where are you going?'

'I've got the breakfast shift again tomorrow,' says Max, pulling on his pants. 'If I stay the night, I'll have to get up at fuck o'clock to get there on time.'

This isn't strictly true. It's barely an extra ten minutes to commute from my place than from his, but I don't want to argue.

He kisses me goodbye and says he'll text me, then lets himself out, and I make the active choice to think about anything else. I have tons of laundry to do. Maybe I'll make lasagna for my work lunches this week. Could I pull off a white jumpsuit?

Minutes later, or maybe hours, I hear the front door open and close again and Leo's and Katie's hushed voices. I turn on my white noise app and roll over into the middle of the bed — the better to ignore the vast Max-sized stretch of empty sheet — and give in to sleep.

CHAPTER ELEVEN

It's amazing what you can achieve once you give yourself permission to go after what you want. I made a list.

- Maximilian Aurelius Fitzgerald: ✓✓✓ *(yay!)*
- A career I love: Possible, pending:
  - regular validation from Margot Camilleri, Head of Accounts
  - at least one cool client, preferably several
- A thigh gap
- Peace from the perma-hum of anxiety between my ears
- To stay close with Bec and Annie until we're so old we resemble English bulldogs

One out of five is good but not good enough, so it's time to get to work.

I wake before my 6 am alarm on Monday and set off for a run around the neighbourhood. But for the hyper-positivity of Taylor Swift and Carly Rae Jepsen in my headphones, it's pretty peaceful. I run — slowly — past quaint houses and dilapidated duplexes, careful to avoid my reflection in the glossy-windowed apartment blocks. Richmond is a mishmash of rapid gentrification and long-term residents unwilling or unable to keep up. A terrace house on one corner will sell for a few million dollars while, a street over, houses larger than mine and Leo's seem to slowly sag into the earth, with peeling paint that reveals rotting wood, and wire fences that are wound tight around the limbs of an ancient lemon tree. It all seems like a project left half-finished.

I'm overtaken by more practised joggers. I dodge uneven pavement and resist the distraction of a curious dog's happily wagging tail. The February sun is quick to rise, and I only make it fifteen minutes or so before a pleasantly elevated heart rate gives way to hacking gasps for air and I have to retreat. I practically crawl through the front door. How many times do I have to do this before my body looks like Kendall Jenner's? Like, four or five?

Once I've caught my breath, showered, and shaved my legs, my real work begins. If I'm going to go after #2 on my list, I need to make some serious changes. No more wrinkled linen shirts and lazy topknots for me. Take a good look, everyone: this is the last time you'll ever see me without my shit together. I spend an inordinate amount of time getting my eyeliner wings even, blow out my hair and remember to put earrings on. I'm on my way at a perfectly reasonable 8:12 am in a crease-proof shirt dress (fast fashion and synthetic fabrics may be destroying the planet but they're saving my life today) with a pair of heels in my bag. By the end of the week, I'll probably have bamboo sheets and a stock portfolio.

I skip the morning gasbag with Bec (***Penelope Moore (08:16): Can't make coffee today @Bec Cooper, have v important arse kissing to do*** 😘) and pick up two coffees from Sexy Barista en route to the office. I have an inkling that the only thing standing between me and Margot's approval is an extra hot soy mac. I should have tried this months ago.

Don't look at me like that. No one is above petty bribery.

My usual workday routine is to get a coffee, check my inbox, and pore over twelve or so tabs of trashy news until mid-morning, when I finally find the will and coherence to answer emails. Then I chip away at my to-do list: commission a homepage banner from the designers, report a loading glitch to the developers, source statistics that assure my client at Clean Juice Co that two minutes on their product page is actually quite a lot, and fantasise about taking a pillow into the disabled toilet for a nap.

Then it's usually lunchtime, and I require sustenance — a banh mi or baked potato from down the road — and a nice little walk in the fresh air. By the time I get back, untucking my shirt to hide my unbuttoned jeans, I'm ready to smash out a few jobs and trot along to a meeting or two. If Helena, my deskmate, is in, we'll chat over an instant coffee and a biscuit (or four). If she's not, I'll keep the biscuits to myself and settle into a long article from *Vanity Fair* or a short story in the *New Yorker*. On a bad day, I'll check on my superannuation and work out when I can retire, then get depressed and eat four more biscuits.

Somehow, after all of that, there's still usually an hour left in the day, and I often have nothing to do but think about what I have to work on tomorrow. By 4:40 I've closed my inbox — who expects to get queries answered that close to home time? — and then I go to rinse out my mug, and I might as well do everyone else's while I'm at the sink, so that kills another ten minutes, and who's watching the clock that closely anyway?

If I time it right, I'm out in the hot breeze of Swan Street by 5:01, and I've forgotten about work entirely once I make it home.

But not today. Not anymore. *Things I want #2: A career I love.* It's time to work at it.

Margot balks as I drop off her coffee at her desk. She frowns. 'Why?'

'I had a freebie from my loyalty card,' I lie. 'Mondays are always a two-coffee day, don't you think?'

'Thanks,' she says, taking a tentative sip.

'Welcome!'

Things I want #2a: Margot's approval. Point: Penny.

Though my brain craves the comfort of inane news about the Kardashians and quizzes to tell me which One Direction member is my soulmate (Zayn, obviously), I stay the course and open my inbox first thing. I rip it off like an at-home wax strip and it isn't even that painful. The pedantic marketing manager at Clean Juice Co wants the design for their new website mocked up in peach pink instead of olive green — easy. Victoria Credit Union wants a newsletter sent out tomorrow afternoon — no problem, I can do that in an hour. Deco Cinemas want a couple of updates to their member portal — nothing the devs can't handle. I'm more productive before 9 am than I usually am all day.

I even forget to have my usual mid-morning slump after a message from Max pops up.

Max Fitzgerald (10:17): What was that Middle Eastern restaurant you were talking about?

Penelope Moore (10:17): Feast of Merit?

Penelope Moore (10:17): Golda?

Penelope Moore (10:17): Maha?

Max Fitzgerald (10:24): Thanks x

Penelope Moore (10:24): Is someone planning a cute little date? ❤

Max Fitzgerald (10:31): Ha x

Things I want #1: Max. Double tick.

I get through the day with the kind of determination I was last familiar with during assessment hell-week at uni. I make a show of eating my lunch at my desk, pinch the soft skin of my forearm to stay engaged in meetings, and don't start packing my handbag until 5:05 pm. Then I do something unheard of: I take work home with me.

At the staff meeting, Margot had asked who would be interested in working on a pitch for an up-and-coming skincare brand, and I'd thrown my hand up for it so fast that I think I disjointed my shoulder. I didn't even flinch when she sent me twenty-seven megabytes' worth of briefing material.

The client seems pretty interesting, which is always a helpful motivator. Evergreen Skincare is a tiny little start-up that has just received major funding, and it needs everything: branding, product names, a paid and organic strategy, an entire website overhaul. They offer just five products: a cleanser, a hydrating serum, a moisturiser, an oil and a sunscreen. No more twelve-step, twice-a-day routines that require you to learn the Korean alphabet and buy a mini fridge for your bathroom.

Considering I take up the entire bathroom cupboard with a Sephora's worth of half-used lip scrubs and tinted moisturisers and brightening serums and cleansing oils, this one has piqued my interest beyond brown-nosing.

Things I want #2b: At least one cool client. Tickety fucking tick.

It's been so long since work made me feel anything other than sad and tired that it takes me a minute to place the feeling I get when I start working on the pitch: genuine excitement. Enthusiasm for research, a rush of ideas, wanting to do more than the bare minimum. I hardly even notice the sun going down as I sit hunched over the coffee table doing competitor recon.

Even though the pitch isn't for a few weeks, I'm already pouring hours into it. I want to give it my best. I'm being more thorough than strictly necessary, but if Margot wants to pay me to wank on about skincare all day and get a new client out of it, I'm not going to let her down.

'Are you *working*?' asks Leo, repulsed, entering the kitchen. 'At this hour?'

'I am a modern career woman,' I tell him. 'Get used to it.'

'Alright, *Working Girl*.'

'Cool reference,' I snort. 'Super current.'

'My mother raised me on strong career women who peaked in the eighties, like Sigourney Weaver and Cher.'

'I like the sound of your mum. Can she join me for a power ballad duet at karaoke sometime?'

'She'd love that. She'd love you. She's probably the reason shrill, highly strung women are my weakness.'

'SHRILL?' I shriek.

Leo laughs, and pulls two Peronis from the fridge. 'What are we working on?'

'Are you helping me with a branding deck?'

'Sure am,' he says, and hands me a beer. 'I'll be your earnest little assistant.'

'Alright, Andy Sachs.'

'Who?'

'Don't pretend you haven't seen *The Devil Wears Prada* fifty times.'

'Try a hundred and fifty.'

'That's what I thought,' I smirk, and turn my laptop around to face him. 'Evergreen Skincare. Five products, cruelty free, made in Melbourne.'

'Got it. What do they need us to do?'

'I guess first of all we have to work out their audience. Who's this for? What're they like?'

Leo looks blank, but it doesn't matter. It only takes a minute for the full picture to come to me.

'I think it's a woman in her twenties through thirties. Probably lives in the inner city. She's in a middle-income bracket, enough to splurge now and then but not so much she's choosing Evergreen over La Mer.'

'What's La Mer?'

'Skincare with diamonds in it.'

'Fuck off. That's not a thing.'

'No, for real!'

'But *why*?'

'Wouldn't you want to rub diamonds all over your face if you could?' I shrug. 'Come on, I'm on a roll here.'

'Sorry, alright. What else?'

'Okay. So, I think, for her, it's a bonus that her skincare is ethically sound. It's not a dealmaker, but it helps. She'll use a Keep Cup if she can, but she's not going to not have a coffee if she's left it at home. So we want to highlight the cruelty-free bit, but let's not hammer it in. It's just a perk. I think the key thing here is the experience of it. It's not a chore. It smells good; it feels good when it's on. It doesn't matter how drunk she is at the end of a Friday night: she's taking off her makeup and putting her hydrating serum on.'

'The only thing I'm doing after a big night is putting away a kebab.'

'Well, that's why you'll look like Keith Richards the minute you turn forty.'

He pulls a face and slaps his hand over his heart, offended. I wink at him. Maybe my dress is giving me extra confidence today, or maybe it's just my great big brain.

'And as far as the tone, well, I'm not trusting the fifty-year-old woman hawking Clarins at Myer in navy eyeshadow and orange lipstick at ten am. If I want skincare suggestions, I'm asking my friends. I think that's how this should feel. Like … like your big sister with perfect skin is telling you, *"This moisturiser will fix all your problems and put five thousand dollars in your account and remind you to call your dad and you'll never, ever dribble toothpaste down your front or fall over in public again."'* I pause for breath and a cool slug of my beer, and I'm thrilled with myself when I manage not to dribble any on my chin. 'And it should be cute, right? I have daggy skin care too, but my Sudocrem isn't sitting front and centre on my bathroom shelf. So if it has a fun little label, every time she picks it up to use it, she's thinking *"This is so cute, I love it."* Ooh!' I gasp violently and Leo jumps.

'What's wrong?!'

I write *'shelfie campaign!!'* on my notepad.

'Women can post pictures of their bathroom shelves and show off how Evergreen fits into their regimen. That way we're levelling up with competitors immediately. The same girl who uses Glossier and Olaplex and The Ordinary and sleeps on a silk pillowcase is using Evergreen. We can make it a cult product. *Yes!'*

'I'll be honest,' he says, 'I don't know what half of those words mean, but I think you're onto something.'

'I'm super-duper smart.'

He laughs, and I beam. There's nothing like the validation of someone thinking you're funny.

I think I had forgotten that I can be good at my job. How nice to rediscover it like this, as though it was here all along, waiting for when I was ready for change.

CHAPTER TWELVE

My enthusiasm for my rebirth as a woman who likes her job stretches just far enough to accept Annie's extra ticket to a Women in Business brunch on Thursday morning. When I run this past Margot — a very well rehearsed speech including six reasons why it would be good for Scout if I took the morning off to go to a networking event — she surprises me by welcoming it. In fact, she's going too, so she'll see me there.

Well, okay! Doing an extracurricular activity together sounds like a major step on the path to bolstering our work relationship. Next stop: respect. Then: promotion.

Morning of, I meet Annie at Southern Cross Station, and we and our heels clack our way to the Rialto to rub shoulders with other professionals and try to inconspicuously stuff croissants into our handbags. It's supposed to be an event all about '*professional women uplifting professional women*', as though the glass ceiling can be smashed with stale pastry and burnt filter coffee one morning every couple of months.

It's a bit condescending, I think, to presume women in business all have enough in common to warrant a single networking event. While Annie works until midnight six nights a week on a four-inch-thick case file for a salacious crime involving a university lecturer, his nineteen-year-old girlfriend and a stolen Prius, I spend my days gossiping with the design team and trying to find the right colour palette for a bottle of moisturiser. What do our careers have in common?

When we arrive, sure enough, the room is full of women making polite conversation while waiting for their turn at the coffee samovar. The pockets of their sensible Cue and Veronika Maine outfits are bulging with their business cards. Fuck. I didn't think to bring mine. They've been sitting in the back of my desk drawer since the day I got them.

'I've had e-fucking-nough of all the Pinterest shit Bec's been sending through,' says Annie through a mouthful of scone. We've found a shady spot on the balcony, away from the slightly crazed woman trying to recruit people into a pyramid scheme.

'You and me both,' I say. 'I thought I was just being a jealous arsehole. But now I have Max and that's all sorted and I still hate how she's been carrying on, so maybe it's just bloody annoying.'

'Mm,' says Annie, delicately. 'Just — isn't it a bit ridiculous? Who gives a shit about bonbonnieres?'

'What *is* a bonbonniere?'

'Fucked if I know,' she shrugs. 'It's just typical of Bec to make this the centre of the universe and insist everyone get on board. It's not like it's even going to go ahead.'

'You don't think so?'

'Any day now, she's going to wake up next to this fucking ... Michael Kors handbag of a human being, come to her senses and pack her bags.'

'He's so basic. I don't think we've ever had a conversation that didn't end with him mansplaining the stock market. And why do they have to merge into one being? They're inseparable! They turn it into a competition: us chaotic singles versus them, the settled adults. Why else do they spend every weekend at Bunnings?'

'It's just about her feeling superior,' says Annie. 'She's not *Bec* anymore. She's not *fun*. More and more, she isn't the person she used to be.'

'Are any of us, though? I think this is like — what do they call it? Your return to Saturn? Somewhere around your late twenties, all your priorities shift and you begin the second part of your life. Maybe this is just the second part of her life.'

'I hope the second part of my life doesn't revolve around homemade flower crowns and someone who bathes in Polo Blue.'

'Are we huge bitches?'

'Yes.'

'Are we terrible friends?'

'Yes.'

'Are we going to have to be bridesmaids?'

'Fuck.' She sighs. 'We are, aren't we?'

'Wedding planning brings out the worst in people,' says a woman at the next table. She's probably in her late thirties. She has a sharp dark bob and her plum lipstick is smudgeless even though she's holding a half-finished coffee. 'I don't think I spoke to my sister for a month after she got married. I needed a *break*.'

'Oh, thank god it's not just us!' I cry. 'We thought we were terrible people.'

'Wait until she starts asking about A- and B-list guests.'

'Good *grief*,' says Annie, looking pained.

'I'm Petra,' says the woman, extending her hand. 'Marketing. That's how you're supposed to introduce yourself at these things, right?'

'I'm Annie, and when we're not being snakes talking about our friends behind their backs, I'm in law, and Penny's in marketing too.'

'We aren't exactly *uplifting professional women* right now,' I say.

'Forget it,' says Petra, waving us off. 'These things are so self-congratulatory. I'm mostly here for the omelette station.'

'I was looking at that!' I tell her. 'But how are you supposed to eat an omelette standing up? I need a table and a knife. They're rooting for us to fail.'

Petra pulls back the lapel on her blazer to reveal a telling yellow stain on the pocket of her shirt, and we start laughing. Her tidy suit and serious court shoes have done a good job of hiding the warmth underneath. I would have been terrified of her if she hadn't approached us.

'What kind of marketing do you do, Penny?'

'Oh, no, it's nothing —'

'It's not nothing,' says Annie, cutting me off. 'Penny is a superstar. She doesn't appreciate her own genius. Tell her about whatsitcalled. It was *amazing*.'

'I helped build the Deco Cinemas website last year.'

'Oh, that was you?' asks Petra. 'I go to the French Film Festival every year. That site needed an upgrade. Nice work.'

'I was pretty happy with it. A couple of nervous breakdowns later. So much functionality to manage!'

'My company is looking for some agency help. Do you have a card?'

'Shit — I mean, shit — sorry! I actually forgot to bring them with me. Not a good woman, not good at business. They shouldn't have let me in.'

'Don't be silly,' she says, pulling her phone out of her purse. 'Why don't I add you on LinkedIn? Maybe we can be the first people to ever network at a networking event.'

With her connection request sent, Petra leaves to work the room, and Annie high-fives me. I'm off on what might be a very long tangent about the merits of *putting yourself out there* and how all you really need to do is *ask the universe and it will provide* when Annie grabs my arm and urgently whispers, 'Microbitch alert.'

She can only mean one thing. I spy Margot's little brown bun popping in and out of sight as she navigates a room full of women over five foot two. Annie knows her from the cathartic routine of tearing her Instagram presence to shreds after too much white wine.

'Were you just talking to Petra de Silva?' Margot asks, brisk as ever.

'Good morning,' says Annie with aggressive politeness. I have to bite my cheek.

'I — good morning,' she says, blinking rapidly. 'Were you? Talking to Petra de Silva?'

'I guess so,' I say, feeling as blank as I look. 'She came over for a chat. She's nice.'

'She's from LVMH,' says Margot. 'What were you talking about? Did you mention the agency? Did you give her your card? Did you set up a meeting?'

'Um …' Against my will, my face assumes an expression that can only say '*whoops*'.

Margot clicks her tongue. 'Honestly, Penelope, that's what these events are *for*. You're here to *promote the agency*, not blab about *Bachelor in Paradise*.'

'Listen —' begins Annie, but I cut her off.

'You're totally right!' I say, brightly. 'I'll find her before she leaves and make sure she knows about Scout's best work. Don't worry. I'll handle it.'

'Good,' says Margot.

Off she goes, all tiny stiletto steps and rigid posture, and I exhale.

'We're not as bitchy as *her*,' says Annie loyally.

'She's never going to like me.'

'Who gives a shit, babe? Who cares what someone like that thinks? I hope she chokes on her fruit cup.'

'You're going to feel terrible if she does.'

'No, I won't,' she sniffs. 'It's not exactly hard to say, "*Good morning, Penny, did I see you making a professional connection with a potential client?*" How did she know *I* wasn't from LVMH? Does she talk to you like that all the time?'

'Kind of.' I shrug. 'It's just how she is.'

'I wish you worked somewhere with an HR department.'

'You're not as bad a friend as you think you are,' I tell her, touched by her loyal indignation. 'You're a very good friend to me.'

'Aw, babe,' she says. 'But we still get to shit-talk these fucking wedding plans, right?'

'Absolutely,' I say, taking her arm as we head to the omelette station. 'Did you see that she wants us to go to Bali for two weeks for her hens'?'

'*For. Fucks. Saaaake.*'

CHAPTER THIRTEEN

'Too early,' Max says into my neck under the cry of my phone. His arm snakes around my waist and pulls me close. 'Stay.'

'I can't,' I groan, silencing the alarm. 'I have a client meeting.'

'No meetings,' he says, kissing my neck and curling his leg around mine. It's a compelling argument. 'Stay.'

'If only. They're *this close* to signing off on the site design. They'd better do it today. It's all minor UX stuff that we can fix during the build, but, *no*, they need two weeks to review it internally, and *"Can you make the gallery scroll vertically on mobile? Can we make* this *yellow* more *yellow?"*. And Margot is always looking over my shoulder and it's — ugh, I have to go in.'

'Boring,' he grumbles, and turns over.

Well. He doesn't get it. There's not a ton of red tape when your stakeholders are dead poets and an espresso machine. It *is* pretty boring.

I get up and make for the shower. Max lives with three other postgrad students, and their place is dated and grubby. The bathroom is tiled in that depressing 70s brown, with cracked plastic taps and a fluorescent light that reveals a constellation of blackheads I didn't know I had. As I try to work up the courage to touch the greying communal bar of soap under the shower's lukewarm dribble, I think longingly of the water pressure at home, my lavender soap, mandarin body scrub and hessian exfoliating mitt. I could just set the alarm earlier and get ready at my place, where I don't have to bathe on tiptoe to avoid tinea, but it's a small price to pay for an extra fifteen minutes of spooning. Max still doesn't sleep at my house, but I'm allowed to stay over here now. I'll take wins where I can get them. And at least here I don't have to offer breakfast to Leo's overnight guests.

Once I'm moisturised and makeupped and dressed, I head down the hall to the kitchen, where Max, in all his bed-headed deliciousness, is hand-grinding coffee for his Aeropress.

'What do we think?' I ask, doing a spin. 'Do I look like a beautiful genius account manager who's definitely going to get her project plan signed off today?'

'Is that one of my shirts?'

'We share a wardrobe now. It's in the boyfriend code of conduct. Can I have sugar in my coffee today, please?'

'It sullies the flavour profile,' he says. 'You only need sugar in crap coffee.'

'But I like my coffee sullied and sugary. I even like a Splenda now and then.'

'Trust me.' He looks repulsed. 'Mug or Keep Cup?'

'Mug please. You get me for five whole extra minutes!'

'Lucky boy,' he says, kissing my cheek and handing me a mug with Mikhail Gorbachev's face on it. I think he shops exclusively at Chapel Street Bazaar.

This has been our routine almost every morning for the past three weeks. After work every day, I stop at home just long enough to water my plants and grab a change of clothes, then I come round here. We watch an episode of *Four Corners* or *The Daily Show*, have sex and go to sleep. Sometimes we spice things up and watch a documentary about the prison industrial complex, or play drinking games with his housemates for which I pay dearly. I can't handle Tequila Tuesdays like I used to.

We sit slurping unsweetened coffee in sleepy silence. He flicks on the television and I scroll through my messages. I don't have the stomach for SBS News at this hour. The group chat is a gentler way to ease into the day.

Bec Cooper (22:49): Ladies, do you fancy a dinner party at mine?

Bec Cooper (22:49): We got a hibachi grill for an engagement present!!

Bec Cooper (22:50): Tomorrow night? 6:30? Bring wine!

Annie Lin (05:29): Ah can't babe, I'm working late tonight & Saturday

Bec Cooper (06:43): Could you postpone? :(I really want you guys to get to know Evan

Annie Lin (06:46): I have an advice due COB Monday, really can't babe

Annie Lin (06:49): Another time x

Bec Cooper (06:50): :(

Penelope Moore (07:13): Sounds yum! I'm in. Max too?

Penelope Moore (07:13): I'll look up some vegan hibachi options

Bec sees my messages as soon as I send them, and three little dots appear and disappear until:

Bec Cooper (07:17): Let's wait until we can all come. @*Annie Lin* maybe next week?

Annie Lin (7:17): Sure x

Oh. Well. Yes, it would be nicer to do it as a whole group. I wish they'd give Max another chance, that's all. They just need to see that it's different this time, then they'll come around.

'Hey,' I say on my way to rinse my mug out. 'Will you come to dinner with my friends? You haven't seen them in ages. It'll be nice to get out of the house for the night.'

'Which friends?' he asks.

'I only have two.'

'Annie and that? I don't know. When?'

'Bec's having a dinner next week. What's wrong?'

'No, they're fine,' he shrugs, eyes still on the news.

'I know they are. They're the best. What's wrong?' A prickle in my stomach tells me I'm preparing for conflict.

'They're just not really my people.'

'Um.' I stall. 'Well, I'm your people. And they're my people. So they should be your people too. That's just maths.'

'Let's stay in.'

'*Hey.*' This change in tone makes him look up. 'Come on. I don't want it to be like that this time. They're my friends, they're part of my life. We can't just not see them.'

'*We* don't have to see them. *You* can see them.'

'No, that's not —'

'Penny. I just find them … draining. All they do is talk shit.'

'So does everyone. That's all anyone does. They're important to me. They're like family.'

He makes an unconvinced face, and it stings. I'd hang out with his friends. If he ever asked me to.

'Look,' I say, floundering for composure. 'It's fine. I know they're a little …' I search for the word, but I can't find any that don't feel like betrayal. 'I'll go alone.'

'See? Easy. It'll be good to have the night apart. Absence makes the heart, et cetera.'

'I've got to go to work,' I tell him. I get the sense that pushing this any further will result in my sleepover rights being revoked. 'Wish me luck with Clean Juice Co.'

'Hm?' he says, already absorbed in the news again. 'Good luck, pal.'

Hm. Not a great pet name. Let's try again.

'Don't miss me *too* much,' I say.

'Have a good one.'

Right. How do I feel about that? Was that okay?

Anyway, he's right, isn't he? It will be good to have a night apart.

But what did that mean? Am I overstaying my welcome? Why doesn't he just say that? Am I being too needy? Have his housemates complained about me? Should I sling them $20 for their utility bill?

I guess I haven't been home much lately. I'm starting to miss Leo a bit. The other night I tried to tell Max and his housemates Leo's story about eating too many special brownies and getting lost in the catacombs while on exchange in Paris, but I didn't do it justice and Max didn't think it was very funny. I don't get the impression Max loves the idea of Leo at all and they haven't even met yet.

Not so long ago I was walking on air at being allowed to stay for morning coffee, so maybe I'm never satisfied. I just don't understand why he acts as though I'm asking too much of him. It's like he only wants us to exist in the bubble of his bedroom, and anywhere else is beyond his realm of interest.

Maybe I'm overthinking it. It wouldn't be the first time.

As we wrapped up our session the other day, Dr Minnick told me to do breathing exercises when I feel overwhelmed, which I found condescending. I've spent twenty-six years successfully breathing and panicking simultaneously, thank you very much. But I want to take confident, positive energy into my day, and I'm jittery enough to give it one more try. I take four seconds to fill up my lungs with air and spend another four pushing it all back out.

One two three four.

One two three four.

I can't tell if it has helped, so I do it again.

One two three four.

One two three four.

One — shit, is it that time already? I don't have time for this. I need to prepare for my meeting with the most pedantic pressed-juice institution you've ever met, whose marketing manager insists that spinach and celery juice doesn't taste like pond water. I need to get them coffee and acai bowls and print out the new wireframes because they don't like working off screens, which I fucking — I mean, it's for a *website.* But it's fine, it's fine, I can manage a printer and a cafe pitstop. I just need a latte to get the bitter taste of Max's single origin Americano out of my mouth. I swallow hard against the lump in my throat. Did I remember to take my pill last night? A pregnancy scare is the last thing I need. God, can you imagine? Why is the light for the pedestrian crossing taking so long to change? Come on come on come on. Argh, *fuck today already!*

CHAPTER FOURTEEN

It's no easy feat juggling my handbag, five coffees, an assortment of breakfast bowls and my office keys, but I'm on top of it. I'm determined to correct my mood. I'll just drop my things off and get to work setting everything up in the conference room.

'Oh!' I squeak, spotting Margot's little brown bun behind her monitor. 'Good morning! Another early bird!'

'Overburdened?'

'It's for the CJC meeting,' I say brightly. 'Are you sitting in? I got you a coffee.'

'Thanks.'

'And I got provisions from Nutrition Bar. Are you sugar-free this week?'

'I want to chat with you this afternoon,' she says. Alarm bells go off in my head.

'Oh? Anything the matter?'

'One pm. I've booked the conference room.'

Oh god. What does that mean? Despite my supreme effort to improve my work and attitude, her chilliness seems to have intensified, and it's hard not to take it personally. More than ever, I've just been trying to stay out of her way. I come in early, do my work quietly, smile in meetings, and try to contribute. I wish she would forget I exist.

When she was out of the office at a management retreat last week, I was sharp and upbeat. Ideas came easily and I got through my work quickly. I closed fifty-nine jobs, when the team average is forty. But then she came back and I began to freeze up again, and I don't know how to stop. Even thinking about it makes my stomach hurt. But I need to be on my A-game for this meeting, so I count my breaths again. I just need a big gulp of coffee and everything will reset.

I take a sip, the lid slips off, and the shirt I took from Max's closet is drenched.

One two three four. One two three four.

One two three four one twothreefour.

Onetwothreefouronetwothreefour.

'Oh, Christ,' I hear Margot say.

I don't want to see the look on her little puggish face. Isn't this embarrassing enough? I drop the cup in the bin and walk straight to the bathrooms to ring out my shirt and have the cry I feel brewing in my sinus.

Once I'm locked in the cubicle and sitting on the closed seat, I put my face in my hands and wait for the feeling to pass. How quiet and safe it is in this cubicle, just me and my wet shirt, nobody making little remarks, no coffee lids leaping to freedom. Now would be a great time to find out I'm not a muggle and disapparate straight back to bed.

With no desire to move and no magical abilities, I figure I might as well reach out for some affection from Max. I'll feel better once we're back in our usual rhythm. I snap a picture of the coffee-stained shirt and send it to him.

Penelope Moore (08:17): :(should've taken your advice and stayed in bed today

He doesn't reply. He's probably on his way to the library. Last night I highlighted pieces of his thesis that needed a bit of work, and he wasn't happy. That's probably what started this. As though I should be punished for his overconfident semicolons. I should find out where he got this shirt so I can replace it. I wish I'd just worn one of my own. It's probably vintage and irreplaceable. I should have asked before I took it.

Though I know better, I tempt fate by asking myself if this day can get any worse. And then it does.

The sunny morning fades to an overcast, humid afternoon, and all these weeks of immaculate eyeliner and forced peppiness feel as though they've come to nothing. The power imbalance in our large glass-walled conference room is palpable, and I can't shake the feeling of being called into the principal's office. I feel the overwhelming need to apologise, but I don't know what for. For the cost of my measly salary? For not being her favourite? For the internet bandwidth I take up?

How I envy Margot's ability to sit in an uncomfortable silence and not rush to fill it up with chatter. Her perfect nails — an understated nude colour on long nail beds, so unlike my bitten cuticles and sloppy at-home manicure — *taptaptap* away on her tablet as she finishes an email and pulls up a reference document. I'm peripherally aware that I have plenty of open jobs I should be working on while she takes her time, but I stop myself from checking the time or looking around the room in boredom.

'I'm glad to see you've been in a better mood these last few weeks,' she says at last.

'I am!' I nod enthusiastically. Ooh, positive reinforcement! This could be like that time at my old job when I was called in for a chat with my boss after interning for two months, and

I'd ruined my mascara by the time I'd even pulled my chair in. Turned out he was offering me a job.

'I just wish I could see that in your work. I know you've been trying harder, but your work is still —' she casts around for the word '— uninspired.'

Oh.

'In what way?' I ask, thrown by this particular accusation. 'I've hit all my deliverables this month. Every ticket in my queue gets closed by the end of the week. I mean, except for Clean Juice Co, but they were dragging out every request — they wanted to see everything in staging and it takes up so much of the devs' time and eats up their budget, and I've explained that to them — but we finally got them to sign off today. I know it took for*ever*, but —'

'But it's your job to manage that,' she says. 'They signed off today, but I had to step in to get them over the line. They should be able to trust you to get it done, but they don't. That's what your job is. And if you can't do that, I don't understand what you *do* all day.'

This isn't a question but a challenge I feel woefully ill-equipped for.

If my friends asked me what I did this week, I could tell them: written insights reports for Deco Cinemas and Park Street Espresso; done a mountain of copy edits for Victoria Credit Union; built a newsletter template for EasyChef meal plans and sent it to their 13,500 subscribers; worked with the creatives to tidy up the Jackson & Smith Realty homepage; triaged a slew of requests to the devs; finished off the Clean Juice Co wireframe updates and had three meetings with them to get their contract signed; spent hours hunched over my laptop organising the presentation deck for Evergreen. But when Margot asks, all I can think about is the pressure building in my temples, and I'm trying to practise my breathing exercises without counting to four aloud.

'I had, um, a lot of bits and pieces, to, um, get through for Deco and VCU, and I, uh, sat with Ed for a while to work on the, um —'

'That should take you an hour, not all day.'

'Um, well ...'

'Penelope, do you like working here?'

'Yes!' I say reflexively. I don't sound convincing. 'Yeah, of course. It's ... I — y'know, sometimes it's tough, but, um, that's just the job, any job, you have good days and bad days, but, I mean, yeah — yes. I do.'

'Most of the time it doesn't seem like you want to be here at all. You have to be prompted to do more than the bare minimum. The work you do is ... fine. I never see you present ideas or go the extra mile.'

'I've been working a lot on Evergreen lately. With the designers. But on my own too. I've been working on the deck for our pitch ...'

'That shouldn't eat up too much of your time. They haven't signed with us. You're throwing hours at them for free. What about paying clients?'

'I mean, a lot of my projects, they're sort of in ... stasis. Like, CJC is good to go now. Everyone else is happy with their campaigns right now. For this quarter, there's not really, um, places for ideas.'

'It's your job to give them new ideas, to generate business for the agency.'

No words come. My head hurts and my neck is hot, and counting breaths isn't doing anything.

'Listen,' she continues, 'I don't mind telling you. The partners wanted to give you the Account Director role, but I didn't think you could handle it, and you're only proving me right. When was the last time you spent the day at a client's office or took them out for dinner? When was the last time you went out and found a new client?'

This isn't Mad Men, I want to tell her. *I'm here to deliver projects, not entertain clients.* There's a reason I never pursued sales. My first job as a teenager was at The Body Shop on Bourke Street Mall, and I got fired because I never upsold customers the full-sized mango body lotion. I figured no one needs that much lotion. I'm here to give people what they ask for, not to sell them shit they don't need. But I can't tell Margot I don't care about Scout's bottom line enough to have an awkward conversation with my clients about tripling their ad budget for no reason.

'You're out of here at five on the dot,' she says, turning her iPad around to show me a spreadsheet with my name at the top of it. 'Actually, often earlier. I asked Kim to track what time you leave, and most days you're out the door at four fifty-five, four fifty-two, *four forty-nine* last Wednesday ...'

'But I get here before nine every day!' I cry, finally, indignant. She's been getting the receptionist to keep a log of what time I leave every day. Really? 'I eat lunch at my desk most days. I get the work done!'

'No one is asking you to get here early. No one is asking you to eat lunch at your desk. But when it's eight pm on a Friday and I'm still here finishing up your work, it's a problem.'

I don't know when she has ever finished my work for me, but I don't know how to argue with her. She's so good at keeping her cool that it makes me panic twice as much. I'm all too aware of my pinkening ears, my quivering lip. The entire office can see me panicking in here. I'm not brave enough to look around. I hope nobody is enjoying the show.

Is she right? Maybe she is. I know I don't love my job. I just didn't know everyone else knew it too. Does Kim mark down my clock-off time and then corral everyone for a daily bitch session about how much of my slack they all have to pick up? Am I such a colossal fuck-up that I'm dragging everyone down?

The partners wanted to promote me. I should find comfort in that. But I don't work with them every day, so maybe they don't see how shit I am at my job. Margot managed to talk them out of it, so they can't have wanted me to have the job that badly.

Am I going to be fired? How will I explain myself in job interviews? What kind of reference would Margot give me? Would I have to go back to uni and study something new and start again in a different industry? Should I just get a job slinging coffees at the cafe near home? But could I still make rent at Leo's? Would I have to move to fucking Castlemaine and live with Dad? I'm nearly twenty-seven years old, for fuck's sake; how do I start over?

These questions scream over the top of each other and I only realise I'm crying when a tear drips cold on my clavicle. My skin is itchy and it's taking all of my self-control not to scratch it off, to dig my ugly chipped nails into my arms and rake at myself until it burns and stings and gives me some distraction from the *thudthudthudthudthud* of my pulse in my ears and my suffocating, overwhelming shame. How do I get away from this? Should I just go home now and pack a bag and get an Uber to the airport? Where should I go? Paris? Or LA or Berlin? What visa would I be able to get? What would I do there? Where is far enough away from this cold fluorescent room and the look on Margot's face and every mistake I've ever made in my life? Have I ever made one good decision? Am I always going to feel like this? Have I ever *not* felt like this? I don't remember, I can't think of anything, my chest hurts, my head hurts, and can I just stop crying? *You're a fucking adult, Penny, stop it, stop embarrassing yourself, get your shit together, you stupid bitch!*

'Look, Penelope,' Margot says in a tone that could be mistaken for gentle, but it only makes me hate her more, 'I'm trying to help you.'

I want to spit *fuck you!* in her face, but I betray myself by nodding instead. She's been out to get me for months. I don't know why she fucking hates me, but she does, and it doesn't matter how many coffees I get her or how many times I try to pipe up in meetings. She's just on a power trip and taking it out on me because she can. How is she allowed to get away with this? Doesn't everyone see what a monster she is?

'This chat is never pleasant. Trust me, I've been where you are. I know you're disappointed about the AD role and I don't want you to be blindsided again. I'm telling you this because I need to see a real improvement in your productivity and your attitude if you want a future at this agency. Be *proactive*. Show me you want to be here. Because you don't have to be. You can leave any time you like.'

All I can manage is a pathetic choked-up little '*okay*' before I leave the room, humiliated and approaching hysterical.

I'm glad to find that most of the office is at lunch and they don't have to see this. I don't want to talk about it; I just want to get out of here. I can feel every remaining eye on me as I cross the room, pick up my handbag and leave. I don't care what time it is. Kim can write whatever the fuck she likes in her snitchy little spreadsheet. I'm not staying here a second longer.

Keep it together. Don't make eye contact with anyone. No one needs to watch you have a full-blown panic attack. You're being a fucking drama queen. Just get out.

I think I hear Margot call my name, but maybe I'm imagining it. Maybe I just want her to, want her to prove she's a human fucking being. I don't have it in me to turn around. I walk out, refusing to look at Kim — the traitor — and I gasp for fresh clean air out on the street.

Traffic surges and an army of raucous school kids takes up the footpath on the way to Richmond Station, and the noise and speed and chaos of it all is overwhelming, and I don't know what to do with myself, and I can't see straight, and it feels like every pedestrian is running at me.

I find myself crouching in the empty laneway behind the office. I click on Max's name in my address book and hit *call* and try to measure my breath in time with each ring. It rings and rings and rings and goes to voicemail, and I resist the urge to throw my phone as hard as I can. I want to break something, tear something up, take all this agony out of my body and put it anywhere else. No one is coming after me, and I'm at once hurt and relieved. I open my mouth to scream, but I choke, and fresh tears come hot and fast. My whole body shakes with it, and I hate myself more urgently than ever before.

CHAPTER FIFTEEN

I don't remember walking home, but I must have because I've made it to the couch. The living room is dim, so it must be late in the day. I'm so tired. My head throbs, and it's too hard to even put a hand to my forehead to soothe it, or to get up to refill the glass of water on the coffee table beside the blister pack of Valium with two newly empty tabs. The dark green fabric of the couch is soft against my cheek. I wonder how much energy it would take to reach up and pull the throw over me. It's warm today, but my arms are cold, and a blanket might be a comforting barrier between me and the fading sunlight. It sounds too difficult, so I don't bother.

I wonder if I'm still upset about the meeting and test it by letting myself remember a little of it: Margot's expression; the sight of my nails pressing hard into my wrist. A lump immediately forms in my throat and my vision blurs. Yep. That settles it. It takes determined effort to close that folder and direct my thoughts elsewhere.

Is it Friday? Do I have plans tonight? I should get up. I should find my phone and ask Max to come round or check the group chat. I should get in the shower, rinse off the day, and reset my senses with warm water and nice soap and one of my good candles. I could order dinner and drown in pad thai. Ugh, no. I can't be bothered.

There's a muffled *ping* from my bag on the floor, and I reach into it to find my phone. It's just a notification about a Net-a-Porter sale. I'm not in the mood for browsing clothes I can't afford. There are a dozen messages in the group chat, but I don't have the energy to engage. I check my chat history with Max and find the messages I only vaguely remember sending him.

Penelope Moore (14:09): Can you call me?
Penelope Moore (14:12): Important
Seen: 14:47

I expect this to sting, and it does.

From outside myself, I watch as I double down on this weight in my chest and dig for trouble. I open Instagram and I only have to search the letter *A* for her handle to pop up in my search history and I find exactly what I'm looking for. I knew I'd find it before I'd even finished forming the thought.

Max's ex-girlfriend's hair is different than it was the last time I visited her profile. What was an icy platinum blonde now has a cotton candy pink hue, presumably chosen to make her look more interesting and subversive than she is. Her slinky kimono jacket is probably from some fabulous vintage shop in the West Village, and those light-wash jeans look like they're no-stretch but practically fall off her anyway. There's no fat on her hips to create a muffin top. Her arm, dark with either a real tan or a convincing fake one, hangs in stark contrast around Max's soft pale neck. Her jawline is enviably sharp and her cheekbones radiate perfect highlighter as she pecks him on the cheek. There's a smear of peachy lipstick giving away where they have attempted this photo several times before.

amber.lou.92 *cute catchups with @maxfitz* 🐱🐱🐱

I don't know what to do with this. I could screenshot it and send it to him and ask him what the hell I'm looking at, but I can't find the energy. I'm not interested in a chorus of '*I told you so*'s from my friends, either. I don't even want a copy of this in my cloud. Despite having hardly moved all afternoon, I'm awash with exhaustion again. Too tired to drag my bones down the hallway to my bed; too tired, even, to be alone with my thoughts. I put on an episode of *Friends* and let the laughter track lull me back to sleep.

'Penny,' says Leo's voice, and there is a warm hand on my arm. 'You okay? Why aren't you in bed?'

The room is dark, lit only by the glow of the Netflix menu. The house is still, and the street is quiet. It must be past midnight. He's in his underwear. He has a tattoo on his stomach.

'I didn't mean to,' I say.

We're whispering.

'What's going on?' he asks. 'Where've you been? Are you okay?'

I nod into the cushion. Keeping my eyes open takes effort, so I don't. 'Had a panic attack.'

'Shit, Penny,' he says, and the sympathy in his voice spurs on new tears. 'Oh, Pen.'

My limbs are heavy, and he pulls me like a ragdoll against him, wrapping his arm around my shoulders. He smells like my lavender soap. I don't have the will or energy to be embarrassed as I let myself cry into his shoulder, and he doesn't let go, and the intimacy of this gesture makes my chest hurt. It should be my boyfriend comforting me not my housemate, and this thought brings another wave of sadness, of resentment for Max, of anger at myself.

Then Leo gets me some water and rubs my back as I drain the glass and set it on the coffee table. My face says, '*thank you*', and his says, '*you're welcome*'.

'Leo?' comes a woman's voice, and we both look in its direction. It's not Mermaid Hair or Jumpsuit Girl but someone new. She's got long red hair and she's pantsless in one of his T-shirts. Her skinny calves look dainty in the moonlight.

'Coming,' he says over his shoulder before turning back to me. 'Get yourself to bed, okay? I promise you'll feel better in the morning.'

I nod and give him an attempt at a smile. He heads back down the hall with her, and I wait to hear his bedroom door click shut before pushing myself off the couch and heading, slowly, for the warm safety of my sheets and another long dreamless sleep.

CHAPTER SIXTEEN

The floorboards creak under the weight of someone trying to tiptoe down the hallway.

It takes me a minute to assign blame for my thudding headache, my dry mouth, the anvil on my chest. Did I drink last night? Get hit by a bus? Inject vodka into my eyeballs?

Oh, panic attack. Right. That sounds more like me. If I had to mainline for a buzz, I'd use a vodka-soaked tampon before I stabbed myself in the tear duct.

Taptaptap comes the sound of knuckles on my door. I glance down to check that I don't have an errant boob popping out from under the sheets before I respond. Turns out I'm still in my work clothes, apparently too defeated to even get undressed last night.

'Yeah?'

The door cracks open. 'Just checking on you,' Leo says, poking his head in and assuming the kind of sad, sympathetic expression you make when you see a stray dog. It's humiliating. 'You okay?'

'Yeah.'

'Do you want to have pancakes about it?'

My immediate thought is to turn him down and retreat back under the covers for the rest of the weekend. I want to have a proper wallowing session, complete with a binge and a movie marathon to seal in the self-loathing. Maybe I could do both. You can't eat pancakes and then go on to have a productive day anyway. They're basically a primer for a weekend spent horizontally.

My thought process must show on my face because Leo says, 'Ten minutes and we'll go to the cafe,' and shuts the door behind him.

It's an effort to drag myself out of bed and get dressed, but I manage. I don't feel the need to dress up for Leo. Comfy (read: unflattering) jeans and my last remaining clean white T-shirt do the trick and even feel compassionate after a week of fitted waistbands and slightly-too-snug work blazers or the short dresses that require hairless legs and the slinky bralettes that I wear to hold Max's attention.

In the bathroom, a wet-haired Leo and I make eye contact through the mirror. He grins with a mouth full of foamy toothpaste, and it's impossible not to smile back. He even lets me smear sunscreen on his face, if only so he can avoid another twenty-minute lecture from me about UVA rays and his skin ageing like milk.

Leo never pulls his shoulders in close to make himself take up less space or worries that everyone in the room secretly hates him, and it's infectious. Being around him is a glass of wine after a long day. Walking to the cafe together, all my panic about Max and Margot and next week's Evergreen pitch is reduced to a faint buzz, like mildly irritating tinnitus instead of life-crippling anxiety.

'What's news?' I ask him after our tattooed and moustachioed waiter drops off our orders. Shakshuka for him, pancakes with banana and Nutella for me. I figure all my leftover panic attack energy will take care of the calories.

'Eh,' he replies. 'Nothing exciting.'

'What, no gossip? What about the girl from last night?'

'I would *never* gossip,' he says, faux-affronted. 'I leave that to you. I live for your drama and hysterics.'

'Mine?!' I cry. 'You're the one screwing everyone in a five-kilometre radius of our house. You're way messier than I am.'

'That's not true. More like ten kilometres. I even went to Footscray for a date once.'

'The west side? You must have been desperate.'

'Desperately desperate.'

'Makes sense, you're hideous. Gotta widen your net to find someone who will deign to be seen with you.'

'Hey!' he says, taking his fork and digging a wedge of pancake into the puddle of Nutella I'd been saving for the end.

'No! Rude!'

'Please? I need it. I had a hard week at work,' he says petulantly.

'What, did you have to actually do your job?'

'I had *two* meetings yesterday and a very dry salad roll for lunch.'

'You poor thing! Kurdish freedom fighters would feel sorry for you.'

'That's what I keep telling people, but for some reason they think that's "*an unnecessarily controversial take*".'

Our dynamic of straightforward silliness is the perfect antidote to yesterday. It's just comfortable, you know? I don't know the last time I had a friendship with a straight guy without fucking it up by getting a crush on them and leaning in to kiss them after ten thousand vodka sodas, only to have them go lobster-red and start stammering about how I'm *really great* but they *just don't see me that way*. Then, inevitably, they start dating a woman with the bone structure of a Hadid sister and delete me off Facebook. Leo's just my friend, and there's no sexual tension or lingering questions to colour our relationship any other way.

'I know you probably don't want to talk about last night,' he says after a while. 'But … you okay? What happened?'

'Oh, you know,' I begin, waving my hand as though to brush off the whole conversation. 'Work. Boys. Existential crises. Faulty serotonin receptors. The endless wait between Carly Rae Jepsen albums.'

'No, come on. I want to know. Is it Max?'

I want to save all my questions about his ex's Instagram and why he never called me back yesterday for when I'm beached on the couch later. I whine, scrunching up my nose in protest at Leo's persistence, but he won't let it drop.

'I'll take that as a yes. Let me ask you something. Why him?'

'What do you mean?'

'Of all the guys in the world, what got you so stuck on that one?'

'I — because I love him. I always have. For years I've loved him.'

'Okay, but why? Is he nice to you? Is he really funny? Does he rescue puppies from burning buildings in his spare time?'

'He's more of a cat person,' I say.

Leo grimaces.

I'm playing for time. What a strange, perfectly acceptable question. Why Max? Have I ever asked myself that?

'I guess because he reminds me of how good things can be. When we were together, the first time, in my last year of uni, we used to stay up all night drinking cheap red wine, talking about films we loved and these great big adventures we wanted to go on, telling each other all our sad little secrets, and he really got me, you know? He liked all the same things I liked. He didn't pity me about growing up without a mum. He let me read his poems. We were in love. We were happy. *I* was happy.'

'And now?'

'Well, that's not fair,' I say, avoiding eye contact by using the strawberry garnish on my plate to swirl patterns in the remaining Nutella. 'No one ever thinks they're happy in the moment. Everyone walks around miserable all the time, and they don't realise how happy they actually were before until they move onto the next unhappy phase of their life. So as far as future me is concerned, I'm probably, like, the happiest I've ever been.'

Sure, sometimes I'll have a great day with my dad at an art gallery or the movies, or a nice afternoon reading in the sun, and I'll think, *I'm so happy right now*, but that's different from broad, lasting happiness. The awkwardness and dissatisfaction of everyday life is just part of being a human. Even if I'm having a picnic in the Botanic Gardens with the girls and we're two bottles of prosecco down and someone has splurged on good cheese and I'm really happy with my outfit, I still have notes on how the afternoon could be improved. I'll wish the sun was a little less hot on my back, or get annoyed by someone's screaming baby, or want the day to last forever because I don't want to go to work tomorrow. Even in my happiest moments, there's room for improvement.

'But you're happy that you're back together?' asks Leo, considering me over his coffee. 'It's what you've been waiting for?'

'It's nice to have him back in my life. Properly.' I shrug. 'I don't have that yucky feeling in my tummy that I'm lying to my friends or I'm one wrong move away from him blocking my number. It's a weight off.'

'You can also look back and be surprised at how miserable you were, you know?'

'I don't know. I'm always happier in my memory than I am in real life.'

'I think that's called depression.'

'No shit,' I snort. 'Can I interest you in an SSRI?'

He laughs, and so do I. I'm glad he doesn't treat my self-deprecation like something to be corrected; that's so boring.

I wear my mental health on my sleeve. I use it like a suit of armour. If everyone around me knows I'm in a thick fog of ambivalence — feeling nothing at all or everything at once, not caring if I live or die then clawing frantically for breath and safety — then they can't hold any of it against me. '*Treat with caution*,' says a sign across my chest. '*I could explode at the mildest criticism*.'

Leo busies his hands folding his napkin into triangles and, after a beat of contemplation, says, 'Sometimes you don't know how shit a situation was until you're on the other side of it.'

'Like how?' I ask.

'Well, it's tiny, but … I remembered this morning how me and my ex used to go out for a big one on Fridays, and she'd go off with her friends and I'd have to stand around all night with all their boyfriends who I just, urgh, hated.'

'I hate being in the girlfriend corner too!'

'Right? And we would get in a fight because I'd want to leave, or she'd think I wasn't participating enough, and then the whole weekend would be a hungover, pass-agg write-off. And these days, I just don't fight with anyone. There are no arguments. My weekend belongs to me. I'm sitting here with you and I'm realising I'm so much happier than I used to be.'

'That's a nice thought,' I say softly, touching his arm. 'Like coming up for air.'

'Not everything deserves to be romanticised. Sometimes you're right to let go.'

I don't know. Every time I look in the mirror, I think longingly of the body I had in old photos and chastise my past self for hating my thighs back then when I should have appreciated what I had. I do the same thing with my old job, which I miss more than ever today. Sometimes I fantasise about the tedious meetings I used to have about the correct terminology for hole punches. Have I done it with Max too, or was I really happier back then? I think I was. I seem to remember laughing more.

But if I think too hard about the things I used to love — like the sweet (often dirty) poems he'd write on post-its and stick to my pillow while I was sleeping — I'll get upset. We don't really do those things now. We don't tell each other secrets, if we even have any left to tell. We barely leave his flat except for the occasional movie night at The Astor, or when I walk him to work on weekend mornings. And if I drink red wine these days, I get a stomachache.

If he goes out with his friends, all of them academics, they usually go to a student bar in Carlton. I don't go because I feel like a rotting nectarine in a crowd of bare-midriffed arts students armed with $10 beer jugs and uncomplicated optimism. So we don't go out, and he doesn't stay at my house, and I can't talk to him about my friends or to my friends about him. On a busy day I can almost forget we exist at all.

But relationships evolve, don't they? Of course it doesn't look the same as it did five years ago. We're different now. That doesn't necessarily signal incompatibility. Someone told me once that if you have to overanalyse your relationship, then you're in the wrong one. Usually it motivates me to keep my mouth shut, as though I need to do my part in fulfilling the prophecy of making Max the right man.

How can a month-old relationship have this many question marks?

'Anyway, if you're happy then I'm happy,' says Leo, giving my hand on his arm a pat, and I realise I've left it there this whole time. 'What do you want to do today? Let's have some fun.'

'My kind of fun?'

'Anything you want.'

'Oh, if those aren't the magic words,' I say, pretending to swoon. 'Even if I want to go clothes shopping, get cupcakes, use your arm to try a hundred lipsticks, and go home and do a face mask and watch *The Great British Bake Off*?'

'I regret everything I just said. You're on your own.'

I begin to laugh, but it's cut short by the telltale vibration of my phone on the table. My screen lights up with Max's name, and I go frantic trying to unlock it, but my thumbprint is tacky with Nutella residue.

Max Fitzgerald (11:44): All good?
Max Fitzgerald (11:44): Come round for a little afternoon delight? ;)

'Can we take a raincheck on our hang?' I ask Leo, who doesn't look surprised or bothered.

'Course,' he says easily, pushing his chair out. 'I'll go pay.'

'No, let me —' I begin, but he waves me off.

'Let me buy you breakfast, you little basket case.'

He says this with such affection that I don't argue. How lovely. Yesterday's worries have evaporated. It appears that a little support and positivity from Leo, a stack of pancakes and a flirty text from my boyfriend can cure anything. I decide to shelve my questions about Amber's post for the time being and force myself to have a good day today. The world is kind and bright again.

CHAPTER SEVENTEEN

This shop is as white as a hospital hallway, and I can't look anywhere without catching my reflection in one of the floor-to-ceiling mirrors. It's barely midday, but someone offers me a flute of champagne and what am I going to do, turn down a free drink? Who do you think I am? I overcommit to the first sip and spill a little, and it doesn't go unnoticed by the lithe, sleek-haired shop assistant. I think I see her wrinkle her nose as I pat the wet spot on my top. If she knew it was from the sale rack at Topshop, she might kick me out of the store.

We're in Armadale, the wedding district, in a bridal shop you can only visit by appointment. Outside, cavoodles are being chauffeured around in Range Rovers, and heavily collagenned women chat enthusiastically as they power walk up and down High Street in Stella McCartney activewear. Inside, there's tulle and organza and lace enough to stitch together a circus tent. Even the mannequins are being dramatic and have been bent into couture poses: concave spines, arms at ninety-degree angles, legs extended to show the full effect of a mermaid skirt. It feels like another planet, given I had to bunny hop over a puddle of urine at West Richmond Station to get here this morning.

Frankly, this isn't what I had in mind when Bec asked if we wanted to go dress shopping. I wanted to go to COS to find something for my presentation to Evergreen next week and maybe a new red lipstick for confidence.

'Is that what I think it is on your neck?' whispers Annie from beside me on this overstuffed white sofa, delightfully scandalised.

'*Fuck*,' I hiss as I whip my hand up to cover the left side of my throat. 'Has the concealer worn off already?'

'Put your hair down,' she whispers, 'or the bridezilla over there will see, and she'll make passive aggressive comments about him all day.'

'I'm going to *kill* Max,' I tell her, pulling my hair free of its bun and raking it smooth.

'That's still going well?'

'Lovely,' I tell her, smiling thinly. I don't want to get into it in the fanciest shop in the entire fucking world. Not that there's even anything to get into. After our little mid-afternoon session yesterday, Max apologised for being unreachable the day before. It had been a busy day at the cafe, he said, and he'd had to leave his phone in a bag of rice overnight after dropping it in a sink full of dishwater. Before I worked up the nerve to ask him about the picture with Amber, we were kissing again, and I couldn't think of a way to explain why I was stalking his ex's Instagram anyway, so I let it go.

'How are things with you?' I ask Annie. 'How was your date with …?'

'Emmy,' she says, lighting up like she's been waiting for the opportunity to talk about it. I know what's coming, but I indulge her anyway because that's what good friends do. The usual surge of hope before the unsatisfying reality. The busted seesaw. The euphoria before the misery. 'Oh my god, yes. The other day we —'

'Are you ready?' calls Bec in a singsong voice. 'Prepare to be *amaaazed*.'

'*Later*,' says Annie, and I nod. Her phone buzzes just as Bec appears from behind the curtain of her dressing room, more fabric than girl. The skirt of her gown — strapless, ivory, tulle — is as wide as she is tall.

'Oh wow!' cries Annie.

'So pretty!'

Bec does a twirl, and we coo dutifully. I feel an odd sense of victory at the tiny roll of back fat sitting above the zipper, and then I have to tell myself to stop being such a bitch. Must be a better friend. Must be a nicer human. I imagine what she might say about me if our roles are ever reversed and feel a pang of regret.

All I know is that my fantasy wedding is the diametric opposite to the one she is planning. According to the group chat, she's having trouble finding a venue that '*speaks to her*' that can also accommodate her bulging 200-person guest list. She cried at the florist at South Melbourne Market last weekend because they couldn't guarantee the availability of yellow dahlias in October. She is considering a costume change pre-reception. She is banning phones at the door.

'Do you love it?' she asks us, accepting a $300 jewelled belt from the shop assistant and fastening it around her waist. She's on tiptoe in front of the mirror — I can see her maroon pedicure peeking out of the bottom of the tower of tulle — and she's twisting around to see herself from every angle. 'I love it.'

'It's very *you*.'

'It's very pretty,' says Annie from behind her phone.

'Can you put your phone down?' Bec snaps.

Annie flinches. 'Sorry, I was just —'

'I know your job is *very important*,' says Bec, 'but can you not be thinking about murderers and rapists while we're shopping for my *wedding dress*?'

'I've never worked on a murder case, actually,' Annie says coolly.

'What do you mean it's "very *me*", Penny?' asks Bec, changing tack. 'You don't like it?'

'No, I do!' I cry. 'I think it suits you!'

'But you wouldn't wear it? You think it's hideous.'

'I don't think it's hideous! It's not what I'd pick for myself, but —'

'Well, I've seen your wardrobe, so that's not much of a compliment.'

'Bec, *enough*,' says Annie, frowning rather hard now. 'We know you're stressed. We know this is very important. We're here to support you, not be your whipping posts.'

'I just want —'

'You can calm down and talk to us like human beings, or you can shop alone.'

Tension fills the room, and for a moment I expect Bec to hurl a diamante tiara at us, to banish us from her sight and this shop and her life, to scream and combust with rage. Instead, something worse happens. Her face folds into tears.

'I'm sorry!' she wails, and I immediately feel overcome with guilt for ever feeling annoyed at her. 'Evan's mum is being such a d-*dick*, and my sister w-won't come unless she can bring her kids — fucking Vegemitey hands everywhere — and I have so many clients right now I don't have enough time to handle them all. I'm g-going to have a-a-a nervous *breakdown*!'

'Hey, that's Penny's job,' says Annie, gently, as freaked out by this sudden change of mood as I am.

'Yeah, having public meltdowns is my domain,' I add with a placating hand on her back. Annie and I share concerned looks behind her. 'Maybe you need a little break, babe.'

'I can't!' she cries, red-faced under her hands. The shop assistant is feeding her tissues, desperate to protect the dress from eyeliner marks. 'I'm a freelancer! If I don't work, I don't get paid! Weddings are so expen-*hic*-sive.'

'Well, maybe prolong the engagement then,' offers Annie from the other side of her. 'Push it back six months, give yourself time to plan it without all the pressure.'

'I'm NOT pushing it BACK,' she snaps, officially entering panic attack territory. I'm pretty familiar with the landscape. 'I'm ready for this part of my life to be *done*! I'm getting married this year and that's final!'

'Okay,' I say calmly, while Annie mimes a request for water. 'Okay, we hear you.'

'What do you mean, "*this part*" of your life?' asks Annie.

'This!' she cries. 'Messy! Broke! Unsettled! Renting! Single! Like, like —'

'*Us?*'

'I didn't say that,' says Bec. She's handed a bottle of Pellegrino and drinks the whole thing in one go. 'I'm just ready. For what's next.'

'Okay,' we say.

'What's next, then?' I ask, fighting to keep my voice light.

'I'm going to buy a wedding dress,' she says with a hearty, resolute sniffle. She straightens up and passes me her handful of wet tissues. 'And there's a jumpsuit for the rehearsal dinner I want you to see.'

Bec collects her composure and all of her skirt and heads back into the change room. When the shop assistant comes by to top up our champagne flutes, Annie says, 'You might want to leave the bottle here.'

CHAPTER EIGHTEEN

'That's it,' I say. 'I've hit a wall.'

'What's the matter?' asks Margot from behind her monitor.

'Nothing. I was talking to myself.'

Dusk is settling over Cremorne, and the streetlamps have just flickered on. I don't think I've ever stayed back this late. I've been slouched over the Evergreen pitch deck since this morning. It's now past 6:30 pm, and the office is empty but for the two of us. There's a pinching pain in my middle back that my shoulder rolls aren't fixing, and my screen is blurry even with my glasses on.

'Is your pitch ready?'

'Yeah, it is.'

'Let's see where it's at,' she says, her chair scraping the floor as she gets up to sit beside me.

After the cursed meeting last week, I fantasised about breezing into the office at 8:59 am with a latte and a power lip, then spending the day annoying the shit out of her with relentless positivity, but I chickened out. I don't even have the guts for malicious compliance.

She has asked me to send her a list of everything I've done each day and said we'll meet once a week to go over it. The pressure of accountability and fear of a volcanic reaction to any evidence of unproductivity is a pretty helpful motivator, actually. I'm annoyed at the dopamine hit I got when she replied to my checked-off to-do list last night with a '*Great, thanks.*'

The pitch is over lunch tomorrow, and it's down to the wire. With the creative team's help, I've created a bulletproof proposal. Using a pistachio-inspired colour palette and a fat, comforting custom font, I've mocked up a wireframe for their online store, created product labels, written web copy, mocked up a social media calendar and reworked their entire brand ethos through a young, peppy, conscientious lens.

And now, after working on it nonstop for weeks, I hate every single thing about it. Why didn't I consider pink? Or lavender? What if they don't think their audience is overwhelmed and panicked twenty-somethings like me but actually a more tranquil pre-menopausal demographic? It's like spending too long on your eyeliner and ending up with one Winehouse-esque mega wing and one skinny little ski slope, but now I don't have time to have a tantrum and start over with a smoky eye. I just have to try to believe in what I've created.

This is more than I would do for any other client, but I really want to nail this. I need a win. Every ounce of my self-esteem depends on it. Maybe if I put this much effort into all my clients, I wouldn't be stuck in performance management hell. I wouldn't have to spend all day glued to my desk, grinning mindlessly like I'm horny for Google analytics.

Margot scrolls through each page, painstakingly reading every sentence and dot point, and I'm strangely self-conscious about all this effort. I suddenly feel overdressed. She taps my screen to point out where I've typed *Evergrene* and I groan internally.

'What've you got left?' she asks. 'SEM campaign projections, competitor reports …?'

'All prepared,' I tell her, switching tabs to show her my data. 'And I'll proofread it in the morning with fresh eyes, and print and bind it before the meeting.'

'Okay,' she says. 'Looks good.'

'Really?' I ask, reluctant to believe my luck. 'You think so? No edits?'

'This close to the pitch, it's as good as it's going to get.'

'Okay. Alright. Great. I think so too. Okay.'

'You can head home,' she says, attempting a smile. 'Good work today.'

The longer I stay, the higher the chances are that I'll open my mouth and say something stupid and shatter this feeling and give her reason to withdraw her high opinion of me for the day. Within a minute, I've powered down my laptop, swung my handbag over my shoulder, and bleated '*Goodnight!*' from the front door. How's that for a good day?

Once I'm free from the throngs of station-bound commuters and striding up Lennox Street in a perfect mood, I pull my phone out of my bag to message Max.

Penelope Moore (18:44): Fiiiiinally finished work!
Penelope Moore (18:44): Have you had dinner already?
Penelope Moore (18:45): I could go for Pho. Want to meet me?
Penelope Moore (18:48): Buzz buzz. Look at your phone. I'm starving. Is the one we like the one next door to the National, or is it the one up further?

I walk past four more streets with my phone in my hand, but there's no response. When I try calling, it rings out. Annoying. I search my memory for any reason why he wouldn't be answering. I think he said he'd be working on his thesis tonight. Did I remember wrong? Was he hanging out with his faculty buddies tonight, or was that last night? I haven't seen him since the weekend. I've been trying to be better about giving him space since our talk last week (*'Absence makes the heart, et cetera'*), but I'm starting to miss him.

When I swing my front gate open, Leo's at the door, stowing his keys in his pocket.

'Hey!' he says, brightly. 'What timing.'

'Must be fate!' I chirp. 'Are you leaving? Hot date?'

'Not for me,' he says. 'I was about to get dinner. Want to come? Save me from a table for one? The waiters at I Love Pho are such judgmental pricks.'

CHAPTER NINETEEN

Good morning! I've been awake for hours.

I went for a run as the sun struggled to rise, too full of electricity to stay asleep past 5 am. I woke Leo up by blow-drying my hair, which he was quite upset about, but he forgave me when I ironed his shirt since I was going to do my dress anyway. He indulged me as I blabbered on about the Evergreen pitch over coffee and strawberry jam on crumpets, and we did a *Top Gun* high five for luck.

He sets off for work on his bike, and I realise I still have two effing hours before I need to be in the office. Right. How do morning people keep themselves busy? Yoga? Affirmations?

I spend an unnecessary amount of time getting my makeup just right. Even though I could do a full face in my sleep, I turn to my god — Lisa Eldridge — for advice. I set my laptop carefully on the bathroom sink and follow along with one of her YouTube tutorials.

Sartorially, I'm not taking any chances. I'm wearing a belted black silk shirt dress. It's my lucky date dress, actually. It's been relegated to the back of my closet since I deleted all my dating apps a month ago. It's a little slinky and the thigh split is approaching risqué, but I decide that it passes for work appropriate if I pair it with a dark blazer and my best and most serious pumps. Don't fail me now, lucky date dress. I need all the help I can get.

To finish things off, I layer on several dainty necklaces and pop little star-shaped studs in my ears. I painted my nails in a fun pastel pink last night, and you can't see where I've smudged it unless you look closely. I wish I'd thought to get them done properly during my lunch hour.

In my bedroom mirror, I smooth out my hair and point at my reflection. 'Be a winner today,' I tell myself as I turn from side to side sucking in my stomach. Should I wriggle into some Spanx? 'No crying, no panicking. Getting this account is the only thing that matters. Got it, Penny? Keep your shit together and get the job done.'

Great, how long did that take? How is it only 6:45 am? Oh, fuck it. I'll just head in. I'm too nervous to sit around the house, and watching Netflix in the morning feels wrong if you aren't hungover or unemployed.

Even though I used Leo's deodorant (men's deodorant just *feels* more effective) and the sky is a mid-season overcast grey, I'm not risking sweat patches today, no sir. I take an inconvenient train from West Richmond Station to East Richmond via Flinders Street and resent paying $4.40 on my Myki for a three-stop trip. Whatever. Chalk it up to the cost of winning new business.

My phone buzzes as I bid good day to Sexy Barista, and I dig through my bag for it. I hope it's Max wishing me good luck. I reminded him about today a dozen times.

Annie Lin (07:04): Skincare pitch today, right?
Annie Lin (07:05): GOOD LUCK PENNY
Annie Lin (07:05): Celebrations tonight at Daughter in Law, table at 7:30 under my name x
Bec Cooper (07:11): Gonna smash it today babe!!

Oh. Well. Well-wishes from my friends are nice too.

> **Penelope Moore (07:12):** Thanks gals!!!
> **Penelope Moore (07:12):** Can't wait to destroy a garlic naan (or four)
> **Penelope Moore (07:13):** Calories don't count on pitch day

When I arrive at the office, I'm surprised to find the lights off. I'm hardly ever the first person in. I flick on the kettle, drop my bag and settle in at my desk, hooking my laptop up to the Bluetooth speakers embedded into the ceiling. The early bird gets to be the office DJ, and it's a Carly Rae Jepsen kind of day. Buoyant, sugary pop is exactly the right mood. I'm barely thirty seconds into *Party for One* when Margot appears.

'I'm about to do a final proof of the sample copy,' I tell her brightly. I return my gaze to my monitor, more confident when she isn't in my line of vision. 'And I thought we could send Kim down to that vegan cafe for lunchy things or little cakes before they get here.'

'Are they vegan?'

'Not sure,' I shrug. 'But it'd be poor form if they are and we try to give them a beef bulgogi bowl for lunch.'

'That's — that's good thinking, actually,' she says, a little surprised. I could levitate.

In a baffling gesture, she puts her hand on my shoulder and makes meaningful eye contact as she wishes me good luck. It's unusually genuine and sort of uncomfortable. I manage a strained, *'um, thanks,'* before excusing myself and getting back to reviewing the same five lines of copy I've been obsessing over for weeks. Can you ever really be sure about *affect* versus *effect*?

I work in a calm, intense silence for a while. The office fills up around us, and someone switches Carly off — rude — and the din of a busy agency serves as white noise while I smash through the last few things on my to-do list. The morning goes by at warp speed, and I become acutely aware of the time as desks begin to empty and the microwave beeps and beeps with people heating up their lunch.

The Evergreen team will be here in ten minutes. I've managed to stave off my nerves until this point, but I'm reaching the limit of the control I have over my emotions. I don't even have time to do an emergency meditation in the toilets. I'd better reapply my lipstick in my phone camera in case they get here early.

There. Perfect.

I round up Kim and get her to plate up the sandwiches and salads. I'm colder than I would usually be to her, but I think I can hide it under the guise of cool, focused professionalism. If she wanted to be my bestie, she shouldn't have been such a sneaky little time snitch. I might hold a grudge against her longer than I do Margot. If I ever get out of here …

No!

No escapism fantasies! Focus!

Getting this account will change everything!

I deposit five copies of the pitch deck, still warm from the printer, at each of the conference room chairs so we can follow along with it on the big screen. The deck is half an inch thick with data and campaign samples. Everyone also gets a branded pen and notepad, a tall glass of sparkling water, and my business card.

A few weeks ago, I called the Evergreen headquarters and had a peppy, overly friendly chat with their receptionist under the guise of getting a headcount for today's meeting.

We'll be meeting with their founder, Julia Garland (with a name like that, why *wouldn't* you start a skincare line?), their CFO, Nelson Young, and the marketing director they hadn't yet hired. I also learned that the majority of their staff are women, which I love. The more I find out about their products and company ethos, the more I want to work with them. As far as today goes, I'm much more comfortable addressing an audience of women, especially when it's about something as near and dear as skincare. I could talk about it for hours, to anyone. To get to do it on the clock is nothing short of a treat.

About halfway through my research, I realised that this wasn't about wanting to appease Margot. I've actually enjoyed working on this project. I'll be upset if we don't sign them. I'd have to swear off their products forever, out of pettiness and betrayal, and my skin has really taken a liking to their hydrating oil.

Before I have time to fully appreciate the symmetry of the conference table setup, my peripherals catch the three of them walking into the lobby. I'm glad I changed into my pumps before I left my desk to set up the conference room; the scuffed-up faux leather ballet flats I use for commuting don't contribute to the competent/professional vibe I want to give off.

I take two deep breaths to bring myself back to earth and remind myself of the most important thing: I can do this. I am smart, capable, and confident. No qualifiers. No filler.

Before Margot and her tiny stiletto steps can make it to reception, I stride across the foyer to meet the team, and my nerves begin to melt into excitement.

'Hi!' I call as I approach, and then — 'Oh! Hey!'

'I know you,' says Petra de Silva. 'Women in Business brunch, right? Penny?'

'Yeah! It's so nice to see you again!' I feel almost ... What is this feeling? Confidence? 'Come on through, guys. I can't wait to show you what I've been working on for Evergreen.'

I'm tempted to sit on my hands. It's hard not to fidget when you're across from people whose very job is to judge your work. I try to arrange my face to look as impassive as possible, and I reckon I can catch my reflection in the conference room's glass walls if I lean a *liiiittle* to the left to get around Petra's head. Hm. Better not.

As Margot introduces herself and begins to hype up the agency, I pick at a bit of nail polish on the edge of my thumb and observe our potential new clients.

Julia suits her name exactly. Her long dark hair falls in effortless waves and her full cherubic cheeks radiate health. She's bare-faced, because when your skin is that good, makeup just distracts from your prettiness. I wish I could pull off a fashion kaftan. She's probably got tarot cards in her bag, and if we had a couple of drinks — home-distilled gin with lemons from her garden, I imagine — she'd tell me all the secrets to womanhood and inner calm. I want her to adopt me.

Petra could not contrast with her more. According to a cursory LinkedIn stalk after the networking brunch, she got her marketing degree from Melbourne Uni, just like me. Then she worked at an agency, just like me, then climbed the ranks at a couple of mega-corporates and got an MBA, all before she turned thirty-five. She then did a stint at an important non-profit and clocked five years on the Sephora marketing team. She hadn't yet started at Evergreen. On my feed now and then, I've seen her posting articles about the importance of sustainability and business and driving the green dollar. She's so fucking impressive. Her lipstick is a vibrant orange-red I wish I could pull off, and her perfectly tailored navy suit is cropped at the ankle. She looks ten feet tall and has the earned and uncompromising confidence I associate with women like Michelle Obama and Ruth Bader Ginsburg. I know instantly that she's the one I really have to win over.

The only man on the whole Evergreen team is their CFO. It's an irritating reality that good ideas come to little without money, and most of it belongs to old white guys and big corporations. From what I could gather about Nelson online, he's on the board of half a dozen charity organisations and a university advisory committee or two. I don't know enough about big business to understand what any of that means, so when he says by way of introduction, '*I'm just the purse strings; these two run the show,*' I respect it.

I'm a bit in awe of them all, actually. I have such respect for an ethically sound company led almost exclusively by women, several of them women of colour, with a no-bullshit product. My constant and desperate need for approval has never been stronger, but I know I need to play it cool and calm. I should be independent and aloof. Like a housecat. Or Rihanna. I'm wondering how I can better channel Rihanna's energy into my everyday life when I catch my name and I realise I've tuned out whatever Margot has been talking about.

Whoops. Quick, pay attention.

'Penny has worked extensively on this presentation,' she's saying. 'I don't think I've ever seen her so enthusiastic about a project.'

I know this is a covert dig at me, but I don't care. It's showtime.

'So, um …' I begin, and my voice wobbles over the vowels. I hate public speaking. My breath rattles as I pull myself together, trying to look confident and apologetic all at once. 'So. *So.* Let me tell you about the brand Evergreen could be.

'We're asked to care about so many things every day. My supermarket shop takes two hours because I have to read the back of every packet to find out if there's palm oil in it or google the parent company to find out if their quinoa is ethically sourced. I really believe we're all basically well-intentioned, but, my goodness, making the right choice can be *exhausting*. If you have a product with transparent practices and good ethics, you've piqued my interest. If it works like I need it to, even better.

'But how does it make me feel when I use it? That's the next step. Maybe *self-care* is a bloated term, but it hits the spot. Maybe it's a little vain, but I think it's deeper than that. It's about confidence. We're inundated with messages about how we're not good enough, that we need to fix ourselves before we can be happy. Is getting rid of this acne scarring on my chin — see, here? You can even see it under my foundation — going to suddenly make me feel fulfilled? Probably not. But it's one less thing to worry about. My skincare regimen gives me permission to stand in front of my bathroom mirror and look at myself for five minutes, and it makes taking care of myself a positive sensory experience, not a burden.

'And with Evergreen I don't have to feel guilty about it. There's no animal testing, no harmful byproducts, no evil corporations dumping chemicals into the ocean … There are so many selling points, you really don't need to work hard to get anyone over the line. Your conscience is safe here. That's the message we should run with. Evergreen is good for you, and it's not bad for the planet.'

Fuck. Yes. Me.

Usually when I talk for extended periods of time it's because I'm nervous, or drunk out of my mind at a party. I talk reallyreallyfast and gesture with my hands a lot. I use *ums* and *ah*s and *kinda like*s and only shut my trap to chug yet more vodka because my mouth is so dry. But today I'm not dizzy from panic or wishing I could crawl into a hole and die. I'm just … calm. For once, I actually know what I'm talking about.

'That's a big message for a tube of moisturiser or a little pipette bottle of serum to convey, but it can be done,' I continue. 'This soft, pale palette reads comforting and trustworthy. It's not frivolous, but it's not boring either. This isn't your mum's ancient tub of Olay gathering dust in the medicine cabinet. It's *joyful*. In a lineup of products on a shelf, it's refreshing and refined. Looking at these product packaging mock-ups — can you switch to slide six, Margot? Thanks — I want to pick them up and try the cleanser on the back of my hand. And I know from the samples you sent us that the experience carries over. It feels good. I don't think my skin has been this clear since, like, before puberty.'

I laugh, and there's a beat of silence in which I regret going off script and making a joke … but then Petra laughs. And then Julia joins in, and they share a significant look, and there's a warm, happy bubble inflating steadily in my chest.

'Right,' says Margot, reclaiming the room, 'let's talk about competitor data.'

And I have a chance to sit back and take a sip of water. I try to follow what Margot is saying, but I'm already going back over my ultra-monologue looking for weak spots, and I don't find any. No huge crater of embarrassment appears. I sneak a glance over at Margot, who stumbles over her pronunciation of Chantecaille, and I chew back a smirk.

Fuck you for doubting me, I think. *And fuck the old me, too, for doing the same.*

I needed to remind myself I could do this. This renewed confidence in myself has stretched a set of muscles I'd forgotten

I had, and it's more than just the shin splints I gave myself running too hard this morning. I belong in this room. I deserve all the space I take up, and I can't remember why I ever thought I didn't.

'It was a real pleasure to meet you,' says Julia, grasping my hand in both of hers as the meeting breaks up. Margot is in conversation with Nelson as he stows the pitch documents in his briefcase, and Petra and Julia have turned to me. I bet they want to give me a gold star.

'Your instincts were exactly correct,' says Petra warmly. I beam. 'You know precisely what this brand strives to be and do and say. We're very impressed.'

'That's so nice to hear. Pitching can be so ...'

'*Hellish*,' says Petra, and Julia nods along. It's so gratifying to have this impressive team praise me and my work.

'A bit,' I admit. 'But I meant it before. That wasn't me gassing you up. I'm genuinely so into your products and the whole thing.'

I'm babbling, but they don't make me feel self-conscious about it. They're looking at me like I have something interesting to say, not like I'm an overzealous kid. We talk a little about my shelfie ad idea and user Q&A campaign, and Julia says she can already picture it exactly and could offer up her garden (I *knew* she'd have one) for photoshoots and brand mood boards. Petra tells a story about a meeting they had with Facebook last week, and I want to stay here and pick their brains and listen to them talk about rosehip oil and data mining for hours.

'We have a few other meetings this week and next,' says Petra as Nelson nods towards the door to indicate it's time they head off. 'But you'll hear from us soon.'

'*Very* nice to meet you, Penny,' says Julia again.

I actually curl my toes inside my pumps to keep from bouncing in place.

I watch carefully as the front door swings shut behind the Evergreen trio, and as soon as they disappear from sight, I can't hold it in anymore, I let out a yelp of pure excitement and a laugh of relief, and Margot looks as pleased as I've ever seen her.

'Well done, Penelope,' she says, and I'm grinning so hard my face hurts, so light and excited that I don't even need her approval now that she has deigned to give it. Not when I have Petra's approval, and Julia's, and, most importantly, maybe for the first time in my life, my own.

CHAPTER TWENTY

I'm useless all afternoon. I'm busy daydreaming about what this win means for the rest of my life. Clearly this is the first of endless good things. I bet Margot will get off my case now, put me in line for the Account Director promotion and stop insisting I bcc her on every email I send. My work will probably be so excellent that the agency will win awards, and I'll be able to springboard off this success to start my own agency — an ambition I didn't know I had until this very second. So powerful is this wave of fortune that after signing Evergreen, I bet I'll grow an inch taller, my hair will get thicker, and I'll probably never have a pimple again. I feel so untouchable that I don't even sneak off to the bathrooms every time I want to check my phone. No, today I am the king of the office, and I can text as much as I want to.

The Outnet is having a further twenty percent off sale, and it seems like a sign from the universe to reward myself. My latest Instagram post — an indulgent selfie because my contouring was on fucking point this morning — has received likes nearing triple figures. There are well-wishes from Leo ('*You'll fucking nail it today! Will bring you home a cupcake to celebrate*'), Dad (a series of naff GIFs all with varying sentiments of luck), my brother ('*I'm such a good brother: I remembered you have a pitch today. Or is it tomorrow? Or was it yesterday? Shit I don't know – hope you smash(ed) it. Do you and Dad want to come here for Christmas? Emirates has a sale on. Mark and I went to Venice last weekend, attached some pics xxx'*), and several new messages in the group chat. Today is a good day.

Bec Cooper (15:04): Can you add another seat to the reso *@Annie Lin?*

Bec Cooper (15:04): Evan wants to come xx

Annie Lin (15:17): Tragedy!! :(I have an emergency hearing first thing in the morn and can't make it tonight. Don't hate me *@Penelope Moore* I'll make it up to you later x

Bec Cooper (15:19): Just the three of us then! Fun!

Hmm. I don't know if I fancy spending a night third-wheeling a date night with the world's most codependent couple. I ask Max if he can come along and make it a double date, but when he can't (***Max Fitzgerald (16:03):*** *Broke this week, can't. Have fun* 👍), I have a vision of myself sitting next to an empty chair, pushing biryani around my plate and feeling outnumbered at my own party. I imagine Evan's face curling into a smirk as Bec murmurs something into his ear, some private joke, with her hand resting on his knee. I feel left out and lonely at the thought.

Penelope Moore (16:10): Let's reschedule

Penelope Moore (16:10): You enjoy a date night x

She sees my message but doesn't respond. Was that too transparent? Might I just as well have said, *'No fucking thanks'*? Should I pop in a series of lighthearted emojis or steer the conversation to something she would like so she has to respond and reassure me that she isn't angry? Then again, she can't honestly think a night spent tagging along on a date is my idea of a celebration. She might enjoy a night hearing about digital disruption and how we're in the middle of the fourth industrial revolution, but I'd rather not. She's probably fine. I don't need to stress about it. There's somewhere else I'd rather be, anyway.

'I brought sustenance,' I sing as Max appears at the door to his building. I shake the heaving Aldi bag in my hand for emphasis. Since he can't come to the party, I can take the party to him.

'I'm really busy, Penny,' he says. He's standing in the doorway, still gripping the handle.

'That's okay,' I say, hopping up the steps and pecking him on the lips. 'I got pretzels and that chickpea curry you like, and oat milk ice cream, and I thought we could —'

'I have a fuckton of notes from my advisor,' he says. 'My thesis is a wreck. I can't hang out tonight.'

'I won't get under your feet,' I say. 'I just want to tell you about my pitch today. We can have a wine and I can help —'

'I said I can't,' he snaps, and I freeze.

Oh god. I've fucked up. Look at his face, all taut; his lips a straight line of annoyance. I shouldn't have come. I should have checked with him first. I shouldn't have assumed he wanted to see me. But we've been off-balance lately and I just wanted to grab hold of any kind of normality, and he's always let me come over and help with his thesis before, and all of this must be showing on my face because he lets out a sigh and drops his shoulders.

'Sorry,' he says, slumping against the doorframe. A couple of kids ride their bikes past me on the footpath. 'I'm just really fucking stressed. I'll message you later, okay?'

'Okay,' I say, struggling to keep my voice light. 'Do you want —?' I hold the bag out for him, and he takes it.

'Thanks for this,' he says. 'That's really nice.'

'You're welcome.'

'Don't be like that.'

'Like what?'

'Like that,' he says. 'All shitty with me. My thesis is important.'

'My pitch was important today too,' I say with a resigned little shrug. My eyes feel hot and I look towards the gridlocked traffic on Nicholson Street, willing myself not to cry. 'I just wanted things to feel normal again.'

'Things are normal,' he says, pushing a frustrated hand through his hair. 'Nothing's wrong.'

'Okay,' I say, but I can't agree. Everything feels wrong.

'I'll message you later,' he says again, and I nod. 'You good?'

'Yeah. I'm good.'

'Good.' Keeping the door propped open with his foot, he leans down and pecks me on the cheek. 'I'll see you later.'

'Love you,' I say, throwing it out there and not really knowing why. I don't want to leave it unspoken anymore. I just want to hear him say it back — that will make everything better, won't it? Hearing it, knowing it's true, something to comfort myself with later tonight when I'm replaying this conversation over and over and searching for its subtext.

'See ya,' he says with a wink, and the door swings shut behind him.

I need to do something to drain all of the nervous energy in my veins. My muscles are starting to ache from this morning's run, and all my laundry is done, and there's nothing on television, and all the clothes shops are shut already, so I can't even spend money to solve the problem. In a moment of desperation, I turn to YouTube. The *Yoga With Adriene* channel is the closest

I can get to peace. Every time I find myself wondering why the hell I said that to Max, Adriene tells me to change positions, and I'm pulled out of my panic spiral just in time.

'Well, this is a greeting I'm not used to,' says Leo as he arrives home, finding me in downward-facing dog.

'Don't get used to it,' I grunt.

'How'd it go today? Smash it?'

'They are obsessed with me,' I tell him as Adriene directs me into a lunge. 'I am incredible. No one is better at my job than I am.'

Leo laughs. 'You should be knighted for services to the marketing industry.'

'Do you need career advice? Because I know everything. I'm the smartest person alive.'

'Who's a superstar? You are!'

'I am!' I cry, and my back leg wobbles, and in an instant, I fall on my arse and laugh right along with him. 'Ow.'

'You going out to celebrate?'

'Max is busy,' I tell him. I hit pause on Adriene.

'What about the girls?'

'Annie's working and Bec takes Evan everywhere, like an emotional support animal.'

Leo groans sympathetically. 'They're getting worse, aren't they? I saw them out the other night and it was like he was trying to eat her face.'

'She wanted me to go along with them,' I tell him, rolling up my yoga mat and feeling no better for it. There's still a restless hum between my ears. 'But I resent paying for dinner and then wanting to vomit from watching them paw at each other all night.'

'You can celebrate with me,' he offers from the kitchen. 'Pasta and wine?'

'Aren't you going out? It's Thursday. Date night.'

'What is "date night"? Are there nights of the week I'm not supposed to go on dates? Have I been dating wrong this whole time?'

'You don't go on first dates on a Friday or Saturday,' I explain, shocked that I know something about dating that Leo doesn't. 'Those are prime fun-time nights. What if the person you go out with sucks and you've wasted a whole Friday night on a bad date?'

'I don't have bad dates,' he says, looking smug. 'I'm such a hot date that I uplift everyone around me.'

'I wish I had the confidence of a straight man,' I mutter, and he pretends not to have heard me.

'Well, now we have to hang out,' he says, producing a bottle of something from the pantry. 'You can't leave me all alone on date night. Everyone would find out what a loser I am.'

'I think they already know, babe,' I tell him. 'It's all anyone talks about. The whole of Melbourne is in on it. We have a group chat.'

'Hey!' he says, pointing the neck of the wine bottle my way like it's a sword. 'Do you want me to make you dinner or not? Brat.'

'Can *you* cook?' I ask, incredulous. 'With ingredients and everything?'

'I can even do it without a recipe,' he says, and I pull up to the kitchen counter looking suitably impressed. 'We can watch *Fleabag*. I'm on season two. That hot priest is making me bi-curious.'

'Oh god, I know,' I say with a sigh. 'I feel that way about Zendaya.'

'Who?'

'From *Euphoria*! It's good! It's about these messed-up high school kids who —'

'Penny. I am a 31-year-old man.'

'Are you? Gosh, you look terrible for your age. I would've said forty-five.'

'Fuck off,' he says, laughing.

It's the first glimmer of sunshine I've had since I shook hands with the Evergreen team, and I take him up on it. I can always use more Leo, this human embodiment of sunshine. Even though he helped me do half the effing thing, he lets me walk him through the pitch, their reactions, even the conflicted look on Margot's face. He's a perfect audience, giving me all the right responses at the perfect time. I skirt over my conversation with Max this afternoon, half because Leo seems to glaze over whenever Max comes up, the same way my friends do, and half because I'm trying not to think about it.

But no matter how much I try to swallow my worries with great mouthfuls of pasta and white wine, or cover over them like the thick green clay mask I talk Leo into doing with me, they're still there. Fleabag pleads with the hot priest and I check my phone, and we're both left wanting.

CHAPTER TWENTY-ONE

Bec's reply to my message yesterday kept me awake long after midnight. There's an unpleasant guilty feeling in my stomach about it.

Bec Cooper (18:37): Ok.

Incredible, really, how three characters can contain such hostility and induce such concern in their recipient. It niggles at me all day.

It doesn't help, either, that I've completely lost interest in my job post-Evergreen. All I want to do is refresh my inbox until their email arrives, something to the effect of '*Dear Penny, you have revolutionised our business. We're organising an honorary doctorate in your name. Thank you for existing.*' Every minute that I don't receive that email is a minute of torture. Who cares about the distinct blandness of Vic Credit Union or Jackson & Smith Realty when I know how much fun it can be to work on a brand you actually like? What's more, I can hardly concentrate on anything because my whole subconscious is busy being anxious that Max hasn't messaged me all day and my best friend sent me the coldest, most passive aggressive text you can possibly send someone.

I mean, does she hate me now? Have you ever received a

message so hostile? Is she going to continue to give me the cold shoulder until I grovel for her forgiveness? Is she — fuck, this is exhausting. What am I so worried about? People cancel plans all the time. *Bec* cancels plans all the time. I bet if I go over there right now, she'll be fine, and I'll feel stupid for worrying in the first place. Isn't it better to be proactive about my anxiety, to stop it becoming a problem in the first place?

> **Penelope Moore (09:51):** Sorry about last night babe
> **Penelope Moore (09:51):** Free this afternoon? I'll pop by your office with treats x
> **Bec Cooper (10:12):** Working from home. I'm not feeling well.
> **Penelope Moore (10:12):** Oh no!! Poor thing. Restorative treats then xx

Refusing to give in to my compulsive tendency to worry, I claim a fake client meeting at 3:30 pm, spend an eye-watering amount of money on an assortment of biscuits and cakes, and head to Bec's glossy South Melbourne flat.

I have a spot of trouble finding it, actually, because it sits among several identical glass-walled towers, and I've only been here a handful of times. I've never really liked it — it's just too boyish, too *Evan*, with its leather couches and gleaming brass kitchen fixtures and a vintage *Playboy* cover blown up and hung on the living room wall. The only sign that Bec lives here at all is the tube of Elizabeth Arden Eight Hour Cream on her bedside table. To avoid feeling like a rambunctious child who threatens stains on their linen cushions and grubby handprints on their sleek appliances, I don't come here if I can help it. In fact, I don't think I've visited since their housewarming party a year ago, when I met Leo.

She doesn't sound great when she answers the intercom and buzzes me up, poor thing, but she looks okay when she lets me in.

'I have presents! Kind of,' I announce, pecking her on the cheek and shaking the paper box at her. 'I got cakes from Burch & Purchese. Have you had their lamington wagon wheels? Fucking heaven. And the gin and tonic citrus tarts! Do you want a plate? I got one for Evan too. I'll get plates, you sit.'

'Thanks,' she says.

'I'm sorry I didn't make it to dinner last night,' I say from the kitchen, searching her cupboards for crockery.

'Uh huh,' says Bec.

'What?'

'Nothing,' she says, again with an unfamiliar coldness. But if she isn't going to say anything about it, then I'm better to just soldier through until we arrive at neutral territory.

'So, I did something fucking stupid last night. I went over to Max's pl—'

'I don't want to hear about him, Penny,' she snaps, and my stomach clenches, and it feels like someone's turned the sun off.

'I'm sorry?'

'I'm so sick of hearing about *Max*. It's been years of this shit. I don't want to hear about him. Neither of us do, me or Annie, but we listen because we love you and we have to, but this is the last time you've blown us off to see him, okay? I refuse to come second place to that arsehole.'

'Ex*cuse* me?' My brain skips anxiety and jumps straight to anger. My brow is furrowed uncomfortably, but I can't move it under the strain of trying to process what I'm hearing. 'Annie didn't even go last night. And I'm sorry, but — how many times have you blown us off to sit at home with Evan?'

'Don't bring him up,' she snaps, casting a warning glance to the bedroom door. 'Evan is not *Max*. Evan is —'

'The most important thing in the world, right? More important than us? You don't get to be all sanctimonious because I skip *one* dinner when you put us second all the fucking time.'

'Skip what, Penny? Decline last-minute Friday night plans to get trashed and listen to you and Annie whine about how you can't find anyone?'

'Oh, I'm sorry!' I cry, with a bark of mirthless laughter. 'It was good enough for you when *you* were single, but you have a boyfriend for five minutes and suddenly you're above us? You're too good for us now, are you?'

'You're a mess, both of you!' she cries. 'That's not real life! We aren't children anymore! It's time to grow up, but heaven forbid either of you date someone with a job, or who's nice to you, or doesn't send you into hysterics on a daily basis. Christ, Penny. Last year you broke up with someone because they made a stupid noise when they laughed! Do you know what it's like to sit there and listen to you complain about these losers? It's so *boring*! You're never going to find someone like that!'

'Are you a fucking expert?' I ask, wringing my hands to keep myself in place. I might swell up with rage and hurt and rocket through the ceiling. 'How do you think we feel about Evan? Did you ever ask? You get into a relationship and suddenly you know everything. What we do and who we see and how we feel isn't important anymore. We don't matter, you're too busy being a full-time girlfriend. There's no space in your life for us anymore.'

'I'm his *fian*—'

'Was our friendship just a way to kill time while you waited for some guy to relieve you of the burden of your sad fucking friends?'

'God, grow up Penny. There are more important things to worry about. People are dying all over th—'

'Oh yeah, fuck, people are dying, famines, the economy, what-fucking-ever. That doesn't excuse you being a bad friend. Don't minimise shit just because you don't want to be called on it.'

'Do you want to know why I cared that you weren't there last night? Do you have the capacity to stop thinking about yourself for one second to wonder why it bothers me this much?'

'That's so unnecess—'

'I was going to ask you to be my maid of honour!' she cries, and I blanch. I suddenly don't know what to do with my limbs.

'I — well, obviously I didn't know that or I would have come.'

'I've wanted to ask you for a while,' she continues. 'But every time I want to talk, Annie is too busy with some gross case about a pervert flashing people on the train or you're distraught over some *nothing* problem, another crisis over some useless guy —'

'If you want to talk about warped priorities,' I snap, 'I'm not the one who had a crying meltdown over a fucking wedding dress the other day.' I'm remotely aware that I'm being petty now, but I'm hurt and angry and *fuck* if it doesn't feel good to make someone else feel like shit for a change.

'And I bet you both went home and texted each other about how much you hate seeing me happy!' she cries, and I actually have to cover my mouth to keep from laughing.

'If you really think we're jealous of your life, like it's so special —'

'I just hate being around you!' she cries. 'When was the last time you had anything positive to say? "*Max doesn't love me,*" "*Margot is mean to me,*" "*I hate my job,*" "*I hate my thighs*" — it's BORING! I've had enough of you! I don't even know why we're friends! Spending time with you makes me miserable!'

You know that split second when you realise your fingers are about to get slammed in a drawer and you haven't got time to stop it, and every muscle tenses in anticipation of the searing pain? That's what this feels like. But it stretches on and on. Time warps in this cold loveless room. She's been cataloguing complaints for who knows how long, storing them up, presumably coming home from any time spent in my company to complain to Evan about her annoying little friend and how she wishes she'd never met me. I can't speak. I just stare at her, blank-faced and clench-jawed.

'You don't need a boyfriend,' she says, twisting the knife. 'You need a psychiatrist.'

'Right,' I croak.

'I don't want to see you until you sort your shit out.' She crosses to the door and opens it, a clear invitation to fuck off if I ever saw one.

'Fine,' I say and, having firmly been put in my place, I leave. I wait until I feel the rush of cold air from her front door slamming shut before I allow myself to crumple into tears. Blue skies have gone grey, replaced with torrential rain and a carousel of cutting remarks echoing between my ears.

There's some sick and painful satisfaction in being handed confirmation of our worst fears on a platter by someone whose approval means so much. Dr Minnick's voice appears from nowhere: '*We love being right, even when it hurts.*'

CHAPTER TWENTY-TWO

You've found me in the middle of my pity party: I'm curled, foetally, on the couch under my favourite blanket. I leaned into my own stereotype and bought a bottle of wine and a tub of Ben & Jerry's, betting on the therapeutic qualities of both to lift me up into a sugar high or dull the buzz of anxiety in my stomach, but they've done neither and now they're just sweating on the coffee table while I stare at my phone.

Bec's not going to call. Why would she?

The logical bit of my brain knows this. It also knows that even if she did call, it wouldn't make a difference: the damage has been done. Any apologies would only be to assuage her guilt about yelling at me, but it doesn't mean she didn't mean what she said.

Knowing that it's unhealthy and unhelpful doesn't stop me from picking at the scab and agitating myself further. I'm digging my nails into my palm as I deep dive into every recent memory I have of us, mining them for every little indication of detachment or impatience or disapproval. All those snarky comments at the bridal shop. Every time she picked up her phone to text Evan, was she telling him how exhausting it is to sit across from me and converse? Is this why he never hangs out with us, because he's primed for how annoying I am and doesn't have the energy for it? Are they sitting in their happy little love nest now, relieved that the obligation of my company has been lifted?

Not that I'm blameless. It wasn't necessary for me to attack her relationship. For months I've put off saying anything about it, hoping that she would realise all on her own that she misses her friends and wants to strike a balance between time spent in Evan's back pocket and time spent with us. I figured that the honeymoon phase had to end eventually, that real life would come calling and things would settle into a new normal. Clearly not. I should have told her that her distance was putting a strain on us, that her shifting priorities were hurting my feelings, and maybe all of this could have been avoided.

She wasn't always like this, just so you know. It used to be that Bec was the one hassling us to stay out for one more drink or five. It was she who organised the party drugs, whose recycling bin clanked like New Year's Day every other Sunday morning, who had two guys named *Tom Bumble* in her phone and invited the wrong one round for a hungover hookup and went with it anyway. Part of the appeal of working freelance was that she could start work at midday. Not so long ago, Bec's main priority was having a good time. Responsibility was boring and romance was disposable. It's like that part of her personality evaporated as soon as she met Evan, and now she barely resembles the girl I used to know.

Soon she'll move out to the suburbs where they can afford a house, and shortly after get two more cats or have a baby. I'll see her once or twice a year, and those times will only illustrate the ever-expanding chasm between us.

I can see how it'll go. We'll be catching up at a playground, and she'll be wearing a puffer vest and calling for Elsa or Noah or Willow or Harper to '*play safely on the monkeybars, darling*'. She won't really listen to our chat except to muse about how she wishes she had time for such mundane concerns as work or dating or anything beyond paediatrician appointments and ballet classes. By the time we reach our thirtieth birthdays — which are really beginning to sneak up on us now — we probably won't speak at all.

Is that how it goes for all friendships in your late twenties? Will it happen to me and Annie too, as her career reaches new heights and her carefully structured days have less and less room for frivolity? Our coming of age has already passed and now there's nothing but wide-open space, hardly anything tying us together anymore. Will our motley little family, hand-picked years ago, simply dissolve to make way for real families and sensible priorities? We'll try to stay in touch, but life will just get in the way. All the conversations about trips to the Barossa or trips to Mardi Gras will never turn into booked flights. The promised catch-ups over dinner won't eventuate. Intentions to grab a drink after work or spend an afternoon shopping or at the beach will ebb, because there's always so much housework to do, or it's such a commute in from Sandringham or Geelong, or someone's partner has hurt their back so '*it's just not a good time, how about next month*?'. And when we do find a moment for each other, too much time and silence will have passed between us, and it will be hard to explain all the little mundane details of our new and different lives, so all we'll be able to do is talk about our happy, wild memories together. And then we'll part ways again, swearing not to leave it so long next time, but quietly we'll feel drained by it, nostalgic and sad and not motivated to waste another precious afternoon reliving a past long out of reach.

Perhaps the golden age of freedom and spontaneity and limitless capacity for one another has already gone, and I'm the last one holding out hope for a return to the comfort of yesterday. Perhaps Bec is right and the sun has already set on relationships like ours. She and I may not ever speak again after this. Maybe it's time for me to find an Evan to get lost in. Not a Max, but someone sensible and nice and, yes, a bit boring because they're safe and dependable.

But what happens if I don't make the grade? What if I never figure it out and everyone moves on without me? I'd learn to adjust to perma-single status eventually. I'm lukewarm on the idea of having children of my own anyway — I'd like a dalmatian or two, I think. I could fill my days with a PhD or something. But what about at night-time? How will I fill up those lonely hours? Who will I talk to? Where does all the love I have inside me go? Where do I put it? What do I do with it?

Leo snaps his fingers in front of my face, and I jump, wrenched violently out of this horrible and sobering prospect.

'What happened here?' he asks, gesturing at the most pathetic picnic in the world. As I try to answer, my bottom lip gives me away, and I crumble into ugly tears. 'Shit, alright.'

'M'sorry,' I wail, fully aware that the number of times he's had to comfort his half-hysterical housemate on his couch is probably into the double digits by now. I'm sure he wishes we didn't have a rental agreement so he could just kick me out.

'Max problems?' he asks with a sympathetic grimace, patting my back awkwardly.

'What? No, I don't — I just, I'm so ...'

'Shit, Penny, are you okay? Want me to go round there and beat him up or something?'

'N-no, it's not about that, not fucking ... Max. Fucking ... No, it's Bec, we had the most awful fight and I just ... It's so shit, it was so bad. We've nev-never had a fight before.'

Through snivelling sobs, I tell him about it.

Once upon a time Leo must have been an excellent boyfriend because he doesn't tell me to calm down, or offer practical solutions, or try to minimise my feelings. He just sits next to me and nods along with a comforting hand on my back while I bawl. Sometimes you don't need or want help, you just need a great big cry. Crying releases oxytocin, according to an old therapist of mine, and is a wonderful stress reliever. I'm practically meditating over here.

'Do you want to order a pizza?' he asks patiently, which is about the only helpful thing anyone can say in situations like this. He's so fucking sweet. He knows me so well. This earnest gesture sends me from pathetic crying to full-on blubbering, and he starts to panic. 'No? No pizza? Fuck, I thought that would help. We can get the good one, the twelve-cheese one! And we can watch *The Great British Bake Off* and I won't complain at all, I swear.'

'You're —' I hiccup, wiping my nose on my sleeve and forgetting to feel self-conscious about it. 'I think you might be my best friend.'

And he starts laughing, which sets me off, and I go from wailing sobs to proper hysterical laughter, so hard it hurts my head and my stomach, and we can barely catch our breaths. *How absurd*, I think. *How ridiculous*. Poor Leo, living with this idiot who oscillates between misery and jubilance on a daily basis, apparently with no middle ground.

'You're a fucking moron,' he breathes, red in the face, arm around my shoulder. 'I think you might be mine too.'

'How sad for you! That's terrible!' I cry, and we redouble, laughing so hard it comes out in shrieks, and we slip on the velvet of the couch and land on our arses on the floor, and we're a lost fucking cause, now unable to laugh at all, just gasping and coughing for air with tears in our eyes. My ears are full of the sound of it and my head throbs so hard I barely hear the knock on the front door.

'I'll get it,' says Leo between breaths, collecting himself and making for the hallway, shoulders still shuddering.

The backs of my hands are covered in mascara, from sad tears and happy ones, and my face feels hot and shiny, and it takes me a minute to remember why I was upset in the first place. I'm barely back to recalling the stony look on Bec's face as I left her apartment before my mind is pulled back to the present.

'Hey,' says Max, and I don't have time to get sad again. 'You okay?'

'Hi!' I cry, getting up from the floor gracelessly. 'Oh, I'm so glad you're here.'

I hear Leo's bedroom door shut.

'Sorry about last night,' says Max. I bounce on my tiptoes to request my hello kiss, but he bumps his smooth, sandalwoodsy jaw against my cheek. I'd contemplated messaging him about my fight with Bec on the horrible claustrophobic Uber ride home from her flat, but after my careless declaration of love hadn't been reciprocated, I was feeling text-shy.

'Do you want some wine?' I ask, making for the kitchen and trying to fix my panda eyes in the reflection of the microwave door. God, I look disgusting. Blotchy and jowly like a deflated basketball. This isn't the image I wanted to greet him with after showing my hand last night.

'Was that your housemate?'

'Leo?'

'Sure, Leo, I guess.'

'Yeah, that's Leo.' I pull a fresh wine glass down from the cupboard and crack ice cubes into it. 'I've wanted you guys to meet for ages. You'd like him. God, it's nice to see you.'

Wine in hand, I perch on the very edge of the couch — a little trick to better allude to a thigh gap — and peck him on the cheek. He smiles, crinkly and delicious, and it makes everything better. Who does Bec think she is, to question our relationship? I didn't even have to ask for his help, he just knew that I needed him and came calling, pulled across the great divide of Victoria Street like the tide follows the moon.

'I wondered if we could have a quick chat,' he says as he sips his icy wine and shifts in his seat, and I reach out to take his hand in mine.

'Quick chat, long chat,' I say, shrugging. 'Whatever you like. I've missed you. Feels like I haven't seen you in a hundred years.'

'Yeah, about that,' he says. The knots in my intestines twisted by Bec give an uncomfortable tug. 'I think we should revisit the terms of our, ah, agreement.'

My brain goes blank. I can feel my pulse in my throat, and I think I start to sweat. 'Is this … are you breaking up with me?' What happened? What did I do? Why did I have to fuck everything up?

''Course I'm not,' he says, but I'm not soothed.

'It sounds like you're breaking up with me.'

'Maybe we could use a time-out. I was thinking that I'm just better suited to ethical non-monogamy, you know, kind of like —'

'Kind of like you fucking whoever you want and me sitting around feeling like shit,' I say, finishing his sentence for him because there's nowhere else a relationship like that can go.

'You're overthinking it. You're always doing that,' he says, brushing me off with a harassed little frown. 'It was just an idea. I think I just need a bit of time to think about what I want. A little breather.'

Funny he mentioned breathing because I suddenly can't. My ears pop and dull out the noise of the room. Max's voice, the whirr of the dishwasher finishing its cycle, the looping trailer for a true crime documentary on Netflix — all I can hear is the sound of my frantic, leaden heartbeat.

His lips are moving, and I can make out words like *space* and *expectations* among what must be a long list of reasons why he doesn't have room in his life for me anymore. He's gesturing with his hands — free, now, from a prison of our laced fingers — and I hear him say, 'Like before, you know? When it was fun,' and I register that I'm nodding because the effort makes me feel lightheaded. I don't know what I'm agreeing to, but he looks relieved.

'Thanks, buddy,' he says, and this pet name — no, this demotion, this slap across the fucking face — brings the room back into sharp focus. 'I'll see you soon, yeah? Come round next week like old times?'

'I guess,' I tell him, hardly feeling my mouth move to speak it.

'Great,' he says. He lands a playful pop on my shoulder and waits for me to assure him that what he's done is okay: a white flag in the form of a forgiving smirk. And when he's gone, both the room and I are empty, and I register a quiet dread and the certainty that nothing good is coming soon.

CHAPTER TWENTY-THREE

For the love of drama, I announce a social media leave of absence.

Mostly I want an excuse to leave the group chat. I don't want to stay in it and watch Bec's name pop up on my phone a hundred times a day, or worse: have *her* go silent and feel the full effect of her absence as Annie and I continue to spam each other with inane updates about our days.

I told Annie privately that Bec and I had a tiff, but I didn't get any more specific than that. After all, many of Bec's low blows were aimed at her too, and I don't want to hurt one friend in the process of bitching about another. If I had to choose between hearing my friends' ugliest thoughts about me and living blissfully unaware, I'd choose the latter.

Meanwhile, discontent has bled back into my life. Back in rotation are my stretchy jeans and rumpled shirts; my hair is held together by dry shampoo and bobby pins. Makeup seems pointless when I'm reduced to waves of tears every few minutes.

When Helena settles in at her desk and asks how my weekend was, my lip wobbles over a weak '*Fine, yours?*', and I know this isn't something that can be fixed by a face mask and a good night's sleep.

By some miracle, when I call, Dr Minnick's receptionist tells me that there's an available appointment at 10:30 am. It's 10:10

now. I've barely finished my first coffee before I'm swinging my handbag over my shoulder and heading for the door without more than bleating '*Meeting!*' over my shoulder at Margot's enquiring frown. I'm counting on the good will earned from the Evergreen meeting to keep her from questioning it. I don't really care. I just need to talk to someone.

After our last session, I had no intention of coming back to Dr Minnick's office. I chalked it up to a bad fit. But I can't talk to Annie, and Leo has disappeared again, presumably tangled in the limbs of someone new. I tried to talk to my dad, but his quiet, repressed brand of support comes in the form of numbing platitudes to trust that everything will sort itself out soon. So this is my last resort.

'Penny-not-Penelope,' says Dr Minnick with a warm smile from her doorway. As I approach her, I notice that today's unflattering Gorman smock dress has a foundation stain around the collar. 'I wasn't sure I'd see you again.'

'Here I am,' I say, unenthused. The room is the same as ever. Same cheap couch. Same intrusive second hand on the clock. Dr Minnick has had a heavy fringe cut, as though she's just binged *New Girl* and thought Zooey Deschanel bangs were the answer to her problems. Perhaps I should have found a psychologist with more experience, someone older and wiser. I'm sure I could find a quirky thirty-something willing to dole out advice at literally any Fitzroy bar, and it wouldn't cost me $125 an hour. Desperation will take you to the strangest places.

'What's new? Anything you'd like to talk about today?'

'I ...' My voice falters. The weight in my chest is so big, and I hardly know where to start. Suddenly, words come flooding out of my mouth before I even think of them. 'I had a fight with my friend, Bec — I told you about her last time — and Max — we got back together — I haven't seen you since then — but we did, then he said … It was going great or, well, it was going *okay*, but now I don't know what I did, but —'

'I need you to take a breath,' says Dr Minnick, cutting me off as I pick up speed. Feeling like a lost little kid, I do as she says, taking in shaky lungfuls of air and letting them out again.

One two three four.

One two three four.

One two three four.

One two three four.

'Okay,' she says, notepad and pen at the ready. 'Walk me through it. What happened with your friend?'

So I tell her about Bec. The story isn't linear: I weave in and out of anecdotes and examples and head off on tangents, and I tear through enough tissues to fill up her wastebin before the clock on the wall reads 10:50.

I tell her my worries about ending up alone — really alone, with no one to talk to but my imaginary dogs and kind-faced strangers who make the mistake of engaging in small talk with me on the bus. I tell her about the loneliness I fear and feel, the way that it is beginning to curl around my bones like a weed, less of an emotion and more of a core truth, this sense of being unwelcome in every room I enter. It used to be that I felt at ease with the people I love and I presume to love me back, but that's finished now; there's nowhere safe left.

And I can talk about all of this in hyperbole and hypotheticals, but when I finally arrive at Max, my muscles of self-containment give out, too tired to carry on after thirty minutes and twenty-six years of holding myself together. I can hear my teeth chatter as I speak, but I'm determined to finish, to verbalise it and get it out of my head. My head throbs as I explain that he wants a break, but it's not a break*up* because he wants to see me this week, and I just don't know what I did to make him change his mind or what I'm supposed to do to help him change it back.

'Boundaries are part of healthy relationships,' Dr Minnick says patiently. 'Max is setting a boundary. He isn't saying you did something wrong. He's just telling you he isn't able to give you what you want from him right now, and you have to respect that.'

That word, *boundary*, hits me in the heart. A boundary is a border wall, designed to keep enemies and unwanted guests out. It's hard and hateful. You don't need boundaries with the people you love. So why is she throwing it around like it isn't a bullet to the chest?

'But why?' I wail. 'Why does he get what he wants? What if my boundary is incompatible with his? Why does he win? He wants time alone and I want time together. I have to squash myself down and need less from him, but he doesn't have to stretch himself to make me happy. Why does what he wants matter more than what I want? Who takes care of me?'

'You do, Penny,' she says simply. 'You take care of yourself.'

'Well, I don't want to!' I cry, misery melting into anger at this useless, unsatisfying answer. 'Everyone else finds someone to take care of them. Why don't I? How is that fair? I'm sick of being the only one who cares about me —'

'I don't think that's true,' she argues gently. 'Your friends — don't you think that Bec's frustrations come from a place of care?'

'Of course they don't! She doesn't care! She doesn't have room in her life for her stupid fucking fuck-up friend anymore, that's what she said! You aren't listening to me!'

'I am listening to you,' she says, infuriatingly patient. It makes me want to hurl this empty tissue box at her head. 'I understand that right now you feel very judged and —'

'Don't placate me. Either admit that they've done the wrong fucking thing, both of them, or agree that it's because they don't care about me, because no one does and no one ever fucking could. It's one or the other, you know it is.'

'Penny, please. Let me explain it to you from a more objective place,' she says then pauses, waiting to see if I'll interrupt her again. I don't have anything clever and cruel to say, so I keep my mouth shut, digging my short jagged nails into the flesh of my palms and relishing in the sharp sting. 'You are surrounded by people who care about you. Bec, your dad, even Max … Just because they don't express it in a way you would like them to doesn't mean the love isn't there.'

'Well, then I don't want it,' I spit. 'I don't want love like that. I only want it how I want it. I don't want a best friend who thinks I'm pathetic. I don't want a boyfriend who doesn't even want me around.'

'You deserve relationships that lift you up, but sometimes —'

'Then why don't I have them? You love that word, *deserve*. Who's monitoring it? Who's in charge of giving people what they deserve? Whoever it is, they're doing a fucking terrible job.'

'You are,' she says. 'You have to be the one to form strong, honest, safe relationships with people who —'

'This is pointless,' I tell her. I'm beyond avoidance. I don't care about being polite or liked or a good patient. She's talking in circles and offering nothing. I could get better advice from a stoned uni student with a self-care Instagram.

Dr Minnick fixes me with a look that says her patience and professionalism are wearing thin, but I don't care. I'm out of here. I don't need this shit. I didn't come here to be attacked. I pick up my bag and leave, making sure to slam the door behind me. The receptionist jumps at the noise, and I think, *good*. She's probably keeping track of what time someone here comes and goes. Bitch.

I hammer the down button for the elevator in time with my pulse — *bambambambambam* — so hard the Braille dots leave indents in my fingertip.

Fucking Jennifer Minnick, with her master's on the wall from a second-rate university, unable to keep from staining her clothes on a daily basis. The fucking hack.

When I finally clamber out of the lift and out onto the street, the sunshine and bustling crowd feel just as claustrophobic, and I have to flatten myself against the warm brick building to keep from getting swept away. It must be close to lunch hour because Collins Street is a sea of corporate wear, hair-gelled men in suits barking into their phones, and sleek-ponytailed women carrying sashimi and bottled water.

Oh, right, work. It's a Monday. I'm supposed to go back to work. I can't remember if I have any meetings today, or what my to-do list looks like, or how it felt to leave that office with a smile on my face just a few days ago. The idea of going back there now, spending my afternoon writing emails and drinking muddy instant coffee and counting the seconds until I can be alone and safe under a blanket in my dark bedroom again — I can't do it. Knowing that I'll pay for it later and lacking a single fuck to give about it, I pull my phone out of my bag. '*Not feeling well*,' I text Margot. '*Back in the office tomorrow.*'

CHAPTER TWENTY-FOUR

From: petra.desilva@evergreenskincare.com.au
To: margot.camilleri@scoutdigital.com, penny.moore@
scoutdigital.com
Subject: Re: Scout Digital Pitch
Hi Scout team,
I write to thank you for your insightful and unique presentation.
Your pitch showed great enthusiasm for the Evergreen brand.
At this time, we have decided to explore other avenues. We
sincerely appreciate your time and effort and look forward to
working together in another capacity in the future.
Regards,
Petra de Silva
Marketing Director
Evergreen Skincare

Well, if that isn't the cherry on top of a shit sundae. I can't wait to see how Margot makes this all my fault.

'What are you frowning at?' asks Annie, returning to our table with drinks.

It's a drizzly Saturday afternoon, and we're decompressing at Cookie on Swanston Street after two intense hours of shopping for a new dress for me to wear on my birthday. How else is my wardrobe going to know I've turned a year older? Half a dozen bags sit at our feet, full of things I don't need and can't afford, but I'm counting on booze and new clothes to rewire my dopamine receptors. The one thing to be said about a traumatic week is that it has completely annihilated my appetite, and if I keep this up for six more days and wear a double layer of shapewear, my new size ten dress will zip right up on Saturday. Little wins, you know? Maybe twenty-seven is the year I finally eliminate my hip fat. It's my cosmic destiny.

'Nothing,' I tell her, putting my phone down and relieving her of one of the espresso martinis in her hands. 'Work. I didn't get that account.'

'The skincare?'

'Yeah, Evergreen.'

'The cleanser sample you gave me really dried out my T-zone,' she says. 'You'll get the next one, babe. Can't win 'em all.'

I wish I could shrug things off so easily. If someone so much as declines my offer of an empty seat on the train, I take it as a personal affront. How do you learn to accept rejection like it's a natural part of life? Was there a TED Talk I missed?

'I fucking hate my job,' I say, drinking half my drink in one sip.

'What would you do instead?'

'I don't know,' I say. 'Maybe it's not my job. Maybe I just hate Margot.'

'Emmy's in digital too,' she says. 'At one of the big agencies. I can ask her if there are any openings there if you like?'

'Did I tell you she's making me keep a log of everything I do all day?' I continue, unsubtly skipping over the mention of the new girl in Annie's life. If we open the door to talking about our dating lives, I'll have to tell her about Max, and I'm not wearing waterproof mascara. 'Can you believe that?'

'You did,' she says, looking a little hurt. 'Is it helping?'

'Helping what? Helping her like me? No. Half the time I have to embellish the list because otherwise it would be like, "*1. Answered emails. 2. Read a profile on Meghan Markle. 3. Considered suicide.*"'

Annie frowns. 'Why don't you ask for more work then?'

'Why would I do that?'

'If you feel like you're not busy all day, can't you ask for more stuff to do? Or see if you can do some professional training — for design or something?'

'I'm not a designer.'

'Or *something*,' she says with a note of waning patience. 'If you have a lot of free time and she wants to measure your productivity, ask for more work. She'd probably appreciate you being proactive about it.'

'She's not going to be satisfied with my work no matter what I do,' I scoff. 'I could bring in a client on a million-dollar retainer and she'd still ask why it wasn't one-point-two.'

'Well, not if you go in there every day this negative.'

I can't help but feel a little attacked. 'Sorry?'

'Hey — no, Pen. Look, I get it,' she says, putting on a diplomatic voice. 'We all wish we didn't live in a capitalist hellscape. But if you go to work feeling like shit every day, people are going to notice. Maybe faking a little positivity will alleviate the pressure a bit. That's all I meant.'

'I'm not paid enough to be positive,' I tell her. 'Positivity from me costs at least six figures.'

'I can't say that I'd love a junior who clearly hates being there either,' she says, trying to sound sympathetic, but I feel offended all the same.

'I can't handle this right now. Can we talk about something else?'

We both sip our drinks, and I have trouble meeting her eye.

'I heard what happened with Bec,' she says.

'Oh, that's a much happier topic.'

'Why didn't you tell me?'

'I didn't want to put you in the middle of it.'

'Too late, babe,' she says. 'I am the ethically sourced, cruelty-free plant-based meat in the Penny and Bec sandwich.' My mood must be showing on my face, because Annie, sounding a little harassed, says, 'She's asked me to be her maid of honour now.'

'Really,' I say flatly, doing my best to keep my face blank. 'I'm surprised she hasn't officially uninvited me yet.'

'Don't say that,' says Annie. 'She wouldn't do that.'

'She can do what she likes,' I say, shrugging. 'It's her wedding.'

The knowledge that they talk about me when I'm not around stings, although only a little. I wonder if they're enjoying the group chat without me in it, talking nonsense together, sharing funny videos and updates about their days like nothing has changed, as though three becoming two hasn't made a difference.

'Don't you think you'll ever make up?'

'I don't know. I don't really like who she's become lately.'

'She was just upset,' says Annie fairly. 'We all say stupid shit sometimes.'

'It's not even that,' I tell her, frowning. 'It's not even that she's wrong, exactly. I probably needed to hear it. But what happens next? For the rest of my life, every time I go to her with a problem, I'm going to worry that she's going to throw it back in my face later.'

Annie grimaces, and we shrug at each other.

'Sometimes things just run their course,' I say, tracing around the base of my glass for something to look at. 'What do we have in common anymore? If I met her tomorrow, would we become best friends?'

'I wonder about that sometimes too,' Annie says. 'I don't like the way she talks to us lately. It's just hard to believe that eight years of friendship can mean nothing. It has to be a blip, doesn't it?'

'Maybe not. Maybe this was just a convenient excuse to blow everything up and end our friendship for good.'

We fall silent, and she's probably wondering what it would take for our relationship to run its course too. I feel a throb of shame at myself. Every time I sidestep the topic of Emmy, I'm channelling the ugly side of Bec I've been resenting all this time. Being a good friend goes both ways. If I want a strong, honest, safe relationship with Annie, I have to work at it. I can't lose her too.

'So,' I say, panicking, 'tell me everything about this new girl of yours.'

'Are you sure?' she asks, uncertain.

'Absolutely. I want to know everything about her. Is she good enough for you? When am I meeting her?'

'Okay,' says Annie, trying to contain her giddiness. 'You promise you won't vomit on me? Because I'm about to tell you a lot of cute shit.'

'How cute are we talking?'

'Penny … I think I have an *actual girlfriend*.'

'Stop the presses!' I cry, and she goes pink, laughing. 'A real one?'

'She has a toothbrush at my place and everything.'

'Okay, stop. That *is* too fucking cute. We're going to need a bottle for this.'

Annie tells me about their date to Heide last weekend and how she fell asleep on Emmy's shoulder on the bus ride home.

She tells me about Emmy's vinyl collection, and how they listened to Phoebe Bridgers until 2 am on Thursday and how it made her almost fall asleep during a hearing yesterday. She says that she'll send a text without drafting it in her notes app first, and how she doesn't feel sick with nerves and doubt when she doesn't get a reply in an hour or two. She says it doesn't feel like all the torturous relationships she's had before. There's none of the waiting and wondering and meticulously creating a strategic version of herself to present when they're together; she doesn't cancel dates when she's feeling bloated or pretend to be in a good mood when she's upset. It's just easy and honest, she says.

All through this I nod and coo and laugh in all the right places, feeling at once elated for my friend and scared of losing her to her girlfriend. And every time my phone lights up with a notification, I get a little sad that it's from Apple News or Etsy and never from Max.

I can't sustain this. I need to snap Max out of this stupid daydream he has about open relationships and show him that I'm what he really wants. He just needs reminding. Leo's advice to be upfront was a bust, so I'm not doing that again. No, I'm going back to my old tricks: my trusty rule book. If I want to rejoin my own happy little love bubble, if I want to be like Annie and Bec, it's time to take control.

CHAPTER TWENTY-FIVE

Rule 1: Never message them first

It's a Monday evening, and I'm sitting around the house chewing my nails and making my way through a sleeve of chocolate caramel biscuits. I scroll through my photo reel to find a picture from a good hair day on a night out with the girls sometime last year. I post it on my story to show how full and busy my life is and compulsively refresh the app until I see that Max has seen it. Right on schedule, I get a message.

Max Fitzgerald (18:49): Hey good lookin
Max Fitzgerald (18:49): Free tonight?

Hook, line, and fucking sinker. An hour and a half later, I reply. Something short and sharp: '*Sorry, just saw this! Busy tonight.*' He replies immediately to ask what I'm so busy with.

It takes every ounce of self-control not to respond right away, to keep from telling him about the halloumi and pesto toastie I had for breakfast and the new book I've started, how I turned all my white laundry grey by accidentally leaving a black sock in the washing machine, that I saw a fat little dachshund on my walk home today, that I miss him. Instead, I make use of my favourite loophole.

I pretend to fall asleep early, before I've had a chance to respond. That way when I message him back in the morning, we're having one long continuous conversation, and I get to skip the shattering trauma of being left on read or — heaven forbid — double messaging him.

Rule 2: Don't be too available

It's late on Wednesday afternoon when Max calls — actually *calls* — to ask if I feel like ordering pizza. *Ordering pizza*, ha.

'Nah, I've gotta get home,' I tell him, mashing my keyboard loudly and clattering things on my desk so it sounds like I'm extremely busy. 'I've signed up for a barre class tonight.'

'Bar class?' he asks. 'I like bars.'

'B-A-R-R-E class. Next time you see me, I'm going to look like Natalie Portman in *Black Swan*.'

'Well, tomorrow night?'

'Yeah, maybe. I'll let you know.'

'Buddy,' he whines. (*'Thanks for your help today, Helena!'* I say to no one. She isn't even in today. Ed from Creative looks up in confusion). 'Don't be like that.'

'Hey, I gotta go. I need to get to Brunswick Street for this class. Traffic's a nightmare this time of day.'

I can tell he feels bad about the other night because some of his messages have regained the slightly smutty quality I love, and @amber.lou.92 posted a thirst trap yesterday and — I know because I've been obsessively checking — he hasn't liked it.

Instead of allowing myself to relax, I use this as motivation to persevere. If I can hold out a little longer, he'll realise all on his own that he loves me too, and that little hiccup will turn into a silly memory. I only have to keep at it for another couple of weeks, and we'll be out of the woods, and everything will be okay again.

Rule 3: Keep your options open

This one is hard for me. How can I resist putting all my eggs in one basket if I only have one basket? It's the *'How do you feel about a destination wedding in Cinque Terre?'* basket, and it demands to be kept full at all times. But these are hard and fast rules for making your emotionally unavailable boyfriend remember that he really cares about you, and they all must be followed.

I download all my dating apps again, enable notifications and post a screenshot of my home screen under the guise of sharing my horoscope.

'Windows of opportunity are going to open,' says Co-Star, innocuous enough. *'Things that seem impossible now will finally be possible.'*

'You have a new match!' says Bumble.

'Don't keep your match waiting, send him a message!' says Tinder.

'Tomas has sent you a message'

'Drew has sent you a message'

I have no intention of actually meeting any of them. The conversations stall after basic pleasantries, and I make no effort to push them along. If anything, this just reinforces how much I need to make it work with Max. I can't date again: the stilted small talk and attempts to build chemistry through GIFs and *Arrested Development* references. Kill me now.

In exchange for eternal happiness and unlimited orgasms, you are required to undergo the traumatic ordeal of peeling yourself out of cheap polyester dresses in the H&M fitting room for all the awkward first dates you have to endure. You must learn how to straighten the back of your hair blindly, suffer through at-home bikini waxes and spend hour after agonising hour staring at your phone willing someone to text you back. It's simply the price of admission. And boy, have I paid. Overpaid. The universe *owes me* Max.

*

All I want is to rewind to two weeks ago, before I told him I loved him and all this doubt and distance coloured our relationship grey, and figure out a way to keep things smooth. But I can't time travel, and this is the only way to regain control. Following these rules is exhausting, but it works. At least, it always has before. A little chase is the only encouragement he needs, and then our relationship rights itself.

Until now, the only problem was my weak will, that I always cave under the curl of his silver tongue a moment too soon. This time, I'm determined to stay the course and see it through to success.

All week I do this: teetering between warm and cold, never too generous with my time or words. I promise myself that when we kiss, I'll be the first one to pull away. I'll no longer draw shapes with my finger on his naked back and ask if he's sure I can't spend the night. I will build it up and up and up until he's the one left all cold and concerned. I'm only giving him a taste of his own medicine, showing him what it's like to feel my waning interest. And at just the right moment, late on Friday afternoon when I'm bored and horny, I pull the trigger and grant him relief, and suggest he comes over.

He's barely finished before I'm wrapping myself in my robe and tossing his jeans onto my bed. 'So, it's my birthday tomorrow,' I tell him. 'Did you want to do something or ...?'

'Sure,' he says, looking a little surprised as I toss his T-shirt at his face. Usually I whine and curl around his back like a baby koala to keep him from leaving so soon. But not this time.

'It would have to be a real date,' I warn him.

'I can probably manage that,' he says. 'What do you want to do?'

'That's for you to figure out. I'm the birthday girl. Can you handle that?'

'For you?' he asks, lacing his boots. 'Sure.'

CHAPTER TWENTY-SIX

I'm surprised that I'm actually surprised when I find myself sitting on the couch in a new dress, a burn from my curling iron fresh on my neck, staring at my phone and willing it to light up with a message.

Stop me if you've heard this one before.

If I start thinking about it, I feel my lip begin to wobble, so I wrench my thoughts elsewhere. I spent an hour at Sephora this afternoon letting the bubbly girl there do whatever she wanted to my face, and I don't want to waste all her hard work. I can't even pick at my nails, because I had those done today too, and the deep charcoal colour will look horrific if it chips even a little bit. My shapewear is starting to dig into my waist, but the dress doesn't zip up without it, so I have no choice but to stay in this spandex prison.

I shouldn't have got my hopes up. Annie messaged me this morning, promising to take me out to dinner next week, when she would have a wisp of free time away from the office. My dad has called six times to sing increasingly off-key renditions of 'Happy Birthday' and to tell me my room at his place in Castlemaine is still waiting for me whenever I want to go and visit. My brother and his husband FaceTimed me from London and sent a doughnut bouquet that I have already made a hearty dent in, with a card that read, '27 *club, baby! Don't fuck it up.*

Love you. Happy birthday! — *Mark and Chris*'. My Facebook wall received the usual slew of well-wishes from people I haven't spoken to in years. No word from Bec. Nothing from Max. If it wasn't for the pink tulips and bottle of Clicquot that Leo gave me this morning and the decadent cupcake I had while waiting for the train at Melbourne Central, the whole day would have been decidedly average.

I check my phone again. It's blank.

Maybe something came up. Maybe he just forgot. We hadn't set up a firm plan. It's hard to argue that Max is late when we didn't have anything set in stone. I could always message him and ask. But why does that feel like defeat? It's like every minute he isn't messaging me is a malicious act. He's probably sitting on the other side of Victoria Street, laughing with a new member of his harem. I don't even know if he's dating anyone else now or if he's just actively not practising monogamy with me. I can't bring myself to ask.

'I thought you were going out,' says Leo, arriving home laden with bags from the supermarket.

'I thought I was too.'

I feel ever more overdressed, sitting here in a dangerously short cocktail dress while he unloads Sapporos and paper towels onto the bench.

'Oh,' he says, understanding. 'That sucks. You got all tarted up and everything.'

I make a noise of agreement and check my phone again. Still nothing.

'Well, we can't waste an outfit,' says Leo. 'Call Annie. We'll go out.'

'No, it's fine,' I say, waving him off. 'I'm just going to call it a night and go to bed.'

'Bullshit,' he scoffs. 'What kind of friend would I be if I let you go to bed feeling sorry for yourself on your birthday?'

'No, I don't think I'm up for it. Really. Everything will be booked anyway.'

'I'll make a call.'

"*I'll make a call*," I say in a bad imitation of his deep voice. 'That's smooth. Who are you exactly?'

'I'm extremely important. Is that a yes?'

I hesitate for a minute and check my phone again. Nothing. It's closing in on 8 pm. Max isn't going to call.

How do I really want to spend my birthday: digging ever deeper into @amber.lou.92's Instagram and feeling sorry for myself or being a dickhead with Leo, a bread basket, and a bottle of wine? I have the power to pull myself out of a bad mood. I am in control of my life.

'Yeah, alright,' I say reluctantly. 'Fuck it, yes, okay. Let's go have some fun.'

It turns out Leo *is* someone extremely important, because within forty-five minutes, we're being seated at Cutler & Co in Fitzroy, where there's often a waitlist for a reservation. It's a glossy high-ceilinged restaurant with sexy lighting and a clientele that doesn't rely on Afterpay several times a month. The prices on the menu are written in a tiny font, as though to say, '*If you need to read this, you don't belong here.*'

'Don't look now,' murmurs Leo after we've settled into our seats, 'but I'm pretty sure we have an audience.'

'What do you mean?'

'The girls at the big table over there — *don'tlookforfuckssake!* I think I ghosted one of them a few months ago.'

'Which one?' I stage-whisper, trying my very best to look at the second table on our left through my peripherals only, and failing. I look like I slept on my neck wrong.

Leo's right. By the window, there's a five-top of identical women, all with hair in varying shades of butter and caramel, all wearing whatever fell off the Sportsgirl sales rack, and all clearly gossiping about the man at my table and his latest conquest.

'The blonde.'

'They're all blonde.'

'Long hair. Red top.'

'You certainly have a type.'

'I do not,' scoffs Leo. 'I'm an equal opportunity scumbag. I'll fuck anyone.'

I laugh and receive identical filthy looks from the left. How dare I, they're probably thinking. What kind of feminist am I, laughing with their collective nemesis? Don't I know what a dick he was to their friend?

'They probably think we're here together,' I tell him, looking scandalised.

'We are here together,' he says.

'*Together* together,' I say. 'They don't know you're my platonic boyfriend.'

Leo smiles, and I'm glad for it. I didn't screen that thought before it escaped my mouth. Sometimes I don't know where the line is with him. Am I supposed to joke with him like a brother? Or is there some invisible divide here, some unacknowledged grey area relating to that bullshit old adage that men and women can't be friends?

Gosh, no, that's a dumb thought. I don't look anything like those women over there. My haircut is far too low maintenance, and I don't have that flirty streak that beautiful, confident people have built in from puberty, the one that Leo has and expects from his partners. Whenever I try to flirt with people, I just end up ranting about whatever topic Trevor Noah covered this week and then wonder why men never call me back. Even for a platonic boyfriend, Leo's out of my league.

'Who ghosts people?' I ask, pulling myself back into reality and sucking my stomach in a little. My Spanx scrape against my navel. 'You can't even spare her a *"thanks, no thanks"* text?'

'Who has the time?' he replies, and I give him an unimpressed look. 'I don't know. Sometimes things just die off. I don't think I did it on purpose. I probably just didn't get around to replying to her last message, and she didn't send another one, and it didn't feel like it was going anywhere. And then I just forgot she existed.'

'That's flattering,' I tell him, rolling my eyes. It's comforting to think that even among the leagues of C-list local influencers, people are getting ghosted and rejected like the rest of us. 'Although, honestly … sometimes the *"I'm dumping you"* message is more offensive than just never hearing from them again.'

'You think?'

'It's like, okay, you've been on two dates, neither of them were spectacular, the texting is dying off, we haven't got another date lined up, and I don't care if I never see them again, and that's fine. But then they don't want to see me again *so much* that they have to verbalise it. Can't they just let it fizzle without actively rejecting me? It's like, fuck off.'

'You should write a dating etiquette bible,' he laughs. '*What Not to Do with Someone You're Trying to Do.*'

'I should, shouldn't I? It'd be a hit. A *New York Times* bestseller a thousand weeks in a row.'

'It might outsell the actual Bible.'

'I bet it would. I'm very entertaining. So talented.'

'*So* talented.'

'And tall!'

'Are you tall?' asks Leo, leaning over to see the length of my legs.

I tuck them under my chair self-consciously and make a *tsht* noise.

'Yes, I am!' I cry. 'I'm five foot eight — unless I'm using the measuring tape men use for their dating profiles, in which case I'm six foot fucking four.'

'I never understood that,' he says. 'If you lie about your height on your profile and then you meet, she's going to notice you aren't six foot.'

'Some short guys have a real complex about it. I don't think women actually care. I think it's just the lie that gets us. I'll date someone my height, but give me some warning or I'll show up in heels and I'll feel like the fucking Hulk and have to pretend not to notice you're a hobbit.'

'So why don't you wear flat shoes just in case?'

'Because then you have the dumpy calves problem.'

'*Dumpy calves*,' he repeats, wearing an incredulous frown.

'Yes,' I tell him with a sanctimonious little nod. 'The kind of calves that make you unlovable and uninteresting. No one with dumpy calves has ever won a Nobel Prize or *The Bachelor*. Probably.'

'The female brain is a fascinating place.'

'Alright,' says the waitress as she reappears at our table. 'How are we going with the menus? Drinks, food?'

'We're ready,' says Leo. Usually a man talking for me would send me into a blinding rage, but when Leo does it, it's gentle and generous. 'We'll do the tasting menu.'

'And how do we feel about wine?' she asks. Even in her simple black work clothes, she's better put together than I am in my elaborate birthday getup. How does she do it? Her neck is lovely and long and elegant. Is that it? Do I have a fat neck? I try to subtly pinch myself below my ears to see if it's excessively flabby.

'Whatever your sommelier recommends,' says Leo, and hands back our menus.

'That's so fucking expensive,' I hiss as she leaves. I think of my bank balance and imagine a tumbleweed blowing across my phone screen.

'Let me buy you dinner on your birthday,' he says, screwing up his face like I'm unreasonable to take issue with a two hundred dollar dinner. 'Just say thank you.'

'Thank you,' I say, and he smiles.

'You're welcome.'

'God, I'm glad that part of my life is over,' I tell him, drinking heavily from my wine glass when it's set down in front of me. It seems a shame to waste fancy wine on tiny useless sips.

'What part of your life?'

'Dating,' I say with a shudder.

'You're done?'

'I'm with Max now.'

'And that's a forever kind of thing?' he asks.

'Well …' *Huh.* I've never thought about it in a long-term way. It never seemed like much of an option, so my subconscious blocked it. I don't have pictures in my head of us arguing about credenzas at West Elm or clutching each other with joy as a positive pregnancy test sits on the bathroom sink. I try to imagine it, but nothing comes. 'I don't know. I guess. Maybe.'

This uneasy thought compels me to pull my phone out of my bag and check it. Nothing. *Active 2 hours ago.*

'I haven't heard you mention him in a while, that's all.'

'We're doing this polyamorous thing lately,' I continue. It's a story I've been rehearsing in my head. 'No one belongs to anyone, et cetera. It's very modern.'

'That's very open-minded of you,' says Leo smoothly. 'Good for you guys.'

I catch a flicker of disappointment pass through me when he doesn't challenge me, doesn't tell me it's a bullshit concept or ask how many extracurricular relationships I'm having at the moment. But then, why would he? Leo and Max could probably do a travelling lecture series on the subject of disposable women. And why should I crave his disapproval?

'Anyway,' I sniff, tossing the subject aside. 'Right, fancy man. What can you taste in this wine? I'm getting notes of raspberry, goon and pretentiousness.'

CHAPTER TWENTY-SEVEN

He holds my hand the whole way home. It's just sympathy. We're palm to palm as the Uber lurches through the post-football Saturday night traffic on Victoria Parade, and I watch the world move on around us. As we stop at a red light, I rest my temple on his shoulder, and he rests his cheek against my head. Another two hours and zero messages later, I feel heavy and sad, barely comforted by the unquestioned affection from the one man who doesn't use my heart for target practice, who treats me like an equal, whose steady rotation of women doesn't affect me and my self-worth at all. A nice man, who never makes me feel burdensome or inconvenient or stupid. How easy it would be to be with someone like Leo, if I could ever find them.

But then, Max *is* someone like Leo. Didn't I just have a very expensive dinner across the room from someone Leo found himself too disinterested in to even remember to tell them so? It's just that in this version, the players aren't glossy, full-lipped beauties but neurotic, intense people who relate a bit too hard to Hannah Horvath. The game remains the same: the one with the power is the one who cares the least.

'Should we have another drink?' he asks as we pull up at home. 'Nightcap? End the night in style?'

'I think there's wine in the pantry,' I reply. 'I can't remember — do you like or hate rosé?'

'I don't mind rosé.'

'Okay.'

The house feels suddenly huge, and I feel very small in it. It's as though I've never been here before. I don't know how to crack this mood now, and I don't want it to linger. It's been so long since we've had to make small talk, but it's all that comes to mind. Leo is radiating pity, and I just want to shake off the feeling and have ten normal minutes with my friend without giving in to this shitty feeling and crying.

Our hands bump as we both reach for the corkscrew in the second drawer, and we let out an awkward laugh at it. It happens again when we turn to the pantry to look for the emergency wine stash kept on the top shelf.

How strange the energy is in the kitchen right now. It's warm in here despite the chilly April evening, and Leo looks as though he's grown uncomfortable in his body, all shoulders suddenly. He always looks so composed, in full command of any situation he finds himself in, with his strong, clear voice and easy confidence, but now he seems to be searching the room for something safe to let his eyes linger on. He looks at the Matisse print on the wall, the lonely green apple in the fruit bowl, the moth outside the kitchen window, but he can't settle anywhere. He seems taller. Broader. More aware of his limbs. He looks at me, and I feel even less in control of the atmosphere than he does.

Wine glasses, wine glasses, where do we keep the wine glasses again? I've lived here long enough. What a silly thing to forget. I set the bottle down on the bench, and he's right there. There's his aftershave, softer now than earlier in the evening. Warmer. Leo-er.

'Is it — um. Don't make fun of me — are you okay with ice in your wine?' I ask, and he's trying not to watch my mouth and failing, and in a second that hangs on and on, I know what's about to happen. And then it does.

There are trillions of nerve endings all over the human body, and every single one of mine ignites, pulses and explodes into golden fireworks when we kiss. My heartbeat thumps in my ears, frantic, urgent, and my hands are full of the smooth muscles of his arms, and his mouth is warm on mine, and his hands are in my hair, against my cheek, on my waist, and I'm desperate for breath but so unwilling to pause to take it, sure that to stop kissing is to stop existing, or maybe that I'm imagining all of this and if I open my eyes it will never have happened and that's not a risk I'm ready to take. His hands — such nice, long-fingered hands — are against the backs of my legs, sliding up my skirt, and he's raining kisses against my jaw, my neck, and the pendant on my necklace is pressing sharply, deliciously into my chest, and it's all so much better and hotter than I ever remember kissing being, and just as he pushes me hard against the bench there's the unmistakable buzz of a phone receiving a text, and we spring apart as if by electric shock.

The room spins, and I don't know if it's the delayed onset of half a dozen drinks at dinner or the herculean effort of my brain trying to process this.

When did this happen? When did watching *Bake Off* in our pyjamas get romantic? Was it somewhere between helping him choose a going-out shirt at Harrolds and last call together on Saturday nights at the local pub? It's like someone has changed the lighting gels and what was blue is suddenly red. Years of over-analysis should have prepared me for this.

Leo. Housemate Leo. Emotional pep-talking, slightly slutty Tinder Platinum subscriber Leo. Anti-relationship Leo, who's so burnt out by his last girlfriend that he's punishing every woman he meets for it. Leo, who embodies everything that

my friends have been complaining about for the last decade.
Fuckboy Leo. Dangerous Leo, for whom women are disposable,
who has decried the merits of commitment for months now.
Leo, who isn't a real option, full fucking stop.

I don't know what to do with my body. I'm too embarrassed
to look at him and see the look of regret on his face, so I reach
for my phone instead.

Max Fitzgerald (23:37): You up?

He's close enough to have seen my screen, and he takes a step
back.

I must be glowing red. Our silence is heavy as I search my
racing thoughts for something to say. I need to paper over it,
tell him it's okay, that it was just a silly drunk mistake. No
harm, no foul. A part of me wants to take him by the belt and
pull him my way, but maybe the moment is gone. I want him
to suggest we have our wines, or to take me to my room, or to
make a little joke and cut the tension, but he doesn't. And I
can't do anything but stand here, uneasy limbs and hot cheeks,
staring somewhere between his knees and the floor, no closer
to finding the right thing to say than ever before.

'Are you going to answer him?' Leo asks in a cold, clear
voice.

'I — well, yes. I should.'

He lets out a dry, horrible laugh, and I register a freezing
dread of shame and scolding.

'What? What am I supposed to do?'

'What are you doing, Penny?'

'I don't know.'

'Yes, you do,' he says, back in control of himself now. 'You're
going to go and see him, aren't you?'

'I don't know,' I repeat, too embarrassed to meet his eye. 'He is my boyfriend.'

I hear him exhale, '*For fuck's sake*', and I want to cry.

'Why would you do this to yourself?'

'Do *what*?'

'He treats you like shit, he stands you up *on your birthday*, and then he sends you a text in the middle of the night and you come running. Is that really how it is?'

'He didn't mean to stand me up,' I mumble, wishing I believed what I was saying. 'There was probably some emergency —'

'There's no emergency,' he says. 'He didn't forget. He just didn't want to come. Stop making excuses for him. The guy's a *cu*—'

'*Don't*,' I snap. 'You don't even know him.'

'I don't need to,' he argues. 'Why are you the only one who doesn't see what he's like? Why do you refuse to believe he's exactly who he says he is? Relationships aren't meant to be like that. You shouldn't —'

'You think you know everything,' I ask, hot defensive anger flaring up in my chest, 'because you've had one girlfriend and fucked everyone on this side of the Yarra? What is that even for? All those women? Has your one failed relationship left such a dent in your self-esteem that you have to take it out on every woman who swipes right on you?'

'Christ!' he cries, laughing humourlessly from the other side of the kitchen, the space between us like some sort of forcefield. 'Where did that come from?'

I don't reply so much as glower at him, jaw set — it's starting to hurt, actually, but it's nothing against the throb of blood in my ears and the searing wine headache beginning to form.

'It's just something to do,' he says, finally, throwing his hands up in exasperation. 'It's just for fun.'

'Who's it fun for, Leo? You?'

'Of course it's fun for m—'

'Because I've been that girl, all of them, those poor stupid girls, hanging on to every word you say, humiliating themselves, completely disposab—'

'Stop being so fucking obtuse!' he cries, beyond frustration now. 'That's exactly the path you're on now. That's exactly who you are to him!'

'Not anymore, I'm not.'

'Yes! Yes, anymore! Right now! Look at yourself, you're in the middle of a bad choice. Just stop!'

'I'm *not*. That's not how it is with Max. It's not —'

'You're standing here judging me, watching me not care about those women the way I stand here watching Max not care about you, and you're sick with it, aren't you, hating him for making you the idiot begging for his attention and hating yourself because you let him do it.'

I hate to be conspicuous. I stress, constantly, about the space I take up in a room or as noisy chatter in peoples' heads. So many of my problems would be solved if I was just invisible. Margot wouldn't notice my fuck-ups, Bec wouldn't be sick of my presence. Some days I just wish I could disappear. But underneath, secretly, there's nothing that touches me more than being noticed. I love when Sexy Barista remembers my order or when Max remembers a book I mentioned months ago and lets me borrow his copy. When I go out to the country to visit Dad and he tees up *Clueless* on Netflix because he knows it's my favourite. Even being sent some video of a fluffy cat, just because someone saw it and thought I'd enjoy it. It's the ultimate compliment: being seen, being heard.

And then there's this.

Instead of making me feel warm and cared for, it leaves me cold and exposed. Leo has heard more than what I say; he's heard what I mean, the way I *feel*, and has spat it back to me with such venom that it makes me pull my arms close, as though to protect my heart from hearing it.

He sees this — my flinch, my freeze — and softens, and it's worse.

His shoulders drop first and then his eyelids. He presses the heels of his palms into his eyes and whines in frustration or regret or hate, who knows, and addresses the floor. 'It's not you,' he says. 'It's me.'

'Okay,' I say, resigned, quiet, holding my shoulders in an attempt to make myself smaller.

'I'm sorry I said that.'

'Okay.'

'You aren't disposable.'

'But they are? Those girls.' There's a note of a challenge in my voice, if only a weak one, but I still can't look him in the face. The floor will have to do.

'I'm — yeah. I'm just trying to have fun and kill time while I wait.'

'What are you waiting for?'

'I can't stand watching you do this to yourself,' he says, exhausted. 'I wish you wouldn't go.'

'You can't sulk because I'm not falling over myself to sleep with you. That's not fair. I'm allowed to not want to be one of those girls creeping out of your room at six in the morning.'

'That's not what this is at all!' he cries, inflamed again. 'Do you really not get it?'

'I don't —'

'How can I make this any clearer? Do I have to spell it out? You overthink *everything*!'

'What are you talking ab—?'

'You know I'm in love with you. Don't stand there and pretend you don't.'

And time has simply stopped, and I can't do anything, and I must look shocked and he looks embarrassed, and silence stretches on forever, I can tell, because Leo tries and fails to break it six times, now seven, and I just keep coming up blank. A thought barely forms in my head before I lose it and another one starts to leak in.

'Say something,' he says softly, eventually. 'I'm fucking vulnerable here.'

'How could you do this to me?' I ask, my voice coming out quiet.

'What?'

I work to keep my breathing steady. Thank goodness for all that meditating. There's a stabbing in my stomach I can't credit to dinner. It twists and aches and turns poisonous inside me. How foolish I was to think anything good could ever stay that way. How stupid I was to believe I could have one relationship not fraught with subtext and landmines.

'What am I supposed to do with that, Leo?'

'I —'

'We're supposed to be friends. Why are you trying to fuck everything up?'

'I'm not trying to fuck everything up. You knew. You had to know.'

'You don't want me. You're just bored of all your easy conquests. You're just stirring up trouble to entertain yourself, and then you'll get sick of me and throw me away too.'

'It's not like that.'

'*Fuck* you,' I spit. 'Leave me alone. Go find someone else's life to ruin.'

And I leave him there in the half light of the living room, stopping only to pick up my shoes and jacket before I slam the front door behind me and leave for safety: anywhere but here, with anyone but him.

CHAPTER TWENTY-EIGHT

I am literally running away from my problems. Figurative action is no longer enough to satiate my need for escaping myself. My whole body is hot and ringing with the memory of what happened last night, and it felt too suffocating to stay in the house and just sit with it, so I've taken to the pavement. I don't care that it's barely 5 am and the sun isn't up yet, that the streets are dotted with strangers at varying levels of sobriety. It's just me and my racing thoughts winding our way through the empty back streets of Richmond. Egan Street, then Lennox, Highett, Griffiths, Somerset. Ugh, I hate it. I wish I could yoga away from my problems.

I don't have any music. I left my phone at home. I was worried that even having it in my hand would compel me to call Annie and vomit up every detail of last night, and right now I can't think of anything I want less than anybody knowing about this. I don't know why this feels private when all those nights spent up in Max's room received precise play-by-plays and when Annie has asked for my input on every thirst trap she has ever posted. I'm not sure why I never talk to my friends about Leo, even in passing. Maybe I thought they would read more into it than there was.

Is? Was?

Maybe I was worried that they would see it before I did, and

I wasn't ready to be honest with them or him or myself. Maybe I just don't want anyone knowing what a silly, giddy schoolgirl I am, instantly developing feverish crushes on anyone in my eyeline with a pair of testicles. It feels like the right choice, now, to keep it quiet. The whole thing feels sordid and pathetic.

I realise, winding down Davison Street then Buckingham, that part of me has known for weeks that something like this was going to happen. Clues were growing like mould spores: nowhere and then everywhere, hinting at something bigger beneath the surface. Since he learned my coffee order by heart, since he started touching my back to squeeze past me in the kitchen, since he started choosing nights on the couch with me over nights at bars with beautiful women. His comforting hug after that panic attack. All our stupid private jokes. Scattered, these things are meaningless. But I can taste his mouth even as I take heaving breaths while I'm passing Citizens Park, and instead of being insignificant gestures between friends, they all become his sweet, obvious tells. I wonder if I've been giving off clues this whole time too. I wonder what they were.

It can't be that just at that moment I was irresistible. I ended up going to the pub on the corner and caught my reflection as I splashed water on my face in the grungy, graffitied bathrooms. I looked like shit, with ruddy cheeks from the wine and great black circles under my eyes from melted mascara. I looked like a drunk raccoon.

Had I asked him to kiss me? If not with my words then with my behaviour? Maybe. Possibly. But calling him my platonic boyfriend was a joke. Did my inflection show my hand before I even knew what I meant? Am I that obvious? Can *everyone* see it?

What does it *mean*? He's obviously confused. He doesn't actually love me. He isn't even emotionally capable of anything like that at this point, he's so used to fleeting relationships and clean transactions over a couple of G&Ts. Perhaps he's just never had a female friend before and is uncertain of the mechanics of a relationship where both people keep their hands to themselves. Perhaps he's just lonely, and I was the easiest target.

It *was* fucking hot, though. I haven't been kissed like that in forever. Max and I never kiss for the sake of kissing; it's always just a vehicle to get us to bed.

Oh god. *Max*. He has been top of mind for the majority of my twenties, and now, suddenly, he's disappeared from my whole entire brain. Poof! I'm cured.

I really wish I'd been nicer to Dr Minnick. This would make for a jam-packed session. But I can't go back now; I'm too ashamed of what a brat I was.

Do I want to kiss him again? Do I wish Max hadn't messaged me at that exact moment? Do I want to know where it would have led? Yes, yes, yes. But it feels more complicated than that. Max and I are — I mean, *were*. Or is it still *are*? I'm struggling to keep track, honestly — complicated insofar as he always keeps — *kept* — me at arm's length, now more than ever.

But I would do that to him too, even if I kept it within the rigid borders of monogamy. Every minute we're together is a battle for control. I always have to be *on*. Not too clingy, not too argumentative; very clever, very quick; always horny, always amenable. It's exhausting when I'm losing but exhilarating when I'm winning. When he pecks me on the cheek unexpectedly, or I make him laugh, or if I've seen a documentary he hasn't, I'm above the clouds. And in the next breath, he'll unlace his fingers from mine, or stare at his phone when I'm trying to talk to him, or say something like, '*Mm, I don't know if you're right about that*,' and my self-esteem plummets beneath the earth's crust and melts into nothing.

I'm looping up towards Bromham Place when I wonder, does Leo have a point? Am I projecting my shit on to the women he brings home, imagining they all want more just because I do? My friends would certainly think so. The way he puts it, I'm being pretty pathetic, trotting after Max like an obedient little pet no matter how many times I swear it's the last time. I've even forgotten to be hurt by this latest disappointment. I've just come to expect it. I think I knew he would blow me off yesterday — I think that's why I didn't reach out first. I was setting him up to fail to prove a point to myself, to use as a weapon next time he and I fight. If he's ever around long enough to have one. If I'm ever brave enough to pick one.

Am I really being my best self? Is this self-compassion? Is this healthy adult behaviour?

I make it back to my street and double over, gasping for air as I clutch a fencepost for support. I wish I'd thought to bring a water bottle. I'm so fucking hot that I'm almost willing to drink from a puddle in the gutter. Low point. Got to get home, where there are glasses and tap water, where I can shower and catch my breath and sneak out again before Leo wakes up.

Sunday stretches ahead, and I don't know what to do with all of it. I can't just walk around with all of this coursing through my nervous system for eternity. I might spark and burn and short-circuit and die.

Will it be so awkward that I'll have to move house? Where would I go? I can't afford to live on my own, and I'm drastically undercharged for rent as it is. Would I ever be able to find another generous setup like this or would I have to live like Max, with three housemates, and black mould growing in the wardrobes? What if I have to move to some far-flung suburb, like Moonee Ponds or Carnegie or the unthinkable — Yarraville? I don't even know if you can get phone reception out there. Do they have trams? Would I need to budget three figures a week to pay for Uber rides back from civilisation after nights out with Annie?

How strange the kitchen looks when I get home. It's exactly the same as it always is. It has no idea it's the scene of a crime. The bottle of wine is still sitting on the bench, and the wine glass cupboard is open. I want to leave it as it is. I want to have it on display in a museum so I can stand outside it and look in and remember the kiss whenever I want. It would be in an exhibition called 'Bad Luck and Bad Habits', and it would include this room, the lecture theatre where I met Max, the toilets at my high school where I discovered my first period, and the dingy house party where I found the untouchable confidence that is brought on by pineapple vodka Cruisers.

I even consider taking a photo of the kitchen while the mood lingers, but I can't think of any purpose it would serve. It would just become one of a thousand mediocre photos in my camera roll, lost among cute dogs I've met on the street, lunches I've enjoyed, rejected selfies, and screenshots of clothes I've forgotten to buy. And, anyway, I may not want to think about last night ever again. I put the bottle away and close the cupboard door, but the energy stays the same. Watchful. Full of secrets.

CHAPTER TWENTY-NINE

'I don't know, Pen,' says Annie. Her kettle lever pops, and she attends to it. 'Shouldn't it all be easier than this?'

I've just drawn breath, having spent twenty minutes bombarding Annie with the details of the last few weeks, including the handy little tricks I've employed to keep Max on the hook. It's early but Annie's always up at this time. As I'd got out of my post-run shower, I'd heard Leo rummaging for breakfast in the kitchen, so I'd dashed from the bathroom, yanked on some clothes and got out of the house in twelve seconds flat. I was a blur of wet hair and emotional avoidance strategy, and Annie's place felt like the only safe place left for me.

Annie started laughing at the mention of Max's new interest in the grey areas of monogamy, but bit back her real thoughts at the warning look on my face and allowed me to continue. I stop my story just shy of the details of Leogate. As far as she knows, Max wasn't able to make it, and Leo and I went out for dinner, had a nice time and went to bed in separate bedrooms, like any other housemates might. All of which is true.

Annie pours hot water into her French press and goes searching for the sugar sachets she keeps just for my visits. I help myself to two cups from her dishrack and take them to the living room.

'When is it *ever* easy, Annie?'

'When it's healthy,' she says, joining me on the couch and filling my cup with rich, strong coffee. 'All these games, all those rules — "don't message them first", "don't be too available" — yeah, they're fun for you and torture for him, but have they ever really worked?'

'They usually work on Max. They have.'

'Have they, though? You're telling me about it because they *haven't*. You followed all the rules of your own game and he still stood you up. On your birthday.'

'He's really close to finishing his thesis,' I argue. It's the first excuse I try on, and it fits okay. I can accept coming second to academia. 'He's probably in a poetry black hole. No concept of time or girlfriends or birthdays.'

Annie gives me a disbelieving look. 'If things were going to work out, wouldn't they just … work out?'

'Good things don't always come easy,' I say after a pause, dragging out my thinking time with a long sip. 'Remember when you were all strung out on whatshisname — Dev? If you crafted your messages just right, he'd ask you out again and things would be magicky for another week or so. He liked you; he was just shit at texting.'

'Yeah, and in case you don't remember, *that didn't work out.*'

'But only because you realised you're gay.'

'A tiny incompatibility,' she concedes, laughing.

'But don't you think it might have, if you'd had the exact same problem with a woman?'

'I don't think so,' she says, with a frown and a faraway look. 'I think there are all sorts of roadblocks in relationships, and they're just little signs along the way to show you that you're on the wrong route.'

'But you can't tell me there aren't couples who have to work at it,' I continue, 'or marriage counsellors wouldn't exist. No relationship can be perfect one hundred percent of the time. Why can't that be the case here? Why is everyone telling me to write it off completely?'

'Of course *sometimes* you have to work at it. But not all the time. Not from day one.'

'If we're always in a state of self-improvement, right, who says I can't just self-improve into being what he wants? If, say, I'm his absolute dream girl except he only wants to end up with a redhead, would it be so wrong to dye my hair?'

Annie begins to laugh. She has to set her cup down to keep from scalding herself, and I'm affronted.

'What? Why is that funny? I'm serious!'

'I know you are!' she says from behind her hands. 'That's why it's so awful!'

'It's not!'

'It *is*!'

'Why?!'

'Because if Max thinks you're his absolute fucking dream girl except for some tiny, ridiculous, temporary thing, then you aren't right for each other! Would you want to be with someone who loves you *in spite* of something like that? In spite of *anything*?'

I frown harder, searching for the right answer and coming up short. She's making it sound like this is pure fact, like I'm ridiculous for wanting to better myself in a way that just happens to align with the desires of someone I want very much. What if it's no burden at all to contort myself into the kind of girl he wants? This could be the push I need to sort through all my neuroses and neediness and learn to like the taste of tempeh. I could start reading real newspapers, not just the headlines from *The Cut*'s Twitter. He could teach me to develop a critical appreciation of Woody Allen films. I could be happier on the other side of all that personal development. Who's to say?

'I hate to be the card-carrying lesbian misandrist, babe,' says Annie when I've failed to respond, 'but who gives a shit what men think of you?'

'But it's not *men*,' I argue. 'I'm not that girl. That's not fair. I'm not out there looking for *any* male attention. It's just one man. Max-man.'

'But what do you think of you?' she asks. 'Do you like you?'

'Please. If I had self-esteem I wouldn't be funny anymore.'

'What's your therapist's name again?'

'I'm only joking. Kind of.'

'Listen, I don't want to be like Bec and tell you to stop seeing him. I just want you to think about what a relationship might look like if things were easy.'

'I have no idea. Easy how?'

'Like … you can triple-text them and not care because you know they're just busy, not ignoring you. You know they're going to be happy to see your name all over their phone. You don't spend two hours getting ready every time you're seeing them. You just feel like *you*, not a performance of your best self.'

'But I only have that with friends.'

'Yeah, babe, because you know I'm not going to tell you to shut up, or stop loving you if you're having a fat day, or think less of you if you aren't *on* all the time. Because I just like who you are, and you know that.'

'Do you have that? With Emmy?'

'Yeah,' she says with a little shrug. 'I actually do.'

'What's it like?'

'It's nice. It's just … nice. Like, she was supposed to come over the other night, but I had a shit day at work and wanted to cancel. But she came round anyway, we had dinner, watched a movie and went to bed. I probably said ten words all night, and she didn't care. I didn't go into a spiral about it — *oh no, I've ruined our eighteenth date, she's going to ghost me, my life is over.* I know that sounds really boring, but it was nice. It was nice in its banality. It's a relief.'

'Shit, that does sound nice,' I say, impressed and a little envious. 'Cheers to that.'

'Vashe fucking zdorovye,' she laughs, and we clink cups.

'Anyway,' I say as I recover from my overzealous swig, wiping coffee from the corner of my mouth. 'Anyway, anyway, anyway. Enough of my complaining. Enough me. More you.'

'More me,' she sighs, slumping back against her cushions. 'Work's fucking endless. I didn't get in until eleven last night.'

'You're joking,' I groan in sympathy. 'That's shit, you shouldn't have to do that — especially on a Saturday night.'

'I don't mind it, actually,' she says. 'I enjoy the work, time goes by quickly. I just look at the clock and suddenly it's fuck o'clock. It takes a toll on my body, though. My arse hurts from sitting at my desk for eighty hours this week. I've been living on cold brew and grain salads from EARL. I haven't been to Pilates in ten days.'

'God, who are you anymore?'

'I'll have an identity crisis without abs,' she laughs, pushing her stomach out for emphasis. I note that, in her company, I don't feel the need to suck mine in or hold a pillow in my lap. 'I start taking classes for the bar next week too.'

'I can't believe you have to take classes to take a test for a job you already do.'

'Well, if you ever murder Max, you'll know your defence is in safe and smart and qualified hands.'

'Stop. I'm not going to do that. It's fine. It'll work itself out.'

'Yeah, yeah,' she says, stretching in her seat. 'Another coffee? I have to get to the office soon.'

'I'll get it,' I tell her, rising with our cups and heading for the kitchen. 'Working on a Saturday *and* a Sunday. Sounds like a violation of your human rights.'

'Did you have a nice night anyway?' she asks. 'Last night, with Leo?'

'Yeah.' I keep my back turned and focus on scooping coffee grounds more closely than is necessary. 'It was fine.'

'He's the kind of person you should be with,' she says, and I freeze. Does she know? How could she? Maybe they're friends. Maybe they have a secret group chat. No, I would have found out about something like that. Annie is worse at keeping secrets than I am, and I'm ready to burst with it.

'I don't think so. He's too ...'

'You could never date someone with better hair than you,' Annie says, and laughs.

'Yeah, man,' I say, and breathe a silent sigh of relief that she's taking the disparaging route instead. 'How do you do it?'

'Emmy has a fucking *mane*,' she says as I return to the couch, coffees in hand. 'She wakes up looking like she's wandered out of the Garden of Eden.'

'How annoying.'

'It's maddening. She's lucky I like her so much.'

Annie starts off on a sweet story about Emmy's failed attempt at a paleo breakfast last weekend, how they ended up having a lovely morning eating lumps of charcoaled banana pancakes out of the pan on the balcony. It's imperfect and silly and easy, and the look on her face as she talks about it leaves me happy and sad in every breath.

CHAPTER THIRTY

My reflection in the cafe window is enough to make me do a double-take. The burst of nervous energy that fuelled my run has ebbed down to nothing, and my punishment for last night's wine and tears has arrived in its place. I came here because I needed an excuse to stay out of the house, and to get an IV drip of caffeine and a stack of French toast at least as tall as I am, not to be attacked by the bloaty, sagging face of a hungover 27-year-old. Have my eyes always looked like they're about to slide over my cheekbones and slop onto the ground? I can't believe wine would betray me like this, when all I do is love it. Talk about an all-take no-give relationship.

I hope the barista doesn't notice that I'm not wearing a bra under my jumper.

'Usual?' he asks, and I nod feebly before throwing myself into an empty booth.

Behind my latte — three sugars; I deserve it — I search for emotional sore spots. Remembering your girlfriend's birthday is a pretty low bar, but Max dug a trench to avoid it. The thought of it brings up a dull thud in my chest, and I grab on to it and mine it for more rejection. I might as well make a weekend of it. Do you actually *feel* a broken heart, or is my left tit just aching from the underwire of the expensive and impractical lingerie I never got to show off last night? Thanks for nothing, Stella McCartney.

'Penny?'

My latte glass clatters onto its saucer and I choke on my sip. 'Oh fuc— sorry, I meant — hey, good morning.'

There stands Petra de Silva with her green juice and head-to-toe Lululemon, radiating health and maturity. She motions to ask if she can sit in the seat opposite, and I nod. That tiny movement feels like my brain is rattling around my skull like a pinball.

'How are you? What are you doing here?' I ask, trying to rearrange my face to look less like shit, and failing.

'I live just around the corner. How are you? Big night?'

I groan. 'Does it show?'

'You look how I looked for most of my twenties. I was always in desperate need of either coffee or wine.'

'Don't say wine,' I bleat, throwing my hand over my face. 'It was my birthday last night.'

'Oh, happy birthday! Did you have fun?'

'Too much, and then none at all.'

She laughs good-naturedly and says, 'I wanted to say what a shame it was that we passed on your pitch.'

'It's fine.' I hope I sound convincing, as though I wasn't completely devastated by it. 'No hard feelings.'

'I've worked in places like Scout before, agencies growing faster than they know how to handle. In my experience, all their energy goes into growing the business, and once they've signed an account, they do nothing to keep them.'

There's a twinge of guilt at the memory of billing my clients for six hours (or fifteen) of work while I scoured the entire Mecca website in the name of Evergreen competitor research.

'I actually want to do our marketing in-house, but the team wanted to see what agencies could offer us,' she explains. 'I'd hate for you to think we passed on you because your ideas weren't good, because they were.'

'That's nice of you to say.'

'I'm not saying it just to say it,' she insists. How does she hold eye contact with such confidence? I can't even order a croissant without consulting the floor. 'Other agencies tried comparing us to Clinique, for heaven's sake.'

'They still test on animals!' I say, incredulous.

'I nearly did a spit-take.'

'Did they do no research on the brand at all?'

'I don't think so,' she says. It's nice to talk shop with someone who isn't doing a performance review. 'But *you* did. You knew all about us, what we're about, what's important to us. I was really impressed.'

'I wanted to. It was fun, actually. The most fun I've had at work in ages.'

'Agency work is either all fun or no fun,' she says. 'Which is Scout?'

I raise an eyebrow and take a long sip by way of an answer.

Petra laughs. 'What did you study?'

'Bachelor of Commerce. Marketing major.'

'And then?'

'A couple of internships, then four years at a big agency. I was a producer. Retail clients, mostly. A car.'

'Then you went to Scout?' she asks, and I nod. 'Why?'

'I needed a change,' I say, and shrug. 'I'd been there for so long. I thought a smaller agency would mean more autonomy. Scout was the first place I applied for.'

'And is it better?' she asks.

Pause.

'Sure.'

'I look at my time in agency as a rite of passage,' she says. 'It taught me how to think on my feet, deal with difficult people and manage my time. You get it out of the way and then move on to a job that doesn't make you want to call in sick every Monday.'

By now I've reached the bottom of my latte glass and feel just as empty. I'd love to call in sick tomorrow. The idea of looking down the barrel of a whole week of Margot makes me want to throw myself in the river. 'Girl found in Yarra,' the newspapers would say. 'Resignation letter found in jacket pocket.'

'It's just a …' I cast a glance around the cafe, searching for the right word in empty coffee cups and a billow of steam from the commercial dishwasher. 'It's a learning experience. Character-building stuff.'

'That's very diplomatic.'

'I'm trying really hard,' I smirk, and she laughs.

I'm considering another coffee and possibly redoing my resume or contacting a recruiter. How I wish I could have a boss like her — someone I *like*, who I can chat to without feeling panicked and sweaty.

'Anyway, work's work,' I say. It's not the height of professionalism to shit-talk your job to a relative stranger. 'Sometimes it takes a while to find your rhythm.'

'Don't let someone tell you you're not good at your job, Penny,' says Petra. She has a special way of cutting through the bullshit and speaking directly without coming off as a dick. 'If you aren't thriving somewhere, it doesn't automatically make you the problem.'

I laugh to fight the discomfort. 'Am I that transparent?'

'I speak your language,' she says. 'When we talk about hangovers or your friend's wedding, you're fine, you're quick, you're funny. But when we talk about your work, you clam up. I know you know what you're doing. I know the pitch was all your work because your boss couldn't speak to any of it. She just read off your slides. There's a disconnect between your ability and the way you perceive it. Something is making you nervous.'

She's being so nice, so generous with her words and her time, and I don't have anything to say back. All I can do is stare at my hands as I pick at a painful hangnail. She reaches out and places a hand on mine to stop me.

'I'm sorry,' I say thickly. 'I'm really off my A-game today. You've seen me with my shit together. It's just — you know —'

'Oh, Penny, please,' she laughs. I know she's just being kind. 'I was once so hungover that I cried watching a Nigella special.'

'Maybe this is the year I remember to chug Hydralyte *before* bed.'

'See, you're figuring it out,' she says. She gathers her phone and green juice and starts to make her exit. 'Now I know you're local, we'll run into each other all the time.'

'Thank you, Petra. For all of this.'

'How old did you turn? For your birthday?'

'Twenty-seven.'

She puffs out her cheeks and exhales like I've just told her that I ran an ultra-marathon. 'It only gets better from here.'

I want to believe her.

CHAPTER THIRTY-ONE

Wednesday.

Biscuits consumed today: seven.

Monthly reports to write: four.

Words spoken to Leo since That Night: zero.

Standard drinks consumed this week: ten thousand.

I should be working on the social strategy deck for Clean Juice Co due next week, but it's infinitely more appealing to just do nothing. Just when I thought I couldn't be more disconnected from my job, an exciting distraction appears in my inbox. Weekly email digests from job boards are like a cyanide capsule. I'm not desperate enough to use it, but it's comforting to know I have an escape route.

How many little kids do you think dream of being a communications manager for a retirement village in Dandenong? But if things got bad enough here … Or what about a content producer for the City of Moreland? A brand manager at Nestlé? A marketing assistant at a recruitment firm …

And then I spy Scout's logo among the ads. I immediately click through.

Account Director

Are you a digital rockstar? Do you live and breathe
UX? Does branding run through your veins? Do you
FLOURISH under pressure?

Scout Digital is a young and fast-growing digital
branding agency in the heart of Cremorne, and we're
looking for YOU!!

Joining our fun and dynamic accounts team and
reporting to our Head of Accounts, you'll build
relationships with national brands, oversee complex web
builds, and help manage a small team.

As our accounts rockstar-wizard-ninja, you will have:
- 3+ years in account management, agency-side
  preferable
- Experience leading projects and multifaceted digital
  builds (Shopify, WordPress)
- Brand identity development know-how
- Marketing strategy expertise
- Committed to giving 120% every day
- A passion for excellence

Benefits include:
- Super cool, centrally located office
- High emphasis on work–life balance
- Free fruit 3x a week

To apply, please submit to margot.camilleri@
scoutdigital.com.au:
- A short (minimum 5-minute) video explaining why
  you're awesome
- A cover letter answering these questions:

> *What is the biggest professional mistake you've ever made?*
> *Who is your dream client?*
> *Which* Game of Thrones *character are you?*
> *If you were an animal, what kind of animal would you be?*
> - A full resume, with minimum 3 references and their
>   contact details
> - Your favourite GIF
>
> *We can't wait to meet you!!!*

I have a few questions.

What is an 'accounts rockstar-wizard-ninja' and how do I avoid ever becoming one? What does she mean by a 'High emphasis on work–life balance'? Margot has been harassing us to add our work emails to our phones, and I'm running out of ways to blow her off. And can you really call free fruit a perk? I practically have to wait in the kitchen at delivery time with my keys between my fingers to get a banana before the creative team pillages the communal bowl. Also, what the fuck?

The senior team is away at a leadership conference all week, so I can't even ask Margot about it. I don't suppose I can forward her the ad and write, '*Hello excuse me what the fuck*'. I'll try the next best thing.

'Helena,' I say, pushing back from my desk and motioning for her to take her headphones off. 'Did you know about this?'

She rolls her chair my way.

'Oh, yeah,' she says easily. 'They asked me if I wanted it.'

'Did they.'

'I'm not interested,' she says, shrugging. 'I think I'm going to go back to uni and study biology next year.'

'Oh, really? That's great. That's different.'

'This job isn't very interesting, is it? I wanted to be a scientist when I was little, so a few weeks ago I went looking online for ...'

My face plays the part of an invested audience, but I'm not listening.

So they assessed the internal team and passed me over, even after all my brown nosing. If I didn't have Seek notifications, I wouldn't have found out until some new guy turned up one day and started bossing me around.

Haven't I spent the last two months being proactive, like she asked? Even though we didn't win the Evergreen account, she was still impressed with my work, and shouldn't that count? I already have *3+ years in account management, Experience leading projects and multifaceted digital builds (Shopify, WordPress), Brand identity development know-how,* and *Marketing strategy expertise.*

I wonder, though: *do* I even want that job?

How different would my day look? I'd be paid better, for one thing. It would reflect my experience and give me a little authority in the office. I prickle with annoyance, actually, noting that Margot could have at least *told us* we would be getting a new manager. '*Help manage a small team*', the ad says. Well, that's just me and Helena. And this job was supposed to be mine months ago. How dare she? Why does she have to be such a petty, pedantic bitch all the time? Doesn't she —

God, do you know what? I just can't be fucking bothered.

Getting that job wouldn't make me love working here. It wouldn't make my clients more interesting. It wouldn't make Margot respect me. On Sunday Annie told me she was working so hard that she hardly noticed working late into the night, and the only time I've felt like that here was when I was working on the Evergreen pitch.

At some point Helena finishes talking about microorganisms and the lab facilities at Monash University and rolls back to her own desk. But I can't focus. I don't have the gumption to care about a social campaign for a cellulite-busting juice made from mango, turmeric, and laxatives.

In my fuck-you funk, I decide I deserve a sugary pick-me-up. I tell Helena I'm going to get some air and head for the cafe. I want a muffin. And another biscuit.

I have to admit, my recent flush of enthusiasm for work has petered out since the disappointment of Evergreen's rejection. No Evergreen, no enthusiasm. I'm falling back into the habit of only speaking when called upon in meetings. And my clients, neglected while the pitch took priority, aren't holding my attention like they should. Except for this upcoming strategy session with CJC, my accounts are in maintenance mode. I'm just going through the motions. I've slapped together an uninspired post-campaign report for Jackson & Smith Realty, written a deeply mediocre blog for Deco Cinemas, renewed the security certificate on the Vic Credit Union login, and felt nothing.

Perhaps my apathy is more obvious than I think, I muse as I cross Swan Street to get to the cafe. Maybe Annie was right, and my attitude knocked me out of the running without me even knowing it. I hate when bad circumstances are my own fault. I'd rather blame the universe's ongoing conspiracy against my success and happiness. I am the centre of it, after all.

I'm still sulking when Sexy Barista cries out at my arrival ('*Signorina! Two sugars!*' God love him) and I take solace in a corner booth.

I suppose I don't even have to go back to the office today. There's nothing urgent to work on, and I'd only spend the afternoon building my fantasy wardrobe on Net-a-Porter. Kim might sell me out to Margot. I'll just say I wasn't feeling well.

But then, what good is a day off without someone to spend it with?

Annie's calendar doesn't allow for impromptu bursts of truancy. Once upon an easier time, I would have ambled over to Bec's coworking space and taken advantage of her flexible freelance schedule, but that's so off limits I don't even walk on that side of Swan Street anymore.

I can't go home, because Leo sometimes works from the dining room table. I'm actually doing a really good job of avoiding him by filling up my free time with extracurriculars. On Sunday afternoon I took in a double feature at the French Film Festival. On Monday I went for a free trial class of Bikram yoga and sweated all the booze out of my system, then replaced it all last night at The Ugly Duckling, where I read a book and steadily dwindled their gin supply with several double negronis.

Once it's past Leo's usual bedtime, I creep home and lock myself in my bedroom until he's left for work in the morning. But for a message on Monday (**Leo Deluca (14:06):** *Can we talk?*), we've been incommunicado. I've decided it's for the best.

I'm sure the moment I left on Saturday night, he was back on Tinder looking for some blondish, active-wearing, iced latte–slurping, Mimco bag–toting real estate agent to keep the other side of his bed warm. I'm sure he was successful too. The idea of yet another beige, personality-less woman in my house makes me prickle with anger. Whoever she is, she has probably been dipping into my Sephora loot in the bathroom before she tiptoes out in the morning. The nerve of him, inviting women like that — totally inoffensive, makeup-sample stealing, casual sex–enjoying women — into my house. Unbelievable.

I suppose I could call …

Oh.

My phone rings in my hand. It's Max.

I haven't heard from him since that text on Saturday night — not even a cursory message to see if I'm interested in a little Netflix and chill — and I haven't felt the need to reach out to him either. But for the occasional pang of self-indulgent sadness when I check my phone and find no new notifications, I've hardly noticed his absence.

Sexy Barista puts my coffee down in front of me, and I make a grateful sound as he leaves again. I stare at the picture on my phone.

It's a moody black and white photo, grainy from the old film used to take it. He's wearing a dark T-shirt that says *Aldente!* with the sleeve pushed up over his pale shoulder. His hair is wild, and his jaw looks razor sharp as he smirks down the lens. I took it on his vintage Pentax at a warehouse party in Coburg years ago, and he has used it as his profile picture ever since. I suppose I should find it flattering, but it feels like plagiarism, as though he's stolen my version of him and published it. If he's not going to be *my* Max, then neither he nor anyone else should have rights to my Max. The idea of someone swiping right on this picture makes me feel possessive. Who are all these other girls, and where did they come from, and how do they get their eyeliner wings even all the time, and why have they descended on the men in my life?

I shouldn't answer it. I should still be angry with him about my birthday. I'm entitled to that grudge.

But what if he's calling to apologise and he wants to make some incredibly romantic gesture to make up for his silence?

It rings and rings.

Well, but. What data do I have to suggest that he is even capable of grand romantic gestures? When was the last time I left his company and felt better for it? What could make it all worth it: the rules, the game playing, the therapy, the pathetic crying in the bath, the high-stakes Instagram stalking, the fight with Bec, the fight with Leo. Could anything?

I'm running out of time. It's going to ring out. What if I don't pick up and he calls someone else? What if my replacement is only a phone call away?

What would Dr Minnick say? She would tell me to stop choosing people who don't meet my needs. She would tell me to practise self-compassion. She would tell me that I have to break the pattern.

'*Shouldn't it all be easier than this?*' asks Annie's voice in my ear.

'*What about all the good things?*' I argue back. '*What about all the time and energy I've put into this relationship? Doesn't that count for anything?*'

'*Look at yourself,*' says the Leo of my mind's eye, frustrated and hurt as he was that night, and I can't shake him off. '*You're in the middle of a bad choice. Just stop.*'

My thumb hovers between two buttons: green and red. Answer or ignore. Choose Max or choose myself. The sick comfort of the familiar or the terrifying pain of the unknown.

Alright, okay. I know what I'm going to do. I'm going to —

My voicemail picks up the call, and a minute passes, and he doesn't leave a message. Sexy Barista drops off a sugar-crusted blueberry muffin at my table, and I reach the sad thought: *I wish I had someone to talk to.*

CHAPTER THIRTY-TWO

It's solely desperation that pulls me back to Collins Street again.

There are six suits ahead of me in the queue for coffee and danishes. Out of pure habit, I find myself checking them out. Even when shit is dire, I'm still on the lookout for an answer to the age-old dilemma: Who do I have to screw around here so I don't die alone?

The one with chic little glasses and a skinny tie is talking shop with the one whose biceps strain against the dark grey of his suit. I'd swipe right on them both. There's the balding executive whose tummy wobbles with every syllable he barks into his phone. Sometimes I wonder if the bar is higher when you're on a dating app, and if I'd be flattered by whoever is brave enough to approach me on a night out. The ugly ones treat you as poorly as the pretty men, so either way you lose. You might as well pursue someone who's nice to look at.

Anyway, the one I'm really making eyes at is the pastry case. I'd like to swipe right on the bright and decadent danishes, please. They are the crow that I'm about to eat. And I'm very tempted to take them to the park instead. Or I could go to the movies and spend the day in the dark while one of the Chrises — Evans or Pine or Hemsworth, it wouldn't matter — takes their shirt off and fights climate change and capitalism with their bare hands. Or whatever those films are about.

But I shouldn't. I'm twenty-seven now. The vodka benders and crying in the toilets aren't cute anymore. People my age are having kids on *purpose*. Annie has a mortgage, for fuck's sake. It's time to get my shit together.

Let me tell you something: accountability fucking sucks. It takes gargantuan balls to show up on someone's doorstep and say, '*I'm sorry. I was wrong. Please let me make it right.*'

Dr Minnick's sleek-bunned receptionist greets me with a polite smile. She's on the phone, arguing with someone about a meter reading, so I give her a thumbs-up and take a seat. There's no one else in the sparse, tasteful waiting room. The table beside me is stacked with *frankie* and *Vogue Living* and *W* magazines, and there's a white orchid bobbing under the breath of the air conditioner. I feel scrappy and underdressed in my jumper and jeans, my scuffed old boots, with the peeling faux leather of my handbag and the box of pastries in my lap.

'Thanks, Jen,' says the patient exiting Dr Minnick's office. He's middle aged and pink in the face, as though, like me, he spends his sessions in hysterics. I hope I sort my shit out before I'm forty-five.

'One hundred and twenty-five dollars today, Paul,' says the receptionist with her hand over her handset. She's no stranger to handing over the EFTPOS machine to crying people. 'Got your Medicare card? Great.'

Dr Minnick's door shuts again. Maybe she saw my name on the schedule today and thought, *Ha, not happening.* Maybe when her receptionist sorts out her meter reading and hangs up on AGL, she'll tell me that my appointment has been cancelled and that I'm no longer welcome in the building, and two surly security guards will appear to escort me downstairs.

That wouldn't be so bad, I think. Then I could eat both rhubarb danishes.

Two minutes pass, and then two more. Maybe she doesn't know I'm here. Should I knock? Maybe I got the time wrong. Was my appointment for 10:15 or was it 11:15? Where's my confirmation email again? I really need to clean out my inbox. Inbox Zero is LinkedIn folklore designed to make us strive for an impossible standard of productivity —

'You can go in,' says the receptionist.

'Oh. Right. Thanks.'

A black nameplate on Dr Minnick's door reads, 'Dr Jennifer Minnick. BPsychSc, MPsych (Clin). APS, CCLP.' I should ask her someday what those acronyms mean. I knock, and for a minute I wonder if she's just not going to answer. Imagine being rejected by the psychologist you see to deal with your pathological fear of rejection.

'Come in,' she calls, and I do. 'Good morning, Penny.'

She's smiling, but it's a little tight. Is the chill in her voice real or imagined?

'Good morning.' I hold the box of pastry out to her. 'Morning tea. If you want it.'

'That's very thoughtful of you,' she says, taking it from me and placing it on her desk. 'Let's get settled in first.'

'Oh. Okay.'

She's redecorated since I was here last. Anything would be an improvement over the grey box of misery it was before. The flamingo pink cushions clash marvellously with the red of the couch and a soft-looking mustard throw. Several brightly coloured candles are clustered on her side table. I actually kind of enjoy it. The colour palette feels more overwhelming than my personal crisis.

'What made you come back?' she asks. Even her notepad is loud today: bright turquoise. 'Last time we spoke, I got the impression that you felt like our sessions were unproductive.'

'I'm sorry about that,' I say, sitting down and addressing the floor. 'I feel bad about it. You were doing your job, and I was a dick to you.'

'I'm here to help you, Penny,' she says, and her fair even voice makes me feel even worse. At least if she was angry with me, I could twist this into some unreasonable, untenable relationship. 'Do you want help?'

'Of course I do.'

'Even if I can't tell you what you want to hear?'

I swallow, and when I chance a glance up at her face, she's not wearing a frown or a scowl but the same engaged, curious look as the other times I've been here.

'Yes. Yes, I need help. I'm sorry I was so ... that I got so upset.'

'You lash out when you feel vulnerable.'

'Yes.'

'Why do you think that is?'

'Because being vulnerable is fuc— it's scary.' I frown.

'Do you think you push people away to protect yourself? Like it's safer to be angry than to let them get close to you?'

Leo's crushed, pleading face appears in my mind. I have to close my eyes and remind myself to breathe. 'Yes.'

'So,' she says with a crispness that I understand to mean she accepts my apology, and that the session has now begun. Phew. 'You've told me before that you resent your friends' happiness. Do you think it's unfair that they've found it? Do you think, *Why not me?*'

'Yes.'

'Well, what do you do about it?'

'About happiness?'

'Yeah. What do you do in your day-to-day life that helps you achieve it?'

This question makes me feel hot and judged and exposed. 'I — I don't know. What kind of question is that?'

'Okay, I'm upsetting you. Let's try it like this —'

'Of course I'm upset. You're saying I'm too lazy to do anything about my mental health, like it's all my fault, like I deserve it because I can't get off my arse and fix it overnight.'

'I didn't say any of that,' she says gently. 'Those are your words. That's a lot of judgment you're carrying around.'

'I don't think those things.'

'Don't you?'

'The things that make me unhappy don't happen because of me.'

'How do you mean?'

'I'm unhappy because Bec fucks off at the first whiff of a boyfriend, I'm unhappy because Max is a withholding emotional narcissist, I'm unhappy because I'm stuck in a job I hate.'

'Okay,' she says, uncapping her pen. 'But what do you do about it?'

'I can't do anything about it. That stuff just happens.'

'Well, whether you cause something or just participate in it, what do you do to offset it or improve it? Take the situation with Bec: that's an unsatisfying relationship. If you can't fix it, then what do you do to find friends who know how to balance friendships and relationships?'

'I mean, I don't — it's really hard to make friends as an adult, everyone knows that.'

'Sure, but do you try? A running group, book club? Is there anyone you work with who you'd be friends with outside the office?'

'I don't know,' I mumble. 'None of those things sound like anything I would enjoy. No one's that interesting. It's probably why I keep going back to Max — all those first dates, the mindless small talk. It never goes anywhere. I don't connect with anyone else. It's exhausting.'

'Okay, let's talk about Max. You called him a withholding emotional narcissist.'

'That wasn't fair of me to say. He's lovely, really.'

'Would you think so if he was one of your friends' partners?'

This gives me pause. That's telling. I think of all the people who have stomped on Annie's heart in the last few years. Flaky Dev, hot and cold Amanda, chronic ghoster Lillian: I hate them for what they put her through. If I ever saw that married girl I'd chase her down and cause the biggest fucking scene Albury has ever seen; I would berate her for her heartlessness, her conveniently broken moral compass, her serious lack of character. And they only dated for two months. Max and I have been doing this dance for years. How must it look to my friends? No wonder Bec ran out of patience. It's amazing she held it together for this long.

'No,' I relent. 'I'd hate him for treating them like that.'

'Would you be happy to watch them return to this person who doesn't make them feel very good?'

I don't respond. Of course I wouldn't be happy.

'And yet you do it to yourself? Why?'

'Because it's been so long,' I sigh. 'I keep going back because of all the time I've already sunk into it. Because what does it say about me if it doesn't work out? What will it all have been for? It has to work out because it *has* to. I need it to.'

Dr Minnick writes something down. 'How does being with him make you feel?'

'Great when it's good. Shit when it's not.'

'When is it good?'

'When he wants me there,' I say, deflating. 'When he has space for me, mentally and emotionally, then he's affectionate and fun, and I feel like the luckiest person in the world.'

'And when is it bad?'

'When I'm too needy. When he's in a bad mood. When I hassle him about hanging out with my friends. Sometimes I'll say something dumb and he'll give me this look like I'm some annoying mosquito, and it makes me want to kill myself.'

'So for it to be good, you have to not have needs, not have friends and always say the right thing?'

'It sounds terrible when you say it like that.'

'Let me ask you a blunt question,' says Dr Minnick, pushing her heavy glasses up her nose to look at me properly. 'Why do you think you stay in situations that make you feel bad?'

'I'm not sure. It didn't start out like this. I just keep thinking that if I work really hard, if I can be really low maintenance, do the things he wants, be more like the old me, then I can turn it all around and it will be good again. He'll love me again.'

'Do you think people deserve to be happy?'

She turns to get the box of danishes from her desk and offers me one. Finally.

'Sure,' I say. 'Why not?'

'Even imperfect people? Even if they get things wrong?'

'I don't walk around thinking, *This person is taking too long to top up their Myki. They do not deserve joy or love or happiness in their life*. I'm not a sociopath.'

'What about you? Do you deserve it?'

'I …' I clear my throat. 'I have some shit to sort out. I make a lot of work for my friends.'

'You don't think you deserve happiness until you get your shit together? That's very subjective. That's a moving goalpost.

What happens if you never get your shit together? You just never deserve happiness?'

I shrug. 'Maybe.'

'The problem is that kind of thinking means you're going to punish yourself forever. You think you don't deserve happiness or love or acceptance, so you make decisions to reinforce those beliefs. You stay in unsatisfying relationships because you don't feel you deserve better. You don't ask for what you want because you don't think you have the right to ask for anything. You just stay unhappy and self-pitying, and then you punish yourself some more, and again, and again, and again. So until we teach you to value yourself, we can't teach you how to make sure other people value you.'

I busy myself with a mouthful of fruit and custard because I don't have an answer, and if I keep looking at her I'll start crying, and I can't remember if the mascara I put on this morning was waterproof or the good Marc Jacobs one I use when I need a pick-me-up.

'What do you see when you look in the mirror?' she continues. 'How do you think your friends see you?'

'Messy,' I say. 'I get drunk and say stupid stuff a lot. Greedy, selfish — I can't even be happy for Bec because I'm too caught up feeling sorry for myself. And Annie's got this new girlfriend and I have to force myself to ask her about her and brace myself for it, because she's happy and in love and all I can think is, *Well, now I have no one.* I make every situation about myself.'

She's taking notes, chewing on the inside of her cheek like Leo does sometimes when he's thinking, so I continue searching for adjectives to describe myself.

'Needy. Clingy. Max says I overthink everything. And cruel,' I say. 'You've seen how mean I can get.'

'Who told you you were all of those things?'

'No one,' I say. 'No one's going to say that to my face.'

'You think the people who care about you are sitting there thinking, *Penny's selfish and needy and cruel*? Why would they stick around if they thought that?'

I'm surprised by the severity of this blow. Just a moment ago, I was — well, not *fine*, but I was holding it together. But suddenly my throat is so tight I'm struggling to breathe, and I feel so hot that the sudden flow of unwelcome tears are glacial on my face. In just one second, I've come undone.

'But they don't,' I tell her, addressing my shaking hands. 'Do they? Bec, Max, my own fucking mum. They all get to know me and then disappear.'

Dr Minnick doesn't say anything, and I can't see her expression because I'm frozen, watching myself shred a wad of napkins in my lap.

'And everyone else,' I continue, 'well, it's a matter of time. My brother's overseas. Dad's hours away, and I never call him. Annie's so busy. She has this full, busy, important, hectic life and sometimes I wonder what would happen if I didn't call — would we ever speak again. Max: I can only hold his interest for so long. And he keeps me at arm's length most of the time, and then I asked for more and he tried it for a couple of months and now he fucking — I drove him fucking nuts, didn't I? And Leo. God. I really screwed that one up. You wouldn't believe it. And now — It's just going to be me one day, isn't it? Just me and a pet who doesn't know any better, after I've chased everyone away. Working some awful, impossible job I hate, coming home to my shit apartment with nothing to do, nothing and nobody. It's just going to be this feeling forever, magnified, getting worse every day that it doesn't get better.'

I reach for another tissue, but the box is empty. They're all a sodden, crumpled heap in my lap. Dr Minnick opens her desk drawer and pulls out a fresh box. In the middle of this dense fog and the heavy throb of my headache, I find the space to appreciate that she has sprung for the aloe vera tissues. No small feat given how many people she must have wailing and sobbing in this room every week.

She lets me cry it out. Time is a whir of colour, and new tears come as I look down the road to a long lonely life. Two minutes or two hours, I wouldn't know the difference.

Eventually I run out of tears, more from dehydration than from resolution, and still it takes me time to look up from my lap. I sit, resigned and exhausted, and wait for something to change.

Finally, Dr Minnick shifts in her chair. 'We're going to get you right, Penny,' she says quietly. 'You don't have to feel like this forever.'

I let out a dramatic, pathetic little wail.

'We're going to work through all of that together,' she continues. 'I'm going to teach you all the wonderful things about yourself, and how to believe them. That you're smart and brave and loyal and funny and kind. And that you deserve better than the way you allow yourself to feel and be treated.'

'You have to say that,' I tell her weakly. 'What are you going to do, say, "*You're a fucking bitch and you deserve this*"?'

'Stop,' she says softly.

'Sorry.'

She has put her pen and pad away, and when I look at the clock on the wall, I see that our session has run way over time. I hope she doesn't have another basket case waiting at reception, growing impatient and anxious as some needy stranger eats into their therapy hour.

Dr Minnick doesn't look concerned. She just smiles and says, 'You don't have to believe me right now. You just have to trust me. Okay?'

CHAPTER THIRTY-THREE

I'm so tired I nearly fell asleep on the tram on my way back to the office. My flimsy autumn jacket is no match for the furiously pelting rain, but I don't have the energy to care. It feels like all the nerves in my brain have been set on fire and hastily extinguished, leaving me burnt and aching. Moving at all is an incredible effort when it feels as though there are concrete blocks on my shoulders and in my boots. But I'm at my desk and no one seems to notice anything different. To them, it must just look like I was running late and forgot an umbrella. Why can't my coworkers sense that I've just been emotionally pulverised? Why isn't everyone rushing to hold me and tell me that everything is going to be okay?

I know that's silly. I know everyone has their own problems, and I can't be the only one in this office who has ever had a brush with mental health. I just don't know how they all hold it together. I want to take a hundred Valium, or stand on my chair and scream, or run full pelt in any direction to get away from this huge, hopeless, helpless feeling. I might have to settle for hiding under my headphones and keeping to myself all day. I'll have to sink into something mind-numbing — publishing requests or data entry — to soothe my burnt-out nerves.

'What time do you call this?' hisses Margot, suddenly appearing at my desk.

'No, I — had an appointment, I texted you about it last week —'

'Your leave needs to be put in the calendar so we know where you are.'

'Sorry, I'm sorry, I forgot I booked it —'

'Clean Juice Co has been waiting in the conference room for ten minutes,' she snaps.

Shit. Shit! I completely forgot I had the strategy session with CJC this morning. I haven't thought about work in days; I even forgot to prepare the deck for them. What the fuck am I going to do?

'Why are you wet? Did you swim here?'

'It's raining,' I mumble, scrambling for a pen and paper, and she clicks her tongue.

'Clean yourself up and get in there,' she says. She turns on her heel to head back into the meeting.

Fuck. Fuck fuckity fuck fuck. I dash into the ladies' and sigh at my disaster of a face. My hair is stringy from the rain, so all I can do is yank it into a severe bun. My mascara has pooled and smudged enough to make me look like Jenny Humphrey in the dying days of *Gossip Girl*. I scrub off as much as I can with the last sheet left in the paper towel dispenser, but now I look even rawer and more ruined than before.

It's getting worse, all of it.

Consulting my pink and puffy reflection, I give up. My simpering compliance with anything CJC and Margot say will be my only tool today.

'Thank you, Penny,' says Margot as I slip into the meeting room, and I try to give something of an apologetic and embarrassed smile that no one matches.

'So sorry, guys, I was just —'

'I've got it,' says Margot sharply, and I recognise that I've been put in my place. She picks up wherever she left off, something about the SEM campaign, I suppose. I can't remember what the acronyms she's using mean, even though I use them every day. I resolve to do some sloppy note taking.

'*SEM user engagement goal 12% increase if campaign target effective audience (fem 70% men 30)*,' I write. '*PM to org new copy, media prod., video (?)*'

Even as I write, I'm not confident I'll remember what any of this means later, and it will surely be embarrassing to have to ask Margot for her help, but she moves on to her recommendations for the advertising budget, delicately dancing around the numbers in a way that I never can. Usually this client is suspicious and argumentative throughout every interaction, but Margot has him purring like a kitten. I try to remember his most cutting remark in our last meeting, remember what it was like to care about meetings and clients and acronyms at all, but everything is moving so slowly, and even blinking feels like such an effort, like there are tiny lead weights attached to my eyelashes, and the room is so lovely and warm …

The door slams shut and I wake with a jolt.

Where am I? Wait, this is work. Who's here? No one. The room is empty. Why is my mouth so dry? Why does it feel like someone has inserted a fire extinguisher hose into my ear and filled up my skull with foam?

The big screen still shows a copy of Margot's notes — no screensaver, so someone was just in here. Or did I move the mouse with my hand when I woke up? Oh shit, oh *shit*, why was I asleep?

I'm pulling at the strings of my memory when I hear the ominous *click-click-click* of Margot's stilettos. CJC. The hard-to-please marketing manager. I'm frozen in terror as I hear the door close behind me. I know I'm doomed.

Margot sits opposite. I can't look at her. I'm staring at a tiny crack in the conference table and listening to the tick of the clock. I never knew a second could last so long.

'I hardly know where to start,' she says.

Hot tears form and I squeeze my eyes shut to ward them off, but it doesn't help.

'Your contempt for your job, your contempt for *me*, your attitude, the dozens of unbillable hours on clients we don't sign, your uninspired performance these last six months, and now this.'

'I'm sorry,' I say through a sniffle. 'I'm sorry. I didn't mean to, today has just been —'

'But it's not just today, is it? It's every day. Something is wrong *every day*.'

'I'm not trying to …' I trail off because I don't know what I'm not trying to do. I pick at the edge of my cuticle, ripping it until a speck of blood appears.

'That's exactly the point. You're not trying.'

All the oxygen in the room has been replaced with callous judgment. I try to take in a steadying breath, but all I can do is take sips of air, and my ever-racing thoughts grind to a standstill. I can't think of anything except the pain in my finger.

Finally, after what must be minutes of silence, Margot sighs.

'Penny,' she says, sounding tired, 'last time we had this meeting I asked you if you really wanted this job.'

'I know you did. I do, I want it.'

'I don't think you do,' she says softly. 'I don't think you enjoy it. I hardly ever see you go the extra mile. I really felt like you were turning things around when we went after Evergreen, and I thought, *There's the girl I hired*. But when that didn't pan out, you lost interest again. You don't get excited when we get a new account, you never walk in with a big smile on your face.'

'Well, I just —'

'If you could be anything in the world, would you want to be an account manager at a digital agency?'

I laugh thinly. 'That's not really how the world works, is it? Dream jobs are, like, foreign correspondent, handbag designer, child of nepotism. That doesn't mean — I don't *not* like this job. It's my job.'

'I love my job,' she tells me. 'Not every day is fantastic. Today, this conversation — it's not my favourite day. But I look forward to coming to work every day.'

I don't know what I can say to that. I can't fathom feeling like that about any job. Surely even the third-generation Kardashians don't spring out of bed *every* morning.

'Listen. I know you think that I have it out for you, but I don't — no, truly, Penny, I don't,' she says, catching my disbelieving little scoff. 'You don't like my management style, but I don't do it to make your life difficult. I believe you're capable, but I never see you apply yourself. You aren't giving me your best, and that's frustrating. When you're in a good mood, you're unfocused. When you're in a bad mood, you're unproductive.'

This feels like a losing battle, so no matter how much this stings, I shrug.

'I'm going to ask you again. Do you like your job here?'

There's a long silence as I battle with myself for the best way to answer her. Saying no means I'm fired, but saying yes will drag this conversation out and I'll have to sit here all afternoon hearing about how she doesn't believe me and all the areas

I need to improve on. I don't know which would be worse: unemployment or staying here one minute longer.

She doesn't speak, just watches me.

'No,' I say, defeated at last. 'I don't like my job.'

'I know you don't,' says Margot. 'I'm glad you can finally admit that.'

Oh god, I hate her. I hate her fake sympathetic voice. I hate the weird ripples of her frown. I hate everything about her. I'd like to revise my answer earlier: Margot specifically does not deserve joy or love or happiness in her life. I want to grab her bun and yank it off her head. I want to howl. I want to throw myself on the floor and have a proper screaming breakdown.

'I think you know this is for the best,' she says. 'Pack up your things and head home. You'll be paid out until the next pay run, but I think you're done here.'

'But what do I do now?' I ask, suddenly pleading. That hot hate has given way to fear and uncertainty. The prospect of having nowhere to be tomorrow isn't a relief, it's terrifying. 'This is all I've ever done. I don't want to start over. This is all I'm good at.' I pause. 'And I'm not even fucking good at it.'

'Starting over is freedom,' she tells me. As I rub my eyes on my sleeve, I see her absently playing with the knuckle on her left ring finger, and I realise there's so much I don't know about her, so many things I never bothered to ask. 'Believe me.'

CHAPTER THIRTY-FOUR

I feel sorry for the Uber driver who has to deal with me sobbing in his backseat, cradling a box of junk from my desk. A pair of patent black pumps I forgot I owned in the first place. Polaroids of my friends. My office mug. Twenty sachets of miso soup and porridge from those weeks I try to exist on nothing else. A frayed phone charger.

This is what my life has boiled down to. Holding a box of crap and crying in the middle of the day, in a ride I can't afford, headed somewhere I know I shouldn't go. What happened, and how did I get here?

Punt Road is gridlocked, so I have ample time to pull at every loose thread.

Can you believe that traumatic therapy session was only this morning? I managed to be brutally vulnerable, get dissected by a relative stranger like a frog in a Year 10 science lab *and* lose my job in just one day. My universe has been spun off its axis. This is one productive quarter-life crisis.

I don't want to think about everything that was said in Dr Minnick's office. I want to lock it up in a box and never open it again. All those things I said — I don't think I've ever even allowed myself to think them. Was I telling the truth? Do I hate myself to the point of self-destruction? Can more sessions with her really change anything? Maybe she was just being nice. Maybe she just wants to keep a client on the books. It was scary and impressive, the way I could tell her something off the cuff and she could tie it back to a larger pattern, one that I haven't even noticed, and I'm the one living in it. What does she know that I don't? Everything, apparently.

Can anyone ever really be self-aware? I used to think so, but now I'm not so sure. I liked to think that so much time listening to the voice in my head had taught me who I am and why I think and feel like I do, but it turns out I have no idea. Who is this defeated, lost little human in the backseat of a stranger's car on a Monday afternoon? Why does she implicitly trust the opinions of those who keep her at a distance, and never those of the people who care about her? Do I respect my friends at all? How do I undo all these years of mistakes and give myself a clean slate? Do I even deserve one?

Nicholson Street has been stripped naked by autumn, its trees standing grey and leafless on either side of the road. Box hedges shield the moneyed-up Abbotsford residents from their neighbours. A woman with an immaculate blow-dry bends down with a biodegradable plastic bag to pick up after her Frenchie. At the cafe down the street, a waiter with a face tattoo deposits turmeric lattes at a waiting table. An elderly lady in a headscarf shuffles along the footpath, a hessian trolley full of groceries dragging along behind her. It's the merging of two different worlds, and I'm between them too: on the precipice of a decision, but unable to bring my arm up to press the buzzer.

With my box of belongings on my hip, I fish my phone out of my damp jacket pocket and call Annie's number. I'll tell her what's happened — just the highlight reel for now. The gritty, miserable details will be better saved for a night on the couch with a case of wine — and she'll tell me exactly what to do.

Annie's the smart one, the level one, the one who can tell it like it is without stomping on my heart in her size eight Louboutins.

It goes to voicemail mid-ring. *Oh god*, I think, *now she doesn't want to hear from me either. No more Annie, no more anyone. I said it aloud in Dr Minnick's office and manifested it into existence.*

Oh, thank fuck. A message from her pops up.

Annie Lin (15:22): In court
Annie Lin (15:23): Call you later

No *x* or *babe* or emoji. Annie loves emojis. Is the subtext to this text that she's so sick of my shit that I don't even warrant a little cartoon heart? I'm on a runaway rollercoaster today. I can't count on anything, and nothing is safe: even the tiniest movement or action could result in a four-hundred-foot drop.

Well, perhaps Annie's unavailability is a sign in itself. It could be the universe giving me permission to be here at Max's front door. Maybe it's a good idea. Maybe this is the great story arc I've been crawling towards all this time, and today's crises have been the push needed to set my real life into motion, the final frontier. I'm picturing it now — Max throwing his arms wide, and me collapsing into them, rescued, wanted, and safe from the storm.

But then … that's not really how anything looks, ever, not even in the cheesiest Netflix originals. What does my life really look like?

When he finds me on his doorstep carrying a Cookie Monster mug, wet and tearstained and blotchy and fragile, will he let me snivel into his neck while I tell him what a horrible day I've had? Will he rub my back and tell me it's not my fault, that Margot is a fucking bitch? Will he help me redo my resume and promise that it's all going to be alright as long as we're together?

Or will he tell me that I'm bringing a lot of negative energy into his room right now and that he doesn't have the capacity to take me on when his thesis deadline is looming? Will he say, 'Aw, buddy, that sucks,' and then will I find myself inexplicably on my knees for him twenty minutes later?

I don't know. I don't know I don't know I don't know. I don't even know if he's home. My memory of his work schedule, once something I knew by heart, is lost.

Penelope Moore (15:26): Are you home?
Penelope Moore (15:27): I really need to see you

As soon as I hit send, he appears at the end of the street. He's a few hundred metres away, but I know it's him by his long stride and the slope of his shoulders, and the red beanie we've been fighting over for years. I see him pull out his phone, pause to read the message on his screen, shake his head, and pocket it again.

Fuck. *Fuck.* I dash across the street to hide behind one of his neighbour's parked cars. How would it be if he found me squatting on his stoop like some kind of deranged stalker who can't take a hint? I'd be whipped out as a funny anecdote at his next poetry reading. 'This next one is about my ex-girlfriend, a psychopath who doesn't get Radiohead.'

Maybe if I just pop over there and explain …

But holy hell, I'm tired. Of so much.

I'm tired of being cool with any of it: being sent home after sex, of overthinking everything I do and say and feel, of being his backup option, of all this shame.

All these months of pretending to be cool with things that smashed my heart into a million pieces. All those drafted and redrafted text messages, carefully phrased so he had no excuse not to reply. The number of hours I've logged staring at my phone or cautiously scrolling through @amber.lou.92's Instagram feed searching for all the things she was and I could never be. The excuses I made to my friends — that I lost Bec over him. All the reasons I invented to explain away his indifference. The wanting, the waiting: it all comes down to nothing, just me squatting beside a recycling bin watching the biggest disappointment of my life searching for his keys at the bottom of his vegan leather backpack.

CHAPTER THIRTY-FIVE

I'm halfway up the street before I realise I've left the things from my desk on Max's doorstep, but I can't go back. I don't have much dignity these days, but what little I have left is worth more than anything in that box.

I feel at once too young and too old for this. People talk about their twenties as this energetic, colourful learning experience — but I don't know when it's supposed to get easier. I wonder if I'll ever get it right, or if I'll still be a hurricane in my forties and fifties, constantly trying on paths and partners that don't quite fit.

The walk back to Victoria Street is a slow disgraced retreat. I don't check my phone: Max isn't going to reply, Annie's in court, and I've pushed everyone else away. As I wait for the pedestrian crossing, I pace the pavement. If I'm moving, I'm not thinking. If I think, it will become real, and I'll start crying and never, ever stop.

Was Dr Minnick right? Have I latched on to Max all this time because I subconsciously wanted to reinforce the idea that I'm unworthy of more? But what if it isn't my subconscious at all? Maybe I *am* unworthy of being loved, and maybe I'm not manifesting these unfulfilling relationships at all. Maybe my worth is being reflected back at me, and I'm getting exactly what I deserve.

This thought hits me like a lightning bolt, and the man at the crossing with me jumps as I let out a bark of a sob.

The light changes and I make a break for it, crossing the intersection and flinging myself into the nearest bottle shop.

I want vodka, but they're charging $70 for a bottle of Absolut, and I don't have a job anymore. I grab the cheapest white wine they have, cry-laugh at the poor terrified cashier as I frantically smack my card against the reader and get back out onto the street in under three minutes. I have a plan now. It's not a good one, but it's a plan.

No one on Victoria Street would judge me for twisting the cap off this bottle and chugging it here in broad daylight, but I keep a white-knuckled hold on its neck and my self-restraint until I make it to my street, up my front steps and through my front door.

There.

Peace.

Safety.

Half the bottle is gone before I've even made it to the kitchen. Leo's not home, so I dump my bag on the table and pull off my wet coat, boots, jeans and jumper right there, making my way to my bedroom in my socks and smalls under the sedation of cheap white wine and trauma.

I fish out the emergency Valium from my underwear drawer and take two with a slug of Riesling. I fall onto my bed, my lovely, comfy, safe bed. It's impossible to believe that only weeks ago I was lying here with Max and he was telling me about the scar from falling off his bike on his seventh birthday, and I drew patterns in his chest hair and thought, *I think I really love you.* How romantic. How wonderful. How foolish.

I replay this scene in my head, watching myself trace my little finger along the delicate white line on his chin, just visible through a day or two's worth of stubble, on repeat for so long that the shadows on my wall fade from grey to black.

Maybe I doze off or maybe I don't, but my mind grinds back to real-time with the mechanical ticking of Leo's bike being wheeled down the hall.

'Weird,' I hear him say from the kitchen. And then, 'Penny?'

'Bedroom,' I reply, not bothering to raise my voice. He must hear me anyway, because there's the soft tap of knuckles on my door before he cracks it open and pops his head in.

'You're home?'

'Yeah.'

'Are you starting a nudist colony?'

'What?'

'You left your pants in the kitchen.'

'Oh.' I wait to see if my brain invents an excuse, and it doesn't. 'Sorry.'

Leo frowns and pushes the door wider. 'You alright?'

'I'm *super.*'

'I haven't seen you in ages,' he says, leaning against the doorframe. 'If it wasn't for the missing Tim Tams I would've thought you'd moved out.'

I don't say anything.

'Look, we don't have to talk about it.'

'Okay,' I say. I expect relief to come from this, his white flag of an avoidance tactic, but it doesn't. I don't know if I feel anything at all.

'You want to do face masks and watch something dumb?' he asks.

'How dumb?' I squeak.

'Dumb as you like,' he says. '*Gilmore Girls* dumb, even.'

Leo is the sun, and he's shining on me. His hopeful little smile is infectious, and my desire to stay drunk and sad and angry forever dissolves. Leo doesn't care about my sins and shortcomings. Leo just likes me with no strings attached. Not like my family, who are biologically bound to care about me. Not like Bec, who only loves me when I don't have any problems to burden her with. Not even like Annie, whose free time and patience will run thin sooner or later. No, Leo is the only one anymore who sees me for who and what I am: just someone trying their almost best and failing a lot along the way.

And everything is better when I'm with him. I can't believe I didn't see that before. With Leo, I'm my quickest and silliest self, and he doesn't mind when I'm not. Even when we're in a bar full of sane, pretty women, he stays engaged in our conversation and I don't spend the whole night sneaking off to the bathroom to apply more highlighter to the dip in my upper lip. We can just order half the menu from Thai Corner, put on our pyjamas and slather our faces in a clarifying mask, and he likes me just the same. Loves me, even. He said so himself.

'Fucking Rory,' he tsks a while later. He uses his chopsticks to pick a prawn out of my fried rice, and when I make a noise of protest, he says, 'I'm helping! You've been saying you want to go vegetarian for ages! You're welcome!'

On-screen, Rory steals a boat because her boyfriend's dad criticised her. I wish I knew how to hot-wire a boat. It seems like a useful survival skill.

'Yeah,' I say. 'Fucking Rory.'

Leo smiles at me and gives my ankle, sitting in his lap, a little squeeze.

Look at him. He's beautiful. He doesn't even get annoyed when I invade his personal space.

'I'm glad I'm home.'

'Me too,' he says, and I know he means it. 'I hardly knew what to do with myself without my little neurotic sidekick.

I had no one to watch *Bake Off* with. You would've been furious at the bullshit that got a handshake during biscuit week. Chocolate chip, *honestly*.'

He makes me laugh. His presence takes a weight off my shoulders, like nothing very bad could happen as long as he's within reach.

Am I dizzy from the better half of a bottle of cheap wine, or is it the smell of my lavender soap on his skin? I watch the sharp line of his jaw as he bites back a smile and calls Emily Gilmore a bad bitch.

How stupid can one woman be? Why would anyone run away from this? This, *this* is the answer. I made such a mess, but here we are now, and that's all that matters. Leo will fix this like he fixes everything else.

He doesn't notice as I take our bowls and put them on the coffee table. He lets go of my ankle easily as I shift in closer.

'Hi,' I say softly, inches from him.

He blinks. 'Hey,' he says. 'What's wrong?'

And then I do it. Quickly, so I can't talk myself out of it, I kiss him. I seem to linger there forever, my lips on his, but he doesn't pull away, so I do it again. I get my hands in his hair, and it's good, warm, soft, sweet, and it makes everything right, all of it, all these long months of fucking up everything I touch, it's all going to be better now —

'We should stop,' he says, hoarse and quiet.

'It's fine,' I say into his lips, redoubling my efforts. 'It's fine, it's great, I promise.'

'Penny.' He presses his forehead to mine.

'I want to. We should. Here, take your shirt off.'

He hesitates a moment, and then we're kissing again.

This will make everything better. I know it will. I've just taken a little detour from the path I was always meant to be on, that's all, but Leo's warm hand is on my waist under my T-shirt, and I don't want to think any longer about Dr Minnick, or Max, or Margot, or Bec.

Maybe he's telepathic, because he lifts me off the couch with alarming ease — where did he get such lovely strong arms from? He never talks about going to the gym — and spares me the indignity of sex soundtracked by Lorelai Gilmore's endless chatter, and blindly, too busy being kissed, takes me down the hall and into his room.

Leo sleeps soundly on the other side of his bed. I watch him take deep, even breaths, and I try to match them with my own. Well, *that* certainly took my mind off things. I could sleep a thousand years on his soft blue sheets, could curl up in the nook of his neck and stay there forever, where it's safe and warm and quiet. When he wakes up, I'd like to ask him about his tattoos: on his collarbone (a bee), his stomach (some kind of wreath) and his inner arm (two sets of coordinates). Maybe he could hold my hand while I get a tattoo of my own – probably some cheesy and emotional song lyric on my shoulder blade, if my friends let me get away with it. It's nice to think of all the things we might do together in the future. I'm comforted by the idea of his arm around me as we walk back from breakfast at the cafe, perhaps tomorrow, or even every weekend, and if I don't spiral too hard and manage to keep things steady between us for the next few months, maybe he'd like to come with me and my dad to London for Christmas with my brother. Yes, that would be nice, but I won't ask him until October, maybe, so as not to spook him, and —

The fantasy screeches to a halt. There are rubber marks where the tyres of this whole tangent have skidded on the road. I've been here before. And I'm almost certainly not the first woman who has lain here in his lovely sheets dreaming about an imaginary relationship he's not interested in pursuing. I try to remember one of their faces to imagine the scene properly, but they all blur together, and I dare not even think of all the sleepovers he had at their houses. Something uncomfortable flares up in my throat. Jealousy tastes sour in my mouth. Maybe they all got the same performance I did. Can he even tell the difference between us once the lights go off and the clothes go flying?

He turns over in his sleep and slumps his arm over my middle, and it feels like a cage.

I can't do it. I can't wake up and have a conversation with him about how he's only looking for something fun and casual, which I've always interpreted to mean *Be cool and relaxed and prove to me, endlessly, that you're worth my time, and know I can take it away at any moment*, but which actually means *Let's fuck on my schedule until I meet someone I want to be with*. And what did he mean when he said we should stop? Was he saying that he knew I couldn't handle another messy faux-casual arrangement? Does he know better than I do what's good for me?

The future flashes before me, and it's all too familiar. Our friendship will dissolve into a fling that he doesn't really want to be in. I'll start searching for meaning in the punctuation of his texts. He'll be vague when I ask if he wants to do something on the weekend. I'll convince myself that I'm overthinking it again, and then he'll say something that confirms I'm not.

Or maybe I'll convince him to make a real go of it, and the temporary high won't be enough to offset the inevitable low, when someday he discovers that he's tired of me, like he did with his last girlfriend and her sweet, ancient cat, and his disinterest will turn to disgust, and I'll be crying again, hurt again, alone again, worse off than ever before.

I slide out from under his arm and collect my clothes from the floor.

Don't look at me like that. This is what's best for both of us.

There are only so many pieces of myself I can give away and replace with wine and jokes and chagrined anecdotes of lovelessness. There's hardly any of me left to give.

I shut my bedroom door and retreat under the covers, where I can't fuck up anything else. If everything I touch turns to shit, when will I learn to keep my hands to myself?

CHAPTER THIRTY-SIX

I wake up before the sun and put some things in a bag. Pyjamas, a couple of T-shirts, jeans, a holey old jumper, underwear, moisturiser. I pick one of Leo's books from the bookcase, and I shut the front door quietly on my way out.

Bless Melbourne's coffee culture for having a cafe open at 5 am. I get a latte the size of my forearm and get through half of it by the time I get to Southern Cross Station. The first train to Castlemaine doesn't leave for half an hour, but my brain is sluggish and my bones feel heavy after the hyperintensity of yesterday, so I don't mind waiting while my body catches up.

Yesterday was a low point like I haven't seen in quite some time. But I don't want to think about that. Every time I try — allow myself to remember Dr Minnick's voice, or the sickly sympathetic look on Margot's face, or Max's cool indifference, or the rise and fall of Leo's sleeping chest — I feel the internal panic begin to take root, and I worry it's a well I'll never climb out of.

When everything gets a bit too much to handle, all the Valium in the world doesn't work half as well as just running away from your problems.

I went on an impromptu solo holiday to Thailand after Max and I broke up the first time, and if you ignore the day or two I spent at the pool silently crying behind my sunglasses and slurping back Long Island iced teas while families with screeching children in neon floaties glared at me for bringing down the vibe, it was a pretty effective distraction. I got through six books in a week and a half. I wrote long indulgent journal entries every day, joined three beach yoga classes, went out one night and made out with an extremely hot and extremely stupid surfer from Brisbane, then came home sunburnt and almost ready to start my post-Max life. I continued drinking excessively and making out with beautiful strangers for several months afterwards. That's just life at twenty-two.

But that isn't really an option right now. I'm unemployed with zero prospects and an obliterated safety net. Wallowing poolside in Koh Samui won't fix anything. The best I can do is show up on Dad's doorstep and numb my brain with police procedurals and home cooking, and spend some time working in the garden alongside him in uncomplicated, unquestioning silence. At least until I'm ready to face reality again.

The train ride takes about an hour and a half, or two cups of scalding hot tea and four chapters of *Norwegian Wood*. Trust Leo to have lovely taste in books. He has drawn an asterisk beside the lines he likes, and even though it gives me a tummy ache, I look for them on every page. It's like having his voice in my ear.

My phone is dead, so I can't call to let my dad know I'm visiting. My arrival will just have to be a surprise. I pick up a sponge cake from the bakery on the high street, fat and tall with whipped cream, and spend twenty minutes walking the scenic route to his place.

The weather is cooler out here, as though there's more air to go around. A bearable Melbourne chill is a finger-numbing winter in Castlemaine. The indecisive April has given way to a frigid May, and it feels like the endless grey sky is reflecting my insides.

Just the sight of Dad's little period cottage, with its overgrown wisteria and bay window, takes a weight off my shoulders. It's so quaint and far away from home; it's like my problems could never find me all the way out here.

'Pepper!' cries Dad as he answers the door. No one else is allowed to call me Pepper. Not even my brother.

'*Papaaaa!*'

'This is a surprise,' he says, pulling me in for a hug. He smells like clean laundry and firewood, like he always has. Eau de Dad. 'Is everything alright? Why aren't you at work?'

'I just … y'know.' But of course he doesn't. I never tell him the ugly details of my life. He has worked so hard to take care of me, it seems cruel to tell him that he's failed. 'I'm taking some leave. I just wanted to visit my dad for a while. Is that okay?'

'It's perfect. Actually, you can make yourself useful,' he says. 'I need someone to help me hang some pictures. I don't have a level, and I can never tell if they're straight.'

'And I brought a cake!'

'This is why you're my favourite. Don't tell Chris.'

I beam.

'C'mon. We'll have a coffee and get to work.'

I know he doesn't believe my vague excuse, but he has the good grace not to pick at it. Dad's not the loquacious type.

It used to frustrate me: I would go to him with my inflated teenage problems and wail and cry, and he would give me practical advice. He always had time to listen. I never felt like an inconvenience. But I wanted insight and wisdom and understanding, and when he didn't offer it, it felt like he was withholding. As I learned to keep my worries to myself, they began to rot inside me, and the decay grew wild and unruly.

Now, though, as a terminally worried adult too overburdened to even begin untangling my own messes, I can appreciate the comfort of a warm silence of a morning spent in the garden with someone who doesn't pry.

Annie gets upset if she finds out that I'm keeping things from her, as though it means I don't trust her with it. Sometimes telling my friends something means discussing it at length, studying it, writing an effing thesis about it, but I need to be ready for that. I need time to let my body process it fully, to breathe it in and allow it to filter into all of my cells and out again so I can understand my emotions without them being coloured by a well-intentioned outsider's perspective. Dad gives me the space to do that. He preached about meditation long before I gave in and tried it. If I want to talk, he'll sit and listen through countless cups of tea, but he never forces the conversation.

Instead we just potter around the house together. We make coffee and put fresh sheets on the bed in my room. We fill the house with surface-level topics, and he's generous enough to keep his questions to himself.

Even though I've never lived here, I always feel at home surrounded by all our old furniture, his patently crap music playing (The Doors, I ask you) and Gary the overweight tabby following me from room to room.

As Dad searches for picture wire, I sink onto my bed and look around at the sweet little time capsule of things I left behind when I moved out of home. Among my Enid Blyton books, compilation CDs and a half-empty bottle of candy-sweet Vera Wang *Princess* perfume, I find an embarrassing photo of me at my school formal in a slinky backless green dress. At the time, I thought it was exactly like the Keira Knightley one in *Atonement*, but now I see that it looks nothing like it. My hair was bleachedto-death white and my tan was more Oompa Loompa than sun-kissed-via-Santorini, but I thought I looked great. That night, I got drunk on sneaky sips of Bacardi from the flask hidden in Matt Johansson's suit pocket. I danced so long that I woke up with great black bruises on the balls of my feet.

Back then, I was set on becoming a photographer. I was sure that one day my name would be in *Vanity Fair* and *i-D* and *Vogue*, despite no evidence of any artistic talent. I figured it would come eventually, fuelled by my interesting life and insightful understanding of the world around me. I would be successful and happy, and I'd have great hair. I would get regular manicures and drink in beautiful bars with fascinating people and I would look incredible in pencil skirts. I would move to London or New York and I'd have my shit together. This girl in her polyester dress had the world at her bruised feet. It all just felt like a matter of time.

This photo was taken nearly ten years ago. I wonder what I'll think of myself when I'm thirty-seven. Maybe this current crisis will be a momentary blip on an otherwise unblighted life. I wonder if I'll be living in a terrace house, finally growing out my fringe, only seeing Dr Minnick for emergencies. I wonder if I'll ever learn to like myself. I wonder if I'll even still be here at all.

Skinny little seventeen-year-old me deserved better than the disappointment that would become of her future. Perhaps 27-year-old me deserves better too. Maybe it's time I start taking responsibility for the hurricane I've become. What would Dr Minnick say to that? Would she agree? I could try ringing her receptionist tomorrow for a FaceTime session. Would she even take my call? As I'm clutching this old photo and lying, literally, in a bed of my own making, I realise that there's nothing left for me to lose. Perhaps it's time to try.

CHAPTER THIRTY-SEVEN

After four days of isolation and country air, curiosity creeps in. I've never spent this much time away from my phone before. The world could have come down around us and I wouldn't know it. Annie must be worried. Leo must be furious. Max must be, well, horny. By Friday night, I work up the courage to crack open the door to my mind and see if I'm ready to deal with any of it. Guilt waits there, ready to wrap itself around my throat. How do I feed the beast? How do I quell the anxiety that believes I'm universally loathed?

'*Counter it*,' says my logical side. It speaks in Dr Minnick's voice. '*Prove yourself wrong*.'

So I turn my phone on for the first time in days, and my screen bursts to life with notifications. ASOS has a sale on. MyFitnessPal tells me it's time to step on the scales. Tinder begs me to come back. Co-Star says, '*Your heart is a house on fire*', and I think, *No shit. Burn the whole thing down.*

Notifications from Messenger are next.

Max Fitzgerald (22:07): Just saw this. You good?
Max Fitzgerald (22:23): Wanna come over?

It's funny to think that this is over now. Over the last year, if I ever allowed myself to fantasise about the end of my relationship with Max, it involved an empowered monologue full of clever, cutting quips. He would tear up, and I would remain composed. He would beg for another chance, and I would deny him. But that's not going to happen. I don't feel much like fighting. I don't feel much of anything, except a little disappointed in this unsatisfying ending to a long and treacherous journey. With an indifference I never thought I would feel, I delete our entire chat history. Gone in a single swipe.

Next: Annie.

Annie Lin (18:12): Hey babe, all okay with you? To what do I owe the pleasure of a middle-of-the-day call?

Annie Lin (06:57): Checking in x

Missed call from Annie Lin (17:27)

Annie Lin (22:30): Hey where are you?

Annie Lin (22:30): Leo is freaking out

Annie Lin (22:31): Did something happen?

Missed call from Annie Lin (22:40)

Annie Lin (05:59): Okay, I spoke to Chris and he said your dad said you're with him. Are you okay? What's happened? Leo won't tell me anything.

Annie Lin (08:00): Call me when you can, worried about you x

That makes me feel terrible. I didn't think about how it would look to Annie, with whom I've been in near-constant contact with for almost a decade. Thank goodness for my brother, even if he is on the other side of the planet, or else she might have filed a missing person's report.

Penelope Moore (19:43): I'm so sorry. I didn't mean to freak you out. Lots going on. Can I call you tonight? Let me know when you're free. Love you.

Finally, I steel myself for the big one.

Leo Deluca (06:07): Where'd you go?
Leo Deluca (06:34): Going to the cafe, will get you a coffee
Leo Deluca (11:19): Are you okay?
Missed call from Leo Deluca (18:55)
Leo Deluca (18:57): Can you call me back?
Missed call from Leo Deluca (22:01)
Leo Deluca (22:43): Annie doesn't know where you are either.
Leo Deluca (09:14): Heard from Annie. Glad you're alive.

The guilt stings like salt and lemon and tequila in a fresh wound. I hate to think of the coffee he bought me slowly curdling on the kitchen bench. There's a symbolism here that I know will cut like a knife if I ever get to the bottom of it, so I don't try. The little green dot next to his picture tells me he's online now, and I wonder if he's staring at my name too.

Penelope Moore (19:48): Hey

He's seen it! There! A read receipt! See, everything is going to be okay. We'll probably just paper over the whole thing, and when I get home, we can pretend it never happened. It's what he'll want. No fuss, no drama.

An ellipsis appears and then disappears. Then it appears again, for a whole minute, and I'm gripping my phone so tight that the tips of my fingers go white. Then it vanishes again, and the green dot along with it.

That'll teach me to go digging for answers. I put my phone back in the bedside drawer and go looking for Gary.

I lose the rest of May in self-imposed exile. By June, I often wake to frost on the lawn and the cat curled up in my bed. I spend my days doing not much of anything, sitting around in a comfortable silence, journaling, picking the polish off my nails, and waiting for all the problems in my life to fix themselves. I proofread the new chapters of Dad's novel. We watch a documentary about microplastics. We take a drive and check out the Bendigo Art Gallery.

It's another week before Dad asks me again, more serious now, 'Are you alright, Pepper?'

'Yeah, I'm —'

He gives me the kind of significant look over the top of his glasses usually reserved for after-school detentions, or the time I got caught stealing his scotch and replacing it with apple juice, and I pause. I take a long sip of Blend 43 to buy myself some time. He waits.

'I …' My voice betrays me and comes out wobbly, and my bottom lip follows suit. Before I have a breath to compose myself, hot tears brim. 'I don't think I am.'

His gentle, genuine frown triggers something inside me, and it all comes out at once.

'I don't have a job anymore, got — got fired but not even fired — I just, I don't — I agreed to quit, I don't know how, but I did. And then I go to see my b-boyfriend, I don't even, not even my boyfriend, and he just, he didn't — I really, I made such a mess, such a mess. And Bec, we aren't even friends anymore because I'm too selfish or slow or, I don't know,

I don't know why anymore, and Annie's so busy all the time, and now she's got a girlfriend so she'll disappear too. And my housemate, Leo — god, Leo. I think that's the worst part, I think I really fucked it up — and it's just like, it's like everyone's life is m-moving on and things are happening and I'm just, just, stuck here and I don't know how to get out, I don't know what to do, I just don't want to feel like this anymore but I don't know how to fix it, I don't know, I'm just so — fucking *sad*.'

I don't know why admitting this is so hard, but it is, and I dissolve into sobs. Fat, choking, heaving sobs into my dad's jumper as he squeezes my shoulder. The sadness is vast and endless, stretches on further than I can even fathom. It has been trying to catch my shadow for twenty-seven years and finally I'm too tired to run anymore, too exhausted to fight it off, and Dad's gentle shushing is at once soothing and proof that he knows it too.

'You'll be alright,' he says softly. 'You're in a rough spot, Pepper. We just need to get you through it.'

'I can't. I can't do it anymore. I'm so tired. I feel so beaten down by it. Everything is so hard, everything — I'm so mad at myself all the time.'

'But why? What have you done that you can't undo?'

'Going back to Max all those times —'

'Max, tsht,' he says, rolling his eyes. 'That jumped-up little —'

'But I did it! He told me *exactly* who he was and what he wanted, and I just ignored it. I feel so *stupid*.'

'Darling, you're young —'

'I'm not that young anymore,' I say, with a sad, thick laugh. 'You had two kids by my age. You weren't out there fucking up everything, causing chaos everywhere you went.'

And look how that turned out, I think, but am not cruel enough to say. Maybe it's genetic. Maybe he passed down the romantic fuck-up gene, and we're both destined to wind up alone in the middle of nowhere. I don't think about my mum often, but I imagine her now, living a perfectly normal life, happier without us around, and I feel a stab of loathing so sharp I have to rip at the uneven edge of my thumb nail to get through it.

'But it's a bit different these days.'

'Is it? Other people get it right. Other people are happy, they're fine, they aren't crying in the toilets every other day. It's just *me*, I'm just — I don't know — *broken*, fucking *useless*.'

'Who told you that?' he asks.

'What?'

'Who told you you were useless?'

'Margot might as well've,' I say, and wipe a streak of snot and tears on my sleeve. 'I don't think I'm very good at my job. I'm not excited about it. So I probably slack off, or I make a mistake and I don't know how to ask for help because it's humiliating. But then I keep trying to fix it myself and it all just snowballs, and I've made a huge mess that I can't clean up, and it's a disaster, and I just — I don't know how to stop fucking up. And it doesn't even matter. It's over now, I don't work there anymore, but what about the next job? How do I even get another job when I screwed up so spectacularly there? I'm not getting a glowing reference from anyone at Scout.'

'You'll get another job, Pepper. So many agencies would love to have you.'

The idea of starting again at another agency makes me want to cry, so I do. Half tears, half bitter laughter seems to send Dad into a panic, so he disappears into the pantry to rifle through the biscuits, and I stay wiping my nose on my sleeve and dreading the hell of job interviews and first days and trying to learn everyone's names.

'What happened with Leo?' Dad asks eventually, after returning with a packet of Kingstons. 'I thought you two were getting on.'

'I ruined it.'

'Maybe when you find a new job, you can move out on your own.'

'No, I meant — we ...' I don't know how to talk to him about this. I've always gone to my brother for boy advice, or the girls, or anyone else. Dad went on one bad date in 2002 and gave up the game for good.

'Oh,' he says, catching on.

'Leo's just ...' I search for the words. 'He's so *good*. He's just nice. He's so happy, it's contagious. I'm not stuck in my head when we're together. I feel like ... the best version of myself. And I just left. And didn't tell him why. He was honest with me and then I used it against him. What kind of person does that?'

'Someone who doesn't like themselves,' he says simply.

'How do you know that?'

'He offered you something you're afraid of, so you pushed him away.'

'But what if I don't deserve it?'

'Why wouldn't you?'

'Maybe I'm an awful person.'

'Maybe you're not in the best position to be objective.'

'Neither are you.'

'That's fair,' he says through a mouthful of biscuit. 'But it's not that binary: good people and bad people, deserving and undeserving. We all do bad things sometimes. If we couldn't forgive people, we'd all be alone forever.'

'I don't know how to fix something like this.'

'You apologise, and you don't do it again.'

'But what if I just keep fucking up? What if he says something nice and I call him a c—' Dad gives me a look '— an arsehole, I mean. There are so many ways I could self-destruct, and what then? I can't promise him something and then fail at it.'

'You know how to care about someone. You need to let someone care about you.'

'Dad,' I say, realising we're at the crescendo of our conversation. 'What about you? You can give me all the advice you want, but you don't follow it yourself. It's just you and Gary out here, and Chris and I worry about you too.'

'Well,' he hesitates, shaking the packet at me, 'I'll do it if you do it.'

'Alright,' I say, feeling hopeful for the first time in days. I take a biscuit. 'I'll help you set up your Tinder account.'

CHAPTER THIRTY-EIGHT

It's with some surprise that my game of phone Scrabble is interrupted with a call from Bec's number the following Tuesday night. I hesitate, finger hovering over the *decline* button. Perhaps it was a pocket dial. Perhaps she's calling to let me know, officially, that I'm out of both her wedding and her life for good. I don't know which would sting more: hearing it or having it in my voicemail inbox forever. I know I'd leave it there to replay on especially bad days, when I feel I need extra punishment. Maybe it's better I get it over with. Maybe it's the kind of thing she won't want to leave in a voicemail. That way, if I just don't answer, she can't ever tell me, and I won't ever need to know.

The call rings out, and I'm saved from needing to choose at all.

And then she's ringing again — so a pocket dial is probably out of the question.

Do I really want to know? Is it better to stay oblivious? How long have I lived with grey areas — shouldn't I be used to them by now? What's another unspoken resentment between old friends?

Oh, fuck it.

'Hello?'

'Hi,' she says. One syllable isn't enough to discern her tone.

Was that an annoyed *hi*? How can you tell? 'I wasn't sure you'd answer.'

'Me either,' I tell her.

'Oh.'

There's a long pause.

'Are, um … You're good?'

'I —' What do I tell her? *I lost my job and you were right about Max and I had sex with Leo and then I ghosted him but also I might be in love with him, how are you?* We haven't spoken in months because she's sick of the constant drama in my life. In the end I go with, 'Yeah. I'm okay. You okay?'

'I'm okay.'

'Okay.'

'I stopped by your house,' she says.

'Oh.'

'You weren't there.'

'Yeah.'

'I thought maybe Leo was covering for you.'

'No — I'm visiting my dad. I've been here a little while.'

'Oh,' she says. 'That's nice. How's he?'

'He's okay,' I tell her. 'He's started adding parmesan to his mash, so that's news.'

'Wow.'

'Mm. Thrilling stuff.'

'Truly.'

'Well …' I say after another quiet pause. 'I should let you go.'

'I called you.'

'Oh, right.'

'Do you need to go? Are you busy?'

'No, no,' I say. 'I'm not doing anything.'

'I'm sorry I missed your birthday.'

'That's okay.'

'Happy birthday, then.'

'Thank you.'

This stiff exchange is beginning to take its toll on my spine, so I settle back against the ballerina-pink sheets of my bed and wait for whatever's next. I don't know if she'll apologise, or if she expects me to, or if she's calling for an argument. I don't know if I have the energy for it. I'm growing sick of this relentless loss. I can always hang up if it gets a bit much. Got to appreciate that safety net.

Silence again. It stretches and fills with unspoken things, and I have to dig my nails into my palm to keep myself from breaking it. I will not be the first to speak. I will not let her out-silence me.

'I'm so sorry,' she says, blurting it out like she was working up the nerve. 'I shouldn't have said what I said.'

'It's fine,' I tell her, more out of habit than anything. 'You had some really — you needed to say it, I probably needed to hear it. I know it must be hard sometimes, with me. I know I can be a bit —'

'Babe, it's just that I would get so frustrated,' she sighs. 'I love you, obviously, but it's like watching an addict go back to their dealer over and over, and it's just like, *stop!* You know?'

'I mean, Max is hardly *heroin* —'

'But the other day me and Evan were watching *Sex and the City* — we're bingeing the whole thing. He's never seen it; can you believe that? We're up to season four — and I just, like, I forgot how crap it is to be single. It's *so* lonely and *so* depressing. Like, who am I to say you can't take comfort where you can get it? It made me so sad for you, like a puppy who just wants their abusive owner to love them, you know? And I was so mean to the puppy for needing their attention when I should have been angry at the owner for not giving it to them.'

'Um —'

'No,' she says, and I can imagine her slapping a hand to her forehead. 'I didn't mean it like that. You're not a dog. I'm not articulating myself well.'

'Yeah, I —'

'I just wanted to say I'm sorry. Really, properly sorry.'

'Okay.' I feel four seconds pass. 'Oh. Sorry. I'm sorry too.'

'That's so nice of you to say,' she says, relaxing at once. 'I hate when we fight.'

'Yeah. It was … unpleasant.'

'Let's never fight again.'

'Sounds good to me.'

'Okay!' says Bec, with such brightness it takes me off guard. 'I have so much to catch you up on. I didn't — it's not *why* I called, but I do need to know, incidentally. If you're coming.'

'Coming where?'

'My engagement party. It's this weekend. Are you coming? I need to know, I need a hard number for the caterer, and it's — well, like I said, I wanted to talk to you anyway, but it's suddenly got a bit time sensitive, that's —'

'Sorry,' I cut her off. I suppose if I'm going to start showing up for myself, per Dr Minnick's advice in our FaceTime therapy session yesterday, there's no better place to start than here. 'Is that it?'

'Is what it?' she asks.

'We aren't going to address the rest of it?'

'We have,' says Bec with a frown in her voice. 'I told you: I'm not mad at you, I'm mad at Max. You aren't still seeing him, are you? Babe, please, tell me you aren't.'

'I meant — Max isn't the only thing we argued about.'

'I know you didn't mean it,' she says. 'It's okay, I promise.'

I laugh, although nothing is very funny. 'That's not what happened, though.'

'You actually do hate Evan?' she asks, incredulous. 'What has he ever done to you?'

'It's not about Evan. It's that lately you've been acting like I'm doing everything wrong because I'm not following the same path as you.'

'No, I haven't,' she says. 'I don't do that at all.'

'Okay, well,' I say with a sigh, 'that's how it feels.'

'Well, it's hard to watch someone make the same mistakes over and over again.'

'I'm sure it is. But that isn't the way to handle it.'

'I'm just trying to point you in the right direction.'

'But what's right for you might not be right for me,' I say. 'Maybe I don't want an Evan. Maybe I want a Max or a — or whoever. Maybe I don't want anyone. You don't have to treat it like you're the authority on what's right or wrong for me.'

'You do that too, you know,' she replies. 'You act like my relationship is an annoying phase I'm going through. You don't like him because you don't take it seriously.'

I consider this for a minute. I suppose I haven't tried very hard to get to know Evan. I remember how hurt I felt when Bec changed the topic whenever I talked about Max, or when she deliberately planned events he couldn't attend — if he ever wanted to, which he would never, but that's not the point — and there's a twinge of guilt in the pit of my stomach. Perhaps it's not a competition. Perhaps we've both been bad friends.

'You're probably right,' I admit. 'Okay, I can work on that.'

'Thank you,' she says. 'I'll work on my stuff too. I'll make time for you and Annie. I'll try.'

'Okay,' I say, and I imagine we're both wearing sad little smiles. 'Deal.'

'So, you'll come?' she asks, her voice small and soft. I could almost laugh. She would only sacrifice her pride for the sake of her perfect engagement party. 'You can have a plus one. Even if it's Max.'

'Yeah,' I tell her. 'I'll come.'

It feels strange to have this conversation and to not feel the threat of tears or the panic of saying the wrong thing and losing someone forever. I don't know. Maybe it's easier to be honest on a level playing field. Maybe the universe is forcing me to let things go. Maybe I'm learning how to do that myself.

I don't know if Bec means what she said. I don't know if our friendship will ever truly recover, or if we'll fall apart again without the pressure of a guest list. Maybe things won't be okay. They might just *be*, and I'll need to make peace with it.

CHAPTER THIRTY-NINE

The 2:30 pm train back from Castlemaine is a long restless trip. I don't feel like reading. Podcasts make time move even slower. I've left oily marks on the window from pressing my forehead against the glass trying to catch sight of the Melbourne skyline in the distance. Gross.

But when we finally pull into Southern Cross Station, I'm not ready to get off. I wonder what would happen if I just stayed here in my seat and refused to move, and circled regional Victorian towns forever. I could survive off Pringles and burnt coffee for quite some time, I think, and if Annie ever wanted to visit then she could just buy a return ticket to Ballarat and still make it home before bedtime.

Passengers shuffle down the narrow aisles, chattering excitedly about a weekend in town. Someone's seeing the Harry Potter play. Someone else is excited about dinner in Brunswick. A young mum can't wait to get to her Airbnb to put her grumbling toddler down for a nap. I sit in my seat until they all filter out. I thought I was ready for this, but now I'm not so sure.

I had two more sessions with Dr Minnick via FaceTime since my big chat with Dad, and she has been encouraging me to feel my feelings. She's helping me realise my patterns and sore points: why something like Margot's disapproval triggers something panicky inside me, how Bec's steady life progress feels like a personal attack. She tells me that avoidance is a coping strategy to avoid pain, and it won't sustain me forever. So here I am. I hop off the regional train and switch to the Hurstbridge line, where I'm promptly forced into some businessman's armpit; the price you pay for commuting at peak hour.

The house is quiet when I arrive. Leo usually isn't home from work until after 6 pm, so there's time to kill before our inevitable awkward conversation. But we need to have it. I need to explain myself.

At least it gives me time to wash the journey off me. I have a long bath, do a mask and a full body scrub, and shave my legs for the first time in weeks. I paint my nails. I curl my hair. I take extra time with my makeup: bronzy tones and an immaculate wing, more glamorous than I feel inside. These inane beauty routines feel like self-care, tiny indulgences after weeks of the bare essentials. They make me feel a little like my old self again.

Despite living on a diet of bolognese, stroganoff, full-fat milk and white bread slathered in salted butter — the diet of choice for single dads the world over — for several weeks, the zip on my party dress closes easily, even without the assistance of my super-Spanx. Bec messaged me earlier in the week to 'suggest' I borrow Annie's bubblegum-coloured Scanlan Theodore dress, but because I'm not a size six and because wearing pink makes me look like I'm cosplaying Jigglypuff, I've settled on a vaguely retro full-skirted little number that looks more expensive than it was, and that will have to do. It's from the section of my wardrobe that used to be dedicated to date dresses. I haven't looked at it in months. That date with the Bitcoin enthusiast in January feels like several lifetimes ago.

All made up, I sit and wait for him in the living room. I note, with a pang, that my little snake plant on the side table is thriving. Leo has been taking care of it in my absence. I have to force down a sip of water to cover the foul taste of shame.

It's inching closer to 7 pm, and he still isn't home. I wanted to catch him before he goes out for the night, but I'm edging dangerously close to running late for the train, and I can't afford to take an Uber anymore, so I might not get to see him until tomorrow. Or Monday, even, if he decides to make a weekend of it and have a double sleepover with whoever he's with tonight. No doubt it's someone pretty and uncomplicated.

The tulips he got me for my birthday have nosedived over the edge of their vase and the water has gone the colour and consistency of a swamp, but I can't bring myself to throw them away. I don't know how to press flowers, either, but I'm so unwilling to let them go that I just leave them here, even with that horrible old flower smell right by my pillow.

But I can't stay home and sulk at a vase of dead flowers all night. It's important to Bec that I'm at her engagement party, so even though I can think of nothing worse than standing alone in a room full of couples and listening to them talk about happily ever afters all night, I'm going. I'll bottle up my well-earned cynicism for when I can come home and eat an entire pizza in bed, and I'll spend the train ride into town practising my game face.

All relationships take work, as they say. And I'm trying really hard to do everything I promised Dad and Dr Minnick I would: I'm trying to practise forgiveness, and hope others extend it to me too. So I'm going to swallow my pride and stand around in my slightly too small heels all night, I'm going to stay moderately sober, and I'm going to be happy for my friend, goddamnit, and I'm not going to have a breakdown and make the whole night about me.

Bec and Evan's love fest is on the fourth floor of a building with a broken elevator, and I'm pink-faced and short of breath when I finally make it. The room is aglow with fairy lights and big vintage bulbs, ideal for selfie taking. White roses and candles decorate the space, an ocean of silver and white. The last round of heavily decorated function spaces I frequented were a series of twenty-first birthdays we all attended years ago, but this is kicking things up a notch. There's a photobooth set up in the corner. Waistcoated waiters do laps holding trays of canapes and champagne flutes. It's all so tasteful that I feel grubby by comparison. I resolve to avoid touching anything for fear of leaving a stain on any of these expensive linens.

Oh, Christ, they've got a massive photo of themselves hung up on the wall. Bec's showing every tooth in her mouth as she presents her engagement ring to the camera, and Evan looks like he's about to give himself a hernia.

No. No, Penny, I tell my reflection in the mirror behind the bar sternly. *Happy for them, remember? Thrilled. For. Them. This party isn't nauseating. It's delightful.*

'Penny! You're heeere!' cries Bec, flying across the room to wrap me in a rib-cracking hug. 'Evan's grandmother keeps trying to waft the waiters away because she thinks I need to slim down for the wedding. I'm *so* hungry.'

'What a bitch,' I scowl. 'You look amazing!'

She's a vision in white, made all the more visible by a very courageous spray tan. It mustn't be easy dealing with the stress of a wedding. If I knew I'd have to look at photos of nights like this for the rest of my life, I'd pull out every photogenic stop in the Kardashian playbook too. I wouldn't eat for a year. I'd drown myself in highlighter.

'Want me to steal ten of the mushroom tartlets and sneak them to you?' I ask her. 'I'll hang by the kitchen door. I'm your girl.'

It's nice to see her. Truly. Even if it's a little awkward. Our eyes meet, and we both feel how long it's been since we saw each other and the awful things we said, but she papers over it quickly with a toothy smile and a glance around the room.

'Isn't this effing nuts?' she asks. 'It's all a bit … *adult*.'

'We're adults now, babe,' I nod gravely. 'These are our *real lives*.'

'I'm glad you're here,' she says, giving my arm a little squeeze. We'll find our rhythm again. Eventually. 'Couldn't have this party without you. Let's not talk about that now, though — Oh! Baby! Pen's here!'

'Our Penny,' Evan says warmly, and we double-kiss cheeks. His face is weirdly hot for such a cold night. It's strange to have this level of manufactured closeness with someone you've kept at arm's length for so long. He has to know by now that my feelings about him have been lukewarm at best, but, for Bec's sake, we're greeting each other like old friends. 'No boyfriend again? Bec told me all about him. I wanted to meet him.'

'Oh,' I say, trying to laugh over the awkwardness. Tonight isn't the night to get into all that. 'No, he, um — just me tonight.'

'Sad,' says Bec, making a good effort at a sympathetic face. I frown, but there's no time to say anything before she's steamrolling over me and screeching in delight as more guests arrive. 'One sec, babe, sorry, talk to you later, I — Greg and Monica! You're heeere!'

The party is full of people I kind of know. Barely familiar faces from our uni days, family members I've met in passing, people I only recognise from Bec's Instagram posts. I'm wondering if I can convince a waiter to give me an entire platter of focaccia pizza to eat alone on the freezing terrace, when I'm saved.

'You got brided too, hey?' says Annie, appearing at my side with a fresh champagne for me. She's in her Scanlan dress, looking taller and distinctively less like a Pokémon than I would have. 'I give it a year.'

'Stop!' I chide her, smirking. 'We have to be supportive. We have to be *nice*.'

'Emmy, come over here,' she calls. 'Penny's being *nice*.'

'Hey!' I cry. 'I'm nice all the time!'

It's stupid, I know, and not how it works, but I take one look at Emmy's dark voluminous curls and doe eyes and think, *I could never date someone prettier than I am*. At least when you're dating men, you can make up the difference with lipstick and a push-up bra.

'It's so nice to meet you!' cries Emmy. 'I've been a bit nervous, if I'm honest. I've heard so much about you.'

'Yeah, Penny,' says Annie, chiming in, 'if you don't like her, we'll have to break up.'

'You hold my fate in your hands,' says Emmy. 'One word and I'm gone.'

'I've never had so much power in my life,' I laugh. I like her already.

'No Max?' asks Annie in a tone far more appropriate than Evan's was. 'I heard she was letting you invite him. I was shocked.'

'Long story,' I say, swigging for effect.

'Can't be any longer than this night is going to be,' she says, picking up a macaron iced with *B&E* and pulling a face.

'No, no, I don't want to bring down the vibe.'

'Oh no,' says Emmy. 'Do we hate him?'

'You know what, Emmy? We *do* hate him.'

'I always hated him,' says Annie.

'Everyone has.' I shrug. 'I was just the last one to figure it out.'

'Tell us what happened,' says Annie. She flags down a waiter for provisions.

'Okay, Jesus, fine,' I say, downing what's left in my flute for gumption. 'I don't want to talk about it after I tell you, okay? I'm going to vomit it all out and then it's done. And for the love of fuck, don't either of you tell Bec tonight. Promise?'

'Promise!' says Annie.

'Actually, it isn't a long story at all. I got fired, went to see Max, Max fucking sucks, went home, had sex with Leo — he's in love with me by the way, or was; not anymore — and instead of dealing with it like an adult, I ran away to the country to ignore my feelings. Ha! Story told in ten seconds flat.'

'Oh my god, *Pen*—'

'Annie, what did we promise?'

'Okay but —'

'That fucking sucks,' says Emmy — and then, to Annie's scolding look, 'What? I didn't promise anything. Good riddance to bad guys and bad jobs.'

'Fucking *cheers*,' I call, and we all toast. Like a band-aid over a paper cut, it stung and now it's over. Tomorrow my friends won't be so generous with their bitten tongues, but they at least allow me this much, and the conversation moves on. We talk about what shows we've been watching, something dumb an influencer posted today about DIY lavender-mint colonics, whether or not it's poor form to commandeer the entire tray of sliders as they come out from the kitchen, and I get to pretend everything is normal again, for at least one more night.

Later, as Evan kicks off a slideshow — *a slideshow* — I'm prepared for the sting of mushy speeches about true love: I'm double-parked with a champagne in both hands. I haven't yet felt the need to fully mourn the true end of things with Max, but all the sadness could be lapping at the floodgates when Evan starts using words like *soulmate* and *finally* and *forever.*

I don't know if it feels like the finish line is even further away now than it was just a few weeks ago — and it really does feel like a finish line, the way people are cheering Bec on and handing out hydration packs of house sparkling like it's the end of a marathon. Now there's more mess, more sessions with Dr Minnick, more emotional wounds to stitch together, more healing than I know what to do with.

Here I am hiding in a corner, all dressed up in a room full of happy couples, with nothing to hold but my drinks. I'll go home tonight to an empty bed in an empty house, and in the morning I'll have to start everything — my career, my love life, my therapy sessions — all over again. I'm tired about it in advance.

It used to be that I could count on Annie in moments like this. She was someone to commiserate with. Someone else who thinks that *Princess Bride* is as traumatic as *Hannibal.* But she's somewhere with Emmy, who seems funny and fantastic, and now she's lost to happiness and coupledom too.

I feel a frown threatening to turn into tears when something pink appears beside me, and then something blue.

'Oh my god,' I whisper as Annie and Emmy each wrap an arm around me from either side. 'Are you two trying to turn me into a blubbering mess?'

'Do you want a cake pop with Bec's face on it?'

'Yes,' I laugh thickly, dabbing my eyes with the back of my hand. 'I'd love to eat Bec's face.'

As we bite into miniature Becs and Evans and lose track of the speeches, I feel silly for worrying. It broke my heart to lose Bec to her relationship, but Annie was right there feeling hurt and abandoned too. It was wrong to think she didn't learn anything from that experience. This is a woman who balances an eye-watering case load with studying for the bar, who runs twenty-five kilometres a week even if she's on her period, who finds time for blow-outs and hangovers and dates and client dinners and a dry-clean-only wardrobe and still has always made time for me.

Maybe couples aren't the problem, I think as I watch Bec proudly present her left hand to anyone in her eye line, as Evan is on his fifteenth minute of the slideshow. Maybe we just make time for the things we feel are important.

'I'll always roll my eyes at happy couples with you,' whispers Annie, reading my mind.

'Me too,' says Emmy in a stage whisper. 'Things like this are dumb.'

'I know I'm being a sook,' I tell them, picking at a bit of fondant-Evan's chocolate hair. 'It's just hard not to feel like a massive loser at something like this.'

'It's okay, babe,' says Annie. 'You're a massive loser no matter where you go.'

And it's a good thing that the toasts are wrapping up and the room has broken into applause, because we start to laugh, and none of us could handle Bec's wrath if we'd ruined her night by laughing and choking on a cake shaped like her face.

I'm wondering how many cake pops I can fit in my clutch, or if I could get a waiter to give me a baggie to smuggle home those arancini, and feeling quite content with my buzz and maybe ready for a nice cool walk to the train station, when I crash into a familiar chest.

'Shit!' I say. 'What are you doing here?'

'Oh, that's nice,' he scoffs.

'I didn't mean — you know what I mean.'

'Do I?'

'*Leo.*'

'I was invited,' he says into his glass, taking a heady sip.

'Oh. Right.' I always forget that he was Bec's friend first. I've grown so close to him in the last few months, and so distant from Bec, that it's hard to imagine they exist in the same universe.

'I wasn't sure I should come,' he says. 'I didn't want to step on your toes.'

'Of course you aren't stepping on my toes,' I tell him. 'Come over there with me and Annie. We have a monopoly on the dessert trays.'

'I'm heading out in a sec,' shrugs Leo, stony-faced enough to make my heart break. 'You've got your people, I don't need to be here.'

'Don't be like that. Look, there'll be cake soon.'

'I already ate.'

'Come on, please? I know everything is — just — shit, just awful between us right now, but it's — let's just have fun, yeah? Old times? Wine bottle karaoke later?'

'No, really —' he says and freezes, looking like he's just seen a ghost. 'I'd better go.'

'What?' I follow his line of sight, and through a wall of Bec's extended family and roving trays of macarons, I spot a vaguely familiar mane.

Is it just me, or does a hush fall over the room as she moves in our direction? One of the cheesier Ed Sheeran songs starts to play through the PA, and I can't tell the difference. She glides towards us, stern-faced. It looks like Leo's promiscuity is coming back to bite him in spectacular fashion. The delicious schadenfreudey drama of it all.

'What are you doing here?' hisses Mermaid Hair, taking Leo by the arm and dragging him into a dim corner. *That's* where I know her from. That morning I ran into them at the cafe, the breakfast date with the weird vibe. What was her name again?

'Calm down, Serena,' he says. *Serena!* That's right. She's a total Serena. 'I was invited.'

'I thought you hated shit like this,' she says, spitting resentment like fire. It seems odd that a one-night stand would involve an in-depth conversation about whether or not Leo enjoys engagement parties. 'I thought you said it was bourgeois bullshit.'

'I'll go anywhere with an open bar,' he says with a shrug, unperturbed.

I slink back towards Annie and Emmy but close enough to stay within earshot. I want to give them privacy, but I also desperately want to see this unfold.

'They aren't even your friends anymore,' she says. 'You said that I could have custody of our friends if you could have Richmond and South Yarra.'

'Fuck's sake, I was *joking*. You can go wherever you want. You're being ridiculous. What am I going to do? Patrol Bridge Road with a water gun?'

The DJ Bec and Evan hired must harbour a secret resentment against them, because some sickly sweet John Mayer track is up next, and I lose track of Leo and Serena's conversation under the whine of a guitar solo.

'Are you watching this?' breathes Annie in my ear.

'I am obsessed with it,' says Emmy.

'Bec pointed her out to me earlier,' Annie continues. 'That's the ex. The big one. She who must not be named.'

'I've been looking at that Zimmermann dress for a year.'

'You'd look great in polka dots,' says Emmy, loyally. She fits right in, doesn't she?

The argument is getting more intense. She's laying into him, ticking off his indiscretions on her hand while he looks increasingly unimpressed. He folds his arms, and any minute now the song is going to change — no doubt to some other drippy worn-out Top 40 hit — and in the moment of quiet between tracks, their little domestic is going to draw every eye in the room, and the focus will shift away from the couple we're here to celebrate. Someone has to intervene.

'Can you give it a rest? It's a —' Leo's talking, but I can't totally hear him over John Mayer's wailing. '— just having some fun and —'

'Yes, please, tell me more about all the *fun* you're having —'

'Leo,' I call, and my clear voice rings like a bell against their whisper-shouting. 'Let's go.'

'We're having a conversation, if you don't mind,' she says, mermaid hair whipping round and catching the light impressively.

She's so pretty that she's actually hard to look at. It's like arguing with Helen of fucking Troy. Still, I manage.

'Leo, are you done here?'

'Yeah,' he says, tugging the lapels of his blazer straight. 'I'm done.'

I hold my hand out and he takes it. He doesn't drop it when we're out of Serena's sight, nor as we weave through the crowd. It's only once we make it out onto the twinkle-lit and mostly empty stretch of Bourke Street that he unlaces our fingers, and he can't or won't meet my eye.

'Thank you.'

'That's okay,' I say.

'Like a little superhero,' he says humourlessly. Can this chill be blamed on the weather alone? 'Able to decimate ex-girlfriends in a single swoop.'

'It looked like you needed an out.'

'I hope that wasn't over me,' says Leo, nodding back towards the party. 'Some territorial thing.'

'No, I wanted to help.'

'I can't imagine whatshisname would be thrilled about you fighting over some other guy.'

'I doubt he'd care, honestly.'

'Alright.'

'Okay.'

A tram draws to a stop beside us, and a gaggle of drunk football fans pile out. I wish I smoked. It would give me something to do with my hands right now.

'I assumed that's where you went,' says Leo as the tram rattles off and we're left alone again. 'When I woke up and you were gone, I figured —'

'No,' I interrupt him. 'No, no, no. That's so over. Beyond over.'

'But was it? That night?'

'Yes. I promise.'

'Ah,' he grins, and there's something bitter behind it. 'Nothing like a bit of rebound sex.'

'*Leo* —'

'C'mon. I'm kidding. It's fine.'

'But it wasn't like that.' He gives me a look. 'Okay, I — My head wasn't where it should have been. It was a silly thing to do.'

'Right.'

'Leo, please.'

'What do you want me to say, Penny? It was a silly thing to do, you said it.'

'Just let me talk!'

'I'm not stopping you!'

A couple of people waiting for a taxi turn to look for the source of the noise, and we remember ourselves. I step closer so we can talk without being overheard and take it as a sign of encouragement when he doesn't step back.

'I'm sorry for leaving.'

'Okay.'

'You mean a lot to me. I was in a moment of crisis and took advantage of our friendship and I regret doing that. But I just — I don't know if you meant what you said. That night. On my birthday.'

'I —'

'No, please. I just can't. You're totally transparent about relationships and what you want and that's fine — it's really fine — I just can't do that. I can't be one of those girls. I'm not built for it, and I can't tell you that I am. I wish I could be totally cool and say, "No rules, let's just have fun," but I can't. And if you say one more thing, I'll write some fantasy in my head about it and I'll ignore everything you say and I'll pour everything I have into it and I'll fuck it up, I know I will, and I'll break my own heart and then —' I look towards the moon to blink back the vulnerability I don't want to show. 'And then we won't be friends anymore, or ever again, and that's so much worse. So just. Please. It's okay, really. Let's just put it behind us.'

Leo takes a long time to reply. He rubs his palms together self-consciously, and I notice the pinprick of a freckle on his index finger, and I have to take slow breaths to hold myself steady.

'Alright,' he says finally, but I can't quite look him in the eye. I watch his lips move as he speaks and dig my fingernails into the vinyl of my clutch. 'You're the boss, boss.'

'That's okay?'

'Yeah,' he says, smiling toothlessly, and I can almost match it. 'Okay.'

'Friends?'

'Sure, friends.'

'*Best* friends?'

'What is this, you nerd, primary school?'

'Yes,' I tell him, with a sanctimonious little nod. 'This is primary school. Say you're my best friend and I'll buy you a Paddle Pop from the canteen.'

'A rainbow one?'

'Obviously.'

'What do I have to say to get a Bubble O'Bill out of you?'

We set off for the train station together, and we get into a heavy discourse about red frogs and green fizzers and friendship bracelets. The air between us isn't quite clear yet, but an early morning fog is a good start.

CHAPTER FORTY

The initial enjoyment of not having anywhere to be on a weekday morning has begun to wane. It's been six weeks since I left Scout, and the sheen of funemployment is starting to wear off. I've hit up every recruiter on my LinkedIn contact list — all seventy-two of them — with a polite and upbeat plea for *any opportunities I might be well-suited for, based on my resume, attached.* Five average interviews later, I've got a couple of mediocre prospects and a measly few hundred dollars left in my savings. Dad has offered to float me until I get back on my feet, but I don't want to accept it. I'm an adult. I need to be responsible for myself. I need to stop buying croissants for breakfast every day, pay out my Afterpay balance, and find a job. Any job.

To kill time between episodes of *Judge Judy* and compulsively checking my inbox for news about any of the four hundred and thirty jobs I've applied for, I've been going running almost every day and often take long boring baths. I've cleaned out my wardrobe and listed everything on Depop. I've defrosted the freezer and organised the pantry twice. I'm running out of *Yoga with Adriene* videos. There are only so many naps you can take before you start to feel like a human sloth.

In my desperate search for dopamine, I even find myself scrolling mindlessly through LinkedIn. I'm a week deep into my feed — mostly meandering posts about work–life balance

and bullshit virtue signalling stories about equity in the
workplace — when I spot a post by Petra.

'*Anyone interested?*' she's written, with a shortlink to
accompany her succinct little update. I click through
immediately.

Digital Marketing Manager
Cruelty-free, sulphate-free, BS-free skincare that
does what it says on the label. Sound good? We think
so too.

    Evergreen Skincare is searching for a Digital
Marketing Manager to join our dynamic and inclusive
Brand team. If you're a quick-thinking, detail-orientated
digital all-rounder with qualifications and experience in
the field, we want to hear from you.

Oh my god. Oh my god. Oh my FUCKING god. Could the
timing possibly be better?

Two hours of thoroughly proofreading my resume and
writing and rewriting my email to Petra, three cups of coffee
and three (okay, six) biscuits later, I think I'm ready.

From: penny.moore.1992@gmail.com
To: petra.desilva@evergreenskincare.com.au
Subject: Catch up & Digital Marketing Manager role
Hi Petra,
*Hope you're well (and coping with this horrendous rain we're
having)!*
    *I wanted to check in and see if you might be free for a coffee
one day soon? Maybe next week? I'm no longer with Scout
Digital and would love to get your thoughts on what my next
steps should be.*

I saw your post on LinkedIn regarding a Digital Marketing Manager role. I fill many of the requirements listed and would love to bend your ear about whether or not I would be a good fit for this.

If not, it's no problem at all. Can't hurt to ask!

Speak soon!

Penny

I have to hit send with my eyes shut or else I'll panic and start second-guessing it, and my draft folder is already stacked high with a dozen false starts. I immediately wish I'd left off an exclamation point or two. I wonder if I was vague enough about leaving Scout.

But it's too late now and worrying about it won't unsend it. She'll either reply or she won't, and if she doesn't, I have an okay feeling about the social media manager role I interviewed for at a plumbing supplies company last week. That would do in the meantime.

I expect to spend the whole day checking my phone for an update, at least until my appointment with Dr Minnick this afternoon, after which I'll continue obsessively waiting for a reply.

But what if she never replies?

What if she never replies and we run into each other at the cafe, and she thinks I'm stalking her, and the poor thing has to move? What if she gets a restraining order against me, and under *purpose* she writes, *'Accused is emotionally unstable; seems intent on eating muffins at local cafe every day until I offer her employment; is obsessed with me'*?

I'm only a few seconds into this nightmare when the telltale *ping* of my Gmail app rips me out of it.

OH.

From: petra.desilva@evergreenskincare.com.au
To: penny.moore.1992@gmail.com
Subject: Re: Catch up & Digital Marketing Manager role

Hi Penny,

Great to hear from you.

Are you free today? 2 pm?

Regards,

Petra de Silva

Marketing Director

Evergreen Skincare

I shriek so loudly that birds erupt from the lemon tree in the courtyard.

I have to get dressed. I have to wash my hair. I need to print out my resume. Where can I find a printer? Leo's mum has one, I remember him saying, and I manage two whole seconds of sadness before I'm back to my manic state. I need a red lip and a blazer and my glasses and six more coffees and do I have time to nip into the city and buy that dove-grey silk shirt from Witchery? It would almost clean me out, but it might be the difference between a job offer or another month spent watching *Dr Phil* and sending out boilerplate cover letters to every marketing job posting on Seek. What time is it now? *Argh!*

The rest of the morning disappears into an elaborate getting-ready routine (wearing tights negates the need for smooth legs, but this is about *confidence*), and I burn through my nervous energy with an impressive if needlessly loud Taylor Swift medley. By the time I finish my guided meditation and the 11 tram turns onto Brunswick Street, I'm only slightly jittery. My pencil skirt is slowly riding up to my underboob area and my heels pinch, but I'm gritting my teeth through it.

You will nail this, I tell the face in my iPhone camera as I check my lipstick on the corner of Moor Street (Moor Street! A good sign, no?). *You have no choice but to nail this. You do not want to work at Wholesale Plumbings Plus.*

Through an unassuming door, unremarkable except for a tidy nameplate of the Evergreen logo, I go from the bustle of Fitzroy into … a greenhouse? Did I get the right door?

Their office is a converted warehouse with a glass ceiling (is that a metaphor? I love it) and enough plants to make up for the deforestation of the Amazon tenfold. There are no trite motivational posters or framed certificates of awards won five years ago, no collagenned receptionist, and absolutely no flat-pack furniture.

A fish tank gurgles where a reception desk should be. Low soft couches in breathy lavender and ballet-slipper pink tones contrast with exposed wood beams, as though the intent is to make you feel at home — if you lived in a treehouse designed by a *Mad Men* set director who loves Charli XCX, which would be my dream come true. Every inch of the place is Instagrammable, and I want to move in.

'Penny,' calls Petra, interrupting my daydream about putting a bed in the sun-drenched conference room. Her flats don't make a sound against the hardwood floorboards, and I suddenly feel overdressed. I wish I had time to sneak to the bathroom and wipe my lipstick off.

'Hey — hi!'

'You found us okay?'

'Yes! Two trams, easy. This place is uh-mazing.'

'We're pretty proud of it.'

'I don't think I've ever worked in an office that wasn't right out of an IKEA showroom.'

She laughs, and someone hands me a glass of water with cucumber in it, and I see that their kitchen has a sparkling water tap and a proper espresso machine and oh my god oh my *god* I want to work here.

'Listen, Nelson is in the office today,' Petra tells me. 'Think you'd be up to switching our coffee into an interview?'

'Really? Just like that?'

'I know it's short notice.'

HOLYFUCKSHITYES is on the tip of my tongue, but I catch it just in time. 'Yes,' I say instead. 'Yes, I would.'

Could I walk out of here with a job? I could start today. Wait, no. I have therapy later. Should I tell Petra I can't start today? Obviously you shouldn't, you idiot. Drink your fucking cucumber water.

We make polite small talk on our way to the conference room — *'How's about this cold snap we're having?' 'Have you tried that new Portuguese restaurant in our neighbourhood?'* — and this feels more like a catch-up with a friend than a job interview. If this continues, I could leave here with my hopes high.

Ten minutes later, Nelson, the self-described purse strings, makes it to the conference room, head buried in his phone.

'Just a sec,' he says, and it feels silly to keep talking about the shit vibe at the All Nations pub near home with him and his pristine suit in the room. It's okay. He already knows my work. This is going to be great!

'Penny, good to meet you,' he says, and I deflate a bit.

'You've already met,' Petra murmurs, giving him a good-natured jab in the side with her elbow. 'At one of the agency pitches.'

'Did I? I'm sorry,' he says, rolling his eyes at himself. 'I'm useless without my PA.'

'That's okay!' I hope my foundation is heavy enough to cover up my embarrassed flush. 'I'm sure you meet more people in a week than I do in a year.'

'So you're from ...?'

'Scout Digital. In Cremorne.'

'Oh, I remember. That was one of the good ones.'

'I brought my resume,' I say, handing it to them. 'I've recently updated my book. It's on my website at the top there. You should recognise a couple of the brands. I wanted to include your pitch as a case study, but I thought that might be a bit presumptuous.'

'What brings you here?'

'I thought Penny might be a good fit as the digital marketing manager,' says Petra while Nelson browses my resume, and I beam. I just redid it last week. I think the font I chose says that I am smart, capable and have impeccable taste in fonts.

'Less than a year at Scout,' he says. 'What happened there?'

Ah. I've been rehearsing for this. Me and my reflection in the bathroom mirror ran through countless ways to say, *'My boss was a sociopath and I had a nervous breakdown in the conference room. Twice,'* without making potential employers wish they had access to a silent alarm button.

'I just felt it was time to explore other options,' I tell him with a taut, determined smile. He scribbles something down in the margin. 'I've been in agency-land for a long time and felt like I'd made the most of it. It's time for me to branch out and really dig deep into one brand, rather than working across multiple.'

'Alright,' he says. 'It's just, we're growing very quickly. What's stopping you from deciding to explore other options in another, what, ten months?'

'I won't.' He raises his eyebrows. I send Petra the quickest of pleading glances, but her face is impassive. 'Evergreen is a brand

I'm really passionate about. Honestly, it was a joy to work on your pitch. I'd love the opportunity to do more of that.'

'All this agency work, nothing in-house. It's a different beast entirely.'

'I've worked really closely with a lot of my clients. A lot of the time I was basically their in-house producer, just with a different email signature.'

'Intern, Junior Copywriter, Producer, Account Manager ...' he says, reading off my job titles from the last five years, and I get the feeling that this isn't going well at all. 'Digital Marketing Manager would be a big step up. Do you think you're ready for a senior role? Any experience with budgets, people management, media buying?'

'Um. Well ...'

There's a lump in my throat that doesn't dissolve in a mouthful of cucumber water. If I pay attention, I can see my hand shaking slightly on the table.

Nelson looks disengaged. I catch his eye wandering to his Apple Watch and realise my one chance at a job I could actually like is slipping away. It's now or never.

'I know I have a lot to prove, but I'm really motivated,' I tell him. 'I've worked on every facet of marketing and advertising with my clients. Brand development through to site build through to post-purchase comms. I've just approached it from the outside, not in-house. But it's the same skill, isn't it, just from a different direction. I'm planning on doing a couple of Google training courses this week. I've applied for a graduate certificate in marketing, which I'd take part-time, in my evenings, over the next year. I'd be happy to go to any training you think would be suitable, work back late, pitch in on any department, business development, HR, whatever — whatever you need from me.'

Nelson and Petra share a look, and, at last, he cracks a little smile.

'Alright, you've got my attention,' he says. 'Tell me, though: why do all of that when you could get a job at another agency tomorrow?'

'I want to care about my work again. That probably sounds silly. I think your team is incredible. These products, this message, I love it. Maybe that's trite, I don't know. I want to work on something that makes women feel good about themselves. I think that's worth getting behind.'

As he jots something down on his notepad, I glance at Petra, and she gives me a stealthy thumbs-up.

Fuck. Yeah.

Nelson asks a handful of other questions — specifics about past campaigns, my thoughts on their latest EDM, weaknesses and strengths, what I think is the most important factor in office culture — and then says we'll talk soon.

As all those coffees hit at once and I vibrate out the door and down to the tram stop, I fall into the easy old pattern of anxiety. When is *soon*? Should I call to follow up tomorrow, or is that too keen? Will it put him off? I shouldn't have said that thing about drinking whiskey and going to an escape room with my pre-Margot boss. That was really dumb.

My self-flagellation is halted in its tracks when my phone pings with a new email.

From: *petra.desilva@evergreenskincare.com.au*
To: *penny.moore.1992@gmail.com*
Subject: *Re: Catch up & Digital Marketing Manager role*
Will be in touch Monday.
Get excited.
P

The lurching tram ride does nothing to hinder the carbonation of hope and ambition and excitement in my tummy. I don't even stop smiling when a guy with the rankest BO I've ever encountered sits uncomfortably close to me somewhere around Spring Street.

Even the prospect of spending an hour getting my insecurities excavated with Dr Minnick can't dampen my mood.

Things always get worse before they get better, don't they? I've had so much to keep me worried this year. There's so much room for improvement in every corner of my life, and pessimism is such a natural reaction when things aren't going your way. Daring to hope for something makes the disappointment all the more painful, so lately I've been too scared to even try. But even the saddest, most resentful cynic in me sees a tiny glimmer of light on the horizon. I keep it measured. I refuse to fantasise about what I might wear on my first day at Evergreen, even as I pass a patterned shirt dress in the window of the Saba on Collins Street. I will not check my inbox until after midday on Monday. I will allow myself to be cautiously optimistic, but *that's it.*

Oh, who am I kidding?

'Ready to get to work?' asks Dr Minnick with a smile, holding her office door open for me. She's got a scented candle lit and a fresh box of tissues on the side table.

'I sure am,' I tell her, and I mean it.

CHAPTER FORTY-ONE

Something I learned today: therapy isn't always a watersport.

In this session, Dr Minnick and I settle into a more palatable conversation format. She asks me how I've been, and I tell her what's been on my mind in the fortnight since we last spoke, and she's a wonderful audience. She gasps and scowls at all the right moments, breathes *yes!* when I describe standing up for myself, and she's appropriately impressed when we wind up at today's events.

'So, what have we learned from this?' she asks. 'The good bits and the bad bits. What have the last few months — Scout, Max, your housemate, your friends' actions at the party — taught you about yourself?'

'Hm,' I say, sipping the peppermint tea she poured me earlier, now ice-cold. 'I'm noticing that I'm quite … passive. I never really thought of myself that way.'

'You think you're pretty direct?'

'I don't know. I'm outspoken sometimes, maybe. I guess I kind of … allow other people's opinions of me to inform my opinion about myself.'

'Yep. Keep going.'

'Well, I guess I've felt defined by, like, external judgments. If someone's into me romantically, that means I'm pretty enough and funny enough. Or if my boss likes me and thinks I'm doing a good job, then I'm smart and capable.'

'And if they don't think that?'

'Then I'm ugly and unfunny and dumb and useless.'

'What if they change their opinion of you after knowing you for a while?'

'I tell myself that maybe I present as pretty and funny and smart, but then they get to know me and realise I'm not those things.'

'Do you ever change your opinion about people?'

'Yeah, sometimes.'

'So then you could change your opinion of yourself.'

'Big ask, there.'

'If someone isn't pretty or funny or smart, are they still valuable people? Do they still deserve love?'

'Sure. Of course.'

'So why does it matter if some guy doesn't think you're cool? If your boss doesn't give you a gold star every day?'

I don't have an answer for her, so she lets me chew on it for a while. She explains the importance of self-compassion, and that it differs from self-esteem, and how it's a constant practice that always feels uncomfortable at first. My homework is to write down my mantra (*I'm having a hard time right now. I'm going to be kind to myself.*) and repeat it to myself as many times as I need to between now and our next session. That seems easy enough, so we shake on it, and the box of tissues is still unopened when I leave.

On my way home, I decide that I deserve a treat. I'm going to get myself an off-brand chocolate bar from Aldi and a bottle of their cheapest prosecco to celebrate my good job news with Leo when he gets home from work tonight.

I'm wondering if it's worth risking it with the Choceur Mountain Bar, or if I should just suck up the extra thirty-five cents and get myself a real Toblerone, when someone wanders into the top end of the aisle and catches my peripherals. Wait, why do I feel —?

It's Max. Oh no, no, nonono. I might be having a good day, but I'm not equipped to handle this.

He spots me before I can duck behind the Haribo display, and I have no choice but to acknowledge him. What is it about Dr Minnick that brings bad news out of the woodwork? Haven't I had enough post-therapy traumatic events to last ten lifetimes? What kind of bad omen is she?

It takes him about four seconds to make his way to me, and my mantra is on repeat. *I'm having a hard time right now. I'm going to be kind to myself. I'm having a hard time right now. I'm going to be kind to myself. I'm having a hard time right now.*

'Penny,' he says, meeting my smile with one of his own. It's strange to see him here, at my eye level in heels. He's not as tall as I thought he was, and the reality is sobering and funny. 'Haven't seen you in for*ever.*'

'Well, y'know. I'm really popular.'

'*So* popular.'

'You're well? Thesis, cafe?'

'Getting study snacks right now,' he says, gesturing to his basket full of popcorn and pears and kale chips. 'Doing the final proofread tonight. Submitting tomorrow. *Fark.*'

'That's great! What an achievement.'

'You want to hang out later? Celebrate with me?'

I breathe out a laugh. 'I don't think that's a good idea. You and me.'

'You're probably right,' he says easily. 'Bit of a car crash, wasn't it?'

'A bit.'

We fall quiet. I'm thinking about the frustrated and confused frown he always got when I contradicted him. He's probably thinking, *What a fucking basket case. Dodged a bullet there.*

I see it now. I've been giving Max the keys to my self-worth, never realising that he didn't want them in the first place. I was seeking shelter in the wrong arms, looking for him to tell me I'm worth his time. To tell me I'm beautiful or clever or interesting or lovable. I was following him around like a sad puppy for a year and a half, begging for him to acknowledge me, and then finding myself unsatisfied when he did. I didn't trust him, and I didn't want him to love me. I just wanted to be right. I don't trust anything that comes too easily.

That's so fucked up. I've had a few hundred dollars' worth of therapy to prove it — Wait. No. *I'm having a hard time right now. I'm going to be kind to myself.*

But I can't do that anymore. I have to be the one to decide I'm lovable and worth someone's time. There won't always be a Max or — and it hurts my heart to think it — a Leo around to tell me I'm okay. I need to fill the space in my life usually reserved for heartbreak and situationships with something better, healthier, more sustainable. I need to fill it with myself.

And then Max and I both speak at once: 'I'm sorry.' And we laugh.

I nod, and he puts his hand on his heart.

'I'll see you round,' he says.

'Yeah. See you round.'

I watch him walk away and I search myself for familiar aches, but I can't find them. In days past, the sight of Max going about his life would make me catch my breath, and I'd be all tangled up in wondering if he ever thought about me when he saw someone with my hair colour, or if his clothes ever smelled of me, or if he saw my post on Instagram and wondered if he should give me another shot. Now, though, I don't see the emblem of my desperately open-hearted youth, not a symbol of hurt and unattainability, not the one that got away, but all of him. Just Max. He's pulling his headphones on and his backpack is slung over his shoulder as he walks towards the checkout, and I think, *There's someone I cared about a lot. I hope he finds what he's looking for.*

I know, without knowing how I know, that everything we had is gone. We can be strangers again, and it's better that way.

'Hey!' I call down the hallway as I hear the front door slam. It's been hours since the Aldi incident, and I've already told the revived group chat all about it, to surprise and delight and awe. Just like I wanted. 'Come here!'

Leo and his bike *tickticktick* up the hallway.

'Everything alright?'

'I got a job today!' I tell him. 'Well, kind of. I'll get the job I got today on Monday. Probably.'

He laughs as he rinses his Keep Cup, but he doesn't offer more. Things have been okay between us. No more arguments. A few more uncomfortable silences than I might like, but, hey, we're easing back into being friends with each other. It'll take a bit of time.

'This is great news! Now you won't have to find a new housemate! I can pay rent again!'

'No, it's great,' he says. 'It's really great. Congrats.'

'What's wrong?'

'No, nothing, it's just —' He laughs. 'Actually, I didn't offer you the room because I couldn't afford the mortgage on this place.'

'Oh. Well. Look at you, moneybags.'

'Rolling in it,' he says dryly. 'No Aldi Special Buys for me.'

'Whatever, you use my thirty dollar blender more than I do.'

'It makes my smoothies taste like burnt plastic.'

'That's just how nutrients smell. That's why you're so luminous. You're *welcome*.'

'Ha.'

He leans against the bench, and we just look at each other. It's not unpleasant. It's just neutral. And I hate it.

'I got champagne,' I announce, crossing to the fridge for something to do. 'Well, maybe more like *sham*pagne. Get it? Want some? To celebrate your favourite housemate becoming a contributing member of society once again?' I pop the cork and squeal, '*Woo!*'

'Maybe another time,' he says. 'I've got some work to catch up on.'

'Oh. Boring. But I've already popped it.'

'Don't tell me you don't know your way around a bottle of *sham*pagne.' Leo smirks and gives me a playful little nudge in the shoulder, and I try to convince myself that that small gesture cancels out all these growing pains.

'What ever could you mean?' I gasp, trying to keep the banter going.

'Congratulations about the job,' he says, giving me a thumbs-up and then a weird little frown like he can't understand why the fuck he's giving me a thumbs-up. He doesn't recover from it and heads towards his room.

Now that I've got an entire bottle to myself, it feels less like celebrating and more like wallowing, so I pop a teaspoon in the bottle and put it back in the fridge.

Maybe I'll just have a bath and do a mask. Or will that give my mind free rein to reel? Perhaps I need something time-consuming and tedious, like giving my makeup drawer a good clean-out. Hmm.

I'm reading Leo loud and clear. It's fine. I've just got to accept it. I can't go getting hung up on another unavailable guy. I'm too old and rumpled and fragile for that anymore. From now on, no matter how hard it is, I will only allow myself to get invested in men who are invested in me. Maybe that's something I should have worked out a decade ago, but, as Blanche Devereaux would say, better late than pregnant. Dr Minnick would be proud of me, so I'm going to be proud of myself.

It's sad that the awkwardness of our night together still clings to us. But what happened happened, and we'll get past it. I'll only let myself think about it ... once a week.

Or twice.

Twice for now, and then only once in a few weeks, when I'm ready.

But this doesn't count.

I still get two more this week.

CHAPTER FORTY-TWO

An offer from Evergreen hits my inbox no later than 9:30 am on Monday morning, and I sign on the dotted line as Digital Marketing Manager by 9:32. There's a three-month probationary period and a decent pay rise. It's enough to cover frequent Deliveroo orders and the occasional splurge on clothing not made from pure polyester. I might even get an intern.

I start the following week and only fuck up a couple of times. I accidentally call one of my new colleagues *Anthony* and not *Antony*, and he just shrugs and says what a pain it is having a name like that, and I don't have to spend the whole week grovelling for forgiveness.

It turns out that I'm pretty good at my job when I'm not terrified of my manager.

In the team meeting on Thursday I suggest that we look into fully recyclable mail packaging, and maybe include a little sachet of seedlings for large orders, and Petra won't stop talking about what a good idea it is. She insists that I take the full hour for lunch. She isn't even bothered when I tell her I'll have to leave at 4:50 pm every other Thursday to make it to my standing appointment with Dr Minnick.

It's a whole world of professional satisfaction that I've never experienced before. Don't tell anyone I said this, but when I woke up this morning, I was actually disappointed to realise that after today I would have to wait the whole weekend before I go back to the office. I hardly know myself.

Both Annie and I are celebrating tonight: my first week at a job I don't hate, and her well-earned promotion to senior associate. We're planning to celebrate by eating our weight in lamb curry at Tonka tonight. I'm in such a good mood about everything that I don't mind when Emmy, Bec and Evan are slated to join. Even Leo accepts when I invite him.

Remember my old lucky date dress? It's getting a second chance at life as just a dress. I'm redefining these old habits. All the bra padding in the world isn't going to make a mediocre date better, and, anyway, my friends don't care how my waist looks. Growth, you know? Body positivity, self-acceptance, perspective, et cetera.

'Can I ask you something?' asks Leo as we pass Jolimont Station a while later.

'Sure,' I say. Heavy, low clouds have mattified the train windows, and I'm using my reflection to tidy up the lipstick on my cupid's bow with my pinkie finger.

'What is this?'

'This?' I ask, looking around. 'This is a train. It's taking us to the city. Do we need to set up a *Thomas the Tank Engine* marathon to teach you what a train does?'

'Fuck off,' he snorts. 'I meant — you're dressed up. Usually I see you wearing Miss Piggy pyjamas with slimy green shit all over your face.'

'That's my true form. That's what women look like when we take our makeup off.'

'I wanted to know —' says Leo loudly, speaking over my self-congratulatory laugh '— what kind of dinner this is.'

'We're having Indian. I texted you a link to the menu.'

'Yeah but. As friends?'

'Um,' I say, flushing with surprise and embarrassment. We haven't so much as watched a television show with a romantic subplot in weeks. He hasn't asked for help with any of his date outfits, and if he's been bringing girls home, it must be after I fall asleep. I've been doing my best not to think about it at all for fear of falling into another situationship on the rocks. 'Yeah, of course. Friends. Besties.'

'Right.'

'What? You don't want to be my bestie for the restie?'

He says, chewing on the inside of his cheek, 'It's nothing.'

'Okay.'

'What?'

'*You* what?'

He makes an annoyed little noise and turns in his seat to stare ahead.

I don't know what I'm supposed to have done to flip this switch from *easy* to *awful*. I'm grasping for an appropriate topic change to get us back to neutral territory, but nothing comes. The train doors slide open on Flinders Street Station, and I'm saved as we focus on joining the throng of exiting passengers instead of this strange silence, chilly even for July.

'I don't think I can do this,' he says as he steps out of the spittle of rain between the carriage and the undercover platform.

'What are you talking about? What's wrong?'

'I'm just going to go home,' he says, idling. The screen above us says the train will leave for Hurstbridge in twelve minutes.

'Why? What did I say?'

Leo seems to fight with himself for a moment. There's a tense look in his eye and his jaw is set, torn between irritation and peacekeeping.

'Tell me!' I say, and this seems to do the trick.

He takes a sharp breath, and suddenly — 'I tell you I'm in love with you and you tell me to fuck off. I don't see you for days, then you come home, have a breakdown, sleep with me, and then disappear. Then you're back, you get between me and my ex, then tell me I'm too much of a — whatever, what's your word? — a *fuckboy* for you to take me seriously and you just want to be friends. I don't even get a chance to process it before you're brushing it off with fucking *sham*pagne and cooking shows and trying to pretend nothing ever happened. I get no say in any of this, by the way. You don't ask me what I think of it or consider what I might want. You just decide all of it and expect me to follow along because, what, I'm capable of casual sex so I don't have any feelings at all?'

'I didn't say you don't have feel—'

'You act like it,' he snaps. I've never seen him properly angry before; he's usually calm to the point of irritation, always balancing out my panic with serenity. A vein in his temple pulses purple. His deep voice draws every eye on the platform. 'You think you're the only one who's allowed to be hurt by the things people do to you, but you're a fucking hurricane.'

'I didn't know I did that.' Do I do that?

'Why didn't you talk to me about it? We used to be honest with each other.'

'But it would have ended up the same, wouldn't it?' I reply, pleading. 'I just wanted to spare myself the embarrassment and you the awkwardness of having to break up when you got bored. Like you always do. I just assumed —'

'For fuck's sake!' he cries, so frustrated now that he's dissolving into joyless laughter, and I feel humiliated. 'What gives you the right to assume anything?'

The rain is now pelting down so hard on the platform's tin roof that we have been reduced to shouting at each other.

People are staring. Someone is filming us on their phone. If I wasn't an unwilling participant in the spotlight, I'd find all this drama delicious.

'I — our friendship is important to me!' I yell. 'I don't want to fuck it up!'

'Maybe I don't want to be friends!'

I feel myself shiver, and it's nothing to do with the torrential downpour. My ankles are wet, and my chest aches with the idea of not being friends with Leo anymore. Who would I talk to? I picture him watching *Bake Off* without me, and a lump forms in my throat.

'Oh,' I breathe, because what else is there to say? 'Okay.'

'Is that what you want?' he asks. His voice is sharp and angry, but he's still considerate enough to think of my needs when I have so rarely extended that kindness to him.

'Of course I want to be friends.'

'You just want to be friends.'

'I just think —'

'Do you know what I think?' he snaps. 'I think this is bullshit. You, this, all of it — bullshit. I think you feel the same way as me, and you're too afraid to do anything about it because you think I'm going to fuck you over.'

'I don't know if —'

'Well, I'm sorry,' he says, steamrollering on, 'but I'm not like Max, and it's offensive of you to assume I am.'

'I never said you —'

'I've never screwed you around. I've never lied to you; I've never blown you off. Haven't I always been one hundred percent honest with you?'

'I'm just scared!'

I don't know why admitting this — something I didn't even know to be true until I said it out loud — makes me want to cry.

'Yeah, you are,' he continues, still terse. 'You're a pain in the arse. You're neurotic and bossy and you can be fucking mean, and I've seen what you look like at rock bottom and I'm still here. When are you going to figure out that I'm not going anywhere?'

I'm clinging to my forearms for comfort, too aware of the gathering audience and their shameless interest. Two people in love with each other arguing in the rain. I think I've read this in a dirty ebook on the Amazon 99-cent list.

The game is up. There's nothing left to hide behind; no chance we can revert back to a relaxed friendship, bound together by no more than a lease agreement and mutual love of pad see ew. No, at last, it's my turn to be honest and vulnerable with him in a way I've never had the courage to be with Max or anyone else.

'What if it falls apart?' I ask feebly. 'What if I fuck it all up? I fuck *everything* up. What am I going to do if I can't have you in my life anymore?'

'Do you want to hurt me?' he asks, his shoulders dropping.

'Of course I don't.'

'Are you going to be nice to me?'

'I'm always —'

'Do you love me?'

I take a breath. '*Focus on the breath*,' says the Dr Minnick of my mind's eye. I know what I have to say, what I want to say. It's not complicated. Actually, it's the least complicated thing in the world. It's one syllable. Just spit it out. *Spit it out, Penny.*

'Yes.'

'Then what's the fucking problem?'

'Oh my god,' I hear a teenage girl hiss to her friends. 'This dumb bitch better kiss him or I will.'

It is acutely annoying for someone half my age to be smarter and wiser than I am, but here we are. The train to Hurstbridge blares its horn to signal its imminent departure, and passengers swarm the platform. In an instant, Leo and I are forced towards each other, chest to chest, and, hey, while we're here we might as well make the most of it. And so we kiss, and it's so fucking nice and sweet and hot and electric and magnetic, and we accidentally bump teeth and laugh about it, right into each other's mouths, and it doesn't feel like a test or like I need to make the most of it at all because there's plenty more to come.

'Ooh, does this make you my boyfriend?' I ask, putting on the sickliest voice I can manage and settling in under the drape of his arm over my shoulders. I don't care how superficial it is; I love that he's taller than me in my highest heels. All the short guys on Tinder can bite me.

'Gross, absolutely not,' says Leo, scrunching his nose and writhing away, grinning. 'I'm unattainable and sexy.'

'No way, that's totally my type!'

'No way, me too!'

'I really like it when someone is just, like, completely not interested in me at all. At *all*. Nothing hotter. Oof.'

'Oh, that's convenient,' says Leo. 'Because I actually don't like you at all.'

'That's okay. I don't always like me either.'

'I'll have to like you enough for the both of us.' He plants a deliberately wet, disgusting kiss on my cheek, and I whine about it. He's my stupid best friend, and it's all fun and easy.

Although Tonka isn't far from the station, our dramatic little performance means we're the last to arrive. This earns us a pointed look from Annie, to whom lateness is a mortal sin.

We settle into our seats and debate naan versus roti (the answer is obviously both), and Leo's hand rests on my arm as he's talking to the waiter about the cocktail menu. Bec sees this and gives me a plainly shocked and questioning look, and my reply is a coy shrug.

'Finally,' says Evan, butting into our silent conversation. 'How long did that take?'

'How long did what take?' asks Leo.

'That. You two.'

'Yeah, she's really not that bright.'

'It's true,' I say, nodding along. 'I'm very good looking, but that's all.'

The whole night is loud and raucous and happy, and I laugh so hard my stomach hurts, and I have to take the belt off my dress. Dinner turns into dessert turns into dessert cocktails turns into after-hours cocktails at a hidden laneway bar, and Annie and I dance to uncool 80s remixes until our hair gets flat with sweat.

I've had just enough gin to keep me in a technicolour buzz, so I can fully appreciate how special it is, just for now, to have it all: a great job, wonderful friends, and an exciting new relationship. None of them have to compete with each other.

Somewhere around my third negroni and under the din of the bad DJ, Leo presses his mouth to my ear and asks if I want to get out of here, and in a night of firsts, I'm ready to leave the party early.

Somewhere around Fitzroy Gardens he asks our Uber driver if he can borrow the AUX cord.

I need to make a note to tell Dr Minnick about all of this: seeing Max and acknowledging the need to forgive him and myself in order to move on to better things; confronting my fear of abandonment and giving in to the faith that it will be alright — or, even if it isn't, that I will be. Just another opportunity to earn therapy points and get praise for all this growth.

Before I can even get my phone out to write myself a reminder, Leo hits play on a Carly Rae Jepsen song for my benefit, and all my thoughts are drowned out by our off-key sing-shouting. When you get to go home with your best friend, high on their aftershave and fuzzy from cocktails, who has room in their heads or hearts for past disappointments? The rear-view mirror is for learning lessons, and everything I want is on the road ahead.

EPILOGUE

'Leo?' I whisper into the dark when we're in my room one night.

'Mm?'

'Would it be unsexy if I go do my night-time skincare routine?' I feel him smile into my shoulder. 'I can't go to my job at a skincare company with a whitehead between my eyebrows like a hormonal rhinoceros.'

He's laughing as he tosses the blankets back and climbs out of bed, and I follow. These days I'm the pantsless woman wearing one of his shirts, and I give myself permission to be smug about it for one whole minute.

It's been a couple of months. Things are going well.

The weather is changing again, and everything is looking greener by the day. There's some metaphor here about my new self blossoming into being. I feel deciduous, and having shed a layer that no longer serves my current form, I'm now growing the things I need to carry with me into the next summer. I feel smarter and safer than ever before, like I'm getting warm lungfuls of air after years of struggling to stay afloat, choking on seawater and waiting for a life raft. Only I came to my own rescue.

Maybe it's bigger than the weather. Maybe it's my Saturn return, and the whole universe is offering me emotional reparations after the self-destructive black hole of my early twenties. It's about time everything started falling into place.

My life is beginning to look a bit more like how I always pictured it: a job that doesn't make me cry every day, a nice boyfriend who doesn't define my self-worth, fewer hangovers, slightly looser jeans. I'm getting better at telling the difference between happiness and validation, nerves and anxiety, drama and excitement.

Leo watches me in the mirror with a fond look on his face as I line up my serums in order of use. I smile at the way he squeezes toothpaste onto his brush, so focused and precise. I'm not even shy when I pull my hair into a severe topknot. He holds his hand out for a squirt of moisturiser, and I oblige.

These little routines make me nervous in the best way. Really, nothing much has changed. I don't feel the need to be perfect or polite, to walk the tightrope between *flirtatious* and *marriage material*. He would see through all of that shit and call me out before I even knew I was doing it. It's just … easy.

A while ago, as we waited for our coffees at the cafe, he made me watch as he deleted all his dating apps and told me what a special, lucky girl I am for it.

And we don't fight, we just talk. The push–pull — the intricate strategy of caring just enough and never asking for more than he's willing to give — it just isn't there.

After his mum popped over for a coffee last week, I blew up the group chat with complaints that he had neglected to specifically introduce me as his girlfriend, until it occurred to me to bring it up with him. When I asked — using the calm, superlative-free script Annie had prepared for me — he apologised and called his mum to correct himself. And then there was nothing left to be upset about, so we went for a run in Fitzroy Gardens and talked about what show we should binge watch next.

As I crawl back into bed beside him, he plants a minty kiss on my cheek. He shifts over to give me the warm spot, and I settle in to sleep in the crook of his neck, and it's nice, so nice, to realise the first guy to happily fall asleep in my bed is the right one, and maybe even (whisper it, because I'm not really supposed to think in future hypotheticals anymore) the last.

Tomorrow night we'll make dinner, watch *Bake Off* and sort our laundry. I'll launch a new line of sheet masks at work this week. I'll catch up with Annie for a drink on Wednesday and hear all about her newest case, and how it went meeting Emmy's parents. I won't go on a water fast before my bridesmaid's dress fitting with Bec on the weekend. I'll make time to visit Dad. I'll go to therapy, even when I have more exciting things to do. I'll meditate and repeat my mantra when I need it. I'll forgive myself and my friends when we fuck up. I'll tell Leo I love him every day, because I do. I might look into fostering a cat.

Maybe a neurotic mess and an unattainable fuckboy will make it work. Or maybe we won't. Maybe I'll be back on the dating apps by Christmas. But we're here now, and that's something.

This probably isn't the end to nights alone or telepathically willing someone into texting me back. It's not the end of loneliness or feeling lost and overwhelmed and confused. I may as well take out the mortgage on Dr Minnick's beach house in my name for all the insecurities I still have to work through. It's not the end of bad habits and the constant buzz of anxiety in my ear. That might never come. But maybe I'll try to stop thinking about endings altogether, and just enjoy these belated new beginnings instead.

THANK YOU TO:

(Deep breath)

Daniel Barnett, Sam Smith, Ainsley Thompson, Taylor Whitington, Keera, Ava and Otto Hoogendorp, Erin Hunter, Nick Tattam, Raquel Gazzola, Rachel Coop, Jake Barber, Emma Webster, Shelley Maher, David Adams, Daniella Bagnara, Ariela Jacobs, Lex Briscuso, Nick Schiffler, Dev Bhutani, Jess Gleeson, Anna Burke and Luke Beck: everything I do is to make you laugh. I'm so glad you're in my life.

The ICW group. Thank you for your objectivity and kindness, suffering through Penny's growing pains, and giving me something to look forward to every fortnight through lockdown. Jock, Eddie, Fiona, Ruhi, Kay, Jack, Carmela and Siobhan, thank you.

Nadine Davidoff for your invaluable direction and enthusiasm.

The wonderful and effervescent Jane Novak. You're just really fucking great. I'm thankful every day for your support and guidance, but most of all for your patience when I start to spiral. I'll never stop being glad I emailed you.

Anna Valdinger, human sunshine. Thank you for loving Penny as much as I do, and for turning my lifelong dream into reality. I can die happy now.

Madeleine James for taking such wonderful care of my baby and making her coherent, and Mietta Yans for designing her beautiful cover. All the team at HarperCollins, whom I love sight unseen. Whenever I'm sad or smug (so, all the time), I reread the nice things you've all said about this manuscript.

Anna Burke (you're so special that you get thanked twice!) and Alex Hammond for your endless confidence and support.

MA and LT for bringing me back to myself. Thank you for convincing me to stick around to see how lovely life can be.

My weird, complicated, and wonderful family. The kids are better versions of us all. Probably don't read this to them though, way too many sex bits. Sorry.

Mum, who would be so miffed if she didn't get a personal shout-out. You're the best. Thanks for that time you didn't feel like taking me to the movies and told me to read *Harry Potter* instead, which made me love reading, which made me want to be a writer. You get all the credit. There, happy now? Love you.

VK for being by my side for every word, and for everything, forever.

All the boys I loved in my twenties, who are searching these pages for scar tissue. Thank you for giving me something to write about.

(Except you.)

(Prick.)

**Read on for an exclusive preview of
Genevieve Novak's new novel**

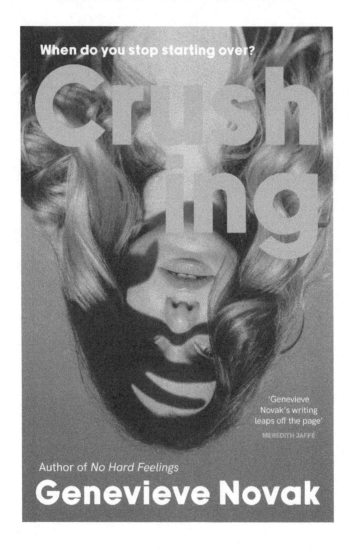

When do you stop starting over?

Crushing

'Genevieve
Novak's writing
leaps off the page'
MEREDITH JAFFÉ

Author of *No Hard Feelings*

Genevieve Novak

CHAPTER ONE

Dumped. Effectively homeless. Failing to black out on the only booze in Nicola's pantry (note to the wounded: when you think you've hit rock bottom, straight gin is the shovel that digs you deeper). Rapidly losing viable eggs. Enemy Number One in this sedate suburban cul de sac, owing to five straight hours of blasting Joni Mitchell's *Blue* album and disturbing the innate peace of the outer suburbs. And for fifteen more minutes, it was my twenty-eighth birthday: the age by which my mother had two kids, a husband, a master's degree and a manageable mortgage in an area where houses now cost north of seven figures. I had none of that. Eddie had even kept the dog.

Sweetie, our greyhound, had watched with pitying eyes as the elevator doors had closed on me and my bags, while my boyfriend — ex-boyfriend — tried to nudge her back inside.

He had explained the problem in excruciating detail as he sobbed in my lap, so overcome with guilt about his decision that I had to be the one to comfort him through it. He had tried, he said, red-faced and sick with himself, he'd really, really tried, but he didn't love me anymore. Then he put on an Ed Sheeran song to try to better articulate his feelings, while

I sat on the couch we'd picked out together and waited for the feeling to return to my extremities.

He'd been having doubts about the forever of it all, he said, squeezing my forearms while I tried to think of all the things I loved, but maybe wouldn't love forever. Really high-waisted denim. A drizzle of chai syrup in my coffee. Binge-watching shows about amateur bakers. Three years together, and he loved me like a collapsed genoise sponge.

Now I was laying on Nicola's living room floor. The baby — Layla, my niece — had been lulled to sleep by the dulcet drone of 'A Case of You'. She had no choice. I wouldn't turn it off. This was my heartbreak party, which made me the boss of the music, entitled me to this entire bottle of gin, and demanded my sister's bottomless sympathy. Mitch, my brother-in-law, had been banished to the pub in solidarity.

I had nowhere else to go. I wasn't emotionally resilient enough for my mum's cloying pity. My only friends, really, were the girlfriends of Eddie's friends, and we weren't close enough that I could get away with crashing on their couches, monopolising their free time with long-winded rants about how much better I could do, and how much he was about to regret losing me until I almost believed it.

Were hotels up and running again now that restrictions had been loosened? I couldn't be bothered finding out. It was much easier to stay here and soak in my misery, annoying Nicola's neighbours, and doing all the things that Eddie hated, like lighting multiple scented candles at once and getting apocalyptically drunk.

'When Mum was my age,' I said, sniffing, 'she had two —'

'— two kids, a husband and a mortgage. You've already used that one. I have a kid and a husband and a mortgage, too.'

Nicola grimaced. 'You're welcome to them. Layla bit me on the nip today. Where's the respect?'

'She's seven months old,' I argued. 'She doesn't know any better.'

'She can't use that as an excuse forever.'

Nicola and I had drifted in and out of closeness as the years passed, but she was all I had left. She was eight years older than me and got everything good in the gene pool: strong eyebrows, good lips, natural athleticism. I was left with half-decent hair and joints that clicked for an hour after I woke up. She got all the good adjectives, too: classic, striking, Grace Kelly-esque, while I got ... tall. It wasn't fair.

And she had the perfect life: an okay husband with all his hair, a cute baby, and a back catalogue of thrilling anecdotes from her days on the international party circuit spanning 2010 to 2020, including one about a lingering hug from Mark Ronson at a BAFTAs afterparty. Before motherhood came calling, she had run glossy, star-studded events in London, living off catered leftovers and energy drinks as she ferried celebrities and their entourages between venues. Her life — new though it was; she'd taken a generous redundancy package when the pandemic had hit, moved home to Melbourne, married Mitch, bought a house, got pregnant and had a baby in the time it took me to grow out a fringe — was as idyllic as smug mummy influencers pretended theirs were, and she never missed an opportunity to grumble about it.

'Seriously Marnie, are you alright?'

'No,' I wailed. 'I'm going to die alone. My neighbours will complain about the smell coming from my apartment and eventually they'll break down the door and find a puddle of stomach acid and eyeballs where my beautiful body once lay.'

'Get over yourself. "Beautiful body". Don't you think I'll notice you're dead when you stop sending me fifty raccoon memes a day?'

I sniffed. 'You're ancient. You'll be dead years before me.'

'I'm thirty-six, you brat. I'm still young and hot.'

'You're geriatric.'

'Watch out, or I'll send Layla and her new front teeth to attack you.'

I crossed my arms over my chest to protect my vulnerable targets.

'I'm devastated. Give me a break.'

She clicked her tongue. 'Do you want the truth?'

'Of course I don't.'

She barrelled on anyway. 'Honestly, Eddie kind of sucks. We all think so.'

'Obviously Eddie sucks, Nicola,' I cried. 'He cuts his own hair. It's his dream to live off-grid in a commune. He calls espressos "expressos".'

'Then what's all this fuss about?'

'Because I loved him anyway.' I felt my face contort into an ugly sob as I said this. 'And he's gone, and I don't know how I keep ending up here. I don't know what's wrong with me.'

'*Oh*,' said Nicola when she realised I wasn't kidding. She slid down onto the floor beside me and heaved my body, limp as a run-over ragdoll, into a comforting, maternal hug.

Breakup number five. That sounded like a lot and felt like even more. Here was another earnest attempt and jagged-edged failure to add to the ever-growing list.

In my mind's eye, I pushed back the plastic chair in the fluorescent-lit community centre meeting room and stood up to face my peers. '*I'm Marnie Fowler, and I'm a serial monogamist.*'

'*Hi Marnie,*' they droned back.

One or two big breakups in your twenties was normal. Three was bad luck. Five, though? Five failed long-term relationships in ten years was a pattern, and the only consistencies I could point to were:

- men
- myself

Obviously men were the problem, always, in every scenario, but I wasn't blameless.

I'd been too opinionated for Ian, who wanted a pliant little ingenue who didn't question our age gap. Too needy for Guillaume, who only signed up to be my heartbreak holiday rebound fling but found himself trapped in an eight-month chokehold of unrelenting affection. Thomas grew bored of me after a year, and Martin couldn't carry all that baggage. I'd failed the girlfriend test all over the world: the wrong woman for every type of man I tried on.

And then Eddie. Kind and unselfconscious. He was supposed to be the nice guy, defined by patience. Not quite funny, but a willing and easily delighted audience. He loved the outdoors, so I loved the outdoors. He loved camping, so I learned how to drive a campervan and got used to falling asleep to the guttural sound of two possums arguing in a nearby tree. Even eighteen months of claustrophobic lockdowns in our prison of a flat hadn't been so bad.

Well, we hadn't killed each other. Good enough. We'd only just got our lives back on track. I'd finally begun to feel safe, even sure … and here I was again. *Again.* I let out a yowl like a wounded animal.

'Oh, my love,' Nicola crooned, stroking my hair. I felt her inspect it for split ends and decide to let it go. 'It's okay, I know, you're okay.'

These platitudes, mixed with how good it felt for someone to care enough to make them, brought on a new wave of tears. I moaned in agony and buried my face in my hands.

'He's the worst of them,' she said. 'Because he seems decent. It's insidious. At least Ian was upfront about being disgusting. Eddie's worse than Tom — sorry, *Thomas*. What a prick. Worse than —'

'Can we not?' I whimpered. 'I don't need a tour of my failures.'

'I'm not! I'm just saying, if we thought Martin was bad —'

'Eddie isn't Martin!' I cried, wrenching myself out of her shoulder nook. There was a splatter painting of mascara on the neck of her T-shirt. 'I loved him — *love* him, I don't know what I d-did wrong. I don't know why this keeps — I —'

'Okay,' said Nicola in that maddeningly soothing mother's voice, reaching out to pull me back to my crying spot as I choked on my words, coughing and gagging on renewed misery. 'It's okay, you're okay.'

I let her rock me gently in her arms as though I was a bereft infant and allowed myself to indulge in all the fantasies that had suddenly been wiped off the table.

The quaint house out by Altona Beach: a period home with an established lemon tree and a yard to raise dogs in. Taking a year off to drive around Europe in a campervan, him making friends with lifelong expats and me making myself sick on pierogies and Swiss chocolate. One very well-behaved child, someday, who would never have meltdowns on the floor of a supermarket or be placated by an iPad. The dream life that I'd been working toward, waiting for, dropping hints about for three full years now had been abruptly cancelled.

'I want to talk to him,' I said thickly. I reached around blindly, running my hands through Nicola's thick silvery shag carpeting to find the cool glass of my phone.

'Nope,' she said at once, grabbing my arm and pulling it away from the search. 'It won't help.'

'But he —'

'Not tonight,' she said. 'Not like this.'

My head throbbed with the pressure of an all-night meltdown. Snot streamed out of my nose and trickled down the line of my lip. I reached for the bottle.

'Maybe that's enough for n—'

'NO.' I snatched it away from her outreached hand and gave her leg a warning jab with my foot. 'Mine.'

'You're going to feel like shit tomorrow.'

'I'm going to feel like shit for the rest of my life!'

I knew, under the glug and burn of gin and the nineteenth replay of 'River', that I was being a tiny bit ridiculous. I was treating a kitchen fire like Chernobyl.

It was just embarrassing. To find out too late that it wasn't safe to let your guard down. To know that someone had made a list and found your cons column was infinitely longer than your pros. To have tried your hardest and come second place without any competition.

'Marnie,' said Nicola, pleading in mixed maternal concern and humiliating pity, 'I need you to take a breath —'

I was mid-swallow when I choked on a sob. My stomach convulsed, and I looked at her in panic. I coughed once. I coughed again, and it morphed into a gag.

'Oh no —' she said, springing into action as dread coursed through me. She hooked her arms under mine and dragged me, legs trailing, to the kitchen just in time for me to —

Splat. Splattysplattysplatsplat.

Gin and bile hit the clean steel of the kitchen sink. It swirled nauseatingly toward the drain, and I watched through streaming eyes as everything I had left in my stomach spilled out of my mouth to join it.

'That's real nice,' said Nicola soothingly as she held my hair back. 'You're okay. It's alright.'

I didn't know if the tears drying on my face were of heartache, shame or a body's natural reflex to mild alcohol poisoning, but it didn't matter. This, I decided as Nicola passed me a paper towel and rubbed my back, was the last time I would ever, ever let myself get this low.

CHAPTER TWO

Heartbreak hysteria looked pathetic in the predawn light of my sister's spare room. The hillock of unrolled toilet paper puckered and warped with tears and snot, mascara smeared on the crisp white pillowcase, the laundry bucket beside the bed, painted glossy with dried bile and gin, and the same Julien Baker song playing on repeat through my phone for the last six hours of fitful, vomity sleep.

I lay there, numb and heavy, and indulged the big grey fog as a treat. I prodded at my bloody fist of a heart and thought of the shape of Eddie's mouth when he told me it was over, and I braced for tears. But all I could think about was the sliver of plaque build-up on his slightly crooked incisor. When was the last time he flossed?

Maybe if I hugged my knees to my chest and pulled the sheet up over my head and stayed really, really quiet, Nicola might forget that she had a spare room or a sister at all, and my body would fuse with the mattress and I'd be found decades from now, preserved, and blissfully, mercifully dead.

Christ. That was bleak for a Friday morning.

I kicked the sheets off in a whiff of angst and contempt and began to stew.

Was I going to crawl into bed and wait for death over someone whose favourite book was the Shane Warne autobiography? Was I going to take long baths in the dark, blasting Phoebe Bridgers and lamenting my wasted time because a man who felt confident that three minutes of kissing and thigh groping was adequate foreplay for an adult human woman decided he could do better? Would I obsess, pine, publish hammy poetry on public platforms, send him steamy texts and then pretend they were for my imaginary boyfriend instead, '*sorry haha*'? No.

Not again.

I caught my reflection in the mirrored wardrobe doors and saw a dishevelled gremlin, one tit having wandered out of the stretched armpit of my singlet, and thought: *This has got to stop.*

I would not become a caricature of the broken-hearted single woman slipping towards an existential crisis and relying evermore on pink wine and a horoscope app.

No, I thought, remembering that losing Eddie also meant never having to hear the anecdote about the first time he ate a jalapeno ever again, *that's quite enough.*

And that was that. Mourning complete.

This was what starting over looked like. Again. Five apocalyptic heartbreaks in fewer than ten years ought to entitle me to an honorary degree in humiliation and recovery.

Don't let Taylor Swift fool you. Getting over someone is not that difficult. All you have to do is focus on every negative thing about them for the rest of your life until you forget to stop actively hoping for their slow and painful death, then get a haircut and move on.

It was thrilling to wake up into a brand-new life and find that the world outside looked exactly the same.

My face looked the same. My clothes fit the same. The sleepy commute into the city followed a different train line, but the beep of my myki, the sway of the carriage, people's blank expressions — they paid no mind to the turmoil and hysteria of an anonymous twenty-somethings' inner life.

I felt my phone vibrate in my pocket, and I fished it out.

Missed call (05:45): Nicola Fowler-Smythe
Nicola Fowler-Smythe (05:45): Don't hate me.
Marnie Fowler (05:46): What?

My phone lit up with an incoming call, which I immediately declined.

Missed call (05:46): Mum (Mobile)

She wasn't dissuaded.

Missed call (05:47): Mum (Mobile)
Missed call (05:48): Mum (Mobile)

Nicola's name popped up in another window.

Nicola Fowler-Smythe (05:49): SORRY!
Nicola Fowler-Smythe (05:49): IT JUST CAME UP
Marnie Fowler (05:49): You are dead to me.

The walk through the concrete labyrinth of Parliament Station and to the corner of Collins Street and Russell was no different than usual. It was too early for most commuters, leaving the streets empty and quiet. The towering office buildings stood as empty as they'd been for the last year and a half. The doorways of designer flagships and price-gouging convenience stores sheltered people sleeping there. A cyclist cried out at a delivery driver who had come dangerously close to knocking them off their bike. Par for the course, no life-altering drama here. I was so unbothered that I forgot to ignore the ding of my phone again.

> **Mum (Mobile) (05:55):** My love … So sorry to hear … R U ok? … ??? …
> **Marnie Fowler (05:56):** I'm fine and I don't want to talk about it.
> **Mum (Mobile) (05:56):** Do U want to move in W me & Trent 4 a bit?
> **Marnie Fowler (05:56):** No thank you
>
> **Marnie Fowler (05:57):** Who the f is Trent?
> **Nicola Fowler-Smythe (05:58):** Hell if I know. The newest squeeze.
> **Marnie Fowler (05:58):** 🙄

Once upon a time, before the wire in a face mask wore a deep red groove into the bridge of my nose day after day, before my cuticles were permanently cracked from constant sanitising, before the world froze, collapsed, and feebly rebuilt itself on the tentative promise of a third, fourth, seventeenth variant, I had a career.

I'd been halfway up the ladder at a hospitality group — a wanky company that owned a dozen chic restaurants more concerned with being Instagrammable than making edible food in decent portions — having clawed my way up from nervy teenaged waitress to business development team leader.

But a year and a half ago, cases grew exponentially and restaurants everywhere closed their doors. Seventy-five percent of our staff were stood down while we waited for the worst to pass, and then it didn't, and then I was let go.

Eddie managed the bills on his own for as long as he could, smiling thinly as I apologised for every tin of chickpeas I dropped into the trolley, exhaling his resentment whenever I ran the dishwasher, murmuring his displeasure if I wasn't in the mood, as though it was the least I could do. My self-worth disintegrated with every polite rejection to a job application, every unreturned phone call to recruiters, every day wasted in front of the television.

Kit only offered me my job at Little George Gastronomia because I was the least annoying person he interviewed for it. He'd once said that his favourite things about me were, in order: I was born before 9/11, and I wasn't afraid of him. If those were the only qualities I needed to retain a job where I got to listen to music all day and offer biscuits to every passing dog, well, I could live with that.

Little George, named for its spot on George Parade, had been operating since the '50s. Kit's grandparents opened it after they emigrated from Italy during the war. It had grown from a poky espresso bar to a piece of Melbourne history. When Kit inherited it from his father two years ago, he had it gutted and renovated, keeping only the heritage-listed green neon sign, the imported tile and the original and highly temperamental espresso machine. I was the only one who could tame it when it was in the throes of a tantrum at peak hour.

Functionally, it was only a small place. Kit's family owned the building: a narrow three-storey space with bright, wide windows and a cafe on the ground floor, decades of storage and forgotten family junk on the second, and Kit's office (slash hiding space) on the third. We had ten tables inside and three out in the sunshine, and a row of bar stools along the long dark wood counter if you fancied a quick pastry and an espresso. In the renovation, he had had the place painted hunter green and white and replaced decades-old furniture with gleaming walnut tables and chairs.

Little George's side-street location, seasonal menu and rotation of chic black and white photographs by local artists in gleaming brass frames across all three walls contributed to the impression that the place was a local secret. A heavy swinging door separated the dining area from the kitchen, which was just as well, or else Sam — a full-time hornbag who moonlit as our day chef — would trap me in innuendos all day long. Monday through Saturday, we served breakfast, lunch and dinner to discerning Melburnians. I worked the daytime shifts, and what my awards wage lacked, I made up for in croissants.

The embroidery on my apron read *Marnie, Assistant Manager*, but my authority stretched only as far as my own set of keys, second dibs on the leftovers and handling needy customers on Kit's behalf. He oversaw the businessy bits, the kitchen had its own system, there were no other front of house staff to manage, and even though I could probably have done the job under anaesthesia, I had no complaints.

I knew I was supposed to want more. I was supposed to go all tingly when my LinkedIn profile got viewed. I was supposed to want a salary that curved upward, responsibility, five-figure bonuses. A career, not a job. According to, well, everyone, I should have used lockdown to retrain in a new field and viewed hospitality as a means to an end: a strictly temporary detour in my road to an acronym for a job title.

But when the morning rush petered out, the dishwasher was going and I was working on a particularly good daydream, I liked my job. The rushes and lulls were predictable, customers were mostly friendly and the biggest catastrophe I could face was running out of oat milk. I liked the early morning walk to open the cafe, and the sweet nonno who camped out at our window table with an espresso and three newspapers every Thursday morning. I liked that I didn't have to think about anything except accurate spelling on the specials board and the crema on my espresso pours. I liked that my body ached at the end of the day, the satisfying *pop* in my ankles when I rotated them on the couch that night. Everyone I spoke to brought me a problem I could solve: coffee, hunger — hell, a bathroom.

It wasn't like this before, when I would spend fifty hours per week panicking about deadlines and budgets and the passive-aggressive barb that Anna from marketing had made in the last team meeting. All of the exposure to the blue light glare from my laptop had given me premature forehead wrinkles. A salary, but at what cost?

I got to take home leftover cannelloni here. People greeted me with a smile. The staff got along, if you overlooked how often we told each other to fuck off. The worst I ever had to deal with was the odd sour-faced customer insistent on complaining. '*This coffee is too hot,*' they'd say, or '*This sandwich is too bready.*' But then they would leave, and I wouldn't have to deal with them again. They were a problem, and then they weren't. Here then gone, easy as that.

I unlocked Little George's doors, disabled the alarm, flipped on the lights and switched on the espresso machine. Soon the pastry delivery would arrive, customers would trickle in, and the day would look like any other.

I blanked another call from my mother. I wasn't in the mood to hear about the number of fish in the sea (rapidly dwindling) or how Trent was the love of her life (more likely, another puce-faced Liberal voter from OkCupid.com). *'Can't talk,'* I wrote. *'Call you later.'* (I wouldn't).

I'd be in good company today. No one enjoyed the indulgence of a bad mood like Kit, and if my hands were busy and my mind was on hospitality service, I'd be fine.

I'd be fine.

I'd be fine.